the YUKIAD

VICTOR SNAITH

The Book Guild Ltd
Sussex, England

The Book Guild Ltd.
25 High Street,
Lewes, Sussex.

First published 1990
© Victor Snaith 1990
Set in Baskerville
Typesetting by Ashford Setting & Design,
Ashford, Middlesex.
Printed in Great Britain by
Antony Rowe Ltd.,
Chippenham, Wiltshire.

British Library Cataloguing in Publication Data
Snaith, Victor P. (Victor Percy) (1944-)
  The yukiad
  I. Title
  823'.914 [F]

ISBN 0 86332 478 9

CONTENTS

Part Two

Part Three

1

DAWN

'Here's breakfast,' the professor called cheerfully, bustling out onto the porch and placing on the table a tray which was far too large for his short arms to carry.

The porch, one of the closed-in type which abounds in Ontario lakeside cottages, lay on the eastward side of the house. Outside the dawn groped its way with shadow-fingers of conifers, still as opaque as jet, over the rim of a small, tranquil expanse of water.

A tall young lady turned from gazing at the scene and smiled gently at the Elsquaird.

In the corner Yukio, half-brother to Bucolia, did not stir in his seat, remaining instead intently gazing at the lakeshore.

The professor gazed across the room up into her serene, ascetic, oblivious face. 'Are you hungry?'

'Very,' she replied amiably, standing perfectly still and inhaling deeply the aroma of the freshly fried food. 'It is very early, isn't it?' The professor nodded. 'It is wonderful here. And I'm sure that Yukio enjoys it, too. I was just listening to the dawn. To one with good hearing like mine it makes quite a symphony. Quite different from the sounds of first light in the city, you know.'

'I can imagine.'

'As kids Yukio, O'Toole and I used to get up regularly to listen to the dawn. Father, too.'

'Who? Dean Smoothe?'

'No, silly. Mother and I lived in a modern subdivision with him. And I was only a toddler then. No, I meant Eli.' Sensing the professor's regret at his *faux pas* Bucolia continued. 'Don't

11

worry, professor — John, I'm not so fragile that I can't bear to think about the Gang of Eleven. In fact I often spend my time thinking about them. There used to be remorse. But not any longer.'

'That's good. Anyway, let's eat, before it gets cold.'

The professor rounded the table and, gently taking Bucolia's wrist, led her to her seat. Taking a plate and a spoon from the tray he crossed to where Yukio was sitting.

The tall young man had not moved.

Professor Elsquaird pushed a wheel of the chair with a deft flick of his foot, causing the vehicle to swing round to face him. 'You're going to enjoy this, old fellow,' he said with a grin.

Yukio's beautiful face stared at him.

The professor, standing squarely in front of the young man, commenced patiently and lovingly to feed him. From time to time he glanced over his shoulder to see how Bucolia was managing. And sighed to see the difficulty with which she sought the cream jug.

Elsquaird returned to his devotion to the man.

Irresistibly his imagination repeated to itself the familiar conundrum: Can a blind girl and a vegetable requite the feelings of a midget?

2

CALAMITY

'God damn id!' Eli Baktrian cursed as he engaged the steering wheel of his four-wheel drive in a convoluted wrestling match. His tyres were slipping in the heavy fall of snowy mush as he tried to speed away from the lights at the bottom of the hill which led to Gasville's non-sectarian Roman Catholic maternity home.

'Your air-conditioner is not working.' The Speaking-Car addressed Eli, interrupting his concentration with those pearls of wisdom which are supposed to show that there is intelligent life at G.M.

'Your clock is reading Eastern Standard Time,' it intoned in a sonorous female contralto.

'God damn id. Shud up.' Eli responded uncharitably by fetching the machine a karate chop with his stump-digited, rhinoceros-hided hand.

'Thank you,' it answered cheerily. 'Your seat belt is required by law to be fastened. Your door is not correctly shut. It is Friday, February thirteenth. The moon is in its first quarter. Atlantic and Pacific tides are respectively . . . '

'If I wan'ed chicken-shid like thad I'd ged me a wife,' Eli shouted at the voice, turning the radio up as loud as it would go, peering out with difficulty and squinting in an attempt to make out the maternity home through the thickly falling snow.

Ms O. Kanada had entered into one of the labour wards of The Maternity House of Sorores Mundi earlier that afternoon, complaining in pidgin sign-language that her time was up.

How prophetic!

Eli had driven her up to the Sorores Mundi himself, before the bonanza February white-out had started, and then he had gone back to the store to arrange for it to be looked after by Wendy-Joe Bulge, a reliable youngster, of home-from-homely appearance, and his most recent pregnancy.

He had discovered that Sarah Delaney had also been admitted to Sorores Mundi that same afternoon and Eli intended to visit his buxom and friendly familiar as soon as he had done the honours for Ms O. In point of fact, both ladies occupied a soft spot in his generally calciferous heart and he was particularly keen to see them this evening.

Although Eli was unaware of the fact, both ladies were resting comfortably in their respective wards after what were, many years later, to be regarded as singular and legendary deliveries, occurring during his brief trip to the deli to sort out Wendy-Joe. Each had delivered in a total of less than ten minutes, without prior warning and completely synchronously (at least, so the rumours of later generations would have it).

Sarah and Ms O occupied small but different lying-in wards, due to the peculiarities of the system by which the Sorores attributed beds. The classification was made according to the contraception of conception. For example, the least well-appointed of such wards were 'M and C (mechanical and chemical) numbers one to thirty'. These comprised the majority of the wards and were little more than an over-crowded, noisy ghetto. This contrasted dramatically with the Delius-permeated, lily-of-the-valley-scented, newly decorated and empty 'A N (au naturel) number one'.

Sarah Delaney, with sorority approval, found herself in the very acceptable 'R number seven', which was a little ironic since there had been nothing rhythmic about Baktrian's rough and ready, definitely au naturel, interference to which Sarah attributed her present condition. Ms O was a short distance away on the same corridor, in 'Interruptus number four'. Both babies, each a boy, had been taken from their exhausted mothers, so that the latter might rest, and had been placed in the infant dormitory together with eleven babies of approximately their vintage.

Under normal circumstances one of Ms O's background and appearance would not have been confined with the Sorores at all. However, as later tellers of the episode would indefatigably reiterate as extraordinary, during her confinement and while under the wing and close attention of Baktrian at his store, she had experienced a vehement, sudden conversion to the Faith. Her own attempts to describe this turn to Christianity were largely doomed to founder amid pidgin-Canadian phrases which were later thought to have described some identification of angels and hunchbacks.

'God damn id!' He skidded again, banging his whitewalls against the kerb; his mouth opening and closing with the effort of concentration, like a rotifer's mastax.

The route by which Eli had become so uncharacteristically fond of Ms O. Kanada had been as unpredictable as it had been inevitable.

* * *

Rising from his conquest in the Alhambra, those few short months ago, just as the broken reel had been spliced and the theatre illumined once more by the mediocre movie, Eli had relieved himself, with his customary post-coital incontinence, over the alligator-skin footwear of Ms O. She had taken this as complimentary, together with the murmured, 'Jewish slut' (Eli was singularly unskilled in genealogy), which escaped Eli as he zipped up and which she did not understand. To Ms O, ever-conscious of her limitless expectations of the new world and particularly mindful of the prophecy involving hunchbacks which she had received from the oracle of a dock-side restroom shortly before sailing, the compliment clinched the coincidence and she resolved, then and there, with traditional inscrutability, to follow this man wheresoever he might lead her.

Fortunately for her tired and diminished financial resources he only led her across the street to an acceptable, but hardly exciting, life as a general dog's-body in his deli-cum-general-store. Possibly it was the prospect of such a regular Judeo-Nipponese treat which softened Eli's heart. Anyway, she could come to little harm for him or herself by living in the studio above the store room in the deli.

All this to happen so swiftly to an inscrutable maid who, up to a year ago, had never been scruted, much less even been away from home overnight!

Ms O. Kanada thoroughly inspected the profile of her

paramour, silhouetted against the movie screen. A dignified outline and not unlike the cultivated countenance of the slightly-bent, maritime medic aboard the *SS Yokahama*, whom she recalled in her mind's eye — for comparison with the hunchback before her — as he sat at the bench in his ship-board laboratory, idly smiling at her, while negligently disembowelling calcareous tubeworms and colourful strongylocentrotus purpuratus amid glass cases and aquaria which bubbled gently behind him from the activities of copper rockfish, grunt scolpins, mossy chitons, warbonnets, wolf eels, shaggy and ringed nudibranches, decorator crabs, oxylebius pictus and gobiesox maeandricus (clingfish) which he had collected during the course of many Pacific voyages.

This anonymous oriental medical's collection would, incidentally, have been very much appreciated at the oceanography department at WHU ('Where?', 'What?' — Westward Ho University, Gasville, Ontario) which, owing to its land-locked location, had ingeniously founded its scholarly reputation upon the study of tinned specimens, their demography, their sociology and psychology. Luckily this had proved to be an area of science in which the Canadian inventive originality could be fostered and thrive, in the absence of competition.

Thus it was therefore that Ms O had risen and followed Eli Baktrian from the Alhambra movie theatre and taken up residence above his store. In fact, it was as they left the show, which was still proceeding, that Ms O learnt two words of Canadian, which might have been very useful and stood her in good stead for many years, had things only turned out differently.

The two syllables were emitted by Eli when Ms O inadvertently trod upon his heel.

* * *

'God damn them, sons of bidches.' Eli skidded again. This time his invective was directed towards the occupants of a fire truck which had just sped past him up the hill, forcing him over onto the sidewalk.

Ramming his foot down hard on the accelerator he slewed his Cherokee round and succeeded in bouncing it back onto the road. With the blackest of expressions on his face and in his heart he sped after the fire truck which had turned in at the Sorores Mundi when it reached the brow of the hill. Eli was intent on giving the young degenerate at the wheel a few well-chosen thoughts on how to drive.

'Damn near killed me,' he was muttering when he turned into the drive of the maternity home and skidded to a halt in amazement, his passage barred by a chaos of cars and bystanders through whom the fire truck was laboriously wedging its way to the accompaniment of sirens and shouts from the firemen, who were pushing into the crowd in an attempt to clear a fire-lane.

Over the multitude Eli was astonished to see the lights of the hospital ablaze and illuminating a gaping hole in the side of the wing which he had been visiting only a few hours earlier.

* * *

The details of the explosion at Sorores Mundi on that fateful February Friday will probably never be known with scientific certainty. At the subsequent inquest on the eleven cherubic innocents as well as the less notable adult victims, presided over by Naomi Weiptz and lasting for thirteen days, many facts came out. Speculative facts, lurid and irresponsible facts, hearsay facts and gossipy-drivel facts were all meat and drink to Naomi, who felt it her duty to extract full entertainment value from this one isolated, exciting incident in her otherwise tedious career upon the judicial bench. Of course, as time has passed, rumour and legend have made their inroads upon the original legalistic account.

Dean Smoothe was just finishing off a straightforward delivery at Sorores Mundi shortly before the explosion.

Smoothe was naturally more accustomed to deliveries on a grander, more bucolic scale. However, on this weekend it had fallen to him to stand in for a friend and Hippocratic colleague in his macaronic profession by the name of Dwayne Testes. Testes' academic claim to medical stardom as the first Canadian to transplant simultaneously four limbs and thirteen internal organs (into a patient who, incidentally, already had a perfectly good set and never recovered consciousness) would generally be considered worthy of coverage by several TV programmes and a ghosted autobiography. However, at this point, we must pass him by with but a few words of explanation. Dwayne had chosen the weekend of February thirteenth to be invited away to a three day drying out colloquium for those afflicted by delirium tremens, of which he was the only local survivor to suffer from a genus known technically as 'delirium tremens colossa inexplorata'.

Understandably, Dwayne had been excited beyond all endurance by the prospect of this weekend and had been practising up for it for the previous month. Consequently Smoothe had been Testes' stand-in on several previous occasions.

Actually, Smoothe did not mind the extra duties very much. He considered his wife to be an utter bitch, particularly concerning the trips (real or imaginary) that he took with Felicite Sox, and it gratified him to aggravate her even more by disappearing on a Friday evening with the evidently lame excuse that he was going to a very late night of deliveries at Sorores Mundi.

He had come by his wife at a key-swapping party during a conference in New York, on the same occasion, in fact, that he had traded in his former wife. It was not as if she did not know what to expect. She had been married to a medical man before. He had been a shrink whose speciality was to disabuse smokers of their nasty habit by what he termed 'abuse therapy'. The latter technique was very expensive and consisted of subjecting his patients to hour-long sessions during which he shouted at them, confronted them alternately with life-size photographs of Adolf Hitler and Mao Tse Tung and deposited ice-cubes in their underwear.

The now Thelma Smoothe had lasted three stormy weeks with him from which she had emerged considerably the richer.

Thelma had, in fact, been rather successful recently in thwarting the Dean's attempts to spend time with Sox, with the result that he frequently caught himself in the pangs of fantasizing about Sox's hairy lips and armpits, her tight army trousers and the scratch of denim on pendulous buttocks.

In the delivery room he had been assisted by a nurse, a somnambulant anaesthetist and a grinning intern, whom he quite liked, as a substitute for a literate conversationalist, despite the fact that the latter's features were a battleground of unsightly seborrhoea. Beneath his pimples and pus there throbbed the incisive mind of a lumberjack.

'What's the small hairy thing between a Scotsman's thighs?' Smoothe volunteered, gazing cheerily round at his companions in the delivery theatre as he washed up from the final delivery of the night. It was time to relax with a cigarette, before anyone could wheel in an emergency case. He reflected that, with the recent waves of liberal anti-fumist legislation, the only 'designated area' in which he could indulge in a quick smoke was the operating theatre.

'Uh? Whad?' answered grinning pus-face. The nurse turned away in an attitude of disapproval, inclining her head sufficiently to catch the punch line. Smoothe lit up and blew out copious amounts of smoke in her direction.

'Another Scotsman!' he returned, smiling with superior satisfaction, elbowing the swing doors open and passing through into the corridor beyond.

He found himself in the corridor in which 'R number seven' and 'I number four' were situated and he crossed over to seat himself on a crate that had been placed by the door of the baby dormitory that was adjacent to the latter.

A slightly built oriental lady, with the customary large teats of a healthy young mother, was engaged in gazing in through the observation panel and was making inarticulate noises of endearment to a cradle containing an oblivious incumbent on the far side of the ward. Smoothe recognized her, even though their previous introduction had been from quite a different viewpoint, in the delivery room. He puffed fumes all around her.

'You should be resting,' he remarked solicitously, without rising from his seat on the crate.

Ms O. Kanada did not seem to hear him, for she made no attempt at a reply.

At the inquest coroner Weiptz had determined that Ms O had been on her way to perform that office so often referred to by a North-American scatological euphemism that would make Winnie the Pooh turn in his grave.

'Hi, sweedie. Hi there,' came a giggling salutation from down the corridor. Smoothe glanced up with a delighted grin. It was Sox herself! He hastily threw away the cigarette and ran along the corridor simultaneously to embrace her and sweep her from sight through the door of a nearby small office and store closet used by the almoner. The Dean did not pause to turn on the light, nor to ask permission, before launching into the lascivious groping that he had been yearning for for days. Accordingly Sox, who with all her qualifications insisted upon being treated like a lady, responded with a knee to the groin.

'Shit, Smoothe you god no manners?' With that she did him what transpired to be the greatest favour of his life. She felled him with a powerful forearm smash to the temple.

At the time Smoothe was in no condition or temper to express gratitude and one second later it was too late.

There was a terrific roar outside in the corridor, piercing white flashes of pain to his head, neck and back. The blast threw open the door, lifting it from its hinges and ripping open the thin partition wall. All that Smoothe felt was one further smashing blow to the ground before he passed out.

When he came to there was glass all around him and a terrific din of wailing, screaming and prayer coming from outside. Sox was looking down at him from two foot up the opposite wall, her eyes staring wide and a thin trickle of blood commencing to run from the corner of her mouth. The official record of the inquest was later to describe her as ' . . . having been victim of an immense explosion which caused her to be impaled upon the extended finger of a metal, prosthetic limb, hurled by the blast, which pinned her to the wall and loosened her fashion jeans and underwear.'

Smoothe rose slowly to his feet, rubbing his head which was beginning to throb, and gazing in silence at Sox, who returned his gaze vituperatively. He stumbled out into the bloodstained corridor; everywhere were gobbets of gore (he stepped on a piece of Ms O. Kanada without realizing it) and before him, in the place where the infant dormitory had been, loomed an enormous rip in the wall through which he could see the shards of devastation — broken furniture, torn feeding blankets and heaps of trashed victims' remains. A lot of the chaos had been flung with lurid stains against the outside wall, a large section of which had been completely blown away.

A screaming crowd was gathering at the entrance to the

dormitory. Patients were rushing in all directions, trying to find help. All around Smoothe could see the genuflecting figures of the sisters of Sorores Mundi, wailing and praying as they smote their foreheads upon hard objects such as broken chair-legs, picture-frames, from which dangled the tatters of some saintly epiphany, and splinters of bed-side lamps.

Further along the corridor Smoothe could see the crumpled form of a bald-headed man. Casting vainly about for some help, Smoothe went over to examine the man.

A brief look sufficed to assure the Dean that there was no hope. The man had been side-swiped by a large piece of the packing crate, which Smoothe now realized was no longer where it had been when he had seated himself on it to have a smoke. He fished out the man's wallet in a very professional manner, which had been instinctive to all his Faculty back in the days of extra-billing. The man's name was Delaney. He looked a little closer. My God! It was Delaney, the Mayor of Gasville and a prominent church-going local farmer. To get a better look he turned the head this way and that.

Looking around once more Smoothe, noticing the splinters of packing-case, began with unusual intellectual or intuitionistic speed, to realize what must have happened so completely to etherize and devastate his immediate vicinity and most of its luckless personnel.

At the inquest Naomi Weiptz had tortuously teased and traced the tissue of tragedy and had eventually come up with the following scenario.

The crate, that fearful rudiment of carpentry containing Delaney's dynamite, had been the cause of the accident. Delaney had bought the explosive for the removal of rocks and he had been disinclined to leave it out in the back of his truck so, for safety, he had carried it in with him when he had gone to visit his wife, Sarah, just before she gave birth. There had seemed no harm in leaving it outside the baby dormitory since he could not take it with him when he went to watch the delivery. He was not to know, nor should one expect too much ratiocination from pregnant fathers when their hour is nigh, that Smoothe's cigarette butt would find its way into the fuses, whose paper wrapping had been torn open as Delaney negotiated the packing-case out of the cramped service elevator.

So much for Naomi's factual treatment of the case. However,

her fine nose for entertainment, enlightenment and testament, had also delved deeper into the fates of the tiny cherubs in the dormitory, and here her efforts were sensationally rewarded — if we are to believe what was later told and re-told as gospel truth throughout the county for many years thereafter.

For thirteen days Naomi's was the hottest show in town.

Concerning the children, she gave over four days to inquisitions, depositions and descriptions, some by witnesses who were not even present at the time of the fracas. Opinions were sought, photographs were passed around, men cried and ladies fainted. Punkers vomited and their girlfriends screamed with misery. Naomi questioned marriage guidance counsellors, occupational therapists, psychiatrists, marine explosive experts, demolition workers, county librarians, chemists, physicists, a mathematician who wandered in by mistake when searching for his inland revenue hearing, a confectionist, three rabbis, an instructor of Scottish country dancing and several native people who gave their names as Broad Scalplock, Mrs Man Who Smokes, Poundmaker, Walking Buffalo, Big Bear, Peter Ear, North Axe, Mrs Old Man Spotted, Pah-pah-kao-paso-wyan, Many Mules, Mosquito and Miko-peasis. The last named had to be brought into the courtroom on a dog-travois because he was too enervated from self-mutilation while doing the Sun Dance.

From all these came the same fascinating tale.

There had been thirteen small babies in the dormitory when the explosion happened. The dynamite-filled packing case was so close to these infants, separated by the thinnest of interior walls, that it was hardly surprising that ten of the tiny sleepers should have been ripped to smithereens immediately. The blast tore open the outer wall, bearing the remaining three out through the aperture with its unspent force. One of these three got no further than the telephone wires, which garrotted the little fellow in flight. His name was lost from the records.

The remaining two babies were later to be called by the names of Yukio Kanada and O'Toole Delaney.

Ms O's child and Sarah Delaney's were not actually discovered until about an hour after the mighty report had echoed all around Gasville. For they were thrown about eighty metres by the force of the holocaust and were only saved from serious injury by the deep banks of snow in the children's playground which faced the Sorores Mundi.

When discovered the two tots were reputedly clasped in a mutual tight embrace. Together in birth, so in life was Sarah's motto with respect to the boys, which was what prompted her to adopt and rear the young Yukio with her own boy.

Although Sarah was a quiet woman, not given to showing her thoughts and emotions too openly, there were times later when her expression led the malicious gossips, tellers of the Yukiad, to point to pangs of regret on her part.

Within days of the disaster the community had initiated a fund for the survivors. This was how, after some vehement discussion about just who had survived what, Yukio Kanada and O'Toole Delaney (aged three weeks, two days, seventeen hours and forty-five minutes — let's not be too silly about their precise ages) found themselves in the company of Dean Smoothe as the sole trustees of the Sorores Mundi Calamity Fund, destined to become a very well-endowed organ of support for the down-trodden, the deprived, the demoralized and the destitute survivors of explosions in South Western Ontario.

3

COFFEE

Bucolia, Yukio and the diminutive professor were taking an early morning pause for refreshments. They were seated around the table out in the conservatory. The breakfast plates had been pushed to one end to make room for the tray which Elsquaird had set down. Bucolia was facing the window, through which the beautiful dawn view could be seen, transformed now into tranquil ordinariness.

Yukio, in his inevitable wheelchair, was reading a book. This operation he could only accomplish very slowly and with extreme difficulty. On his head he was wearing a helmet, a hideous contraption to the forehead of which was attached a long wand — an antenna by means of which he could turn pages, using only his head and neck, and then laboriously trace out in minute increments the passages which he was reading.

To complete the reading of the slim paperback which currently confronted him might take the young man as much as six months of consolidated effort.

The professor leant over and wiped Yukio's chin.

'There are some parts of Eastern Europe where the people are small and stocky,' he continued his conversation with Bucolia.

'Even squat — not much taller than me! When I was young and much exercised by those sort of concerns I used to think that I would be less miserable were I to move to Baku.'

'Baku?'

'A sea-side resort, very old, on the Black Sea.' The professor chuckled. 'I know nothing more about it. I just fancied the name. Most probably I would have arrived there only to find, Gulliver-like, that the natives were giants.

'And when I was young I would not have taken that at all lightly. I used to be, foolishly as I now see, most offended by anyone who was taller than me. And since that was everyone I used to retreat to my second line of defence — the conviction that at least I was more intelligent than everyone else.'

The professor burst into laughter, as if he had made a great joke. The blind girl directed at him her most charming smile.

'But you are,' Bucolia assured him.

'Maybe I was — but it was all too damn silly to think so. And now we will never know.' He laughed again, a low corporeal reverberation, and grinned at his companion's handsome, sightless face.

'The main thing about being a mathematical genius is that it is an airy, light and graceful talent while you have it. A delightful, preoccupying game that you can play with puzzles in your mind — totally absorbing, and impressively mystifying to those who cannot think as quickly as you. It is a scarcely noticeable source of unlimited enjoyment, like a new outfit, only better. However, it is for that very reason that one notices one's genius most when it starts to evaporate; when it won't perform the old tricks quite so fast; when the memory — mine was excellent once! — starts to spring a few leaks. When you're a bit older you will begin to discover that it is becoming harder to remember names. Then you'll understand a little better what I'm talking about.'

'You still have a better memory than I do. But I know what you mean. Yukio, O'Toole and I used to be telepathic.'

Elsquaird raised his eyebrows in surprise but made no comment.

'Tell me about the day when Yukio's real mother arrived.'

'Do you really want to hear all that again?'

Bucolia nodded.

Elsquaird settled back in his chair, drawing his coffee-mug to his chest and glancing first at Yukio, who was still reading absorbedly.

'Well, there was nothing special to notice in Gasville on that day. She just slipped unobtrusively into town. Eli was probably the only one who even saw her arrival. Gasville was a very sleepy place in those days, you realize? In point of fact, if you had ever travelled in Southern Ontario back then it would come as no

surprise to learn that Highway 05, as it swept into the metropolis
of Gasville, hell-bent on conjunction with RR9, was not an
exciting experience.

'Gasville, pop. 5000, twenty-six clubs.' The professor smiled
as he began to tell off club-names for his blind friend's
amusement.

'Kiwanis, Rotary, Lions, Jaycees, Mocha Temple, Sisters
of Oblivion, Sorores Redemptibus, St Andrew's Knights, Rebus
Caelorum, St George's Dragons, St Patrick's (Alternative),
Morris Beauchamp Geriatric Homes, Beauchamp Morris,
Vallee Morris, Ginger Morris, Home County Morris, the
Society of Saint Vincent de Paul, Morris Dancers des Estados
Unidos, Gasville Morris Dancers, P.E.G.S. (Political Experience
of Gasville — Seniors), F.A.G.S. (Football Association of
Gasville — Seniors), B.A.G.S., B.U.G.S., T.F.G.J. (Tooth
Fairies of Gasville — Juniors), Noster Dominus del Flores (S.J.)
and the Gasville Second-Hand Auditorium . . .'

4

MS O. KANADA

The day is still remembered, talked of, chewed over, spewed over, scratched and spittooned over. Throughout his life when the syrup was running and Eli Baktrian had settled down to a thick coffee, after an even thicker piss, he would recall that first afternoon — a dusty summer afternoon, that humid sort of Gasville afternoon that causes bank clerks to hurry into the john at lunch to change their underwear and spray their loins, pits and tonsils in readiness for the ordeal of professional proximity.

The other one, O'Toole, never was worth quoting but Baktrian, to the end of his days, was never to tire of Yukio's: 'My first intelligent thought was of death.'

Later there were reminiscences of sun-spots, eclipses and more than a score of Gasville worthies mentioned the perihelion of Mercury.

There was every sort of rosicrucian, post-equinoxial, Gaussian punditry concerning the heavenly behaviour — its singularity and its multiplicity — on that fateful day. In fact it was hardly fateful; demographically speaking its only significance was that the Gasville population rose by one and a mite (or point zero three per cent) that day.

Eli Baktrian was standing on the porch of his deli-and-hardware thoughtfully cutting a series of notches with his sabre into the superstructure of Southern Ontario's Last Remaining Link With The Past — in other words, an historic public monument in the form of the last hitching rail in Ontario.

He was contemplating his contumely.

The sabre itself has little or nothing to with dishonour — or

27

death for that matter — although Eli's father, himself a veteran
of the camel corps in the War to End Wars Ending Wars, had
been a steadfast avowson of the opinion that the weapon had
seen service in the hands of an obscure aide-de-camp of General
Lee, one Gascoine Beauregard no less.

He was, in a detached manner, indulging himself in the
disgraceful amusement of thinking unthinkable sexist and racist
thoughts.

'Whoops, steady boyo, thad was a partic'ly large notch, damn
near splid the post!'

Why did he persist? And was he not at *two* Meetings on the
weekend? On most in fact?

His Osh-Gosh's were uncomfortably tumescent. He glanced
furtively the length of Dundas to ensure that no Rooneys or
other scummy peepers had him in their binocs. Missus Delaney,
too, was inclined to giggle at his bulge when he was striving
to attend to business and serve her with Old Fort in the deli.

An ample woman was Sarah Delaney — and an intelligent
piece for one of the papal persuasion. To tell the truth she had
lapsed.

She and her husband, Paddy, the Mayor, had lapsed so much
that not only were they childless and cheerful, but they had taken
to coming occasionally to a Meeting. They had been there,
herself with a large and saucy cleavage and himself with a
freckled tonsure, kneeling devoutly all the while Eli had
harangued them on The Evils Thereof.

'Drink, I say it is a horrible vice and too used. Every town
has an abundance of taverns and ale-houses haunted by malt-
worms night and day. They sit at the ale all day long. A world
it is to marvel at their demeanour — swilling, gulling, carousing.
With the spirit of the buttery they are possessed. Some vomit,
some piss under the board, some fall to cursing and blasphemy.

'Meat and drink moderately taken corroborate the body,
refresh the arteries and revive the spirit. Immoderately taken
they abuse the body. Do they not falter and froth at the mouth?
Do not all their hands and organs shake, as if from a dropsy,
shaken with quotidian fever? It dissolves the whole man at length
so that of what he does when drunk he remembers nothing when
sober. A man who takes strong drink resembles the brute beast
rather than a man!'

There had been a universal matronly groan of approval from

around the room at his last stirring line.

Technically speaking, Eli Baktrian was a hunchback. More accurately he was what might be termed hunchsided. All in all he considered himself to be not at all a bad-looking man. Frequently he would contemplate the face on the front of his head and conclude that it was rather dignified, not to say austere; rather sad, not to say melancholic, even becomingly swarthy and weatherbeaten. Many were the loose hours that he had filled with such self-speculation, mulling desultorily over the pictures of his vellum-bound, dog-eared copy of *Big Ears' Book of Arthurian legends and mediaeval trivia*. Daydreaming . . .

The crookback hight Eli was seated, advanced upon the shoulders of an mighty host, peregrine at his glove, encompassing with reverent gaze, and full manly thereto, the Priors, the Reeves, the Warden of the Walls and those others of his yeomanry. Generous was his entertainment, both noble and gentle, and what degree soever, this entertainment being not inferior to any place, both for the goodness of their diet, the sweet and dainty nature of their lodgings, and generally all things necessary for travellers, and withal this entertainment continuing, not willing, not commanding, any man to depart upon his honest and good behaviour.

His lands are girded almost rownd with the renouned River of Weer, in which, as in a Glasse of Crystal, he might once have beheld the beauty, but now the ruine of his walls.

To his provender was added mighty tribute of these Lords and bondsmen, as here listed, 600 salt herrings, 400 white herrings, 30 salted salmon, 12 fresh salmon, 14 ling, 55 kelengs, 4 turbot, two horse loads of white fish, and a congr, plaice sparlings and eels, and fresh water fish, carcases of oxen salted, so brought, a carcase and a quarter of fresh, a quarter of an ox fresh, brought from the Gasbury towne in a tumbril, 7 carcases and a half of swine in salt, 6 carcases fresh, 14 calves, 3 kids and 26 sucking porkers, 71 geese with their feed, 14 capons, 59 chickens and 5 dozen pigeons, 5 stones of hog's lard, 4 stones of cheese, butter and milk, a pottle of vinegar, and a pottle of honey, 14 pounds of figs and raisins, 13 pounds of almonds, and 8 pounds of rice, pepper, saffron, cinnamon, and other spices, 1300 eggs.

All this brought they in and treasures withal. A pyx of black crystal, containing the sponge, and a piece of the sepulchre of the Lord, and the stone upon which Jesus sat in the judgement seat of Herod. A piece of the tree, under which were three angels and Abraham, in beryl, white and hollow, and withal a wonderful structure.

And the Lord Crookback raised, in recognition of this plenty, the Mace of the Raby Bucks. Smiting thrice the table, above the salt, signalled this retinue to take its ease. And, making the sign with his beringed forefinger, turned and quit the Hall, followed by his hounds, Eldfreyn and Athelred.

A man's best friend is his dog, and there is no friend like an eld freyn.

These homespun homilies were homespinning through Eli's headpiece and he hummed contentedly as he nonchalantly twirled his historic heirloom, intermittently notching:

> When I was a young man and still in my prime,
> I used to go skating all of the time,
> I'll tell you tales of desperation and woe,
> Of wild skating expeditions I know.

In front of the Cracker Barrel fishing tackle and gun emporium, named in a moment of nostalgic wistfulness, Eli could see the emerging, languid, stringy elegance of 'Sheikh' Abdul Akbar Jahman, bending slightly to give ear to a portly companion, who was gesturing in Eli's direction. Abdul was no local boy! Although Jahman's immigration sounded like another illustration of Middle Eastern investment, he had in fact lived in Ontario since teenage. His parents had settled there from Calcutta when he was fifteen — the misnomer 'Sheikh' was the traditional Gasville epithet for anyone of his pigmentation. A shrewd businessman and a very successful farmer, he had bought out Agamemnon Pince's sugarbush and a section of the neighbouring land.

For one of them, Akbar's not so bad, Eli conceded.

He played a neat fiddle (last year's runner up at Shelburn in the novelty section — Saint Anne's Reel, Cotton-Eye Joe, Miss McCloud's Reel, Adolf Hitler's Hornpipe, Old Mother Flanagan, The Bummer's Reel, Bum on the Turnpike, the Maiden's Bum, Sheebeg Sheemore and Christmas Day i' da Morning, all played with the handle of a bissom for a bow and he himself balancing on his head the while) and he would help a good guy out whenever he could. He had been the first on the scene when Titus Pinch had done away with himself with a disused powerline which the Gasville community had erroneously assumed to be out of juice. The 'Sheikh' had given Titus mouth-to-mouth for the best part of an hour, in the dark, before Titus' old lady had put six ounces of buckshot in his ass, taking him for one of the coloured snoopers that were always coming around, inspectors from the Ministry of Agriculture.

As the pair turned and gazed in his direction Eli casually remarked to himself that the other man was adorned with a hat that should have been left at the Calgary Stampede. He found such idiosyncrasies distasteful. Better to replace the offensive headgear by a more respectable red baseball hat (with a plastic turd on the peak) as befits an agrarian gentleman and Gasville sophist.

An approaching dusty swirl of haze heralded the arrival of the afternoon Gray Coach from Toronto, via Villetown, Paris, Venice, Hamburg, Rome, Pompei, Princeton, Glasgow, Fifeville, MacBeathville, Macdonaldville, Camerontown, Elginturd, McCustard, MacMustardbury, Waterloo, Townville and several other pointless points east.

Sweeping into the city square, not one hundred metres from the very spot on which Eli stood, transfixed, gazing at the entourage, came this sleek, silver-bodied super-monster of a superluxury travel facility. (What did we ever do before their air-conditioned loveliness was at our beck and call? Fifty dollars to New York, one way — and who would ever want to return?)

Sometimes Eli treated himself to this sort of clandestine heresy, ignoring the societary overtones of his nonconformism.

The coach had stopped, its doors swung open and the driver was already putting out the passengers' valises.

Marjoram Jahman was the first passenger to alight. A strong, willowy lady of considerably more than average height, her face as fetching as a young girl's, although she was nearer forty than fourteen. From her mountain of parcels and packets Eli assumed that she had been to New York (or was it Boston?) to see her relatives, the Aklappa dynasty. Akbar was hurrying over to embrace this winsome vision of loveliness and presents.

Just the thought of that hug caused Eli a tumescent twitch.

Second down from the coach was an astronaut. Recognizing the hypervinyl jogging suit and polyvinylchloride knee waders of a jock from the local college (WHU — Westward Ho University) Eli complacently viewed this replica of extra-terrestrial invasion, which swaggered away down the street, waving to a trio of co-eds who had emerged from a cafe and were trotting, with Hollywood-starlet giggles, wiggles and hair-bouncing towards his enplasticated mass of masculinity.

Another tumescent twitch.

Next down was Gasville's response to radical chic, in the form of a debonair individual in a grey herringbone suit, scented handkerchief in lapel pocket, who (unbeknownst to the campus-ignorant Baktrian, who calmly voided his rheum in a juicy glob of expectorated disgust at this perfumed pansy) was an influential macaronic mentor from the Faculty of Veterinary. He was entitled Dean Twain Smoothe, the Director of Bucolic Insemination. As with medical schools all over the province, it was customary at WHU to subdivide the veterinary faculty into many sub-units of breath-taking importance and international stature, in the interests of world-leading efficiency (and costliness) with the result that Smoothe was the Dean of Insemination, Milda Rattacks was his second-in-command and Principal of Insemination and their headline-arresting unit of three was topped off by a Ph.D student, Felicite Sox, Vice-Principal of Insemination. This scholarly trio was ably and mightily assisted by fifteen secretaries, telephone girls, tea-ladies, physical plant men and receptionists.

The Medical Faculty at WHU subscribed to the perspicacious view that medics should not be too clever and Dean Smoothe endorsed this with his own policies. Just as pigeons are better, he contended, than human beings at the tedious task of checking production lines for faulty silicon chips so was the stupid Hippocratarian better suited to the tedium of the production line of corpus derelictus than his smarter fellow man, who should perhaps seek gainful employment as a philosopher or mathematician.

Smoothe could rightfully take some pride in the clockwork-like efficiency of Insemination. He liked to ruminate on the rows of cow sheds, housing cows inevitably to become gravid, to dream wonderingly about Mozart and Haydn, whose works penetrated the sheds each evening; soothing, lulling, comforting the inmates and preparing them for the great Friday Night Special that was their fate. It was with incredulity and intense satisfaction that Smoothe estimated that forty pounds of spermatozoa would simultaneously, every Friday night, amid coordinated moos of delight, gratified grunts and paroxysms of penetration, in that vast labyrinth of cow-sheds, be released and speed with the fallopian breaststroke towards their ovarian targets. And that was not counting the animals! Copulation without population was anathema to Smoothe.

As always with Smoothe, whenever travelling to places far-flung, exotic, expensive and usually climatologically temperate in the pursuit of his path-breaking research, Miss Sox was along for the experience and it was her suntanned form that emerged next from the bus. She was tall and slim, her face pleasant enough, although it resembled that of a male youth and even sported a thin blond moustache, which Sox neglected to shave when she was doing her armpits.

'Sox! Sox!' came the ringing English baritone of a rather dashing personage in the form of Dragan Weipzt, campus philanderer par excellence and husband emeritus to the local coroner, Naomi Weipzt.

'Hello, Smoothe, Felicite. I've brought the Bugatti,' he casually waved in the direction of a gleaming green 1936 roadster. 'We can all squeeze in at a pinch.' He gave Sox's withers a playful tweak, picked up her bag and led them away towards the transport.

The strains of Weiptz's campus-renowned, legendary Dick song floated back over his shoulder in a cheerful and mellifluous baritone.

Watch your Dick,
Watch your Dick,
Watch your Dick,
Watch your di-i-ic-tion.

Eli's gaze shifted with some interest to the final passenger to get down from the coach.

This passenger was clearly one of them, he told himself. She had the build — he surveyed the heavy buttocks and breasts. Tumescent twitch. Definitely one of them, with the face of a Japanese. What a combination! What a motmot of lineage! What a lustable mixtion of attractions.

Here was something good coming his way. In an expectation

of good fortune he slid his sword and buckler through the open door of his store, flipped the sign to BACK SOON and quietly closed the door, returning his attention to the new arrival, this metempsychosis, the Nippo-Hassidic vision that had brightened up his day.

Usually they had breasts as tiny as the nuts on a Calgary drill sergeant, but here they were bobbing in front of his very eyes. Undeniably Ms O. Kanada, for that was the very name of this weighty wonder of womanhood, was quite a — he searched for a description — hunchfront.

'He who sups wi the de'il mun hae a lang spoon' and Eli's was feeling longer by the minute.

Ms O. Kanada picked up her bag in an attitude of preoccupation and headed for Gasville's most grandiose example of post Norman architecture, the Alhambra movie theatre and pigeon-roost. Fortunately, at this moment, the pigeons had flown off to some other idyllic locale leaving the Alhambra looking its very, very pigeon-shite-free best. Which was awful.

Undeterred by the posters displaying what was showing Ms O advanced, went up the peeling steps and bought a ticket. In she went, picking her way through the traditional garbage and popcorn debris to a place of concupiscent seclusion on the back row of the deserted auditorium.

Ms O — an appellation that had resulted from an inconsiderately-timed exclamation during her belated christening in the saloon bar of the *SS Yokahama*, at the age of twenty-two, on the voyage to join her pre-Canadianized relatives in Vancouver — was heavy with gravid thoughts. She had been christened by the ship's MD, as it happened, a portent of gravidity and delivery combined. A rather good-looking man of middling years he had been. Most unusually for a resident of the Land of the Rising Sun he had been a hunchback. Anything but dapper, trim rectitude was so unexpected an experience that she had realized the ominous presagement of his anomaly.

Indeed, it was with an immense sense of fatality that she had been seduced by this very hunchback, not two days later in the ship's third-class life-boat, swinging out over the stern-churned Pacific.

Gazing at the screen, which happened momentarily to be empty due to a break in the celluloid, her mind ran back over that oceanic rapture of delight. Hot breath on one cheek and sea-spray, champagne-sparkly, on the others. The prosopalgia of a cheek pressed against the davit of the craft, a one-eyed glimpse of the moon from beneath its tarpaulin. A moment of transportation with her hunchback of destiny.

And him an MD all the while!

* * *

Oblivious to being watched Ms O had sauntered to her reveries, concerning Nipponese delights, amid the dustiness and accumulated popcorn debris of the Alhambra. Had Mother never warned her to beware of the uninvited tumescent attentions of hardwear wheeler-dealer hunchbacks in the hinterlands of the North American subcontinent? Evidently not, for the briefest cursory glance over a diminutive but exquisitively shaped shoulder would have revealed the Imminence Grise, personified by Eli Baktrian, shutting up the shop and preparing to cross the bustling Gasville thoroughfare in the direction of the Alhambra.

Baktrian stepped into the road, his eyes on the form disappearing into the movies.

'God Bless Ya, stupid Brother, and keep yar soul in torment! Watch where ya goin', Son of Satan.' This zesty jibe originated from atop a Mennonite buggy, which was bearing down upon Baktrian with all the intent and inevitability of three kilometres per hour. He jumped back, cursing.

'Sonofabitches! Never use the hitch-post. Whoever heard of hitching to a parking meter? Horseshid.'

He crossed swiftly to the side door of the Alhambra and let himself in with a pass-key that he had providentially copied while undertaking a similar commission for the Alhambra then-commissionaire, Jack Butz deceased, three years earlier on the occasion of Jack's having forgotten for the fourth time which flowerpot contained the spare. The key-copying had been intended to save Jack's oft-exhumed avocados from wilting while, at the same time, giving Eli the opportunity for gratis cinematographic entertainment and self-gratification.

The auditorium was very dark, the film being temporarily

interrupted, as he entered. He paused momentarily to get his bearings.

He could vaguely discern a human form reclining in the back row. Inevitably, being currently the only incumbent, the shape toward which he groped his way was none other than the daydreaming Ms O. Kanada herself.

'Trollops! They're all th' same,' intoned Baktrian. 'For whad we're aboud t' receive . . . '

He advanced with popcorn-crunches and a mentality mindful of mediaeval missionary merriment. Dapper in imagined sallet and bevor, Great Basket and barbut, an eagle gules volant in an argent field emblazoned on his mail, equipped with halbard, pike, mace, morning star, gipon, pole axe, lance and scabbard. He envisioned the peeling 'Southern Ontario tacky' decor perhaps as resplendent machicolations, merlons and embrazures of some Norman barbican or glorietta, with portcullis and crenellated gardrobe — a ha-ha beyond the postern.

All in all, suffice to say, the roughcast advances of Baktrian rampant were about to be received by Ms O. Kanada with the same ocean-going, life-boat invoking, hunchback-inviting, medicine-man's double-bill resulting, prosopalgiac deja vue and tendresse that is commonplace, frequent and even inevitable amongst the ennui-beridden of Gasville when the film goes kaput.

For Eli it was just another instance of the foeman baring his steel — the previous occasion being that morning during his sharpening of Sarah Delaney's Taurus mower at her Paddy-absent and otherwise unattended homestead on Esplanade RR 63.

5

ASSUMPTION OF POWER

Eli Baktrian's head lay cradled on his forearms; the council chamber of Gasville, Ont. was in turmoil about him. The other councillors were engaged in heated debate with Sarah Delaney, who was arguing the case for Eli's mayoral candidacy. The casual observer, had there been one, which there was not, would have surmised that Eli was sleeping innocently.

In fact, quite the reverse was true. He knew what was going to happen and was listening attentively.

The building which housed the meetings of the Gasville aldermen stood tall, gaunt and wooden at the very eastern end of the main street. It had been painted in camouflage stripes as a pacifist, anti-Vietnam protest by the former owner, Martin Martin, who had farmed prosperously in the neighbourhood until that unexpected day when he had garotted himself with a piece of fencing wire on a very slowly moving 1929 Massey-Ferguson, in first gear.

Eli himself had been so surprised by Martin's demise that he had been moved wisely to remark, 'Mennonites don't often garotte themselves.'

To commemorate its former owner, whose family nobly gave the building to the town, the hall had had a spire added at the northern wall and was now affectionately entitled 'Martin's Byre', an appellation to which attested a plaque which visitors encountered just beside the front door. The plaque had been carved personally by the late Paddy Delaney himself and graphically depicted the four seasons of farming life arranged in a circle around a central, small, ploughing figure who was engaged in self-garottation.

Inside the former byre was an ample council chamber with twenty-five seats arranged in the traditional circular pattern. The walls were decorated with cherry-wood panelling and the overall effect was one of comfort, light and harmonious warmth.

'Sometoimes you can be the demon of an idjit-man, t'be sure, Thomas Snuze. Just because Paddy was my late husband don't mean, Oi'm thinkin', that I can't speak up in this debate. I won my seat here, same as you!'

Sarah was engaged in an exchange of political banter with Tom Snuze, the convenor and himself a mayoral candidate. Besides Eli he was the only other man in the room.

Snuze had been fighting hard to be the next mayor, Baktrian reflected, although it was all to no avail, of course. Eli smiled to himself as he mused over what was inevitably going to happen.

Snuze was a fighter all right. If talking could have won him the mayorship he would have got it certainly, for he had hardly let any other person get a word in during the course of the meeting so far. A meeting which had lasted for more than an hour. He was a tall, thin man with a slightly sagging face topped by a distinguished mop of iron-grey hair. He had a deep, mature and pleasant speaking voice. By dint of daily exercise and weekly prayer he kept himself in physical and spiritual good shape. The superficial observer would have picked Snuze for the next mayor over the prostrate Eli Baktrian by odds of ten to one. However, comme tous les nords-americains, he had that fault of all faults, that penchant which leads film-stars, lawyers and ballerinas alike to be shunned like lepers.

He had gas!

Of all the explosive possibilities which might have resulted therefrom his was, mercifully, perhaps one of the more benign. Nevertheless, Thomas Snuze, born Tomas Mordecai Schnauser in AusfarhtHimmelberg Pa., was a belcher. Not a secret belcher. Not a take-it-out-in-the-open-air-and-look-the-other-way belcher. Not a weekend belcher. Not a social belcher. He was the sort of belcher from the friends and acquaintances of whom the demands of close friendship extorted the scale of effort and dedication which in former times would only have been necessary in order to accomplish the labours of Hercules. He was an extremely malodorous and continual belcher.

Brrrp! There he went again, very audibly.

'No one wants a belcher for a mayor,' thought Eli to himself with a smile.

Actually, Snuze was the Custodian of the Art Works of Westward Ho University (CAWWHU) which just goes to show that excessive flatulence does not wholly militate against making it to the top.

'Ladies. Ladies.' Snuze was trying in vain to restore decorum to the mass of female councillors who had all now risen to their feet and were shouting at him so loudly as to drown a tremendously reverberant, thirty-second blast of flatus.

Eli raised his head to inspect these women. With the exception of the full-bosomed Sarah Delaney they were all of that same species of hard-bitten, sun-lined, tight-jawed, flat-buttocked, middle-aged Ontario career lady. They sold real estate in Rome. They sold jacuzzis in Pompeii or Cambridge. They sold expensive kitchen trinkets in their Elmira boutiques or stocks and bonds in Toronto. They were all so very elegantly turned out. All so masculine. However, that did not prevent Eli thinking the unthinkable about them; as he gazed round the council chamber from under hooded eyelids he felt the familiar tumescent twitch.

There was little point in all their chicken squawking. Eli knew how it was all going to turn out. He had been told a prophecy; privileged to share a very convincing premonition.

He had come early to the meeting, two hours early to be precise, in order to collect his thoughts and to rehearse what he was going to say and the manner in which he would deliver it. There was no question in his mind that he wanted to become the next mayor, that he was pre-eminently suited for the job and that once he had it things would start to hum — ca ira, ca ira, ca ira, as the French revolutionaries would have it. In fact he had gone so far as to enlist the help of three friends from up the Bruce peninsula, should he be successful. They were to be his immediate advisers under the collective title of 'Trustees of the Board'. These three comprised a gigantic Scotsman, who wore two gold earrings, and was called Preston Pans, along with two eastern European immigrés by the names of Zhilin and Penz. Each one an expert in his own field of human endeavour, although none of them held a university degree. Not even one from WHU.

While sitting quietly in his place, in something resembling his recent posture with his head on his hands, he had become aware of a nearby and malodorous presence . . .

'Eli Baktrian?' the old woman croaked in the strangled accents of a nonagenarian chain-smoker, who was looking down at him with a Player's extra-strong hanging out of the corner of her lips with complete disregard of the Gasville bye-law designation of the council chamber as non-smoking on peril of a fine of £100 ($50 US).

'Yes?' He knew the woman well, for this was old grandma Martin. She lived in the basement of the Martin Byre, having stayed behind when the rest of the family had moved away after the tragedy of Martin Martin. She was a scabrous individual, straw-dry, bitter as a wicked fairy and cold as a Gasville winter. There were many tales rife in the area concerning her prophetic powers so that what transpired next came as no surprise to Eli.

'Wanna be mayor, eh?' No reply from the wary hunchback.

'They don't make mayors out of Injuns in Gasville, eh?' She squinted at him questioningly, her head inclined to one side and her large earlobe hanging loosely down onto that shoulder.

'You're not Cree, Assiniboin, Sarcee, Blood, Beaver, Slavery, Peigen, Ojibwa, Sioux, Stony or Blackfoot are ya?'

'No.' A cautious, irritated reply.

Grandma Martin placed a large tea-bucket on the desk in front of Eli. It was the sort of communal tea-brewing utensil which saw service in the trenches of the Somme. The legend 'Cpl. Martin' was inscribed on its sides in fading letters.

'Sure, you ain't. No more'n my Martin Martin senior was. But that don't matter none, 'cos the mayor'll either be a belcher or a hunchback. Wanna see?' She pointed to the bucket. Without any surprise Eli nodded in agreement. She spat out her cigarette butt onto the floor and commenced to murmur rhythmically to herself while agitating the mess of cold tea-leaves by moving the can gently round in circles.

Eli was beginning to wonder whether the old crone had dozed off when she looked straight at him and said, 'No belcher will ever sit in the mayor's chair.'

Shit on your wrinkled old face, thought Eli.

'On yours too,' she replied amiably with a toothless, stench-filled grin. She paused and chuckled to herself.

'Like Napoleon, fire will be your beginning and fire will begin your end. But you won't know the one from the other. Unlike Napoleon it will take only three to finish you.' She stared hard into the tea-can now, holding it very still.

'Watch the three, even if you can't help it. But beware especially the one who is a cow!'

The old lady sat down on the chair next to him and gazed at him with a large, satisfied smile.

Jesus, stupid old broad, he thought, peddling this perplexing crap. It was clear that she thought he was going to make it to the mayorship. So what? He could have told her that without a bucket of cabbage-water, horse-piss and tea-leaves. It occurred to him, watching her as she rose from her seat and shuffled off out of the chamber, that ninety and prune-dry does not raise even a flicker of an urge. Senex and horrida, but perhaps reliable anyway.

After her exit Eli peacefully had settled down again to his rehearsal of his speech.

Eli's reverie of recollection was interrupted by a terrific reverberation caused by the fact that Snuze had just fallen from his seat. He lay on the floor, a very sorry heap of male-flesh, smelling like a urine sample and rubbing his jaw ruefully where Sarah Delaney's fist had struck him.

The meeting was in uproar and all around female fists were menacing.

Oh, shit, thought Eli as he rose to his feet and bellowed at the top of his lungs, 'Shud up and siddown! All of you.'

He sucked in a deep breath and prepared to let them have his prepared Tusculan prose.

'God only knows why I should wanna be your mayor — you behave like a herd of heifers jostlin' for the bull — bud I do. So there. I'm only a single man — and if I had a wife, she'd only be a single woman, until we got married.'

He waited for the polite titter to run its course.

'Being mayor ain't no easy job, but I'm ready for id. Ready to give id a try and to do the best I damn well can. I can't say that id'll be easy to follow an act like Paddy Delaney. He was as handsome as a filmstar, as narrow as a Jew, gave us the technology of the Americans, had the morals of a Welshman, the cunning of an Arab, the physique of an athlete, could fighd like an Irishman, had the diplomacy of a Frenchman, the money-sense of a Scot, the diligence of a Russian, the manners of an Englishman, the intellect of a Canadian, the courage of a bullfighder and German efficiency. I, on the other hand, have the looks of a Jew, am as narrow as an American, understand technology like a Welshman, have the morals of an Arab, the cunning of an athlete, the physique of an Irishman, fighd like a Frenchman, have the diplomacy of a Scotsman, the capitalistic skills of a Russian, the diligence of an Englishman, the manners of a Canadian, the intellect of a bullfighder and the courage of a German!'

There was a round of applause to indicate that he was warming up his audience of tight-buttocked, middle-class, entre-preneurial house-fraus.

'But I have one thing to offer, and thad is — the future. Elect me and you shall see. Ad the stroke of midnight, while Ontario sleeps, Gasville will awake to a new leadership, to a new life and to a new freedom! No more genuflections to those m-fuckers in Ottawa and Toron'o! Free trade righds for tobacco farmers — stuff these lousy newspapers that won't prind smoke adverts, we will no longer cow-tow to the opinions of the medical high-priesthood and their idolators! Every freeholder shall have his rightful fief, every tithe-holder his grazing rights and no city-dwelling horse's ass is going to grind him down! A moment like this comes rarely in history. Led's step oud of the old and into the new regime! The history of Gasville has been a tale of mistakes, calumny and error — the only action left to us is reaction! Elect me and you elect Pans, Zhilin and Penz — there's good value for money — my sheriff, bum-bailiff and reeve! I pledge myself to miss no more opportunities. Missed chances are like lost friends! Sometimes I think of a lost friend. Not dead, eh? Just lost. Somewhere in this goddamn universe, but I can't find him! In those moments the sweat breaks out.'

With this Eli swayed visibly and wiped his forehead with his forearm.

His voice wavered.

'In those moments a black terror shakes me like a kidden an' I feel I'm being buried alive — I feel, "Oh, Christ, Nod yed! Nod yed!" '

Eli shook his fist in the air with these final words. And promptly collapsed into unconsciousness.

Sarah Delaney leapt to her feet, shielding the prostrate form of Eli.

'Well, isn't that a man fer yer? What more could we want from a mayor? Who's it going to be, girls? Baktrian for mayor, says I.'

'Baktrian! Baktrian! Baktrian! Baktrian!' chanted the assembled multitude of alderwomen. And that was that!

'And now that we'll be havin' ourselves a new mayor,' continued Sarah Delaney at the top of her voice, 'The forst t'ing he can do, when he wakes up, is to perform a weddin''.

'Whose?'

'Mine, I'm going to marry the mayor! Haven't I always been the mayor's wife? And won't I be needing a man, now me husband is dead, to help care for those two wee babes, O'Toole and the tiny bairn that I've gone and adopted? And, to be sure, I'll be needing him for a smidgen of the other, too.'

They all laughed uproariously at her last quaintness.

And so it came to pass, then, that the first thing Eli did upon regaining consciousness was to get married. A move to which he had no objections, and considerable inclination — although he resented the fact that Grandma Martin had not deigned to forewarn him about the imminence of this remarkable and happy event.

6

SAVING GRACE

Dean Smoothe pulled in to his reserved spot in the parking lot of the WHU Institute for Buculo-Inseminology. The evening was very dark but the snow had ceased to fall, leaving three or four inches on the ground. He looked over towards the cow sheds which were his destination. He was en route to an assignation with his favourite Jersey, Grace. He had chosen Grace for his critical experiment because of her positive penchant for procreation. She had a positive attitude. She was also a fine milker; slow, solid and plentiful, so that he could be sure of getting a glass of the good stuff from her to console him through the long hours of his nocturnal vigil.

Grace, poor dumb bovine, had no idea how famous she stood to become, if all went as smoothly as Smoothe planned!

He had conceived the plan for his experiment while still crawling, nauseated and with aching skull, about the store-room of Sorores Mundi on the night of the explosion.

An 'in utero bucolae' birth! It would be a medical first! Both he and the late Sox would be crowned with glory. Visions of the P.L.U.G.V.A.C. Prize for Creative Inseminology, or the A.X.T.R.A.X. Medal from the O.M.B. Perhaps even a share of a Nobel Prize?

Confident that Sox would have no objections he had immediately begun going over the details in his mind.

A few hours later, having paused to let the seeds have their way, he had wheeled the recumbent, late Felicite Sox into the mortuary of the Sorores Mundi maternity home. They arrived unobserved, the building being still in hectic chaos as the sisters and orderlies sought to calm the patients and to assess the damage.

Smoothe had lain the victim out for her post mortem.

He realized that he would have to square this unconventional activity with the coroner, Naomi Weiptz, but he could see so reason why she should have to know all. She hardly ever did and, on the rare exceptions, she invariably did not understand what she knew. He had resolved merely to persuade the coroner to appoint himself as officiating post-mortuary in this case. A little dash of innuendo to the effect that Sox was believed to have been pregnant, juxtaposed with some reference to Naomi's philandering husband, Dragan, ought to suffice to clinch the arrangement and to ensure coronerial silence until the result of the experiment was known.

The mortuary of Sorores Mundi had been empty when they arrived.

This was generally the case of late. It was used for very little else except the disposal of abortions done upon Inuit mothers — there being too much public outcry these days if the Press got wind of a Caucasian abortion.

In no time he had succeeded in making the incision and, kingsize filter-tip smoking from the corner of his slightly twisted but determined grimace, in delivering Sox of several sections of bouncing fallopial apparatus — as much as he could get into the A and P bag which he had brought along for its transportation.

Oops! She would not mind the cigarette ash which he inadvertently dropped inside, after all she had been a heavy smoker herself.

He had wrapped her up and slid her away into cold-storage.

The A and P bag had been very heavy.

One never could be sure about pregnancy; the whereabouts of those precocious little sperms! His alcoholic colleague, Testes, swore by a broth made from puppies, which he administered as a 'spanish fly'. He claimed also to have used it upon consumptives with considerable success, not to mention pronounced side-effects.

As Dwayne would frequently say, 'Just give me ten thousand consumptives and I will be able to predict, with unfailing accuracy, which ones are pregnant. To the very delivery date, the sex, chromosomes, the whole thing. Of course, if you give me only one — well, God only knows!'

Testes always amazed Smoothe by the sheer wizardry of his intuitive medicine. He was invariably correct. For example, it had been Dwayne who had discovered the Pakistani goal-keeper with the arm-pits which could heal! The discovery had won Testes a much-coveted medal awarded by the leading consortium of deodorant manufacturers. Fancy that! Arm-pits that could positively suck up pus!

Smoothe had grabbed the bag with its plaintive but important contents and, slamming the door of the mortuary, had sped out the emergency exit (it did not matter if another fire-alarm went off that night) to his car. He had motored off with urgency to find his package's fertilized treasures and then to implant them, to the strains of the Einerkleinenachtmusik, in the willing and responsive Grace.

The implantation had not been easy, but it was successfully behind him now. All that remained was to wait calmly and to tend the four-legged patient conscientiously.

Smoothe tidied away the car's cocktail cabinet, turned off the VCR and the quadraphonic stereo, finished his drink, the third scotch he had consumed on the short drive from his home, put the dirty glass into the glass-washer, alongside the others, and turned it on, switched on the car-alarm and activated the eye-level acid-spray system which he hoped one day would give some would-be automobile-felon a nasty shock.

The phone rang. 'Damn. Who's after me at this hour?'

'Hello, Mister Smythe?'

'Smoothe.'

'Fairly. And what about yourself this evening?'

'Dean Smoothe.'

'I'm sorry to bother you at this late hour Mister Smythe ... '

'Smoothe.'

'This isn't an advertising promotion and my name is Euphoranastasia Anthrax. And I'm a disabled person ... '

'What's your O.H.I.P. number?' Smoothe turned on the tape recorder.

'Two zero zero seven six seven three two and we are a group of disabled persons who just choose to make our living over the telephone.'

'That sounds like a swell idea Euthanasia ... '

'Euphoranastasia, and so we have gotten together a list of articles that we are prepared to retail to your door at discount prices. We specialize in vitamins, herbal teas, light bulbs, dictionaries, bean sprouts, ice-cream makers, yoghurt scenters, plastic explosives, rifles, switch-blades, authentic S.S. daggers, fur hats, seal-skin boots, calf-leather gloves, radios, car tyres and second-hand Jim Needles LPs. Now I don't want you to decide at once without thinking about it — this is not some half-baked promotional rip-off — so what I want you to do is ... '

'What's your disability?'

'Hydroencephalitis.'

'Hydroencephalitis?'

'Hydroencephalitis.'

'Hydroencephalitis?'

'Yes, Hydroencephalitis.'

'What are you taking?'

'What?'

'What are you taking for it?'

'Suppositories.'

'For Hydroencephalitis?'

'No silly. For piles.'

'Have you got piles?'

'Oh, yes. We've got vitamins, herbal teas, light bulbs, dictionaries, bean sprouts, ice-cream makers, yoghurt scenters, plastic explosives, rifles, switch-blades, authentic S.S. daggers, fur hats, seal-skin boots, calf-leather gloves, radios, car tyres and second-hand Jim Needles LPs and I'm going to send you our brochure this very evening, all you have to do to order is ... '

'Miss Alcatraz, I'm in rather a hurry, but I've got two bits of news for you.'

'Oh, yes?'

'First of all I've already got all the S.S. daggers that I am ever likely to need but if I should be overcome with an irresistible urge for more I can always buy dozens — and it won't cost me a penny because I'll put it on my research grant as "Surgical Implements". Third of all I suggest you try some of those vitamins — B or E, I can't remember which, on those haemorrhoids, crushed up and pushed up.'

'Oh, thank you, and have a nice day. Where shall I send the brochure? And what was second of all?'

'Second of all Miss Two zero zero seven six seven three two ... '

'Euphoranastasia Anthrax.'

' . . . this has been a medical consultation, and my advice is to keep up the good work. I like to think of hydroencephalitics selling light bulbs. My secretary will send you the bill in tomorrow's mail.'

'Oh!?!'

'Good night.'

With that Smoothe clunked down the phone, entered 'one hundred and fifty-two dollars — Euphoranastasia Anthrax' into the secretarial recorder, pushed a fresh cigarette into the corner of his mouth and heaved himself out of the car. Taking care not to squirt himself in the face with hydrochloric acid.

> Oh, give me dat Nobel Prize,
> And while you're at it
> give my pay a rise.
> Introduce dem movie starlets to me,
> I wanna have a good time
> Like ol' Christian B!

Smoothe was in a cheerful mood, humming to himself a refrain from a ditty which he had penned in readiness for the opening chapter of his memoirs. He picked his way carefully across the parking lot. Since he was still wearing dress shoes he had to circumnavigate, here and there, the piles of snow left by the ploughs.

It was Friday night and the Mozart could be heard emanating from the cow-shed towards which he directed his steps. The lighting was subdued in there and as he drew nearer he could hear the strains of the weekly orgy of buculo inseminology, part of a project to induce off-season calving.

He pushed open the door and stepped inside, beating his arms on his torso for warmth and blinking to get accustomed to the gloom. He could see Grace's peaceful head nodding to the music in the stall at the far end. A second glance revealed to Smoothe that Grace was jumping from side to side.

Jumping?

He put down his alligator-skinned brief-case and stealthily picked up an aluminum milking-pail. He tip-toed down the shed towards an enormous pair of sneakers.

'Out! Out you damned expressors of sperm!'

The pail came down with an ear-splitting crash against the wall of the stall. Grace jumped with fright. Daisy jumped with terror and began to go into labour on the spot. Spotless jumped, Hercules jumped. (Damn silly name for a cow? No, Hercules was the owner of the sneakers.)

'Hercules Stockhausen, get your pants on and get the hell out of here, or I'll give you an A minus!'

Stockhausen and his companion scrambled ruefully for the door, hotly pursued by about twenty other couples who were striving to keep their faces hidden — at the expense, sometimes, of revelations elsewhere.

'Go back to alpha, beta, kappa, chi — and screw yourselves, in Greek. Leave my cows alone! Miss Searle, go home and study — I thought you had better things to spend your time on. Next time go to the chicken sheds. They have Brahms.'

'You are a spoil-sport, Dean.'

Smoothe spun round, startled, to find himself confronted by Dragan Weiptz.

'How do you like my camera, Dean.' Dragan held up a gleaming telephotographic contraption for his colleague's admiration.

'I got it in Hawaii, at the duty-free store, during the Conference on Third World Biochemical Dependency.'

'Turkey.'

'No need to be rude about it, old man.'

'I thought that conference was in Turkey?'

'Oh, was it? Ah, well, er, the plane was delayed due to bad weather so that Searle and I never made it to the lectures ... '

'Not Searle? She's one of our best students. Weiptz, you piss me off sometimes. How could you do it?'

'It was all right. It came off my grant.'

'And I suppose you're in here peeping again?'

'Fast film, two thousand A.S.A.,' responded Dragan with a smile. 'And you needn't look so superior. It was my strain, you see ... '

'Strain? Where does it hurt?' Smoothe reached unconsciously as if to switch on the recorder.

'Not that sort of strain, thick-head. My culture. My germs. Searle and I had to stop off in Honolulu to set them down in the warm Pacific to begin their long swim to the West Coast.'

'What for?'

'Didn't I tell you? It must have slipped my mind.' Dragan shook his head slowly in contrition.

'I meant to tell you, because you're just the one who would appreciate these little buggers. They're completely indestructible. And fatal too, in the medium term. They're transmitted in the bloodstream — marvellous, eh? Just think of those tiny blue and red varmints getting on the head of a hypodermic? Before you can say Euphoranastasia Anthrax you'll have an epidemic on your hands that will wipe out half the fruits, fags and drop-out drug-artists in California! Neat, eh?'

'Christ, Weiptz. You ought to be locked up.'

'Well, don't you look so smug. You're not exactly the phantom of the operating theatre, are you? What about that abortion last month? The one where you amputated?'

'I didn't charge.'

'Not double bill, maybe. But I saw the O.H.I.P. claim with my own eyes.'

'Well, that was one individual mistake. We all make them. It's not the same thing as genocide!'

'Talking of that, did you hear that the horny hunchback hardwarer has been elected the new mayor? I think we're in for the chilly blast of the winter of right-wing discontent. They say that his mandate was "Every man shall have his fief"!'

'Maybe we should get the old guy out to the institute and blind him with science. Perhaps he would drop the taxes on the buildings.'

'Stop fief, I say,' retorted Weiptz with a chuckle, as he paused at the door to adjust his lens-cap.

'Euphoranastasia Anthrax, did you say?'

'Yes, just a lady with an excessively large cranium and a chronic case of piles. I saw her this afternoon.'

'I didn't know you handled cases of piles?'

'Only with sanitized gloves.'

'What did you give her?'

'Vitamins for the rear-end and a cranial catheter. And, of course, a bill for one hundred and fifty-nine dollars, naturally.'

'One hundred and fifty-two.'

'No, no. You always forget the tax!'

Dragan slammed the door behind him and disappeared, whistling and humming a passage from Verdi's Requiem, out into the night. Smoothe turned back to his task of inspecting

Grace.

'How are you, Grace, old girl?'

'Not so bad. How's yersel'. Your friend's a bit of orl right, ain't 'e?'

'What the devil are you doing here?' Smoothe snapped with considerable irritation. Were they never going to leave him in peace? 'You're a hooker aren't you? I've seen you in the Faculty Club.'

'Nobody's perfect. And anyway, I've got a Ph.D!'

'Where from?'

'WHU.'

'What in?'

'Physical science.'

'Engineering?'

'No, gymnastics.'

'Have you ever had anything to do with inseminology?'

'All the time, dearie.'

'Then you're hired. Grab this bucket. The pay's good, you'll like the job. Your predecessor just came to grief in an explosion.'

'I'm not sure I want anything to do with inseminology, if it's done using explosives.'

'Come on, help me milk this cow. Then maybe we can go to the movies. Explosives are obsolete, we're using spermatozoa these days!'

7

TRAIN

It is not unreasonable to expect the train from Toronto to be delayed by an hour. This has happened to me many times. Each occasion has found me listlessly awaiting its arrival and wondering what to do. After all, the thing has only come from seventy miles away with the result that none of us waiting in the station can fully believe that the suspense can last longer than a few more minutes.

On this occasion we, Yukio and I, have been allowed onto the platform because I mentioned to the inspector that we were here to meet a blind friend.

'No problem! Just go up there and take a seat,' the official answered affably, opening the automatic door with his foot so that I might more easily manoeuvre Yukio's chair up the ramp.

So here we are.

Yukio is intently absorbed in that book about the French revolution. He has been struggling gamely with it for several months. I read him a couple of chapters in the evening, if I have the time, in order to speed up the process. Nevertheless, I rather think that he prefers to read it for himself.

So here we are! The boy and I in the VIP circumstance of sitting out here in the open air while the rest of the patient crowd is enjoying the warmth of the ticket-hall. We did not expect to be out here for so long. The weather changes so unpredictably around Labour Day and at this moment we are experiencing just how cool a mid-September afternoon can become when the northerlies start to blow.

Yukio has good warm, young blood but I think that I am too old to be out in this kind of weather. I wish I had put on a thicker coat. Fortunately I brought a spare blanket to cover the boy's knees and I dressed him in a down parker. I also brought along Yukio's toque, which he is now wearing because the hood on his jacket is extremely impractical in view of his reading-helmet.

His helmet looks quite unobtrusive under the woollen hat. My God, it is cold.

Here I am, stamping about for warmth like an old fool when we could so easily go back inside with the others. But then the locomotive would arrive and we would be at the back of the queue, unable to get through to help Bucolia.

So here we stay! Although I am far too old for this, particularly since my miniature stature militates against adequate bodily heat storage. These lumbering giants probably do not know just how lucky they are — they never pause to wonder why they never feel the cold in their blubber-coated, ample frames.

Small men, midgets like myself, usually avoid the chills of old age by the simple expedient of dying young. In that respect I am past my time. I try not to dwell on that thought.

To pass the time I have been trying to recollect a quiz which they once set me in the course of some foolish fun and games at the Drewchester Calithumpian. Eli was alive; in fact the entire Gang of Eleven was there. Some kind of public relations exercise ... TROGONOPTERA ... That was it! My part was some sort of Brains Trust general knowledge competition. I was put against one of the Simpsons, I think. No, it was Spine, or something like that. Aghh, sometimes these names just refuse to be recalled. So I am gratified to have remembered the question — 'What do trogonoptera, gentoo and the Picasso fish have in common?' And the answer was the Quebec Aquarium. They all lived there.

Everyone was astounded that I could get that puzzle, but they need not have been. In those days I used to know the decimal expansion of pi to one-hundred and fifty places.

Even now, through regular memory practice like this, I can do much better than most men one third my age.

Still no train.

Bucolia sent me a rather sweet note. She is practising with a new Braille typewriter and consequently makes rather a lot of errors.

She wrote:

```
 FORGiVE THE TYPiNG. THE RiBBON iS TERiBLE TO
CHANGEE. BUT SOOM YOU WiLL BE THERE TO HELP
ME.
       LOVE TO YUKiO AND YOU. SEE YOU TUES 1 P.M.
```

I can feel the crumpled note in my pocket, but I will not read
it again for fear that it might blow away.

8

EXERCISE OF POWER

'Haggis!'

'Dinna come tha' wi' me, yer yella yid!'

A heated intellectual discussion was taking place in the Gasville city hall. More precisely in the Mayoral anteroom.

The protagonists in the argument were Pans, Zhilin and Penz, who were clustered about a glass contraption, which was the object of their enquiry.

They were watched silently by a trim, but rather wrinkled, gentleman in worsteds, who was evidently awaiting the pleasure of the mayor.

'But wull tha' aver gut bark to weer tha' started, at a', at a'?' remonstrated Pans. The big fellow was so agitated that he was tugging at his earrings so hard that the dapper observer feared for the integrity of his ear-lobes.

The instrument about which the trio had foregathered was, in fact, a very interesting invention of the two eastern Europeans, who had been proudly showing it off to their colleague when the argument had ensued. The exhibit consisted of a perpetual motion machine. It took the form of a circular glass tube, which was in itself a superb testimony to the dexterity of Messrs Zhilin and Penz, into which had been placed some beads. The beads were rather colourful and they were dashing about, never stopping.

Thus far Pans had taken it all in his stride.

What was giving him the difficulty was the manner of their motion.

Each bead fitted perfectly into the circular tube — black, green, blue, red, mauve, white, they were all moving about at exactly the same regular, and rather sickening, speed. They made a dizzying blur of activity that in itself would have unsettled many a more sober man than Pans. They sped along, except when one happened to bang headlong into another one, at which time — and this was the blissful, harmonious simplicity of the design — they collided perfectly elastically, each one reversing its direction and otherwise continuing on at the same velocity.

'Marvellous! Marvellous!' murmured the neat bystander, who was wearing upon his lapel a discreet badge bearing the legend, 'MATHEMATICS CANADA' subscribed with the motto 'hic iacet bummus qui de nulla mathematica cognovit'.

'But wull tha' aver gut bark, at a', at a'?' reiterated the Scottish giant, menacing the two inventors with his fist.

Zhilin and Penz were noticeably non-plussed by the question. Particularly by the 'at a', at a'.

'I have it, I have it!' exclaimed the watcher, clapping his pink palms and striding over to the machine.

Penz and Zhilin tactfully moved aside, permitting the stranger to stand between them and the Scot.

'Wa' yer wa', rat-face?' Pans genially enquired of the newcomer, who by this time had placed one finger upon the throbbing mass of glassware and Heraclitian flux. He carefully consulted his wristwatch, which he had set to the egg-timing mode.

'Ping. Ping. Prrrrripp!' went the watch. The effect was evidently very satisfactory, because the unknown gentleman breathed a satisfied, 'Aaagh.'

He moved his finger to another place and repeated the operation.

'Ping. Ping. Prrrrripp!' faithfully repeated the watch.

'Aaagh!'

He moved the finger to a third spot, this time moistening his finger tip before placing it. The three men leaned closer, aghast and captivated by this novelty. But the manoeuvre was only in order that the fellow could clean a spot of detritus from the glass. Penz instantly jumped forward to offer his Kleenex.

Finally the man looked up at his audience and smiled broadly. 'The configuration of beads,' said Sherloch Humes, for that was indeed the identity of the mysterious individual, 'is guaranteed to have exactly replicated itself by the year two thousand and nineteen.'

They were agape with admiration. Zhilin and Penz hugged one another and jumped up and down for joy.

'Two zouzand, nineen! You hear himp?' they chorussed at Pans delightedly.

'Actually, chaps,' added Sherloch. 'If I may permit myself a little inexactitude, my investigations lead me to an educated guess that the first replication will happen sometime tomorrow.'

'Tomorrow! Hear himp? Tomorrow!'

The inventors hugged Humes, unsettling his deerstalker and causing his pipe to fall from his breast pocket.

'Zo zorry.' Zhilin hastened to retrieve the lost article.

'Wha' dee is tumorra'?' growled Pans, who was clearly not entirely convinced.

At that moment the discussion was suddenly interrupted by a loud crash, followed by the opening of the door to the Mayoral suite and the speedy ejection of a smartly dressed male of evident African origins. It later turned out that he was a dealer on behalf of some unknown locality of Third World persuasion, rumoured to be Georgia.

His name was Mandola Magabutne, or so his tee-shirt advertised, and underneath the name a discerning eye could just pick out the words, 'Small munitions, armaments and defences in the cause of peace and freedom'.

'Don' do dat no mo', waart trash', responded the man to Eli, who followed him into the room.

'Don' yuh "trash" me, soot-face', retorted the Mayor, with his characteristic dignity, which the whole city had come to know and love during his few months of office.

'Gonna take id or leave id, filth?' he added.

'Ah'm takin' it, man. Just deliver dam' soon. An', waart hunchback trash . . . '

The speaker got no further. The cheery exchanges must have reminded Preston Pans of Glasgow, because he suddenly sprang to life and dealt the negro a crushing kick between the shoulder blades.

'Pans!' called out the Mayor in alarm, too slow to stop him.

'No, no, Zhilin. Don' cud him, fer chrissake.'

Eli helped the dealer up.

'Don' hurd 'im, fellas. This guy's just made us a damn good deal, for them ol' cow sheds near the university. We're gonna have us a li'l facd'ry, oud there. Helpin' along the down-trodden of the world.' He bellowed with laughter.

'Yuh godda deal, black felluh. We'll have thad place in production quickr'n a Yank's erection.' He offered his handshake, which the abused visitor surprisingly took heartily.

'Ah godda deal, man. An' don'yosel' fuggit, nah.'

With that Eli waved the man towards the door, eased a hand down inside his jeans to give a momentary relief to the hydroseal cyst that was acting up and had inflated his scrotum to the size of a soft-ball.

'Uuuhm,' he gave a sigh of relief and closed the door behind Mandola Magabutne, who rejoined the following Parthian shot from out in the corridor.

'Yo' day's gonna come, big fellah. Yo wade'n'see.'

Eli turned, fingers still down his pants' front, to the other visitor. 'Whad we god here?'

'It looks to me like an orbifold complete with contractile and digestive vacuoles', replied Humes, thinking that the other was referring to the machine.

'Shud thad darn thing off,' Eli pointed to the invention.

'Oh, zat vill neffer zzhtop. No, zir' answered the shining Zhilin, with a gratified grin.

'Then led's go in my office' said Eli.

The visitor introduced himself.

'Sherloch Humes.'

'Hi,' said Eli, shaking hands in deference to the formality of the occasion.

'Weer's y'fraen' wat's name?' giggled Pans.

Pans was beginning to enjoy himself and would dearly have loved to knee this cocky, smiling flower in the groin.

'Y'd nae be smilin' thae',' he thought to himself with grim satisfaction.

'I have come to invite you to take a mayoral turn about my mathematical institute — Institute Mathematics Canada,' Humes was saying. 'What do you say? It would mean such a lot to the chaps, you see?

'I particularly want you to meet our latest recruit. Professor Elsquaird. We got him by the merest chance from the Amadeus Institute for Defence Systems, where he was applying Timmins thirty-fifth conjecture on automorphic random walks to modelling the demographics of race and stature. I don't mind telling you that the President ... '

'Ugghh?'

'Rafe Catcher, you know, the President of WHU.'

'Oh? Whad? Where?'

'Anyway, Catcher was quite right. It was a real coup to get someone of his stature away from a prestigious outfit in the US like the Amadeus. Of course, when I speak of his stature I mean mathematically speaking. Physically, I, er, well, physically he's a midget, in a manner of speaking.'

'How big?'

'Perhaps this.'

'Goddamn, Jesus thad's small.'

'I wenderrr wa' saze tha' penae' orn a laddie tha' wee?'

'A manikin, I zink.'

'Exactly. A manikin, and just terrifically bright.'

'Iss he ein Jew?'

'Do you . . . , er, I mean, actually I believe he's Aryan. But, of course, what with his stature being so tiny one doesn't like to ask, does one?'

Pans was roaring with laughter. 'Uf he worrr, thae'd nae be verra muckle thae' Rarbbee cud chop orff thae' wee one, wi' oot takkin' 't'a',' the giant bellowed with evident mirth, as he imagined the perplexed official beating his brow against the nearest Sh'ma.

'Are they all small?' Eli pursued with aroused curiosity.

'Who?'

'Mathematicians?'

'Er, no. I should say that, er, oh, a goodly percentage of them are almost normal-sized. And, of course,' he spoke with measured pride, 'Canadian mathematicians are bigger than most.'

He added, 'But the main thing about Professor Elsquaird is that he is very, very bright. They say that he was the top of his year, I think it was eighty-three or four, at WHU. His functions had to be seen to be believed, so my colleagues tell me who were here at the time.'

'You weren'd there?'

'No,' a touch of professional pride corrupting Humes' usually inscrutable expression, 'I was brought in to direct Mathematics Canada, you see, so I never teach students. Not even the bright ones — well, you can see how it is? If I don't teach the dumb ones, I can hardly ask to teach the bright chap that happens along once in a decade, can I, even if he is a midget? Fair's fair!'

'How much d'ya pay him?' Eli ventured with matter of fact directness that clearly disconcerted Humes, who glanced round twice before writing a figure on a piece of paper and passing it to the Mayor.

'He ain'd so brighd,' chuckled Eli, passing the paper to the others.

'Mether Maire, a' cud dee bet'n thae bae pimpin' doon Bloor Street. An' anely a' wikkens,' gaffawed Pans.

'Well,' defended the confused Sherloch, 'a prof doesn't get paid a Prince's ransom, you know. Not unless he's onto some medical wheeze, ha, ha, ha!'

'Medical. Thad reminds me,' Eli interrupted. 'We'll be happy to dust yer place over, an' we'll skin two skunks wi' th' same knife. We'll drop around tomorrow, after we's all been to see them Deans about Cow Medicine and Cow Sheds. It's a deal, Mr Holmes, goldarn it, Humes. An' I'm idching t' see this midged of yer'n. Till tomorrow, then.'

With that Eli waved to Penz to take the guest out, quickly. Accordingly the door had closed behind the gracious Humes before he could formulate an appropriate parting encomium, which, perhaps, he got to deliver to the secretary in the hall.

'Ged oud the rye, I think we've godda celebrate a li'l.'

Pans got a bottle from the filing tray marked 'immediate'. 'As thae' sae' in Bootvi' Californiae', hare's thae' Horrn of Zeus,' he laughed as he poured himself a third.

'Horn of zis? I rather have Horn of zat,' with which Zhilin went over to the 'pending' and opened the vodka. He did not seem to need a glass.

'Fellas,' Eli raised a toast, 'Here's t' liddle, black, shiny, profidable, medallic arms.

'Mind you, you have t' tread careful when dealin' with thad half-assed administration from down there. They behave like four-year olds — and four-year old what? They wand arms, id's sure as hell they wand arms, but id's as slippery as alligador turds t' ged a deal worked oud. Godda tread 'em real nice.'

'But you abuse zat one, rufen ihm ein black wog . . . '

'Sure. Thad's pard of id. Ya godda do thad, they're used t' id from their own whide, goofy Presiden'. They expecd thad! Bud there you are — all seddled. Fifdy thousand a year, so many new jobs, nighd-time flying righds etc., etc., — all sealed and seddled — then jusd yuh ask for one thing too much. Just ask them for three dozen dirdy phodos — their Presiden''s god boxes of 'em — of their whidest, brighdest young pieces of ass. And goddamn, if the whole deal ain'd off, and the black guy roaring like a baby — excep' he's talkin' embargo-shmargo and kiss my fanny. Nope, id ain'd easy. But I done id!'

* * *

'Just tell m' good dawg blue,
If he should happ'n thru',
Thad Ah've gorn to Califo-o-ornia.

Young Tommy shod his paw,
Shod his uncle, shod his maw,
Goddamn id makes me so sore,
Thad I cain'd take any more.

Jusd tell m' good dawg blue,
If he should happ'n thru',
Thad Ah've gorn to Califo-o-ornia.'

Eli was feeling extremely cheerful and, as a result, the walls of the Gasville Mayoral suite reverberated to his lusty sonorities. In fact they came from within the door labelled 'Caballeros Rusticanos' behind which their originator's cheerfulness was starting to metamorphose into anger as he wrestled with an undisciplined fly zipper. To disguise this from the outside world he began to bellow even louder.

'Yuh kin take my lo-er-rr-ve
An' throw't oud the door,
But ah jesd don' like yuh
Killin' m' paw,
Goddamn I cain'd take no more.'

Zhilin and Penz were busy in the corridor while their boss abluted and Pans occupied himself next door in 'Senoritas Amorosas', where the mirrors were better for cosmetics.

The duo in the hallway were telling off weaponry, stuffing grenades into the pockets of their long black, European coats, plastic into the linings, pistols round the waistband of their pants.

'Haff you zer syringe und der poisons.'

'Poisons? Poisons, is it? Verfor zem poisins isst, nar?'

'Fur dem schicksa cowsss — dummy. Fur clearin' zer cowshedszs!'

'Ahh, jah.' Penz nodded seriously.

'All von zem?' There was a note of remorse in his voice.

'Sure, all — all. Vot vee gon't'do mit cowses?'

'Zey could kip zem zu hospital, vahrscheinlicht?'

'Ve'll zee.'

At that moment, with lots of ostentatious flushing from the former, 'Caballeros' and 'Senoritas' swung simultaneously open and they were joined by Pans and the Mayor — both mean and ready for action.

'C'mon.' Eli Baktrian led the way swiftly out of the building.

He was an impressive figure, virtually straight, striding towards the four-wheel drive, Mayoral transport. There was a limousine but he did not feel that it suited his be-denimed, fashion-tailored, pre-shrunk, pre-dirtied, pre-urine-soaked leisure suits that he had taken to wearing since assuming office. Also his spurs caught in the carpet of the limo, as he had found out on the evening when he had given the first of his six, short-lasting secretaries a ride home in it. She had eluded him, dodging out into a blizzard, leaving him impaled to the floor of the passenger lounge by the rowel of his spur. Since then he had reserved the spurs for ceremonial occasions.

Eli touched the key in the lock. It stuck.

There was a loud wailing of a war-time siren, Pans dropped instantly to the ground. 'Doon, damn yer, doon.'

He pulled Eli to the ground with one mighty tug, his other hand contained a grenade, the pin was already between his teeth. The sweat was all over Pans's face; wild-eyed he was rapidly twisting his head from side to side. Listening. Feet were running, running in their direction. Breath could be heard wheezing, voices calling.

Pans could hear their awful foreign jibberish, he could sense them behind every tree, he could *smell* the enemy snipers nearby. He knew what these bastards would do to his mates, cut off and defenceless in that alien, jungle sweat-box.

'Bastard. Here's tae yew!' He sent the grenade arcing away out of sight over the top of the cars in the parking lot.

Wooomph! Instantly Pans was on his feet, scrambling over the four-wheel drive; he could see the feet of the enemy now — sneakily poking out from beneath an Isuzu. Swerving to one side he raked the ground around those feet with a burst of rapid-fire.

Finally he straightened up, cautiously, and stealthily approached the enemy feet, which had not moved.

The sirens had stopped.

'Goddamn, yer dumbo. It was the car-alarm. B'Jeeze, yer've gon'an' croaked some poor bastard. Jesus! Jesus!' Eli bent over the prone body, casting an anxious glance around the otherwise deserted parking lot. He felt in the uniform pocket of the obese victim.

Pans was leaning against the vehicle, mopping his brow and breathing deeply. The flash-back of his Korean service had subsided, returning him to his usual affable self. He momentarily cast an eye over what he had done.

'Aw, tak' the wee beggar 'n' poosh 'm'n a wee boosh,' Pans suggested, casually disinterested now and merely trying to be helpful.

'Okay, yer kin do id yerself,' Eli stood up; he grunted with recognition as he examined the enemy driving licence. 'Yer've doggorn shot some guy called Wyadd Erpees, damn ass-hole.'

Eli pocketed the driving licence and climbed into the driver's seat, ready to set off for the Institute of Buculo-Inseminology, which loomed like the Chicago Standard Oil building, marble-clad and shining, in the distance, visible miles away from the WHU campus.

'Dump him over there. Then led's ged goin'. I god cow-sheds to deal with up there.'

Penz thoughtfully stood and stared in the direction being indicated.

The others quickly re-grouped. Pans dumped the corpse and took the precaution of opening the barrier to the lot and leaving a sign — 'HAD TO GO FOR A CRAP' in the window of Wyatt Erpees' booth at the entrance to the car-park.

'Penz, quid day-dreamin' and hop in.'

Having gathered his flock, Eli gunned the accelerator and roared out of the parking lot on an errand of such audacity that

9

MEETINGS

Two minutes ago I had almost decided to take Yukio back into the ticket hall. However, I have just noticed that he is smiling. He has not been complaining about being cold. In fact, he is very good natured — as comely within as without — and he is still engrossed in his book, but I think that I can detect a smile.

Yukio does not smile very often.

His doctors do not have an explanation for it. They attribute it to the blast. That is, they relegate his unsmiling appearance to that dustbin of symptoms which they imagine to be explained by smothering a bomb. What do they know of hand grenades?

I am inclined to seek a more cosmological explanation, one which fits in with my surmised origin of his current, unusual expression. He is almost grinning!

My hypothesis is that this unfamiliar look is a vestigial part of that telepathy between Bucolia, Yukio and O'Toole of which Bucolia has told me on several occasions.

Here, to bear me out, is a train pulling into the station. 'Come on, old chap, shall we go and see whether we can spot your sister?'

I see her! She is standing at the door of the carriage which has just passed us by. Her beautiful smile is pale with that statuesque beauty of a young, blind face on an autumnal afternoon, staring straight ahead through the glass. The train is slowing. I get the wheel-chair in motion.

'I bet you that she'll stop just by the pillar, Yukio!'

I have to run for a few paces in order to keep up with the coaches.

'Bucolia! Bucolia!'

How stupid of me! She cannot hear me until the conductor opens the door. Anyway, I am hardly in the sort of condition to run and shout simultaneously.

'Bucolia!'

This time she hears me.

'John? Is that you. Where's you're hand? Ah, thank you. Is Yukio here?'

'Yes. It was he who spotted the train first.'

Bucolia is making a puzzled frown.

'Yukio knew that your train was here even before it reached the station. He was grinning like the Cheshire Cat.'

'I would have liked to have seen that. I haven't seen him smile in a long while.'

Phrases like that, when they come from Bucolia, for whom I am almost guardian as well as chaperone, disturb me. I would rather that she never made mention of sight.

'Me neither. Let's get off this platform quickly. It's too damn chilly out here. Is this all your baggage?'

The cold wind is causing the crowd to jostle amiably and briskly from the platform into the passenger hall. We are being carried along with the surge. Bucolia is holding my wrist gently as I propel Yukio's chair. I cannot steer, nor do I have any choice of speed. We will be swept out into the street by this surrounding matrix of giants. Invariably, when in the throng like this I feel a pleasantly soporific humour enveloping me. It comes with the closely encircling warmth of this multitude of large bodies.

'Excuse me! Excuse me, please!'

I have decided to push our way out of the doors onto the main street, since almost everyone else is trying to go through the revolving doors which lead out to the parking lot. My car is out there, too, but we will not be able to navigate the doors. There is a ramp up to the front entrance. The going is easier now that we have escaped the masses.

'Are you tired, Bucolia?'

She smiles at me, but it is a weary smile. 'I'll be glad to get home and put my feet up.'

'That won't take long, all we have to do is ... '

'Is something the matter, John?'

Across the street there is a large crowd gathered outside the offices of Agriculture Ontario. The outpost of the Ministry for Agriculture is housed in a recently-renovated Victorian church.

The white brickwork, with inset panels of red, has been cleaned and the sidewalk surrounding the Italianate structure has been refinished in interlocking clay bricks. The small plaza created in this manner has been adorned with simulated reproduction gas-lighting. In this elegant but limited space the horde of men — I can see no women down there — is shouting and brandishing farming implements.

Two policemen on horseback are holding their steeds in check a few yards away. I can recognize the man who is confronting the farmers. It is the local Agro-Ontario representative.

'What's happening, John? What are they shouting about?'

'I think we should get you and Yukio out of here.'

'No, tell me what's happening first.'

'Come on, Bucolia. Let's get out of here.'

I am very uneasy about that mob. Several trucks have just squealed to a halt, blocking the road. About thirty men have jumped down from these vehicles and joined the press.

'Go home! Go home! There's nothing I can do for you guys! Go see your Minister. Go an' put a flea in the politicians' ears. I only push the paper around here.'

'Fucker!'

'Who're you calling names?'

'You — shid fer brains. Yer wouldn' know a fron' loader if I drove it up yer ass.'

'Yeah, id's nod yer farm thad's goin' down. Id ain'd you who's losing land whad yer folks've worked for generations.'

'Stuff the bum in the trash! He's righd, we din't come to mess with this crap.'

'Led's stick it to the Ministry!'

Someone has smashed the big window bearing, in large golden lettering, the legend, 'Ontario Ministry of Agriculture'. For a few seconds the word 'Agriculture' is still precariously intact, but now it has gone — smashed into shards by a salvo from a shot-gun. A squad of police cruisers are cordoning off this part of the street. As the policemen on foot are moving in the mounted officers have started to push their way into the crowd.

'My God! Bucolia, let's go. Do as you're told. Take my hand and follow me!'

Behind us the group is turning ugly. We are fleeing none too soon. There is another shot. I can see the farmer who fired it. He has hit one of the horses. The rest of the police are sprinting towards the man. And more of them have arrived from somewhere that I did not see.

'Run, before we get shot.'

This time Bucolia is obeying me.

We have reached the corner of the station building — one step round it and we will be safely out of sight.

Looking back briefly I can see fighting everywhere. The police are less numerous although better armed and more disciplined. The farmers are angry and they will not be routed easily. One of the riders is down, pinned under a shrieking, wounded horse. The animal has fallen upon its master. Its rear legs are useless. It is scrambling in vain with its forelegs, its neck twisted round at an unnatural, gruesome angle, its panic-stricken face turned in a scream at the grey sky.

'Go! Go!' I am bellowing in a frenzy of fear, as I push the other two in front of me. My God, I started all this. When will I have paid enough?

10

BUCULO INSEMINOLOGY

Dean Smoothe was pacing up and down before the six elevators which served the Institute of Buculo Inseminology. He repeatedly glanced at his wrist-watch and then down the hall to where the gags and giggles of the secretaries could be heard emanating from the nurses' lounge.

'Pipe down, ladies, this is supposed to be a hospital!' he bawled hopefully.

Finally, since it looked as if the Mayor and his party were going to be late, he strode over to the open doorway of the lounge. He stuck his earnest, handsome head inside.

Behind him, simultaneously and silently, three of the elevators arrived and disgorged the Mayor, Preston Pans and Haim Zhilin.

The nurses were absorbed in a board game, Nurse Failure was about to shake the dice.

'Nurse Failure, can't you lot put that away, the Mayor's on his way. How are we going to make a good impression with that racket going on?' He strode over to the table.

'What is it, anyway?'

'Trivial Percy,' giggled a young nurse, whose plump but not undesirable figure he had not noticed before.

'Please don't be cheeky, my dear,' Smoothe smiled, in that best bedside manner of his. 'I'll play a game with you later,' he winked at the novice, 'But right now ... '

He was cut off by the jingle of spurs in the hallway. The Mayor pushed his way in and flopped into a chair. 'One helluva join' ya god here, Doc.'

'Ay, a faen set of th' wee broads, tuoo,' echoed Pans, leering round the door-jamb.

'Ach, ein board-game, jah? I luff zees games,' Zhilin clapped his hands gleefully and squeezed himself into a place at the table. '"Ow vill vee play 'im, jetzt?'

'Ermm, I think that the ladies were just packing up and returning to work.' Smoothe virtually snatched the board away, scattering the Percy cards. Everything stopped for a moment of mutual admiration of Failure's backside, crisply starched and seam-straining, as she searched under the settee for the fallen dice.

'Grrr,' commented Pans.

'Rena, leave that. We'll find it later. Gentlemen, I'd like you to meet my senior nurse, Rena Failure ... Mayor ... and these gentlemen?'

'Pans.'

'Zhilin.'

'Pleased to meet you, I'm sure,' curtsied Ms Failure with a dazzling smile. 'Shall I prepare the Experiment, Doctor Smoothe?'

'Good idea. We'll be along shortly.'

Rena managed to press past the closely attentive Pans in the doorway and bustled off into obscurity down the heavily carpeted corridor.

Smoothe led the way into the corridor, which was long and spacious with tasteful sculptures and works of art adorning it at regular intervals.

'I'm so delighted that you were able to come. Medicine is a very expensive science and I think that a soupcon of liaison between town and gown can't but be beneficial to both parties. The general public doesn't realize just how important we are. My motto, you know, is, Cows today, tomorrow the world. And with the Mayor behind us, my, my! Who knows what might happen? A fund, an appeal. Oh, yes. If we could just make the citizens of Gasville pay more — attention, I mean — to cows.'

'Sure, Doc. Thad's why we're here. 'Cause I remembered them cows.'

'Wonderful, wonderful.' Smoothe started off down the hall, beckoning the rest to follow.

'We have an Experiment just along here that will really impress you. It could be a first for WHU. A first in the world. The bovine in question, whose name happens to be Grace, is resting in her stall, but we've got all her charts in the experimental lab, this way.'

They turned the corner.

'We're going to be the first unit in the civilized world to stimulate an in bucula pregnancy resulting in a human foetus. Pretty neat, don't you think. I should say that Gasville will be damn proud of our Institute when we bring home the prizes!'

'Did zis man say, zey haff a human baby borning being — inzide von cow?' Zhilin was amazed.

'Exactly, Herr Doktor,' said Smoothe, forgetting himself. 'The foetus belonged to my ex-Assistant Director, Felicite Sox. Poor girl, she was impaled by the arrow of God, during that awful explosion at Sorores Mundi.'

'Last Monda'?' queried Pans, whose attention was partly preoccupied with staring ahead in an attempt to find out whither Nurse Failure had disappeared.

'Sorores Mundi Hospital. You remember the explosion last winter? Well, Sox was one of the unfortunate casualties. But I managed, by some very tricky surgery, to save her foetus.'

'An' ya pud id in a cow!'

'Jah, ihm say zat. In ein kuhe. Misha, moshe. In ein kuhe!'

'Nearly there.'

They turned a second corner.

'My God, what's this? Nurse, nurse, what on earth is this?'

Smoothe was staring transfixedly at a gorey mess on the carpet, prodding it with his alligator-skinned toe. The soft thud of running fallen arches were heard from several directions. The first on the scene was a young woman in civilian attire.

'What's this — an organ, an organ, for Christ's sake.'

'People are filthy beasts,' remarked the girl sagely. 'They're always dropping things.'

'But a smelly, steaming organ. Who left it here?'

'It must be Testes again, filthy scum.'

'Er, no. I think it comes from the small of the back,' replied Smoothe. 'Anyway, Betsy, get someone to clean it up.'

At the fringe of the group Pans suddenly had a realization of recollection.

'Ut's wee Betsy, dinna yae 'member me. Preston, eh lassie. Ah 'member yaesel', th' hooooker wi't' Ph.D. Dinna yae 'member, Zhilin, yaesel', masel' and Penz, las' hogmanay? Betsy, eh lassie, menagera' a'twa, las' hogmanay on Dundas?,'

Pans fetched the girl a friendly belt of comradeship across her shoulders.

Betsy responded with a smack from her handbag, which she still carried just in case of emergencies like this one.

'I remember you, dirty pigs — all three. An' where's the other four-eyed ass-licker?'

'That will be quite enough, Betsy, thank you,' interrupted Smoothe rather testily.

'In here, gentlemen, please. The previous Director used this as the art-storage room, "state-of-the-art" you know. He loved it very much. Unfortunately, one day he was accidentally locked in. It coincided with Yom Kippur, so he was in here for eight days. By the time that he was found he had become quite, quite deranged. He kept repeating, "Clean out the art-storage room, clean out the art-storage room." It was very tiresome, although I have the incident to thank for my present position as Director.

'Mind you, my predecessor was a very fine man. And an excellent administrator before that unhappy incident. It was his idea to raise research funds by the annual Organ Transplant Competition, Fete and Dinner/Dance. That has become so popular that we have been raising as much as a hundred dollars per double ticket and three hundred from the competitors. Everyone is secretly a transplant surgeon at heart. Switch heads, arms on knees, breasts on backwards — they just love it. And the crowds really roar when there's a little slip. I remember the lady with the tongue in her cheek — well, perhaps that was a bit gruesome. Here we are, anyway.'

The trio was ushered into a brightly-lit, windowless room containing boards with charts and graphs upon them. One, labelled 'Grace's Udders (temp.p.h.)' at once caught Zhilin's eye. Pans wandered the length of a row of cages, which were stacked commodiously against the far wall.

'Bu' th' wee beasties arre a' deed, mon?'

'But of course, you see they have been helping us in our experiments.'

Eli stepped over and peered in. 'Bud, shid, you budchered the bastards!'

'Yes, that's what I said. In the experiments. Absolutely essential to conduct experiments on animals, of course. How else do we cure humans. Anyway, let me describe to you this experiment with Grace. I'm certain that you'll be positively enthralled. You see, no one has ever produced a human being from a cow before.'

Smoothe paused momentarily, as if reflecting.

'I believe that they gestated a foetus in a man. But that was in the POW camps, and you know the sort of thing those heartless bastards got up to. But here we are concerned with civilized experimentation, not freakery. Bollas, in Peru did try it with a hedgehog, so I hear. But again, you can't believe anything that you hear from some of those swarthy swindlers. However, I can assure you that there is nothing phoney about this experiment and that we are using a cow called Grace; not a boa-constrictor, a gazelle, polar bear or anything gimmicky. A straightforward cow, because we have discovered that you can learn a lot from cows. And, anyway, I had to find something quickly, and Grace was the nearest available animal with big udders.'

'A'v fel' tha' desp'ra' masel' on occasio',' agreed Pans.

'Well, let's see. Perhaps you'd better look at this first. It records lactation ... '

'Led's nod horseshid around, Doc. I opine we'll just git over whad we come fer. Yer know all thad crap aboud cooperadin' with the town? Well, we gonna accept thad ad face valyuh. Yessir, we're gonna misappropriate them cow sheds o' yern. In fact we're doin' id righd now. OK?'

Smoothe looked from face to face in blustery panic. 'But, but ... '

'Ain't cause fer no buddin', Doc. Jes' consider id done.'

Smoothe had finally recovered himself sufficiently to assert his authority as Director of the Buculo Inseminology Institute and as a Member of the Medical Association.

'I forbid it. No, no. If that's your game you may leave forthwith!' He pointed to the door, against which Zhilin was leaning, a contented smile slowly osmosing its way across his face.

'Aw, c'mon, Doc. Id ain'd worth id, makin' a fuss over a few cow sheds.'

'No. No. No. No! What about the experiments? What about the cows?'

'Do the experiments agin'. Id'll serve t' check oud yer results. As fer them criddurs — I 'magine thad Penz has todalled them already. He wen' down there with the poison aboud thirty minutes ago.'

'Never,' insisted Smoothe.

'Pans.'

Preston stepped forward and held three shining coins up for Smoothe to see.

'Silverrr dollarrrs, d'y'ken? Thae gang herrre 'n' herrre 'n' herrre,' Pans inserted one coin between each of the fingers of his right hand and held the effect up before Smoothe, for his inspection. Slowly Pans closed his fist.

'Ugh.'

Quick as a flash Pans had fetched Smoothe a mighty, silver-dollared blow to the abdomen. Smoothe doubled up instantly, to the extent that his head was down to a spot whence he could have looked the second Scotsman straight in the eyes, if his mind had been on jokes at the time. However he was more concerned with the rising feeling of nausea and the dread that he was about to puke over himself.

Wham. A rabbit-punch smoothed Smoothe onto the carpet. Zhilin was hastening over from the doorway.

'Don' cud him, Zhilin. Zhilin!' Just a trifle too late, came Eli's command. Zhilin had Smoothe on his tip-toes against the wall, a strop-razor against the left ear from which the smallest suggestion of a slice had been nicked.

'So long, Doc. I guess yer see our poin' of view?' Eli beckoned his colleagues with a nod of the head. He opened the door.

There was a hullabaloo outside that they had entirely failed to notice. Women were shrieking, voices were shouting and above all this rose an immense mooing.

'Jesus.' Eli, Pans and Zhilin sprinted down the hall. Smoothe struggled to his feet and limped after them.

As they turned the corner the trio stopped, bursting into gales of laughter. There, issuing from all six elevators at once and streaming crappily down the office-ways of the Buculo Inseminology Institute was a very appropriate herd of cows. At their back, yelling and waving his arms, was Penz. Somehow he had succeeded in persuading many of the inhabitants of the cow sheds into the elevators and thence to the third floor.

'I ran out of poison,' Penz shouted by way of explanation. 'Anyvey, I donn li' killink zem zo many like zis.'

'Oh, help. Help.' Rena Failure came briskly out of the dispensary pursued by a Jersey with a crumpled horn.

Smoothe panted up. Horror of realization spread slowly over his pain-tortured physiognomy.

'Oh, my God! Grace! Grace! Where are you old girl? Grace, dear.' He pushed his way into the herd and started snatching at identification tags, heedless of the mire on his alligator skins.

'Oh, Christ, the experiment. We'll have to do a Caesarean. Grace, damn you, where are you! Nurse, help. Help, get me Testes.'

Pans, with a guffaw, obligingly complied.

'Ouch.'

'Drop him, Pans,' Eli growled.

Thud.

'Sha' 'a' kick th' wee mon i' th' heed, while hae's doon?'

'C'mon you three, let's git ouda here.' With that Eli and his advisory committee took their leave. Smoothe was scrambling to his feet amid the debris.

'Testes. Testes.'

'I thought you said "small of the back"?'

'Get Doctor Testes — I don't care where he is or what he's doing. Tell him I want him down at the cow sheds at once — a matter of life and death, literally. Tell him to bring his gynaecology knives. Rena, get the incubator unit. Betsy, get the lamps and the clamps. Hurry. Move. Move.'

Smoothe dashed from cow to cow, still no sign of Grace. She must have been poisoned in the shed. Oh, my God!

11

THEORY OF POWER

'Ugh! The wee do-oo-er is jammed,' Preston Pans gasped to the other three as he tried the handle of the door above which were emblazoned the words 'Mathematics Canada'.

The building, which was far from large and had taken the quartet the best part of an hour and a half to find, was a one storey shed tucked in between the vaulting spires of Home Economics and the Institute for Business Management Research, Industrial Innovation, Cosmological Planning and Phrenologistical Ecology.

'Rats!'

'Where iss?' asked Zhilin.

'The wee harndle ha' come awa' in m' harnd. Pet yae wee showders to th' do-oo-er.'

Accordingly they all heaved together with the result that the entire group, and the door, collapsed inward with a lurch which admitted them into a cramped lobby filled with mathematical shapes. On the left there were green, blue and red ellipsoids. Zhilin picked up the nearest one and blew from it a cloud of dust.

'Iss covered mit dust on its osculatink plane,' he remarked sadly and set about dusting off the rest of the exhibits.

'Penz, kommen sie hier! Ein bottle von Felix Klein,' he held up a glass object that looked far from bottle-like. In fact it seemed to have been ruined during its manufacture and was all twisted in upon itself.

'Och, 't's a' ballsed up, mon. Y' cannae see?'

'Nein, nein. It is ein Felix Klein bottle. Oi, oi, oi, what a mind zat Felix Klein!'

'Mind or none, he ain'd so gread ad glass-blowin', if yer ask

76

me,' Eli remarked casually.

'Zis is no ordinary bottle,' Zhilin hastened to explain. 'You vill see that him intersects himzelf. Ja? Vell, zat iss becoss him vill not embed in der tree dimensions. Not mit out zelf intersectionsss. But you putting ihm in der fier dimensions, zen du vollst zee. Zen der zelf-intersections vee remooff kann.'

'I see, so in them four-dimensional places this darn thing becomes a boddle thad I kin pud m' whiskey in?'

'Ach, no. Viskey vudd out-fall gekommen, becoss even der unorientable survace cannot separate fier-space. Einstein hass ziss proofed.'

'Hod shid boddle,' muttered Baktrian in disgust. He set off down the narrow, dirty and ill-lit passageway, in which they were constrained to follow in single file and then only with difficulty for the hulking frame of Preston Pans.

Bang. Bang. Swoosh, swoosh, bang!

The group turned the corner to encounter a singular individual who was smashing a tennis ball repeatedly against the partition wall, with the aid of a tennis racket. He was dressed for the occasion in shorts and tennis shirt that must at one time have been white. Unfortunately the once pristine and immaculate sportswear was now neglected, unwashed and threadbare in places.

Since the man did not appear to be about to stop his service practice the visitors were obliged to squeeze past him as best they could. Such was the press that Pans must inadvertently have kneed the sports enthusiast in the groin three or four times because, as they left him, he was collapsed on the greasy linoleum floor, grasping himself in the verissimilitude of agony. His racket lay beside him and he groaned in a whisper as his balls rolled away down the not inconsiderable slope of the passage.

Ignoring his plight the adventurers pressed on. Ahead of them dusty light issued from a doorway beside which rested the sign, 'Mathematics Canada', which must once have fitted with dignity into the frame, now broken, above the door.

From the office the newcomers caught the sound of animated conversation.

'But, Director, where *is* the centre of the plane? Existentially speaking?'

'I suppose the damn thing is plunked right in the middle. Where else?'

'But every point is the middle of the plane. Because it is infinite in all directions.'

'Dammitall, man, you can't have it all ways. If every point is the centre then we needn't worry. Just guess. Pick the damn thing with a pin.'

The listeners could recognize the distinctive tones of Sherloch Humes. Humes added an after-thought. 'Perhaps it would be a different matter if we tried to prove it. I wouldn't be at all surprised to find that I could demonstrate that no centre exists at all!'

'Every point is the centre and then you prove that it doesn't exist?'

'Yes, one can prove anything about something that doesn't exist. Of course, if there was a group acting in such a manner as to preserve a lattice ... '

'Lettuce, what have fruit and vegetables got to do with it?'

'Not a lettuce, a lattice. You know, like the lines of a cross-word.'

'No cross words, gentlemen,' giggled a female voice that sounded very familiar to the eavesdroppers, who now made their appearance.

'Hi, Prof,' Eli waved in salutation. 'Sorry we're so doggone lade, bud we jes' losd our way somehow.'

'Ah, Mister Mayor — and your colleagues, too. Super. Roberto, you other chaps, the Mayor's here.'

'Uniforms on,' Humes called down the corridor; so saying he reached behind the office door for a crumpled lab coat with the legend 'Mathematics Canada' stitched carefully in red around the lapel. 'Mathem' ran up to Humes' right ear and 'Ada' emerged from beneath his finely-chiselled left ear-lobe.

''M afeard we croaked some dude with tennis balls in the hallway,' the Mayor apologized.

'Ah, yes. Well, never mind. That was probably Cosmo. He's really not on the faculty any more. Awful shame. Such a brilliant, brilliant mind. The trouble is that he's too clever to endure finality with the rest of us. To march forward to the bitter end. He stays put in nineteen seventy — in the days of two postal deliveries per day, mini-skirts, the defeat of small-pox and the year that he made his famous discovery. It concerned the bladder, you know. Perhaps you heard about it at the time? He devised a mathematical model for the bladder.'

'Ah sure hope id weren'd modelled on them goldarn Helix Clean boddles in the lobby.'

'Eh!?! Well, of course, it hit the headlines once the breweries heard about it. Actually we'd gone to press three weeks before in the *Globe and Mail* science column, even though the doctors who were testing the model hadn't got the experiment working. Of course, the medics pushed us into the premature advertising — they didn't want to get pipped by some American smart-alec. I well recall the local headlines:

'W.H.U. BLADDER-BUFF BEGGARS BIG BAD BLADDER BUGS'

They took it very seriously. Unfortunately the experiments failed in the end. Mathematically the trouble turned out to be that in three dimensions one can have an unoriented normal bundle and still be cobordant to the Klein bottle.'

'Durn me if I didn' know them boddles weren' no damn good!'

'Quite. Well, that finished Cosmo. The University Hospital at once held a Press conference and palmed all the blame on him. Hundreds of indignant bladder-sufferers camped in protest outside the office of the President — the *University* President — and Cosmo was given the sack. Rotten luck really, which is why we let him bang around in the hall like a perpetual motion machine.'

Penz turned to Zhilin with a broad grin.

'I zink zis von vill 'aff returnt zu posionne orig-ginale by zwei zousand nine'een!'

'Oh, very good,' chuckled Humes, 'two thousand and nineteen! Very good indeed!'

'Anyway, late or not doesn't matter,' he resumed. 'Fact is, that it's damned decent of you to drop in like this at all. Not every department gets a Mayoral visit, by Jove.'

'Most don't deserve it,' remarked the swarthy individual who had been the other half of the dispute over the whereabouts of non-existent centres. This person had a husky voice and wore the crotch of his trousers very low, but otherwise Eli could see no prima facie reason for disliking him.

'Yes, let me introduce you, Mayor, to one of our faculty. This is Roberto Buzartis. Buzartis, this is Pans, Zhilin and over there,

Mister Penz.'

'Mighdy damn well pleased t' make yer acquaindance, Mister Booze Ardis',' the Mayor offered his manly, mayoral handshake.

Buzartis took it with a limp, greasy hand.

'Bu-zaar-tis,' he mouthed with voluptuous, meaty lips like steak slices, 'Bu-zaaa-aar-tis. As we say in my family, the emphasis is on the art rather than the booze.'

'Bu-zaar-tis. Bu-zaar-tis. Bu-zaar-tis. Bu-zaar-tis ... ' continued Zhilin and Penz, heads together consultatively, each intently listening to the intonations of the other.

'There are four of us here, plus secretarial staff,' explained Humes. 'Myself and Elsquaird, to whom I'll take you imminently, constitute the Research Institute. Roberto, here, and Jim Slag do the teaching. Very important duo they are, too. Without them where would we be? Eh, Roberto? Oh, yes. Quite as important as the research which Elsquaird and I do. Quite, quite. Why, Bob and Jim teach the rudiments of calculus to the rudiments of nineteen thousand, five hundred students.'

'Not that they're very grateful,' inserted Buzartis. 'They're always complaining. They don't like my accent. They can't understand calculus. They signed up for the wrong course. They don't like the class sizes — neither do I, but I've tried every trick that I know to drive the students away. When it gets too bad I ask them just what they expect, in way of education, when they're paying less than a dollar a class. You pay more than that for the two seconds that it takes a tax consultant to show you where to sign your name.'

'Right-o, Bob. Scout around and see if you can find Jim. And tell him to put on his uniform.'

'He'll not be here. I'll look, but I bet he's at Ada's. And I don't have the number because he's scared witless that I'd give it to some students. Which I wouldn't do. Not for nothing, anyway.'

Buzartis ambled off.

'And don't forget your uniform, Bob!' Humes called after him.

Without being noticed a young lady had ventured out of the copying room, which gave off the back of the office.

'Hello.'

'Ah, Mayor. Meet the real boss around here. Miss Rena Failure, she's our head cook and bottle washer. She handles everything.'

The quartet were silently gaping at the lady; a dribble of spittle was making its way unremarked down from one corner of Pans' open mouth.

Eli gathered his wits first.

'Howdy, Miss Failure. Pardon me being rude an' all, bud didn' we all jes' meed over in th' Cow Department of th' hospidal?'

Miss Failure laughed heartily at this one, throwing back her head and revealing a very attractive long, smooth, white throat.

'No, no,' she laughed. Humes was snickering quietly, too. 'You met Nurse Rena Failure over *there*. She's my sister. We're identical twins, you see. And my mother thought that it would be such a pain to distinguish us all the time, so she gave us the same name. I suppose it was her little joke. Her retribution for our being two twins and not letting her know in advance.'

'Ay, twuns ca' offa' send a wee lassie off hae' chump.' Preston Pans replied sympathetically. He was secretly wondering if this one's buttocks felt the same as her sister's. It seemed only reasonable — identical twins. He resolved to find out.

'There was a call for you, Mayor. Your secretary left a message that she has had a lot of complaints from the motorists in the parking lot. Something about shooting at their tyres.'

'Sure, honey. Thanks a lot. I'll fix it when I get back.' Eli frowned meaningfully across at Pans, who was still concentrating on anatomy.

'We only have a small fraction of this building, just four offices and these secretarial workrooms. The rest of the building is given over to the Graduate School of Strategical Journalistic Analysis.'

He pointed down the corridor.

'You can see where the clean paintwork starts. That's G.S.S.J. They've got a thousand grad students. In fact we got Rena after she'd graduated from there, didn't we Rena?' Humes smiled thoughtfully into space.

'Most of them are blondes, about five ten, a hundred and twenty pounds, white Caucasian and training for TV. They study hair-do, microphone posture and smiling in their first year. Rena took their course on answering the telephone.'

'Does zee cook und bottle-vosher, vosh dem Felix Klein bottles?' interjected Pens, innocently.

'I'll have to admit they don't get washed very often,' replied

Rena, laughing again, much to Preston Pans' delight.

'The same goes for the plastic ellipsoids.'

'Well, come along, gentlemen. I think I should introduce you to our celebrity — Professor Elsquaird. This way.'

The others followed him, reluctantly in the case of Pans, down to the office at the darkened end of the corridor, where the lighting had failed. Humes knocked.

A muffled crash could be heard, almost at once, from the other side of the door. It was followed by a shout that sounded like, 'Bloody chalkboards.'

Humes rattled in alarm at the door, which came open slowly to reveal Professor Elsquaird looking down upon the intruders with a far from benign gaze. The quintet strained to look up at Elsquaird. Craned their necks, twisting heads to one side, to look at him.

He was indeed a midget. Hardly a metre. White, Caucasian — actually a little on the yellow side — and God knows what he weighed. He was holding fast to the top of the sliding blackboard, which he had ridden as high as it would go. In fact, further examination would have revealed that he was not so much holding on tightly as trapped.

'What on earth are you doing up there?' Humes asked in astonishment.

'He sure ain'd taking a piss,' replied Eli sardonically. 'Pans, ged th' poor basdard down. Bud,' he snapped, 'don' break him.'

Having restored the professor to his usual, dignified perch on top of the filing cabinet, they were able to resume the normal pleasantries of introductions all round. Elsquaird apologized for the fracas and explained that his hand had been caught in the board handle as he pushed it out of the way on its upward traverse.

'Good job you came along,' Elsquaird admitted.

'Tell me, prof,' Eli began, hesitatingly at first. 'Does mathemadics have a theory of Power?'

'Nuclear, electric — wind?' Humes interrupted.

'I think, Sherloch, that our Mayor means us to infer that he is enquiring about *political* power. Am I not right, mister Mayor?'

'Bulls eye, prof. Jeeze, yer may be shord, bud y'ain'd dumb.'

'Well, watch out for the statistoquacks,' Sherloch interjected further. 'Their's is the way of utter balderdash when it comes to political predictions.'

Elsquaird flashed an irritated glance at his director, who silenced at once.

'Funny that you should ask. As it happens I have a complete mathematical vision of Power. You could call it a programme. Some pieces are in place, some theorems are proved, others await proof and revelation. It is based on the theory of schemes.'

'Of finite type?' asked Zhilin, with rapt curiosity.

'Any type, my friend, any type at all.'

'Schemes, eh.' Eli nodded his approval. 'Good. Good.'

'Schemes are a little like the crania of topology with little light bulbs of algebra, called sheaves, stuck all over them.'

'Sheaves, very good. Very agricuidural.'

'I combine this with the theory of mixed motives — which does not yet exist — but we are encouraged by the boundless fruits of its hypothesis.'

'Mixed modives. Thad sounds jes' dandy t' me.'

'A'm no sae sh-oo-er aboot a' the' fruits,' snarled Pans.

'Dumb ass, *fruids* nod fruids.'

'The experts don't doubt my motives,' continued Elsquaird.

'Nor do I,' replied Eli.

'To them my motives are as real as sliced bread! And I unify it all in the theory of Tenacrean categories. Which don't exist, either. But just you wait!'

'What a brain,' put in Humes. 'See what I told you? He thinks about things which don't even exist yet.'

Pans nodded, he was engaged in pondering a duplicity of things that did not exist yet. In fact, truth to tell, he was not listening to the celebrated professor or to his boss.

'Ten acres. Hod shide, if thed ain'd jes' whad ah've bin lookin' fer. I see, ten acres. A sord of strip farming. Socialism. Every shidhead'll have his ten acres, every free man shall pay his tithe, every tithe-holder shall have his fiefdom. Perfect. Ah gid id!'

Eli strode over to the midget and looked up into his clear, brown and fearless eyes.

'Say, shord-ass, wanna be my Minister fer Power? Id pays twice whad yer'll gid fer wiseacr'n id here.'

'Mayor,' said Elsquaird, in an instant so short that no mere mortal could have cogitated in it — but Elsquaird evidently calculated his *cogito ergo sum*, 'I like your style. You've got some balls. And you've got yourself a deal.'

Elsquaird vaulted down from the filing cabinet, unhappily landing in the waste-bin. Eli beckoned. 'Pans, gid him oud.'

He added,' A deal id is, son. Bud ther'ain'd nothin' in id about m'balls. Now ah think yer should show us th' rest of yer place, prof, afore'n we have t' gid.'

'Er, yes, I suppose so,' spluttered the amazed Humes. 'You gentlemen have flabbergasted me, I think.'

Humes led the way out of the office and back along the hall. In the rear of the group Zhilin and Penz, attempting to pronounce the word 'flabbergasted', whispered quietly to one another. 'Blibbinkcustard. Blibbinkcustard. Blibbinkcustard. Ja.'

12

DELIVERANCE

Panic-stricken, Smoothe raced ahead of the phalanx of scramblers, each laden with medical clamps, blankets, rubber sheets, oxygen masks, coats, sweaters and scalpels, which hurried along after him.

'Get me Testes! Get me Testes!' Smoothe called imperiously in all directions.

However, for all the shouting, he arrived at the cow sheds to find no Testes.

The sight that greeted him was nightmarish, representing as it did the tragic termination of months of experimentation.

There was neither time nor opportunity to waste on such maudlin reflections. If only they were in time to do a successful Caesarean, they might have the first truly bucolic human being — there had been attempts at frauds and swindles in the profession, particularly in the United States, where the technology was readily available.

Grace was lying on her side, a stiffening hind leg raised in the air, as if preparing to make a breech delivery. She was still warm. All around lay cow-corpses with wide-eyed, euphoric gazes directed mindlessly at the ceiling. Quietly, gently, soothingly, Mozart's Requiem was piping in over the PA system.

'My God, Testes, hurry — where are you?' Smoothe stamped his foot impatiently.

By now the equipment had caught up with him; with a struggle they got Grace onto a makeshift operating table, cleared space around it and set up the incubator for the premature offspring.

Smoothe paced to and fro — he looked at his watch; there

remained only a matter of minutes .... . They might already be too late. He lit a cigarette, drew on it once and threw it away.

'Testes?' He ran to the door and hurled it open. There, lying on the ground, was Dwayne Testes, the medical miracle. Pissus como newtus — pissed as a newt. Testes had fallen from his BMW (continental quadraphonic sports model with additional gearing and ejector seats) which he had contrived to bring to rest by colliding with a bank of garbage.

'Oohh, God,' moaned the fallen surgeon.

'Where the hell have you been?'

'Jus' paus-s-sed for some liquid refreshment.'

'You're paralytic!' screamed the desperate Smoothe.

'Sure, buddy, fuddy-duddy! You sh-h-hould s-s-see me when I'm drunk,' rejoined Testes, with a grin. As he looked up his face revealed a cut over the left eye, but there was no time for trivialities like that.

Smoothe dragged Testes inside and hauled him over to the remains of Grace. The latecomer was gazing, wide-eyed at the carnage surrounding them. At least fifteen cows were keeled over, in stalls or out on the main floor, in positions of finality and supinity.

'Testes,' Smoothe roared with an unmistakeable note of authority, 'Caesarean this beast. Now. As fast as you can.'

'Holy cow!' Testes scratched his head in bewilderment.

'Shhhh, have some respect for the dead. Rena, get ready with the tools.'

Testes took a tool.

Testes in action was a marvel to behold. Smelling like a distillery, seconds earlier unsteady on his feet, now — steadied by a nurse — his deft hands flashed to work. Such was his expertise, so remarkable his training, so trivial the task in hand, that his dexterity and confidence remained undiminished; in that manner which is characteristic of his highly-trained profession he literally tore into Grace's uterine regions. Those hands, which had so often trembled with lust over the arched, downy neck of a nubile third-year pre-med, were now rock-solid. They had become the hands of the Great Architect.

In what seemed the briefest instant, but in reality was a long, sweating agony for the attendant, pacing, praying Smoothe, Testes was done.

'Voila! Damn me, it's a girl.'

'Waah, waah, waah.'

At the familiar cry, that clarion of international fame and success, Smoothe took command.

'Into the incubator with her, Rena. Check the temperature. We can't afford to lose her now.

'This is my daughter, Bucolia Smoothe,' he added impressively.

'Sweet Jesus,' remarked Dwayne, a little more sober by now. 'What have you been up to in these cow sheds? Horny, used to mean one horn, not two.'

Disregarding his colleague, whose task was now over, Smoothe laughed, joked and handed round the inevitable cigars.

Finally, when the incubator was running steadily and everyone had milled around it, goo-gooed and gazed in, Testes, Rena Failure and Smoothe were able to relax atop the soft carcass of the venerable Grace and to enjoy their cigars. Testes pulled out a leather-bound flask from his jacket pocket and passed it round.

'I needed that,' Smoothe reflected after taking a long swig.

'By the way,' he added, 'I made arrangements for the television and the Press to be here. They should be arriving very soon, because I stressed what a scoop this would be. It's a good job that we pulled it off!'

In fact, Rena Failure had scarcely time enough to adjust her make-up before the crumpled, genial figure of the Press appeared through the door in the person of Sebastiano Antuigliu. He was followed by two novices and a tall, smiling, blonde girl with a television camera.

They got straight to business. Smoothe described the background, his inspiration, indispensable ingenuity and masterliness which permeated the whole project, its international impact and its immediate and overwhelming relevance to the techtronics industry, including its place in assisting the Canadian effort to resist and overcome the Third World Japanese industrial challenge.

'Is this a first for Canada?'

'Absolutely.'

'Will this win you a Nobel Prize?'

'Oh, I hadn't thought of it that way. Umm, perhaps I might at that.'

'Is this your greatest scientific achievement?'

'Yes.'

'No.'

The latter remark came from Testes who, usually a crowd-dominator at Press-conferences, was beginning to awaken to the realization of the opportunity that he was missing by his quiescence.

'No?'

'No, I think I've done better. Don't your remember the Testes affair?'

'Last week? — assault in the ladies' lockers?' enquired the tall blonde girl.

'No, no. Wasn't it transplants?' interjected Sebastiano.

'Correct. Don't you remember it. Four limbs and thirteen internal organs, transplanted into one vict . . . - patient — in one operation. They said it couldn't be done.'

'Isn't the record now sixteen limbs and forty-five internal organs?' asked the ingenuous blonde.

'That doesn't count,' protested Testes vehemently. 'Bloody show-offs. They used a set of Siamese quadruplets and essentially replaced everything that they could get off. Needless to say, the rejection problems were massive and not all the transplants took.'

'How many took?'

'I don't remember,' admitted Testes.

'Fifteen limbs and forty-two organs,' offered the helpful, smiling blonde, steadily aiming the camera at the nearby carcasses.

'What are all these dead cows?'

'Where?'

'These.'

'I think they are only anaesthetized.'

'I don't think so,' insisted Antuigliu, crossing over to a Friesian and prodding it with his toe. 'There's rigor mortis here. This one's had it all right.'

'I imagine that it is some experiment,' assured Smoothe. 'It is probably F.A.D.S. research, which has to push on so fast that we've been obliged to make a laboratory out of the cow-sheds.'

'Oh, I see,' replied Antuigliu hesitantly.

Smoothe made a mental note to have the sheds cleared before the coast-to-coast Press-conference that he had set up for the following morning at nine. Also, by an oversight, it would happen that he would forget to tell Testes about this conference until noon on the morrow.

Perhaps it was fortunate for Smoothe that the interview was curtailed at that point by the arrival of thirty or more Morris dancers, who had been attempting to dance in the parking-lot when they had heard about the great event and had drawn near, Magi-like, to see it. In their gaily coloured costumes, ribbons dangling, buttocks dangling, flowers on their hats and heads, all the clubs were there — Morris Beauchamp Geriatric Homes, Beauchamp Morris, Vallee Morris, Ginger Morris, Home County Morris, Morris Dancers des Estados Unidos, Gasville Morris Dancers. They were all well represented.

'Aahhh,' sighed Rena Failure as she watched the capering Morris dancers picking their way through the cow carnage, as they danced Highland Mary, Black Joke and Bonny Green Garters to the swirl of the bagpipes and the squeeze of the wheeze-box, and the scrape of the fiddles. Unnoticed, Mozart continued his Requiem.

13

CHRISTENING

The occasion was the christening of Bucolia Smoothe, tiny, jaundiced celebrity of six and a half weeks of age. In the grandiose Victorian splendour, beneath a peeling ceiling, complete with hammer-ended beams and flying buttresses of the Gasville Anglican Basilica were assembled, by unignorable ordinance, the entirety of Gasville's interesting parties.

On the front row, in pride of place beside her husband, sat Thelma Smoothe. Although they were scarcely ever seen in public together any more and although there were rumours, her bearing was dominant and determined, overshadowing Dean Twain Smoothe. Smoothe was wearing his iron-grey pin-stripes, to be measured for which he had had to go all the way to Fergus; tasteful, tranquil, timid grey beside Thelma's towering infernal red, topped with Ontario, radical chic boas in flame and mustard.

In fact, with one iota more of cosmetics Thelma could have been easily mistaken for a towering Toronto tart, a Bloor Street beauty, an aging Amazon.

As it was, Thelma merely looked rather tired as she presided over a gleaming row of smile that would have done credit to a Ganges gavial.

At Smoothe's elbow quietly cowered Milda Rattacks, his pimply but otherwise wholly unexceptional Second-in-Command, with Rena Failure and three of the nurses at her right. A place had been left on the front row for Testes, who was, after all, to be the Godfather, but he had been unavoidably detained (by his customary midday delirium tremens).

On the other side of the front row sat Eli Baktrian and his

90

wife, Sarah, formerly Delaney, nee O'Donal. The Mayor's entourage spread backwards down that side of the church and at his feet, sleeping soundlessly, lay the inert bundles which were O'Toole Delaney and his adoptive half-sibling, Yukio Kanada.

Officiating was the Reverend Michael Chreist, BA (WHU — Phys. Ed. Class of 19XX), the Vicar of God.

The vicar, an impetuous and ambitious young man in his thirties, sandy of beard and temperament, and thirsty of inclination, to the extent that on some weekends the congregation had been obliged to mime the sacraments, gazed down upon the assembled multitude with an intrepid stare of blue-steel.

Unfazed, Preston Pans stared back and blasphemously muttered, 'O, Chreist.'

He did not like the vicar, with whom he had recently had occasion to differ in the course of the latter's attempt to prevail upon the town hall to close Pans, Zhilin and Penz' favourite brothel.

Barging in to the Mayoral anteroom unannounced, the vicar had introduced himself.

'Chreist!'

'A' wouldna be sae shit-face blasphemin', laddie. Tha' be unco uncivil of yae. An' ma maties bein' th' verra pillar o' th' presbytera', lak' masel'.'

Undeterred by Pans' obstructive bulk, Chreist, a former WHU running back, used to rough treatment at pagan hands, had dodged around the Scot. Leaving his fetid dog, Apostolic Succession III, to smell up the carpet, Chreist had darted into Eli's office before they could stop him, closing the door behind him, in front of Pans and his pals.

Thus the young vicar had insinuated himself unfavourably into the lives of Pans, Zhilin and Penz. Penz, disgusted at this brash North American had contented himself with a lethal injection of formaldehyde, administered to Apostolic Succession III during his master's absence and effective before the day was out.

Gazing innocently up at the blue-eyed vicar, Penz wondered idly whether the incipient Divine suspected anything about the fate of his pedigree pup.

Chreist returned the congregation's communal stare with that generic expression of detachment and rapture to which ordinary mortals can never hope to aspire, and which the promising pupils of the pulpit perfect only after prolonged periods of practice.

Above the divine countenance was suspended an extremely enlarged portrait of a cow.

Grace!

In loco materno, the bovine bearer of baby Bucolia!

The organ music swelled, climbing, overwhelming the voices, erecting huge pyramids of sound above the brave, brazen beatitudes of the choir and congregation as they joined in their appropriate animal anthem — Amazing Grace.

Unconcerned by her surroundings, gazing sidelong at her new husband, mayor and hunchback, undistracted by the unwholesome cathedral, whose interior had been deturpated by decades of neglect — and, some ingrates would have it, had not originally been very pleasantly wrought — the music lifted Sarah.

It stretched out to her monumental, saintly centremost soul, to the young virgin of Cahir that had been herself as a girl, to the spirit of the rural Irish amidst whom she had been born and raised. To the pale beauty who was to be found on warm summer evenings haunting the walls of Cahir castle, gazing down upon the soothing, babbling, tumbling repetitious river which fell through the town.

Sarah's mind drifted back to the Summer of the English boy. She had met him upon those Cahir castle ramparts. Side by side they had gazed out over the river's turbulence, wordless and concentrated — parallel and peaceful.

Perhaps a month of such chance, coincidental gazings had passed before so much as the exchange of one syllable.

When she had mentioned the good-looking stranger to her father his response had been a leering grin. 'Has yer man totched yer bottocks, then?'

Sarah had fled to her room, in tears, unable to reply.

Gradually that summer the pair had discovered their shared, similar sensibilities. The boy — he never did reveal his name — turned out to be English. He was studying medicine at Trinity College, more (Sarah gathered) from obedience to parental authority than from Hippocratic conviction. He was staying with a retired aunt, who rented a nearby farmhouse, and supporting himself for the vacation by serving as ticket collector, custodian and groundsman at the castle.

Theirs had been the most Euclidean of Platonic relationships.

He had read the poets to her — with such a passionate delivery that she had several times been moved to tears.

To be an actor was his cherished ambition. Or a playwright. Or a writer, like Wilde or Joyce.

He discussed Spencer — not Tracy — with her; enlightening and charming her as if she had been every wit as learned and knowledgeable as he.

Sarah had adored his flushed expression of elation, almost anger, as he recited for her. She would have listened to him until eternity!

One day, never explained, his purple body, with bloated face and striving hands, was found floating in the river below the weir. He had been strangled with his own sphygmomanometer.

Sarah could not bring herself to go to the funeral, but her father and uncle had taken themselves shamelessly off to the wake.

''Tis the only dacent t'ing t' do fer yer man, t' see him off clanely t' t'other side, don't yer know?'

Neither of Sarah's parents were in any way qualified to understand her. Her mother watched with repeated amazement the incomprehensible magic which reproduced daily this complete, washed, starched and immaculate young lady — ready even before she herself rose at dawn.

Sarah's father, on the other hand, might have developed a glimmer of appreciation for his eldest child, if he had not been so immersed in and rancidified by his own rotten luck.

During the 'troubles' the young Brendan O'Donal, who was living in the Belfast of his birth, had been imprisoned in the Crumlin Road camp, along with many another Irishman indifferent to serving in the forces. Collectively known as 'conshies' most of the prisoners, like himself, had no generic conscientious objection to violence, to fighting (for what did they do regularly on a Saturday night?) and to warfare. Rather they shared the personal, private concern that they should be left alone. And if they must be interfered with then was it not logical, to any sane man, that they were likely to survive the interference of their fellow-countrymen, the Crumlin guards and warders, better than the malicious tomfoolery of the British and the Bosche?

In Brendan O'Donal's case this presumption had turned out to be far from accurate, leaving him a bitter man, even after his ultimate move to the south.

The Crumlin camp had not been large. It occupied an acre of wasteland which had served formerly as a refuse tip, and into the place were crammed as many as three thousand men, sleeping in shifts, three men assigned to each bunk. The pressure for space was unbearable, to the extent that there was almost a sigh of relief following any fatality or misadventure that befell one of the tight-fitting community.

Several of the guards (the personnel at the camp were merely NCOs, because of shortage of officers) took it upon themselves to harden the prisoners and their circumstances by nude and nocturnal forced marches. During his first winter in the camp, Brendan saw many stout hearts crumble and expire beneath this treatment.

The trio of guards who were the most diligent in the pursuit of this torturing regime were three fellows from the County Meade, who had come north to volunteer and had been rejected for regular service on grounds of ill health. It was difficult to imagine what sort of physical examination had resulted in this verdict. For example, despite the scarcity of food for both guards and prisoners alike, the first of this trio, Seamus 'Paddy' Weinsteinberger, was a giant of a chap, who must have weighed over two-hundred pounds. The other two, the brothers, Sammy 'Paddy' and Danny 'Paddy' O'Riley, were not so enormous but they were both wiry and strong. When it was necessary, they could each toil for six hours at a stretch at the mass grave just outside the fence; they had even been known, in their impatient disgust with the rate of progress, to elbow the work party of prisoners aside and to set to themselves, by way of example, spading the remains of the luckless into the pit with a will.

Weinsteinberger and the two O'Rileys were collectively referred to as the 'three Paddies'. And the three Paddies made their rounds at dawn each morning, usually finding fault with the bunk or belongings of some defenceless inmate. Resistance to their attempts to steal the prisoners' food and cigarettes was met with detention and torture, although few returned to tell of their experiences in the NCO's hut.

For some reason the three Paddies were extremely cordial and tolerant to the young O'Donal. They did not steal his food and they offered to share his cigarettes with him on several occasions.

Sammy even brought him flowers!

It had not aroused Brendan's suspicions, therefore, when Seamus had appeared at his bunkside one night, motioning him to silence, and had led him outside the hut. Once there the guard had explained to Brendan that he, in fact each of the 'three Paddies' shared his sentiments, was awfully sorry to see such a nice young fellow in such a tight spot. Weinsteinberger had explained the plan of escape, the conditions of the deal and, smiling broadly in the darkness, had made very explicit just what the 'Paddies' were asking in return. Young O'Donal had never done that sort of thing before; in fact for a hard-drinking Catholic he was extraordinarily attentive to the commands of the priesthood.

However, even Scotus Eriginus would have sodomized himself to get out of the Crumlin camp.

After spending the night in the NCO hut, Brendan was led to the inner gate just before dawn. The gate was swung open by a grinning 'Paddy' and closed behind his departing prisoner. He found himself between the two fences, before him the outer gate, beside which he could see no-one.

O'Donal started round in panic. Behind him he could make out the 'Paddies' approaching the wire, he whirled round as a search-light from the outer conning tower was switched on.

'Oh, shit!' Why had he not noticed that the customary lights were all out as he was being led through the gate?

He started to run. Gasping, gaping, grunting, grabbing at the wire. Climbing like a white, sun-lighted lobster up the tall outer fence. There was a sound of shots firing. Many shots. They seemed quite distant, as he continued to climb. His breathing hurt, searing hot came each breath, but he forced his legs and hands to climb.

He never reached the top of the fence.

In fact one of the very first rounds had caught him in the spinal chord, had caused him to drop back to the ground like a stone. And there he lay, passed out, his legs and arms struggling to work, flailing in the dawn air, much to the amusement of the 'three Paddies' who surrounded him, gazing down at him and guffawing, their weapons once more slung carelessly over their shoulders.

Brendan O'Donal's only piece of good fortune that night was to have remained sufficiently alive to have been taken to the

Shanklin Road hospital rather than to the camp burial pit. And
for this slice of luck he could thank the milk of human malice
— the fact that the trio considered a cripple to be more of a
novelty than a corpse.

Every bullet has its billet.

The one that Sarah's father collected in that distant dawn
would leave him an agonized cripple for the rest of his life. On
good days he would be able to walk with a stick, cursing each
step, and on bad days he would resort to alcohol and a wheel-
chair.

But even in a wheel-chair one can get to a wake!

After the war he had bought a small dairy-farm with the help
of his pension and managed to find a good woman to marry
and mother him, uncomplainingly, out of pity.

He would have loved to have joined the exodus of earnest
emigrants who enthusiastically eschewed Erin's erstwhile, eternal
Eden.

To bolt from Britain-buggered Belfast with its battle-benighted
backways and saint-studded Shanklin Road, sacked by a
cemetery-straining soldierly citizenry of sadism.

Many of his fellow victims fled across the Irish sea, to London,
to encounter Edgeware's enmity towards the paralytic Popish
Paddy, prostrate patron of some pub, passing precious pearls
of piss drunkenly in his moleskin pants.

O'Donal went south because he never could understand what
drove his fear-feebled fellow fiddlers into the British arms which
had buggered the Irish as badly as had any Bosche. And there
he would wait impatiently for the day when, from the IRA,
would come word that retribution had sought out the 'three
Paddies' and bombed them, and their families, to oblivion on
his behalf.

Even that news did not turn him into a cheerful man — only
Guinness could do that!

Such a mean-spirited man, her mother's millstone, was not
even a little warmer towards his six children, whom he expected
to obey him and to carry out as many of his chores as whimsy
dictated — each command echoed with some reference to his
immobility.

''T'is not iv'ry dee dat yer man shoots y' up th' rearend wi'
his tomfool sten-gun, coss th' livin' deelights outa th' spalpeen!'

Of all the children, being the eldest, Sarah bore the brunt

of her father's perpetual sense of swindlement. Her mother took as much as she could bear — shielding her daughter as best she could. There was a lot to put up with — his drunkenness, his animal-like conjugal appetites, his foul-mouthed speech in front of the children.

Spurred by a premonition that worse would soon be coming her way from the old man Sarah had begun to look for a man, someone who would take her far away, someone who would be poetic and learned, a gentle and broadspirited antithesis of her father.

The death of the English boy had been a great blow, although she knew from the start, deep down in her heart, that they were unsuited and planets apart. After him she started to search in earnest, lowering her standards with the unsuccessful passage of time.

Her lack of success did not reflect her unattractiveness. In fact she was a fine, straight, broad, tough figure of a girl, with an intelligent face and the type of fine hips and buttocks that were sought after by many an honest farmworker. Her attempts were thwarted more than anything by the minute supply of eligible males of the correct age; too many of them, she found, would emigrate just as they were becoming friendly — and she could hardly speed matters along by advertising in the *Cahir Free Press and Daily Chronicle*.

Thus it turned out that she received with relief and reckless abandon the eventual advances of Paddy Delaney.

Delaney himself was significantly older than the girl, but apparently still eligible, having spent some years in the Merchant Marine and other nomadic professions.

Paddy was naturally a kind-hearted soul, who could charm a smile out of the most misanthropic, even from Brendan O'Donal on occasion!

Sarah took to him at once and within a matter of days of meeting him was toying with his troubled, tousled, tawny, tonsured topknot. He had many entertaining tales to tell, and they almost substituted for the passionate poetry of her previous platonic paramour. Delaney had sailed for sheep-shit-shovelling sites of sullen, strenuous struggle in Scotia Nova and for the syruppy serendipity of Sydney and Singapore. He had battened down his fair share of hatches — the hope of the helpless, hurrican-harried, hastening for Halifax N.S. in some creaking

sloop, groaning in the ocean swell like a hedgehog, hardly a
heedful harpy of hope, running before the North Atlantic storms.

He had haggled with the hedonistic hookers of Halifax, so
different from the hardened heathen harridans of Heathrow.

In this manner Paddy Delaney had become acquainted with
the northern reaches of Canada. There he had visited many Irish
villages and communities, carousing with the promiscuous
Paddies of the parish and their ladyfriends. He had listened
cheerfully to their familiar Erin brogue and had found himself
partial to these pregnant postulants of pill-plagued Popery,
peeking pitifully at the Protestant's plaything in the Pharmacy.

Thus it was that, when once more at home on his native soil,
he found himself often opting for Ontario offal until finally he
decided to show a photograph of Toronto to Sarah.

''Tis th' de'il of a place, I'm t'inkin'. Would ya'self be up
t' tryin' a trip t'th' place, now?'

It was the long awaited question, and if it was not, then Sarah
did not pause to reason why. Without so much as a glance at
the photograph, by way of reply, she slid a hand inside his fly
— her father in front of the fire being asleep and everyone else
being at church at the time.

They were wed two days later and had fled the County
Tipperary by the end of the week.

'Waaagh! Waaagh!'

Sarah's inattentive, daydreaming recollections were rudely
interrupted by the crying of a baby. It was O'Toole. No sooner
had he started to cry than Yukio had also joined in the row.
With experienced dexterity Sarah reached inside her blouse and
flipped open her copious maternity brassiere and had stuffed
the boys successively inside her shirt before the congregation
had had time to locate the origin of the commotion. Inside the
shirt, muffled and immediately feeding contentedly, the boys
were restored to tranquil oblivion.

Sarah turned towards her new husband. A weird man, she
reflected, and one whom she did not attempt to understand,
save by intuition. A tense man, a desperate man and definitely
strange he was — but inexplicably attractive.

The previous night, for example, he had risen from the bed,
in the middle of the night, alarmed, screaming and being chased
about the bedroom by the Angel of Death, shouting at the top
of his lungs:

'Wer are y'all? I'm here, damn yer! Wer are yer — Pad Hayes? Tom Goodey? Ray Bennedd? Barbara Brown? Wer in Hell are yer? C'mon back fer Crissake!'

She had heard him racing down the stairs and around the living room. Finally, and fortunately without waking the boys, he had returned, minus the phosphorescent Angel, exhausted and sweaty, collapsing onto the bed to snuggle against the weighty arm of his newfound spouse. It still came as a welcome surprise to Eli when he experienced Sarah's proximate familiarity — in a bedroom rather than a barn full of mowers.

Eli tried to make light of Sarah's attachment. 'I guess, in'x'plick'bly, she jes' had a sofd spod for m' hardware! Heh, heh!'

Nevertheless, subcutaneously Eli was aware of the good fortune that befell Sarah's friends. The New World had matured her into a desirable lady, who had been known to break the nose of a cow-hand who became too familiar. The mayor realized that beside him was a staunch and formidable ally, who might well prove more reliable than the phalanx of new talent, assembled in the rows behind him, which formed his expanded entourage, to become known eventually as the Gang of Eleven.

Eli turned round to the two men sitting directly behind him and, indicating the elevated picture of Grace at the front of the church, whispered with a broad grin:

'Every puzzle has ids pizzle!'

In the row behind him was Pans, Zhilin and Penz, compressed tightly with two newcomers. It was to these last two that Eli had whispered. They were Norman the Mormon, from Salt Lake City, and Roddin the Norman, from Chicoutomi. The latter's real name was Corpse, Roddin Corpse. He was very disappointed with, and often argumentative about, the inability of the Gasville residents to pronounce his name.

'In Quebec we sayin' Corrrr, Rodanne Corrrr! Corrr!'

However, these sketchy French elocution lessons were largely in vain. Except occasionally for Preston Pans, the rest persisted in addressing him as Mister Corpse.

Elsquaird mispronounced on purpose, just to be irritating to the Quebecois, whom he considered privately to be some lower form of life.

'Damn Frenchies, they eat their Polish sausage in the street!'

'Pizzle, pizzle, pizzle?' muttered Penz, sotto voce, who had slowly managed to reassemble the whispered syllables. 'Wass ist dem pizzlen, jetzt?'

'Aw, pipe down, Penz,' called Baktrian. 'If yer don' know, yer kin waid till efder the show — then 'll tell yer.'

And with that reprimand the mayoral retinue fell silent. Glancing at their watches, they pretended to listen to the Reverend Chreist, who was still droning, moaning and mooing on about the brotherhood of man and his beastly brethren.

14

BOMB

The bright Ontario sunlight insinuated its way down through the heavily foliated maples, speckling the sidewalk with a mute kaleidoscope of patterns which were stirred gently by the warm morning breeze. Gasville was a silent sieve of birdsong, in the tranquil manner which is peculiar to small North American farming communities just before the congregation exits from its Sunday morning devotions, shriven enough to last for another week.

Watched by an eye of amber-cold sternness through a sprocket-driven automatic-focus telescope, secreted in the depths of a hard maple which stood directly opposite the Anglican Basilica, the people began to stream forth from the Smoothe christening.

Photographers stopped the happy trio on the basilica steps, where they were joined by the tardy Godfather, the talented Testes, who mingled with the Smoothes, adopting various positions — holding the baby, kissing it, smiling over it, grinning over Thelma's shoulder, holding Bucolia aloft like the Stanley Cup and so on.

They were joined by Milda Rattacks and the Failures. Testes even insisted upon a snapshot of himself with an arm round each waist of the Failure twins.

Eli Baktrian, meantime, escorted Sarah through the sacristy to the parking lot. Preston Pans followed, carrying the cot containing the two sleeping boys as if it were merely a basket of grapes. The pair helped Sarah into the four-wheel drive and securely fastened down the boys' travel cot.

''ll see yer jes' as soon as ah gid done wi' muh meedin' ad

101

the townha'' Eli explained as Sarah started up the engine.

He watched her departure through wrinkled, tightly sun-screwed eye-lids until Sarah was out of sight and then the Mayor motioned to his colleagues to follow him to the front of the church, where was waiting the gleaming Mayoral Pullman which he had recently acquired.

The crowd at the front of the basilica had thinned. Only the Reverend Chreist remained on the steps, stretching himself, with widespread arms, in a deeply-breathed appreciation of the marvellous fresh-air of an intoxicating Ontario morning. With a broad smile on his face he watched benignly as, one by one, his parishioners started up and drove away. Finally all that was left was the Mayoral Pullman, standing beside the kerb, presided over by Stanley O'Vayshun, the chauffeur who came with the car. Beetle-black and beautiful the car stood there, its engine purring gently, its doors open and its air-conditioning roaring.

The slim, negroid figure in the maple tree opposite the basilica stirred slightly and moved forward to obtain a better focus upon the figure of the Mayoral hunchback.

'C'mon, let's go.'

Swiftly Elsquaird slid down from Zhilin's shoulders and darted inside the limousine, followed by Norman the Mormon, Roddin Corpse and Penz. Eli slid into the front seat beside O'Vayshun. Preston Pans was about to enter the car when something on the floor of the car caught his eye, causing him momentarily to pause. He picked up the object, which was a football. He was about the throw the ball away when a thought crossed his mind. Grinning, he turned to face the church steps and called out.

'Heh! Chreist, mon! D'yae the-enk yae ca' cartch th' wee ba'? Hare y'are y'wee pansa'.'

The ball seemed tiny in his massive palm as he turned it over and then loosed it in a tremendous arching throw along a trajectory that curved so far away that any lesser man than Michael Chreist could not have hoped to reach it.

'Aaaaggh! Go! Go! Go!' yelled Chreist as he sprinted down the basilica steps in pursuit of the flying ball, his surplice streaming out behind him. Down the steps he went, sure-footed as a mountain-goat, once again transformed into that heroic form — the running back — so familiar a figure in Ontario myth and legend. Dodging a fire-hydrant for which Pans had had high

hopes, ducking and feinting past invisible defenders, Chreist
caught the ball with a deft left hand and raced on towards a
glorious touch-down beneath the maple which contained the
telescopic negro.

The touch-down never came.

There was a tremendous crack, an explosion.

'Norman — nod you — you! Norman! Gid darn. Hid th'
gas, Stanley O. Gun id, led's gid ouda here.' Eli screamed as
he dropped flat to the floor of the car.

'For Chrissake, go!'

The Pullman revved up and, with a squeal of burning tyres
and skidding wheels, Gasville's Mayoral gang fled the scene of
the accident. As the limousine sped away Preston Pans looked
back at the dwindling site of the blast through the rear window.

'Th' wee foo'ba' 'xplorded, d'yae ken? Wull, ah naivrr.
'Xplodin' foo'ba's. Whor nex'? Ah the-enk w'll no see yae
Mister Chreist agae'. Unco strange, m'the-enking. 'N't sims
tae huv felled tha' wee tree!'

In the solemn Sunday silence left by the departing limousine,
a silence punctuated only by the birdsong, the widespread
Reverend Chreist, one-time WHU running back par excellence,
fluttered his mortal remains in the street beneath the blasted
maple — the street wherein he had been the Vicar of God and
where he had missed his final touch-down by the merest whisker.
The defence that had brought him down was ten pounds of
plastic explosives. Ten pounds only did it take to down the genial
giant who had, in his heyday, dodged hulks of three hundred
pounds and had thrown them off like insects.

If the Mayoral group had paused to inspect the remains of
the disaster they would have witnessed the body of the slim negro
slip noiselessly from its branch and fall to the sidewalk. The dead
man landed easily, and almost comfortably-seeming, in the
posture of a sprinter at the starting blocks. His head was down,
his back arched, and he maintained a balance on the knuckles
of his hands, with his left leg stretched out behind him. The
deceased wore blue jeans and across the back of the remains
of his tee-shirt were printed the words:

GEORGIA TECH

Silently a black car turned the corner of the street, which was still as quiet and undisturbed as if nothing had happened. At walking pace the ghostly vehicle came down the street, unhurried but somehow urgent. It came to a halt beside the negro on the ground and a window slid noiselessly open. A deep voice barked a command to the driver.

'Git dat fella in dee trunk, dam' fass' man.'

'Yessuh, yessuh, Mando, suh, rahrt 'way, suh.'

'See wot dem waart trash done gonan' done, fellah? Dey won' do dat no mo', no sirree! Once is 'nuff!'

Thus it was that when, two minutes later, the police arrived at the spot they found no arboribund telescope trainer. Consequently when Eli, over breakfast on the following day, read an account of the incident in the *Chronicle* he learnt nothing of the manner in which Preston Pans had rid him of an unwanted spy, nor did he discover whom such a spy might be spying upon. For Eli the next day would be merely Monday — wash day, business day, a production day at the arms plant, sunny, cloudy with a high of twenty-six celsius, a ten per cent likelihood of rain and high humidity.

15

FACE

Her face is saturated by the speckled fragments of light thrown upon it in a perpetually dancing Brownian motion thrown by the lace of small branches in the tree beneath which she is seated. Beautiful. Blind face. Unlined and sanctified. Beatific expression. Intense and proud face. Lovely face. Tanned skin effulgent in the early afternoon sunshine, filtered by the foliage. Her skin is radiant. Does it concern her that here, at my remote Ontario lakeside cottage, where we are more likely to encounter a black bear than a man, that here I am staring at her in ecstasy? What does she imagine that Yukio is up to? How does she picture what I am up to?

Blind beauty attended by her midget and her handsome vegetable.

We three have been an inseparable trio since the scuffle outside the train station. Bucolia is as independent as she is prepossessing but I have insisted upon accompanying her on her trips to Toronto for treatment. Demonstrations similar to the one we saw have been flaring up frequently in Ontario towns and cities recently. Frequently and violently.

My God! Most of the time I simply force myself not to think about it. I just tell myself firmly that it cannot be my fault. Not after so long. Years have elapsed since my involvement.

Yukio does not resent being left behind. He is still captivated by that book about the French Revolution. He reads it at an infinitessimal rate, but unflaggingly and anywhere. At this moment he is down by the lakeshore, beneath the shade of a similar maple. When I left him he was sitting with his head lain so far over to one side that I thought first that he had dozed

105

off. However, when I went to remove the book so that it should
not fall into the water, he moved. The antenna on his helmet
trembled. Very slightly. But sufficient for me to spot it. I am
very familiar with the nuances of Yukio's fragile, faint
communications. He commanded with a whimpered squeal that
the book be left where he could see it.

Sometimes I see the three of them together, mentally conjuring
their fond remembrance to an assembly in this valley. Bucolia,
Yukio and O'Toole. Each very fetching in his own way. And
telepathic?

She is turning her face in my direction. It is impossible not
to think of that tragic, statuesque glance as a 'look'. Bucolia
is looking my way. The sun-speckle-play around her sensuous
lips is imitating a smile. On her brow the shade has created those
familiar smudges at the temples, where she always had them
as a child. They suggest the incipient horns of a young heifer.
Her mouth is opening. Pure black crystal laughter.

'John? John? I do believe you've fallen asleep! A post-prandial
nap, at your age! John?'

There is a hint of uncertainty in her resonant voice, the faintest
vibrato of alarm. I am dazzled by my sightless, dear companion.

I cannot think of any reply.

1

TRINOMIAL PLAN

The Mayoral inner sanctum was quite crowded. Rows of chairs had been arranged and a small blackboard had been erected at the front. The members of the audience were watching, with differing degrees of attention, Professor Elsquaird as he described his plan and intermittently illustrated it with a diagram or a sum.

Eli, seated at his desk off to the left, was at the front of the room, looking past Elsquaird, who was standing on a packing-crate, at the audience. The audience consisted of his hand-picked personal staff. At the back sat Preston Pans, Zhilin and Penz, all of whom had heard the discussion of the plan from its earliest inception and to whom it had by now become a commonplace. On the front row, grimacing with concentration, sat Roddin Corpse with Norman the Mormon at his side.

Norman (the Mormon) was a tall, slim, good-looking man, who would have passed for twenty-five, except for the effect of three long scars on his right cheek, whose livid lines shone out of his otherwise baby-smooth, sun-tanned face. He was blond, an extrovert and a lady's man, with straight fair hair, which he wore rather long. He had a habit of sweeping back his hair when it fell over his eyes. His seemingly charming character exuded nonchalance and languor to the point of idleness but beneath this misleading exterior he was physically tough. He considered himself to have great powers of mental and physical endurance and a quick, unconventional mind. He had, for example, commanded a battalion of Eritrean, Italian and Abyssinian mercenaries in Ethiopia at Gondar against a fascist foe, to whom he had deserted for a doubling of his salary. He had then proceeded to wipe out his former command, relying

109

on the speed of his judgement and his knowledge of the tactics and habits of his one-time subordinates. Quite unconventional enough, Norman had thought, even for a soldier of fortune.

The scars had not been earned in warfare, but rather in a Cairo nightclub, in a brawl over some lover. It was now so long ago, and the whisky had been so good that night, that Norman could no longer remember the sex, let alone the name, of the object of his desire on that occasion!

By comparison with Norman the Mormon, Roddin the Norman looked like an ape. In reality he was not overly anthropoidal. It was merely that he was massive, while being considerably shorter than his neighbour, and that he wore his sleeves rolled up, his shirt unbuttoned to his copious gut, and thereby revealed an immensity of very thick, black hair on his forearms and chest. He was concentrating hard on the lecture and was the first to ask a question.

'Ouat ees zees 'coeffision orv ouest?''

'Waste, my dear Corpse. Waste!'

'Corrr, Corrr. En Québec eet ees Corrr.'

'Absolutely. And the coefficient of waste is best described by a diabolical example. You'll love it. Suppose that we have ... '

On the second row Stanley O'Vayshun nodded and, wiping his brow with the back of his hand, he leaned across his neighbours, who were a rather ordinary looking couple — the Ontals, Doris and Horace — and whispered something to a swarthy individual at the end of the row. The latter was Sid Ra'in, an orthodox believer who was dressed in a thick, black woollen coat, despite the harmattan-like heat, on his head a black homburg from which long sidelocks protruded, greasy and sweat-ridden. He wore his fringes outside his coat.

Sid was Hassidic. A quiet and lonely man was Sid, but with an intelligent face which was adorned with massive eye-brows, currently knitted in deep concentration.

'Bot, wart iss mein task?' Sid asked in a thunderous baritone, raising his hand politely as he loosed the query.

'I'm glad you asked that, Sid. Although I was hoping to save that until ... Ah, here he is. Come in Jaime.' Elsquaird beckoned to a flaxen-haired youth who had just peeped in around the office door.

'Sorry, I'm late,' came the cheery apology, as the newcomer dumped himself down behind Horace Ontal.

'Due thart th' nonce muir 'n'll boogar yae laddie,' growled Pans, under his breath.

'Gentlemen, and lady,' smirked Elsquaird, 'we are now all met. Our late arrival is Jaime Laudenklier. Take a good look at him. You'll be working very closely with him, and indeed with everyone else in this room.

'Pay attention, please.' Elsquaird continued. 'We are the Gang of Eleven,' he chuckled at himself before resuming his narrative. 'Together we are going to take over this region, for the benefit of the community — and perhaps — a little smidgeon for ourselves.'

'Bot wart iss mein share?' Sid butted in.

'Evens Stephens, Sid old friend. Evens Stevens, pro-rated for length of service, less fringe benefits at sixteen per cent before tax, benefits to be compounded daily without regard to holidays, except for Victoria Day, when it should fall on a Monday. Is that clear?'

'Oh!' Sid was gazing perplexedly at his toes and knotting and unknotting his fringes as he weighed up the proposition.

'It's OK, I guess. But wart if mein ... '

'I think that we'll postpone the fringe benefits,' Elsquaird interrupted him.

'Don' worry aboud yer fringes, Sid,' ordered Eli in a low growl, surveying the group through half-closed eye-lids.

'To continue, perhaps you will momentarily regard the cartography which I have displayed here.' With this the miniature Professor skipped down from the box which had been his rostrum, picked up a long pointer from the foot of the blackboard, and proceeded to give them a guided tour of the locality.

'This is the area which we are going to take over first. I expect that we can accomplish this within three months, as the area is mainly agricultural.'

'That's quite a lot,' ventured Doris. Horace nodded in agreement.

'I was asked to provide a mathematical model of power,' retorted Elsquaird, rather huffily.' I believe that I have come up with such a theory, but mathematics does not conceive of power as static. It is dynamic programming of the highest calibre. In fact I doubt whether anyone else, living or dead, before or since, has made such an extensive, daring and brilliant

analysis. As a consequence of the theory we must either expand
or contract. D'you understand? We have to pursue the dynamic
— not the static — stability. And, by taking over this area
marked in red I believe that we will catch the crest of the wave,
so to speak, and take the tide to greater things.'

'Are we goin' t' sea?' asked O'Vayshun.

'Be-alt urp, Stan, f'Chrissake, laddie!'

'H'wer yer telling to belt up?'

Hands pressed Stanley back into his chair.

'Shhh!'

'Thank you! May I continue?' Elsquaird paused to give
further interrupters time to commit themselves.

'As I said, ninety per cent of this area is agricultural and it
has been grossly neglected by the Provincial and Federal
authorities. As a result at least fifty per cent of the farms have
gone into liquidation and been taken over by the city-dwelling
professional classes, who do not farm the land. Our first step
will be to appropriate their farm land. We will divide it into
strips, after the manner of the feudal system, levying tithes upon
those to whom we rent the land, on behalf of the current owners
— all for a further commission, of course. In addition we will
offer the lessees our insurance service against those uninsurable
calamities which always befall farming landowners who have
no previous experience.'

'But 'ow d'we know they'll buy it?' asked Horace.

'Zhilin!'

'Becoss iff zey don't buy — zen bad sings vill be kommen
zer vey,' laughed Zhilin.

Pans and Penz joined in, guffawing uproariously with such
vigour that they soon set everyone off, until finally the entire
Gang of Eleven were rolling off their chairs, kneeling helplessly
in the aisles, clutching stomachs and begging for the laughter
to stop.

Elsquaird recovered himself first. 'They'll buy,' he chuckled
grimly, 'they'll buy or else.

'Experience has repeatedly shown that, just as it is inadvisable
to let landowners become too powerful, it is essential to clip the
wings of the Church.

'Take it easy, Sid. I only mean the Christian Church —
pagans need fear no ill, at least in the first instance.'

'Oh? OK.'

'To exact tithes of the Church and the townspeople simultaneously we will institute a lottery — GASWIN — which will be operated on the same compulsory, take-it-or-leave-it, basis. And we will top it all off with the GASSAVE PLAN, a savings scheme which we can institute through all major employers, particularly the university — they'll be quite easy to mislead, I know all the members of their pension panel.

'We will each have a lot of work to do, as you may well imagine. Each of you has been picked for his — or her (smirk, smirk) talents. When it comes to persuading the ''customers'' Hassidic Ra'in will appeal to the European ethnic elements, Monsieur Corpse — sorry — Corrrr, will take the Francophone community, Zhilin and Penz take the intellectuals, Preston takes the Scots and, together with Norman (the Mormon) works on the gays. Norman also takes the Latter Day Saints, Seventh Day Adventists, Baptists (Complete and Partial Immersion) and the Friends. I, myself, will take small people and the mayor will deal with officials and bent people. Stan can do the Irish — and you may as well take the Anglophone Catholics, too, Stan. All right?'

'Sure.'

'Herr Laudenklier will do the youth, the Canadians of no fixed ancestry and those of Teutonic extraction. Horace and Doris will charm the families when all else fails . . . '

The room was warm and Eli's eyes were closing despite himself. Behind his closed eyelids he was lazily watching his Arthurian existence, which had been creeping up on him more frequently of late . . .

The crookback hight Baktrian, Lord of the Cinq Porters, Emblem of his Race, Knight of his Order, was seated, advanced upon the shoulders of a mighty host of small persons, peregrine at his wrist and hound at his ankles. Compassing the court with a glance of steel, he signalled the troubadour to play.

'Which, sire?'

'The fish.'

'Any special fish, sire?'

'Varlet, cheek me not — you knoweth the righte damn fish!'

'A description of a Strange and Miraculous Fish, caft upon the fands in the meadf, in the Hundred of Worwell, in the County Palatine of Chefter, or Chesfhiere, sire?'

'No, foolish bastard, spawn of lice-plagued loins. By my

trowth, I meanst to have a description of a Strange and Miraculous Fish, cast upon the sands in the meads, in the Hundred of Worwell, in the County Palatine of Chester, or Chesshiere.'

'Why, sire, didst not thou say so sooner? Verily I know it well.'

And without further ado the troubadour, who bore a startling resemblance to Dragan Weiptz, began to sing out in a mighty, mellifluous baritone.

> 'Of many marvels in my time
> I've minded heretofore,
> But here's a stranger, now in prime,
> That's lately come on shore,
> Invites my pen to specifie
> What some, I doubt, will think a lie.
>
> Oh, rare
> Beyond compare
> in England nere the like.
>
> It is a fish, a monstrous fish,
> A fish that many dreads,
> But now it is as we would wish,
> Cast up o'th sands i'th meads,
> In Chesshiere; and tis certain true
> As tasty a fish as graced a dish,
> Which bailiff, reeve and sherriff, too
> Would fain serve up,
> In a tastie stewe.
>
> His Cods are like two hogsheads great,
> That seemeth past beleefe,
> But men of credit can debate
> What I describe in breefe,
> Then let's with charitie confess
> God's werkes are more than men can guesse,
> With Cods like that no man maye stand
> With safetie 'pon the Chesshiere strand.'

'B'our lady! Stop! Stop! 'Tis filth, sire,' dared a young priest, pushing himself forward from the ranks.

'And who be ye?'

'Oswald, bum-bailiff to my Lord Bishop, sire.'

'And why art here?'

'To represent my Lord in the court, sire.'

'Pox on't. M'thinks I had the damned court forgot!'

Eli beckoned his reeve to approach. 'How goes yer reevin'?' enquired Eli, full genially. Not awaiting reply he asked, 'Dost wanna arm-wrestle fuh th' pinks, eh?'

'Not right now, sire — I fain must commence the reeving and thyself the judging, sire.'

'Aye, sooth to say, 'tis as thou sayest. With whom d'ye start this day, David?'

'Here, sire, is the first list of sinners presented,' with which the reeve unfurled the first of a batch of scrolls which he was carrying.

'William Yule has not received Communion for a year or more.

Elizabeth Ewsten of Elginturd is vehemently reported to be with childe.

Dorothy Wilson was delivered of a child unlawfully by Richard Carlton, student commoner of the College, as she sayeth.

Mister Meade is presented for not receaving the Communion at Easter.

Thomas Sturman is reported by his wife that he and Mary Rayner do live together incontinently.

Mister Brampton (vicar) is presented for not Catechizinge our Servants nor our Children, neether having anie minister Resident in our parishe.

Edward Lithell of Melbourne is presented for having been at the fayre upon the Sabathe.

Thomas Campion is presented for begetting his wife with Child before they were married.

The Vicar and his curate are presented since neether did use the clokes appointed for them.

Andrew Osborn is presented for that he had carnal copulacion with his Wife before the daye of their marriage.

We payne oure Minister as he him selfe saithe is not licenced by his Orders to preache and yet he preachethe.

Will Breastbone is presented for absenting him selfe often tymes from the Churche.

Nicholas Campion is presented for cartinge uppon Hallowmas daye.

Thomas Adleson is presented for suffering of play in his house ye twenty-ninthe December, being Sunday.

Wee present Elizabeth — singleton of the parish — for committing fornication with one John Tomlin as is supposed and as the common fame goeth.

Mistress Meade is presented for goinge out of the church two Sundays together and being called back by the Minister shaked her hands at him and spake some contemptuous speeche against him and so went away.

'How dost find them, M'Lord?'

Eli stroked his chin with his left hand, rocking to and fro on his dais and humming quietly to himself the while. Verily he changed hands — his face lighting up, a broad smile spreading across it.

'In sooth I find thus and in sequence respectively eache to his or her lot.

Cut off his balles.

Cut off her fancye man's balles.

Cut off Richard Carlton's balles.

Cut off Mister Meade's balles.

Cut off Thomas Sturman's balles.

Cut off the vicar's balles.

Cut off Edward's balles.

Cut off Thomas's balles.

Cut off both theyre balles.

Cut off Andrew's balles.

Cut off the Minister's balles.

Cut off Will's balles.

Cut off Nicholas' balles.

Cut off Thomas' balles.

Cut off John's balles.

And cut off Mister Meade's nose!'

'Nose, sire? Wherefore his nose?'

'Doltish oaf! Whither thy braines? Didst we not have away with his balles with th' first cut!'

'Verily, master,' responded the Reeve, David, downcast at his owne remission.

'What comest next?'

'Sire,' the reeve brought forth a second scroll and commenced to read therefrom. 'Item that any person who shall suffer any ducks to come into the Common Brooke shall forfeit for every such offence six pence to Eli, Lord of the Manner. Item that every inhabitant that shall not cleanse the Brooke or rivulet which runnes through the towne soo far as is abutting upon their land at such time or times as shall be appointed by the Churchwardens of the saide towne shall give up, relinquishe, lose, forego and forfeit for everie such offence three shillings and fourpence to Eli, Lorde of the Manner. Item that any parson shall not . . . '

'Person?'

' . . . parson, parson, parson shall not let out or suffer to runne anie of their sinkes or puddles into the Common Running Brooke from the foure of the clocke in the morning until eight of the clock at nighte upon pain of paiment of sixpence to Eli, Lord High Reeve of the Shire and Lorde of the Manner.'

Eli stamped his foot upon the floor, shouting out at once. 'Agreed! Let it be so, may it at once be done and finely done! Next item, David.'

'Last willes, sire, to whit — to Mister Chichley one rynge of goulde from his wife, to Mistresse Sterne one ring of gold from her son, to Mistress Wood a ring . . . '

'Yea, yea, yea. I approve all these damned ringes of goulden gold. Next item.'

'To Mistress Pryce from Mister Pryce, as followes, one cowe, two horses, two bullockes one pied and one browne, one heifer, foure poundes in monie, one gode carte, one . . . '

'Yea, yea,' snapped the Lorde, snappishelie, 'so be it, even to all the animals that went within the Ark of Noah. Next!'

'Item, John Seintgeorge and his servants under his orders broke the pound of the manor by armed force and removed two geldings which had been impounded for straying in the cornfields. They broke the Lorde's peace and are therefore ordered to be present to heare the Lorde's justice.'

'Stand forth Seintgeorge and thye dragoons.'

Forward shambled an assortment of victims, cripples, beggars, shaved and clean, a motley crew and at their head, proudly, stepped the arrogant, unrepentant Johannes Seintgeorge.

'Seintgeorge!'

'Sire,' responded the latter with a cheeky smirk.

'I would fain have from thee an answer to a question.'
'Certainly, sire. Anything, M'Lord.'
'How camest ... wist,' Eli paused and cocked an ear.
'Methinks I heard a voice.'
'Canst not be, sire.'
'Well, as I ... there t'is again! Didst not heare it?'
'Nay, sire.'
'Nothing at all, sire.'
'Never, sire.'
From all sides came murmurs of assurance. 'Methought I
heardst a person say — could it mayhap thus? — a person say
that

> "Doris Ontal will be indispensible in forcing
> farmers from their homes. She has the defences
> of a skunk."

What beest this "skunk", thinkest thou?'
Again, from all quarters came murmurs of ignorance.
'Then, bye oure Lady, if the voice didst not say verily

> "Show them, Doris. Give them a corker to stink
> out the place. It won't matter if we have to
> adjourn for the afternoon, we're all done."

Ne're mind then. Where was I?'
'The question, M'Lord.'
'Aagh, yes. Tell me ... ' Eli paused once more, this time
cocking his head from side to side and sniffing noisily.
'Tell me ... ' sniff, sniff, sniff, sniff.
'Tell me ... hast any of thee gotten shite on thy hosen or
shoon?'
'No.'
'No, 'pon m'soul.'
'Never, sire!'
And so on round the Hall.
'My God, in truth, there beest an awful noisome stinke herein!
A mighty stink, a blessed odour of fartinge and potent beyond
... beyond ... beyo ... '
Eli opened his eyes.
'Wake up, boss,' Stanley was shaking him by the shoulder

and endeavouring to help him to his feet. 'We've got to get out of here for a while, boss.'

'Meeting adjourned,' called Elsquaird, in a strangled voice that was muffled by the handkerchief which he was holding over his mouth. 'Jaime, open all the windows, and then let's get out of here. Leave the door.'

Leading the sleep-dazed Baktrian with them, the group of eleven filed out of the door as swiftly as they could manage.

'Fer Chrissake, leave th' damn door open.'

'Weel done, lassie. Wi' a blast lak thart, we'll nae hae' need o' th' atomic bomb!'

2

GANG OUT

The afternoon was miserably, cruelly and unbearably hot and humid. Not a whisper of a zephyr suggested itself. The animals were so quiet that Eli, had he not been totally indifferent to their welfare, might have been driven to suppose that they had expired. He did not feel so great himself, even though he could usually withstand the worst that any Ontario continental summer could offer without having to relinquish his bib-front denims for something looser and lighter. He was laying back in his porch chair with a row of beers ranked beside him in differing stages of consumption. Along the porch were carefully placed eleven other chairs. All these were empty, except for the armchair at the far end of the porch in which Sarah was lolling. With a bone-handled fan she was casually stirring the air above the cot in which the two baby boys were lying, in a sluggish, almost trance-like state of sleep. Even Yukio and O'Toole were silent, such was the oppression of the weather. Normally they would have been screaming for the breast, each striving to out-do the other in his lung-bursting, tearing, squeezing struggle for attention.

Sarah fanned the boys without regarding them. She was watching her husband with her attractive, almost sexual, slow scrutiny.

Eli and Paddy were such different men, Sarah reflected. Neither one the worse nor the better, perhaps. Unusually for Irishmen, she pondered, Delaney had not been much of a one for the body, nor even for the drinking. Not, that was, since their marriage, although doubtless he had been a devil back home in Tipperary. He had been a serious man, she believed, neither scheming nor malicious, and certainly not intelligent.

Rather he had been dependable without being jealous. In short, she surmised that his fate was so plainly obvious as to have been clearly to be anticipated; although no one had predicted it, not even Grandma Martin. He had lived contentedly and happily until the inevitable explosion — the sort that had, in various ways, with several types of detonation and limitless varieties of force, carried off many of his countrymen.

So content had her man been that he had never taken her to a city in all the time that they had lived in Canada, except to pass through Montreal and Toronto on their initial voyage of immigration.

Sarah sighed. In truth she had never set foot in a town any bigger than Cork City.

'Bedad, Cork was the divil of a big plee-ace,' Paddy Delaney used frequently to say, mopping the top of his head with a handkerchief and grinning with appreciation.

But he had been wrong. She had always known that. Now she had a man who had promised to take her to cities that Paddy Delaney had never even heard of — Detroit, East Lansing, Ypsilante and, best of all, to Toronto's downtown shopping malls!

As she watched him Eli stirred. His attention was directed downwards and out into the dust of the drive-way that fetched up at their farmhouse front door. To her he was an intriguing enigma. Sarah could sense, if not recognize cognisantly, Eli's mixture of violence, complicated ambitions, sometime stupidity and straightforward horniness. Sometimes he could be withdrawn, immured and impenetrable. Right now he was silent. One by one he drank the beers she brought him without looking in her direction at all. Without rancour she thought to herself, in imitation of the manner of her own mother, that he might just one time have murmured a 'thank you'. But why should he? The words were almost unknown even in the polite parts of Gasville's rural society.

Against the sun's glare Sarah drew down her eyelids to form the narrowest slits through which she continued contentedly to watch her man, who, after all, she felt sure, had put the curly-haired O'Toole into her belly.

Eli, on the other hand, was disregarding his wife. His attention was riveted upon the only movement in the entire hot afternoon scene before him. Out in the shimmering waves of solar energy two squirrels were playing over a piece of bread that had been thrown out onto the midden after lunch.

One animal, the larger and younger, had the crust. His movements were confident, swift and vigorous as he pulled the prize from the older squirrel, which, although quite full grown and by no means tiny, bobbed and weaved like a small supplicant, hoping to charm away some of the food by wit and experience. Time after time the smaller creature would approach, dance, wave his tail, feint and then dart in at the target; each time only to be deftly shrugged off at the last moment.

Eli watched this perpetual frustration exercise with amusement until it began to bore him by its repetitiousness. Grinning knowingly to himself he lay back in his chair and — momentarily, it seemed — closed his eyes.

Suddenly the tantalized animal shrieked, so shrilly and unexpectedly that it caused Eli to start upright.

'Hod shide!' He exclaimed, 'W'll uh niver.'

On the ground before him squatted the old squirrel, eating the piece of bread with rapid, tearing gestures. The bigger, younger squirrel lay two feet away in the dust. Dead.

As he stared at the furry corpse, against his will but scarcely without knowing it, the Mayor took another, minute Arthurian slip . . .

Crookback Baktrian, Porter of the Cinq Lords, Bailiff of the Eastern Realms and Remnant of the Raiment of his Race turned over the squirrel's corpse with his toe. Eleven whitish, fattish, sluggish larvae abandoned the dead thing and, forming a proximate circle about the body, began to travel, wriggling obesely, diametrically outwards.

The crookback Eli watched the expanding circle of slugs, mightily interested in it was he.

'Sire, 'tis an omen,' suggested the Jester, Obsidian, drily, biffing his Lord and Master with the pig's bladder.

'Methinks yon bladder stinketh, Obsidian.'

'Dost want t'significance, M'Lord.'

The hunchback Lord was systematically squashing at the slugs with the toe of his shoon.

'These are mightily robust, Lord, that e'en thou canst not splatter them.'

'Call the dogs to eat them.'

'Call the dogs.'
'Call dogs.'
'Dogs.'
'Dogs.'
'Dogs.'
The command echoed away down the corridor of the castle.
'Dost want knowledge of its importance, sire?' grinned
Obsidian, coming very close and leaning upon his Lord's arm.
'Uugh?'
'The portent, sire. The portent,' the Clown pointed to the
ring of slugs, which had by this time reached a diameter of some
two cubits.
'Ay,' Eli responded wearily.
'Methinks it meaneth that thy ears are going,' answered
Obsidian slyly.
'My ears are going?'
'Art they, sire?' the Clown grinned. 'Then shall we try an
experiment.'
'What ist? This thing — expertinent — what ist?'
''Tis simple, sire, Verily will I make sundry noises, and verily
wilt thou tellest to me their types and specifications.'
'I bet thy first noise will be an blaste of foule wynde,' grumbled
Lord Eli.
'Ha. Ha! Ha. Ha! See, see,' shouted the Clown, jumping
and somersaulting with glee.
'See, there be nothing wrong with thine ears.' Obsidian
clapped his hands to his stomach and rolled over right mirthfully
at his joke.
'Seest thou, Lord. Hee, hee! There be now't amiss with thine
ears. Now't wrong,' he paused from his hilarity and, still
recumbent on the floor, wither his fit of merriment had reduced
him, he looked up expectantly.
'Dost not get it, sire?' he asked disappointedly.
'Dost not get it, sire?' he repeated, this time with a note of
apprehension in his voice.
The Lord Baktrian scowled. Obsidian saw the expression and,
startled, looked frantically around the Hall, from face to face,
for succour.
'T'was an fulsome joke.' Eli looked around.
'Was't not right fulsome and dreadful? Blasphemous and
without respect for superior from an inferior?'

There was a murmur of assent from the court. 'Here's a joke
for thee, Obsidian.' The Lord beckoned forward the black-clad
figure who was seated by the fire, his hood covering most of
his face. This individual's arms were bared, revealing enormous
muscles and multifarious scars and tattooing. He approached
the Clown, who at once began to slither away across the floor
as fast as slither he could. Twas not a wit fast enough! Fast as
an arrow the big newcomer moved and in two swift paces had
the Clown by the shoulder in an iron-hard grip that brought
tears to Obsidian's een.

'Here's a jest for thee, shite-joker,' Eli thundered.

'One eye, Mister, take one eye. And let that teach thee a
lesson, Obsidian.'

The Lord rose to his feet, chalice of wine in his fist. 'I give
thee a toast, Obsidian. A toast,' all raised their goblets.

'Here's thumb in yer eye, Obsidian!'

The Lord laughed a mighty laugh from deep within his belly.
'Here's thumb in yer eye!'

The crowd roared with approval, repeating the lines from man
to man lest they should not have heard.

'Aaaggh!'

The scream startled the knight from his reverie. It was Sarah's
scream at the sight of the dead squirrel in front of her. Eli ignored
her remonstrations. He noticed that the Ontals had arrived and
were seated beside his wife, goo-gooing at the babies in low
voices.

'Aw, shide,' Eli grunted to himself, closing his eyes once more.

The Mayor relaxed by degrees, turning over and over in his
head the details of the plan, the prognosis and the prospects.
He was not the simple sort of happy fool — disgraces he
considered them — the crème de la crème of Gasville, of the
damn Province, perhaps of the whole stinking mess — who
expects to push people around without resistance. On the other
hand he intended to do a lot of pushing around, in fact all was
ready, and he had in mind to do it through the medium of
municipal Gasville, Ont., and not through brown-nosing his
way down the corridors of Queen's Park. The revenue from
the armament manufacture had begun to come in and for once
in the history of the region productivity was in advance of the
estimates. The revenue from the deal with the scum, Mandola
Magabutne, had already been spread about in bribery of selected

police inspectors, fire chiefs and judges throughout the neighbouring towns. In the event of any complaints when he began in earnest to pressure the landowners to part with their land Eli knew that his contacts would either stop the complainants or at least make sure that he, the Mayor, was appraised of eventualities and perhaps consulted on the subject of arbitration.

Eli knew well enough that when authority speaks the populace listens and believes. Was he not the representative of authority, a reasonable man, a wise and sympathetic ear to whom all his citizens had limitless access? Who defies authority? The middle-class mind is a miasma of apathy and coma; it is a bundle of sensual cortical fibres which are having a perpetually good time. To persuade the rich city-slickers who had bought up the countryside, to disabuse the crème de la crème — the rich and thick — of their farming pretensions was virtually his bounden duty. To take from the ranks of these ambitious and upwardly thrusting hordes of wrinkled, pink-handed, perfumed professionals with their recently wife-swapped, nubile and sun-bronzed twenty-year-old, credit-card waving, ass-wriggling debutantes was going to be a pleasure as well as his foremost duty. They would hardly know that their land was being stolen. Elsquaird had wrapped the deal up in more intellectual red-tape than most of these dumb-asses could understand. They were, in principle, to get back what they sacrificed three-fold by the terms of Elsquaird's 'Trinomial Plan'. Its logic was irrefutable and after they had signed the contracts the Gang of Eleven could lean hard upon anyone who attempted to change his mind and default.

Yes, Eli nodded to himself, the stock-broker, the consumer-consultant, the labour-leader, the political-pundit, the TV-tootsie and the paper-pusher-professional would yield to his authority of violence without a word, without even a raised fist. A person, such as one of these new arrivals to rural Ontario, is isolated, while force is integrated and united, at once beautiful and breath-taking. How many prophets of old had gazed up in awe at the coming of the Hammer of God, watching with such fascination that they failed to perceive until it was too late that the damn thing was going to smash in their stupid skulls?

Later that afternoon the Gang of Eleven was scheduled to take care of all the farm-owning computer consultants in one move, one land-slide of signatures on the dotted line as had never been seen before and whose import would rival that of Magna Carta.

Tougher to handle, but fortunately far less numerous, were the real farmers.

That morning the Gang, driving two motorbikes and the Mayoral Pullman limousine, had gone to visit and persuade Sheikh Abdul Akbar Jahman and his willowy wife, Marjoram. Theirs was a large farm, set across seven hundred acres of rolling fields, with a lake and a healthy profit margin.

When they had drawn up at the house, which was very large and modern, with a double garage and wash-house which was sculpted in imitation of the Taj Mahal, they had initially received no reply to their door-knocking and bell-ringing.

'Sh'll 'a' bailt in thae' wee dooo-oor?' asked Pans, whose patience was inversely proportional to the pigmentation of the person for whom he was waiting.

'Lumbering fool,' retorted Elsquaird. 'We have come here to charm and cajole. When I have done that — and only then — shall I decide whether you are to exercise your musculature on these people. For now, treat them very nicely, dumbo!'

'Och, lusten tae m', yae wee turrrrd . . . ' Pans' retort was lost to posterity because at that moment Marjoram Jahman opened the wash-house door, jumped out and slammed it behind her, leaning back on the door, eyes closed, complexion paled and breathing stertorously as if she had had an alarming experience. From the other side of the door could be heard a series of violent blows against the door.

'Gee, what th' shid is in thar? Is some dude playin' horn-ass?'

Eli signalled to Pans, Stanley and Jaime to surround the wash-house, which they did silently, quickly and stealthily. Jaime dropped to one knee below the window, Pans flattened himself against the wall beside the door out of which the frightened woman had just emerged and O'Vayshun darted out of sight to cover the rear door. Laudenklier and Stanley had unobtrusively materialized automatic sub-machine guns from the linings of their jackets.

Eli grabbed the terrified lady by the shoulders and half-pushed, half-dragged her away from the building. 'Whad'e do t'yer? Careful Pans, 'e sounds like a big dude. Go! Now!'

Simultaneously Pans beat upon the door with his shoulder

and Jaime Laudenklier vaulted in through the window, shooting ten rounds in the direction of the intruder's noise even before he had landed on the floor. It was dark in the wash-house, since one of the shots had taken out the light. The stranger was still banging at the door and wall with thunderous blows and belts. Suddenly both doors burst inward and the wash-house was flooded with light. Stanley O'Vayshun blistered eleven rounds into the offending noise-maker's enamel coating before Pans, flat on the floor beside the source of the bother, which was right beside his door, managed to shout out.

'Stan, yae fuel, 'tis anely a wee washer, dinna shute naemoo-oor. Yae'll mebbe kull masel'.'

The three commandos straightened up, gazing at the washing machine, which was jumping about the room and banging repeatedly against the wall. Now that the doorway was clear the errant machine was attempting to jump through it into the yard but could not make it because of its restraining electrical flex.

'Bogger ma-ee,' said Stanley quietly, pushing his chauffeur's cap to the back of his head so that he could have a good scratch. Jaime opened the lid of the machine, at which point its noise and its gyrations died down. He reached in and redistributed the load, pulling a handful of lingerie out and waving it triumphantly out the door at the rest of the Gang. As he closed the lid the motor began once more to purr and whirr, docilely this time.

'Must've been these, eh? Causin' the motor to overheat, ja?'

Everyone laughed, excepting Marjoram Jahman, who was too confused by this suddenly-arrived batch of visitors to make an editorial comment.

'Where's th' Sheikh?' Eli asked.

Marjoram pointed towards the house from which, now that the other din had diminished, came the sound of a hoe-down. Someone was playing a fiddle to the accompaniment of some hot-licking guitar.

'Who's playin' the guidar with th' Sheikh?' Eli asked. 'We come t' see Abdul, eh? Is he with some dude?'

'No,' spluttered Marjoram, gradually recovering her composure. 'Indeed, my goodness no. Abdul's fiddling with himself.'

'My God,' put in Elsquaird in a loud voice. 'And while

playing the violin, too!'

'Ziss mann habt more talent zan zem Hindu hero, Mongi Slim!' agreed Zhilin, turning to Penz, who nodded in agreement.

'Effen Genghis Khan nicht fiddle vile Rome burnt gekannt, tak.'

'We'll jes' 've a w'rd wi' th' Sheikh,' the Mayor went on to explain to Marjoram Jahman. He led the Gang of Eleven across to the house, walking in without further knocking or ceremony.

'Eh, eh! Abdul,' Eli called out in a jovial, friendly manner which was loud enough to suggest that he was here on business.

'Eh, Abdul, who's yer godden t' play th' axe fer yer?'

'Good morning, gentlemen and Madam Ontal,' Abdul Akbar Jahman greeted them as he strolled into the entrance hall. He was carrying his fiddle and bow tucked beneath his right arm; a large, open smile of welcome appeared on his face, which was lean and handsome and was topped by an elegant silk turban of flaming red, which he wore when he wished to relax.

'It was I my veritable self who was indeed playing the guitar,' Jahman explained, 'I record myself on an apparatus of the highest fidelity and then attempt to do myself the utmost justice, my goodness, my gracious!'

Pans made an unidentifiable remark to himself which attracted Jahman's attention.

'Oh, no. Mercy me no! I prefer to think of it as guitaring with myself, as you would perhaps say — ''Axing with my own person'' — in order to avoid the double-entendre, you understand?'

'Oh, yeh?'

'Indeed.' Jahman smiled again, revealing the most perfect set of pure white teeth.

'But did I not detect that you wished to discuss something? It must, my goodness, be very important to bring so many exalted personages to my humble door at this time of day. In what manner, and with what expertise or favours, can I be of service to your honourable selves?'

'Ah ain'd gonna mince aboud, Sheikh,' Eli began, in his slow and convincing manner, ''cos yer know thed ain'd m' way, eh? I ain'd gonna dosey-doh, ardsy-fardsie around with th' carrods an' peas while leavin' th' real mead till id tastes like horse-shid. I'm gonna tell yer th' deal pure an' sim'le.'

'My gracious me, you have certainly whetted my appetite, mister mayor, your honourableness.'

'Tha' wee broonie's unco muckle eno' tae wet yae underdroo-oo-ers!' Preston clenched and unclenched his fists, eyeing the farmer ominously. He would have liked to begin by breaking that fine, aquiline nose. Pans had little patience with his boss's subtleties.

'Tae-el th' wee basta' warts tae happen tae hae if hae doesna' coooooperate.'

'In a nudshell,' sighed Eli, at the impatience of his lieutenant, 'we wanna make a deal fer all yer fields. We're gonna take 'em away, divide 'em into strips an' them strips'll be ren'ed out t' yerself and th' rest. Yer'll pay rend fer 'em and ... '

'By the beard of the prophet! What thomas-foolery is this one, my heavens!'

The Sheikh was on his feet, legs apart and arms stretched high into the air. He towered over the hunchback mayor. It was fairly clear that, startled though he was, he did not intend violence to anyone — yet. Nonetheless Stanley O'Vayshun thought it wisest to tackle first and ask questions later. Accordingly Stanley tackled the farmer with a full-force, knee-clutching rugby dive that smacked of Ireland versus Wales at the Cardiff Arms Park on the third Saturday after Martinmas. Down went the offending offender, his bow and fiddle were neatly caught by Penz as they flew out of their owner's hands. Stanley, having left his adversary prostrate with his aquiline nose pushed thoroughly into the heavy puce pile of the carpet, stood up and dusted himself off to a Russian serenade from Penz, on the violin, and a thunderous standing ovation from the rest of his colleagues.

'You have disfigured my humble husband, I am betting,' screamed Marjoram, appearing at the door and, seeing Abdul Akbar down for the count, collapsing to her knees beside him, inspecting his brow and aquiline nose with a soothing, soft and aquiline hand.

'Neinsirree, mit ihm vee don' zissfigurihm, vee 'elp ihm figure ziss,' explained Zhilin, holding up a copy of the contract which awaited the farmer's signature.

'Hier ist ein damn fein frog,' added Penz.

'Frog-shide,' shouted the Mayor, irritably.

'Der frog auf der bow von violin,' murmured Penz

apologetically, attempting to hand the bow back, frog-end first, to Jahman, who was in no position to receive the present. Finally Penz stuck it into the fallen agriculturalist's turban.

'Led's ged on,' Eli barked. 'Tell him th' deal, El!'

Elsquaird stepped forward importantly and, ignoring an uncouth, sotto voce remark from Pans, proceeded to treat all and sundry to a concise and lucid outline of the plan.

'We will take your land ... '

At a groan from Jahman, who attempted to get to his feet, Pans pushed the fellow back to the floor, dragging the wife away and forcing her to take a seat by the fireplace.

' ... take your land and rent it back to you, to be farmed in strips in the traditional manner of all good feudal demesnes. However, you will easily be able to pay your rents from the profits that we will offer you from the rents of three other farms in the area. Each of these farmers will be happy to pay their rents to you because each of them will be deriving threefold rents himself, from others so inclined, and so on. We, the organisers, will undertake to see that no-one, not even you, defaults upon his payments. Our commune will satisfy everyone's socialistic longings for the kibbutz, it will appease their resentment at the growing number of bankruptcies amongst farmers and the intolerable level of executive-white-paper-pushing-trash which is daily infiltrating the rural areas of Ontario in alarmingly large numbers. Our scheme will soon extend beyond Gasville, it will soon embrace Villetown, Paris, Venice, Hamburg, London, Rome, Pompei, Princeton, Glasgow, Fifeville, MacBeathville, Macdonaldville, Camerontown, Elginturd, McCustard, McMustardbury, Waterloo and even Townville! Our clients will become more and more numerous. With you there will be one, paying you there will be three more, paying them will be nine, paying them twenty-seven, to them, eighty-one, then two-hundred and forty-three, then seven hundred and twenty-nine, then two thousand one hundred and eighty-seven, then six thousand five hundred and sixty-one, then nineteen thousand six hundred and eighty-three, then fifty-nine thousand and forty-nine, then one hundred and seventy-seven thousand one hundred and forty-seven, then five hundred and thirty-one thousand four hundred and forty-one, then one million five hundred and sixty-four thousand three hundred and forty-three, then four million seven hundred and eighty-two thousand nine hundred and sixty nine, then fourteen million three hundred and forty-eight thousand nine hundred and seven, then forty-three million forty-six thousand seven hundred and twenty-one . . . '

'Goodness gracious me, there are not that many . . . '

'Do not worry, Mister Jahman. The baby boom will take care of all that. Why, even just a few weeks ago — of course, being swarthy you were not invited — we witnessed the christening of a darling little babe that was mothered by a cow!'

'Wha' h' means,' put in Pans, whispering loudly into the ear of the still-recumbent incumbent, 'is tha' a' thae wee laddies, if tha' get 't up wi' doggies, sheepies, pooooossies, th' odd cooo, an' e'en woggies lak yae'sel' ca' soon hae th' numbers up tae far'y-thre' million.'

There was a low rumble of agreement, accompanied by vigorous nodding of assent from all quarters.

To cut a long story short the debate continued for quite some time, Jahman being a tough customer to convince — as always happens with the first sale. Elsquaird dutifully and comprehensively explained the agricultural, ecological, ethnological, entymological, sociological, dermatological and eschatological benefits of feudal strip-farming. He explained, with sample calculations performed at lightening speed by mental arithmetic, the tithes, the taxes, the levels of amortization, subdivision of bonds and deductibility of dependants. He even went into the details of the lotteries that were to be founded in the Gasville area and, with graphs and histograms, showed how feasible and solvent the whole scheme was bound to be. There would even be money left over, he insisted, to finance a Gasville junior hockey team.

When Jahman remained unconvinced Elsquaird offered to play him a game of Nim, double or quits, for the whole of Jahman's farm. He generously agreed to let the farmer use his own matchsticks and to play best of three, or indeed, best of any odd, prime number of games.

Jahman was adamant.

They threatened him with broken fingers, his at first and then his wife's, with broken violins, broken bows, broken knees, broken toes, the itch, the pitch, the palsy and the gout.

The threats fell upon an impassive resistance. 'No! Goodness me, no!'

The Mayor scowled — this was a foul joke, which was going on too long.

'Here's a joke fer you, dusky-face,' he beckoned to Pans, who was seated by the fireplace, holding Marjoram Jahman in restraint.

'Here's a joke fer you, shide-coloured! One eye, Misder Pans, take one eye!'

A gasp and a scream came from Marjoram. With a sob she called out, crawling towards the mayor, 'In gracious goodness, not an eye. My God, anything but that!'

Eli stayed Pans with an imperious wave of the hand. He was certain that the deal was almost made.

It was time to call in the ultimate deterrent — the Ontals!

'Doris, Horace. Call in yer kids!'

From the parking lot were called Boris, Norris, Maurice and Florence Ontal. They were duly lined up beside their parents. Zhilin, Pans, Penz, Jaime, Stanley O'Vayshun, Elsquaird, Sid Ra'in, Norman the Mormon, Roddin and Baktrian stealthily sidled to the door. When the rest were outside Eli turned in the doorway to confront the bemused Jahman and his wife.

'Ya' kin stay pud, Sheikh. An' don' goddam well come ouda here till yer ready t' sign. OK. On'als — id's all yers!'

With that Eli turned his back and darted outside into the fresh air.

All these happy recollections were swilling about in the Mayor's brain as he dozed on the porch.

Recollections of how, hardly two minutes later and choking into handkerchiefs held to their faces, the Jahmans had emerged from the house in complete capitulation. The first customers of the Gasville strip farming commune!

'OK. On'als — ad ease, cease fard.' Eli had bellowed, approaching the defeated landowner with a contract and a pen.

In his slumber the Mayor smiled at the sweets of success. He could feel the porch tremble under the footsteps of his Gang of Eleven, arriving like falcons to his wrist. They were taking their seats upon the porch beside him, awaiting his pleasure and swigging from the beers that Sarah handed round.

Eli, relaxed and comfortable in his leisure, reflected upon the neat sterilized functioning of the brain. How beautiful were his remembrances of the morning versus the actuality of it. In retrospect there was no violence, no near-misses with the twisting of wrists and fingers, no women's screams, no rape-threats, there was just a precisely executed sortie. There was no weakness, no rumour, no doubt, no speculation, only crystal clarity and the appearance of certainly — that (often illusory) certainty of victory. As he napped the Mayor mumbled to himself, 'If y'ask a dude t'do two things ad th' goddam same time th'l screw 'em both up.'

'Too true,' agreed Elsquaird, who had taken the chair beside Eli and who thought that the epigram was addressed to himself. 'Only the other day, at the A and P checkout, I got away with three chickens for the price of one just because I happened to ask the cashier-girl if she had had Bosian statistics. She gave me the three chickens, five plastic bags and a cuff round the ear with the advice that a kid like me should not be worrying himself about her statistics.'

Elsquaird laughed. 'I took the chickens and left her my card.'

'Ugh?' Eli woke up, rubbing his eyes with the back of his fist. 'Ugh? Oh, sure, chicken-shid. Led's gid goin'! C'mon yer mule-asses, led's go gid them compuder turkeys!'

3

GANG ABOUT

The Augustinian Hall had been hired at the Computing Centre for Holistic Information Processing. The Gang of Eleven were arraigned before a crowd of assembled professionals, who had come there of their own accord in response to a cordial invitation from the Mayor and Lady Mayoress of Gasville. A bus had been hired and had been used by Pans, Stanley, Horace, Roddin Corpse and Norman the Mormon to collect those who had responded with regrets for absence or had merely advised the Mayor where to put his Trinomial Plan.

Coffee, port wine and sherry were set out, together with cigars and cigarettes, beside which was placed the inevitable notice:

> 'Coffee, port wine and sherry together with cigars and cigarettes, beside which is placed the inevitable notice, has been deemed by the Surgeon General to be injurious to his health, maybe yours too. In fact, too much boozing damn nearly killed him on several occasions!'

The participants were encouraged to socialise and to enjoy themselves. The party consisted of all the farmer-professionals from the vicinity who could be located by means of their connection with their computer-consultation activities as described in the Yellow Pages. There were numerical analysts, systems analysts, business systems consultants, teachers and doctors. There were professors of biology, phrenology, topology, topography, geography, stenography, pornography, pronography, phonography, humanities, urbanities, absurdities, fine arts and economics. There were labour consultants, stock brokers, brewery owners, marriage guidance counsellors, musicians and, in the corner engaged in an animated debate, an entire echelon of ex-gaol birds.

Zhilin and the Mayor ascended the dais and clapped their hands to bring the crowd to order. The others of the Eleven, with the exception of Elsquaird, had quietly spread out down the sides of the hall. Even to the casual observer, the presence of scarcely-concealed automatic small-arms was obvious about their persons. Preston Pans, for example, was wearing about his neck a string to which were attached a dozen tear-gas grenades. Jaime Laudenklier was nonchalantly paring his nails with an ex-SS dagger which he had drawn from within his shirt. Stanley had a bull-whip tied around his waist and a cross-bow slung over one shoulder. The Eleven were watching the assembly with an ominously silent concentration.

'Hi, there,' Eli began. 'Hod shide, ids so goddam good t' see yer thed 'm gonna hand yer righd now over t' Professor Elsquaird, who's gonna 'splain yer th' doggone brillian' Trinomial Plan.'

'Why, thank you, Mister Mayor, your Worship,' Elsquaird smiled as he stepped up to the lectern, climbed onto the packing-crate which had been provided for the purpose, and faced the audience with a look of determination and inspiration about him.

'You people have been chosen because of your connections with modernity through your activities as computing consultants in those many and varied spheres of important intellectual and commercial life of the Province. It also happens that each and every one of you owns farmland! This happy coincidence is going to permit you, each and every one of you, without exception, to participate in Gasville's new and radical, socialistic farming collective plan — which is called the Trinomial Plan after the manner in which it works.'

The midget paused for the sake of effect.

Not an eye blinked, not a muscle stirred except for a surgeon-general who was coughing his guts up in the back row and wishing that Stanley O'Vayshun would let him get out into the corridor so that he could get a glass of water to help him re-compose himself. Stanley, working to orders, roughly pushed the coughing, retching individual, an expert on computer-aided addiction-therapy, down onto a chair and wickedly wagged the bull-whip at the man, by way of a warning against further attempts to leave the hall.

'You will each give up your farmland to the collective, in most
cases you are not tilling the land anyway, and in return you
will receive rents from three other farms which are within the
scheme.'

There was still no reaction from the assembled multitude. Eli
wondered whether they might not have fared better in the
morning with Jahman if they had given him some alcohol before
starting discussions.

'The land will be rented out in strips, each field being
subdivided according to the tried and true tenets of feudalism.
Everyone will want to join! The scheme is so attractive and the
profit-margin so robust and appealing that no-one will be allowed
to refrain from joining up! Our scheme will soon extend beyond
Gasville, it will soon embrace Villetown, Paris, Venice,
Hamburg, London, Rome, Pompei, Princeton, Glasgow,
Fifeville, MacBeathville, Macdonaldville, Camerontown,
Elginturd, McCustard, McMustardbury, Waterloo and even
Townville! Our clients will become more and more numerous.
With each of you there will be one, paying you there will be
three more, paying them will be nine, paying them twenty-seven,
to them, eighty-one, then two-hundred and forty-three, then
seven hundred and twenty-nine, then two thousand one hundred
and eighty-seven, then six thousand five hundred and sixty-one,
then nineteen thousand six hundred and eighty-three, then fifty-
nine thousand and forty-nine, then one hundred and seventy-
seven thousand one hundred and forty-seven, then five hundred
and thirty-one thousand four hundred and forty-one, then one
million five hundred and sixty-four thousand three hundred and
forty-three, then four million seven hundred and eighty-two
thousand nine hundred and sixty nine, then fourteen million
three hundred and forty-eight thousand nine hundred and seven,
then forty-three million forty-six thousand seven hundred and
twenty-one . . . '

'Hooray,' shouted Horace Ontal spontaneously, who was
sporting a flame-thrower and wearing, like a scapulary, a fire-
resistant shroud in camouflage colours.

'Hooray! Hooray! Hooray!' The others took up the chant,
first the Eleven and then more and more of the audience until
the Augustinian Hall was ringing to the rhythmic bellowings
of an incensed and insensible crowd.

'More booze all round,' Eli yelled above the bedlam and at once his team leapt forward with decanters of gin and whisky, pouring to left and right into the cups and glasses which were thrust out towards them in a frenzy of appetites; some persons even managed to find a second glass to hold forth and occasionally, in cases of extreme assiduity, as many as a third.

In all the turmoil no-one thought, as had Abdul Akbar Jahman, to challenge the arithmetical foundations of the Trinomial Plan!

'Now that you have all got something to drink,' Elsquaird continued, 'we are ready for our special offer. I must ask each one of you to proceed to the next room, where you will see a number of desks bearing names. Please take the seat which corresponds to your name. At your place you will find a little brain-teaser for you. Attempt this and, having finished, hand the result in as you leave. Success in this puzzle-solving, at which you will all excel, I am sure, as computer experts invariably do, will entitle you to a lifetime of special individual and corporate emoluments under our plan. In short, do the problem we have set you and you will be rewarded with shares in the Gasville Agricultural Commune. Best of luck — and enjoy!'

Without a word the mass rose, synchronized like one man, and filed through into the quiz-room.

The contestants seated themselves, pulled out their calculators and their felt-tipped pens, combed their hair and cleaned their teeth, straightened their underpants and sniffed their armpits.

They began to concentrate. Breathing slowed, tooth-sucking started. People took off their shoes, loosened their ties and their belts. Some smiled at the page as they read it while others frowned at it in concentration.

Slowly more and more smiling faces revealed themselves. The smilers relaxed and stretched, leaning back in their desks. The gradual 'smilathon' spread until it was unanimous.

Were they bringing their mighty intellects to bear on the problem, crushing it like match-wood in an inexorable mental conflagration? Had they seen it before and were they steadily recalling the key to the puzzle? Had they solved it in three different ways already and were they just going for the jackpot? Had they all got the puzzle by its pizzle?

Not quite!

These were people accomplished in the art of problem-solving and practised in its rigorous ways. This was a crowd of self-confident professionals, to whom puzzle-solving was their daily bread — and a well-buttered, thickly-sliced loaf it usually proved to be. And at this moment, when all was quietness and smiles, the truth of the matter was that they were all stuck!

Most of them were suffering the bowel-loosening trauma of being unable to understand the statement of the question. These were asking themselves such questions as:

'Why me? I used to be a whizz at math at school!'

Many were sure that their complete lack of penetration could not be due to a blunt instrument but rather to some malevolent deity who could not speak or write in plain English.

Common thoughts were:

'Tovius Slithius! Yuk! Yuk! Yuk!'

'Jaberwockius Vulgaris! My God! Yuk! Yuk! Yuk!'

'Mimsius! Mimsius! Mimsius! La, la, la, la!'

The perpetrators of thoughts like these began to roll back their eyes in their sockets. They began to hum in crazy, monotone intonations which one associates with the victims of shell-shock and dysentery.

As the shock began to wear off the first noises began. At the beginning there were just a few moans, then these metamorphosed into choked sobs and finally came the first mad scream.

'Aaaaaagh! Aaaaagh!'

In the middle of the room a dress-for-success brunette had stood up, torn off her wig and cast it to the floor and was following this by tearing off her garments, only to reveal a rather lanky man in ladies' underwear. Off to one side a burly, balding bruiser was belting away at his neighbour in frustration.

'Who set this pig-shit problem anyway!'

'Lay off! For God's sake, it wasn't me, you know.'

Similar outbursts were beginning on all sides. Each incident growing more violent and zany than its predecessors until finally Elsquaird, with the aid of Pans' stentorian voice, managed to instruct the Gang of Eleven to usher the assembly out, obliging everyone to sign their contract before leaving, and to collect up their puzzle papers.

Only one contestant remained calm. This was not because he had managed any better than the rest in the matter of the problem. In fact he had not even attempted to solve it. This individual was Walter Polushun, an Artificial Insemination Consultant.

'But I don't have anything at all to do with computers,' he protested angrily.

'I'm grateful for the whisky, but what the monkey's asshole am I doing here? I work with my bare hands!' Graphically he mimed the climax of his day's work.

Finally Elsquaird managed to placate the man.

'I am awfully sorry to have inconvenienced you. We must have looked you up under A.I. for Artificial Insemination when we intended to look under Artificial Intelligence.'

The explanation did not meet with a great deal of satisfaction, although they finally managed to get rid of the man by promising him . . . a ride in the Mayoral Pullman limousine, a solution of the brain-teaser and three rounds in the ring with Preston Pans, if he did not quiescently accept alternatives A and B.

When all the multitude had left Elsquaird collapsed up onto a chair, released an enormous sigh and put his head in his hands.

'I must have made the puzzle too hard,' he said despondently.

After a suitably long silence he revived.

'Never mind! Where are all those scripts? It is clear what we have to do! Ontario Educational tradition is, after giving terrifyingly difficult exams to all comers, to give them all full marks. Jaime! Get your pen and start writing, "WELL DONE! FULL MARKS FOR A BRAVE ATTEMPT!" on every script. Then parcel each one up with an Agricultural Commune of Gasville bond. My God, what a way to earn a living!'

Despite the uproar and the outcrop of self-flagellation the afternoon had been an enormous success. Forty signatories had been obtained that day for the Gasville Agricultural Commune. Business was underway!

4

GANG AWAY

'Ooo-eee-aaagh! Aagh, . . . wee lassie . . . aagh. Wha' noise annoys a' oyster? Aagh-ooo-eee, a wee noisy noise annoys a' oyster! Ooo-aaagh-eee, wee nottee boys destroys a' oyster!'

Preston Pans chuckled cheerfully to himself as he scrubbed and soaped, showered and sang. He was cleansing himself from his crotch to his cortical canals and indulging himself luxuriantly. Gone and past for him were the armpits of the via dolorosa and the lice-ridden crevices of the Glasgow harlots with whom he had spent so much of his youth. Instead he had recently charmed and negotiated his way to a ménage-a-trois with the two Failure twins, Rena and Rena. He had every reason to feel elated with his performance in all respects because the Gang of Eleven had successfully carried off an afternoon of promotional competitions at the Drewchester Calithumpian, a traditional form of Ontario gladiatorial combat, a general knees-up and a day of suicidal drinking and fighting which was held annually in the City of Drewchester (population nine hundred — with three clubs). This day of cavorting escapades had a mighty, long and dignified past. It dated from nineteen sixty six when it had been inaugurated by mistake one Victoria Day. In all its long history the event had never seen quite such a spectacle as today.

Consequently Preston Pans, still in the shower room of the Drewchester arena, hockey-stadium and funeral parlour, was treating himself to the All Canadian version of that ritual — the Great North American Shower — a pastime consuming some ninety-five minutes, a kilo of soap and one hundred gallons of water (sufficient to irrigate a thousand hectares of Algerian Sahara for a week — all the way from Boussada to the Atlas

140

Mountains) not to mention the bucketfuls of pommades with
names like Brutus, Fabricius Parvus, Aggrippa the Hunter and
so on, with which Preston could look forward to dowsing himself
at the end of his protracted wash.

Pans closed his eyes and fondled his soapy parts, allowing
his mind to ramble back over the afternoon's events.

The Gang of Eleven, together with Sarah and the baby boys,
arrived at the Calithumpian in good time, but not so early that
there was no crowd to welcome the Mayoral party, which
consisted of the four-wheel drive, the Mayoral limousine, with
Stanley at the wheel and the Mayoral family inside, enjoying
the smoke-windowed air-conditioning in the company of
Elsquaird, Zhilin and Penz. Doris and Horace rode the
motorbikes, with their off-spring riding pillion, Boris behind
Doris and Maurice and Florence squashed together, holding on
ferociously, behind Horace. As they rode, the freshening air
whistling past their heads, the Ontals passed navy-bean
sandwiches, for which they had an unparalleled and relentless
appetite, back and forth between them. Doris particularly felt
herself in need of a little snack to fortify her for the ordeals to
come.

Once assembled on the makeshift stage of the Calithumpian
Arena Eli treated the gathering to his 'Ah ain'd gonna mince
aboud' speech.

Eli's penchant for public-speaking was beginning to grow on
him, much after the fashion of a wart, with the result that he
had begun to enjoy his Mayoral appearances, even though his
orations were not always Caesarian, nor always in the best of
taste nor under the best of control. However, on this occasion
all went unremarkably well, as a tribute to the effect of the
considerable practice which he had been getting recently in
delivering this particular speech.

The only noteworthy happening came at the point at which
Eli raised his arms wide to the sky and cried out in a loud voice:

'Thuh' is a tide in th' affairs of men which, taken ad
th' flood, leads on t' greadness!'

Immediately it sounded to many nearby listeners as if, from
the carry-cot wherein resided the supposedly slumbering Yukio
Kanada, a powerful voice called out: 'Grape nuts?'

Eli paused only momentarily, glancing in the direction of the babies, and then he plunged back into his speech.

Some say that those words from the cradle were Yukio's first political prognostication. Although, in order to be truthful and impartial in this, it is only fair to say that some others reply: 'Rats!'

Anyway, to continue, Eli carefully explained to the attentive rustics just what the Trinomial Plan was all about. He described the abundant benefits which would accrue to the neighbourhood as a result of the plan and handed over to Elsquaird, who intimidated the masses with the arithmetical details. To this day Drewchester residents recall vividly the sight of that animated manikin as he concluded his peroration in favour of the plan.

'Friends — and as I conclude I know that I may call upon you as my friends, just as you may call upon me as your friend — as the poets have so aptly put it:

> Every bullet has its billet,
> Every puzzle has its pizzle,
> Every muezzin has his mizzen
> And every community needs its
> Trinomial Plan!'

With this last cri de coeur the Professor shook his tiny fists in the air while Roddin and Norman the Mormon seized him by the ankles and raised him high aloft above their heads.

'Aayy, go easily there, Corpse!'

'Co-orrr, co-orrr — or I durnk you on zee floor 'ard.'

'Co-orr then. But hold tight!'

The spectators cheered heartily and flung their baseball caps in the air, puzzled by the description of the plan but carried along by the speaker's enthusiasm. What did it matter if one threw up a Labatts and only caught a Molson Export when the hat came down?

Despite the heat, the Mayoral retinue were wearing long and heavy clothes, which looked rather unusual on all but the Hassidic Ra'in. These clothes concealed an arsenal of small arms, automatic rifles, short-stem bazookas and computer-aided, detonation-encoded grenades.

Doris Ontal concealed a water-cooled sten-gun down her jogging pants while Horace Ontal similarly concealed its ammunition and Boris hid its tripod and sights.

The first event of the afternoon did not require weapons.

Once the ceremonials were over the crowd made its way outside to the open air stage. On this had been set up two microphones — one very tall and one very small — in readiness for the first competition, which was a challenge General Knowledge and Guessing Match between Elsquaird and the local champion, James Spume.

The Drewchester town-crier called the meeting to order. 'Oyez, oyez, oyez! Now hear this, now hear this, now hear this. It is my pleasure, it is my pleasure, it is my pleasure, to introduce the battle, to introduce the battle, to introduce the battle, of the great minds, of the great minds, of the great minds, Jim Spume, Jim Spume, Jim Spume and and and Elsquaird, Elsquaird, Elsquaird ... '

Finally this pertinacious perpetrator of prolixity piped down, down, down and the competition was under way.

The crowd hushed. Each contestant was to ask one question — with ten seconds to find the answer. Spume won the toss and opted to bat first.

'What are Troggonoptera, Gentoo and Humu-humu-nuka-nuka-apuaa and what do they have in common?'

Spume stepped back from his microphone and beamed evilly across at the stunned midget, who seemed to have gone into convulsions and was jerking the minute mike around and finally fell with it to the floor.

Saddened by the sight of a midget cracking up under stress the crowd remained silent, a few of them crossing themselves. Here and there lips moved in prayers of propitiation. One old gentleman pulled his garbage-bag tightly around him and gazed heavenward.

A voice boomed out ominously. 'Ten seconds remain before you must respond, ten seconds remain before you must respond, ten seconds ... '

Wide-eyed and panic-stricken Elsquaird scrambled from his entanglement with the electrical cables, smashed the microphone with his fist and gazed wildly about him.

'Nine, nine, nine, eight, eight, eight, seven, seven, seven, six ... '

Veins bulging at his temples, red-faced and perspiring copiously Elsquaird rushed across the stage and launched himself in the most prodigious high-jump of which he was capable. 'Two, two, two, one, one ... '

Elsquaird soared through the air, reaching a clearance of at least two feet, aimed at the towering microphone of Jim Spume; he caught it in flight and dragged it down breathlessly with him. Just in time he panted out the words: 'Some ba-astard had turned my mike off.'

And with those incriminating words of indictment began the best, most furious series of duels-to-the-bitter-end which the Drewchester crowds were destined ever to see.

Having no time to gather his breath, Elsquaird launched forthrightly into his answer.

'The Troggonoptera is simply another — rather strikingly beautiful, I admit — but just another optera. Just another flutterby — just like naprocles jucunda, heliconius brazo (a real beauty), anaea Alberta (a Canadian favourite), parides neophilius, morpho catanecrius, danaus flexippus and stone-ground wheatius thinnieus! The gentoo is a little more tricky — and has nothing to do with gents!'

'Ooooh! Aaaagh!'

'Like the blackfoot, the king, the macaroni, the littleblue and the rockhopper the gentoo is a — ... ' Elsquaird paused until he had complete silence. 'Penguin.'

There were cheers and calls of encouragement from the rest of his colleagues. The locals stood in numbed silence, marvelling at the midget's virtuosity.

'Much more difficult is the Humu-humu-nuka-nuka-apuaa, which is better-known as the Poisson Picasso to the French. It differs in many ways from its relatives, the kissing gourami, the spotted alligator gar, the long horn sculpin, the sixty million-year-old coelocanth, the spectacled caiman, the chrysomil pictu, baluga, clown triggerfish or even the lungfish, which can estivate itself for four years at a time, until it has entirely eaten itself up! But it is still merely a fish!'

'Tha' a' luke thae same w' Fraynch fraes,' bawled Pans from the crowd.

'And now we come to their commonality, their shared property, their missing link. But, mon Cher Watson, c'est plus simple, n'est ce pas' Elsquaird grinned from ear to ear.

'The Poisson Picasso gives the hint! They are all creatures which may be found in the Montreal Aquarium — and they are to be found nowhere else together in the entirety of North America!'

Spume was cursing under his breath and gesticulating crudely to the electrician on the mixer-board for the public address system. The latter was holding up his palms, as if expecting rain, and making a shrug of a face, which seemed only to infuriate Spume further.

'My turn, I believe?' Elsquaird waved for the applause to cease.

'My question for Mister James Spume of Drewchester, which he must answer in ten seconds to tie the match, is:

'How do Martians greet one another passionately?'

'Starting now, ten, nine, eight ... '

Spume was gesticulating to the referee, who paid very little attention since his view was completely obscured by Preston Pans.

' ... Three, two, one!'

In desperation Spume jumped forward and lifted Elsquaird up in a bear-hug.

'Like this?' Spume gave the midget a smacking kiss on the mouth.

'No, you old fag,' responded the wriggling professor.

'Like this,' he shouted into the microphone and then fetched the Drewcastrian a kick to the groin which landed with a perfectly sickening thud.

As Spume collapsed the professor wrenched himself free and strode to the apron of the stage.

'Hurrah! Hurrah! Well done!'

Indeed, such was the popularity of the plucky little, witty wizard that it was full five minutes before the applause from the afternoon's first event subsided sufficiently for Elsquaird to be declared the winner.

Preston Pans, leaning back against the shower-tiles, smiled knowingly to himself as he luxuriated in the pastime of soaping his nipples. First the left, round and round in an anti-clockwise direction, then the right one, also anti-clockwise — taking several minutes over each one. After that he repeated the procedure in the reverse direction. The effect was most soporific.

The other events had gone well, also, he mused. His colleagues had carried the day in all the contests, maintaining the boss's demand for a high profile for the Trinomial Planners, without arousing undue acrimony. It was true that the soccer game had developed into an overt show of the purity and the presence of power and that the foot-shoot came very close to degenerating into a needle match, but the ferret-down-the-pant-leg contest had been, as all would assuredly agree, the sweetest, most lady-like win of the whole afternoon.

Each of these contests had their far-fetched origins in the mists of Drewcastrian antiquity.

After Elsquaird's victory the next event on the schedule was the ferret-down-the-pant-leg competition. For this the competitors were marched up onto the stage with military precision. In all there were nine men, of whom the favourite was Lothar Spume, brother of the unfortunate James, who had so recently met his match in the manifestation of the midget mathematician. The tenth contestant was Doris Ontal, representing the interests and the sentiments of the Gang of Eleven. In particular, Eli had instructed her unequivocally.

'Give 'em shid, Doris! Hod shid!'

Doris was wearing her motor-cycling outfit, consisting of a large, pink jogging suit with Join The Trinomial Plan printed in flowing blue lettering across the buttocks of her pants. On her head Doris was still wearing a scarred, black crash-helmet which bore a Jolly Roger on the forehead, complete with skull and crossed bones, and the Trinomial Plan legend on the back in fluorescent yellow.

As the ten jostled for position on the stage, being introduced by the repetitious town-crier, exchanging quips with one another and eyeing up the opposition, the ferrets were brought in and held up for the cheering audience to appreciate.

'Pedigree, pedigree, pedigree, ferrets, ferrets, ferrets ... ' chanted the wearisome crier. The names of the ferrets, their sires, their dams, their grandsires, great-grandsires, their times, their starting odds and all the other salient information concerning their current form was laboriously read aloud. In all there were twenty animals, two for each competitor. For example, Lord Fitzmount Brazenby Lampshutte IV weighed slightly more than a bag of sugar, was unbeaten in distances of ten seconds, fifteen seconds and twenty seconds. He had caused Grievous Bloody Harm on a dozen occasions over distances of thirty seconds.

Lord Fitzmount was held aloft, wriggling and snapping his

nasty little choppers, as sharp as a narwhal's maxillary tooth, at the handler, who at one point, presumably for some reason not unrelated to his Lordship's delivery of a sharp bite to the man's wrist, almost dropped the rapacious rodent.

After the introductions of the contestants and their fierce, red-eyed, smooth-furred, lightning-fast adversaries, the rules of the imminent struggle were explained to the crowd.

Each person was to be allotted two of the animals, which would be introduced up the trouser leg of the individual, after which the aforementioned leg would be sealed at the bottom with twine and at the top with a rope sash. Some of the challengers chose right-legged tactics and some chose left-legged ones but universally they shared one trait — namely they all fell very silent and serious-seeming as the ferrets and their handlers approached them for loading.

Lothar Spume, a large and unshaven man, gazed down at the two animals that he had drawn. His jowls were slightly green in hue as he, otherwise calmly, cast an eye over the two ferrets. One of them was Lord Fitzmount Brazenby Lampshutte IV!

Doris Ontal, on the other hand, was seemingly quite taken with the two small, white animals which had been assigned to her. 'There, there. Don't ooo 'orry, deary. Ooo's gon'ta be all right.'

Lothar Spume, as the judge counted down for the loading, defiantly shook back his Rastafarian dreadlocks, touched his Rosicrucian deadbolt, which hung about his neck on a tight necklace made of curtain-wire, and closed his eyes.

Spume had won this game every year in which he had entered. No-one had ever outlasted him with a pant-leg full of ferrets — and he was damn well sure that they were not about to start outlasting him now!

The truth of the matter is (it is hard to say such a thing about the brother of one so righteous, upright and God-fearing as James Spume, but to each Seth there is a Cain and to each Esau there is an Eyesore) and it has to be said — someone has to admit it — that Lothar Spume was hardly intending to play fair. In fact, as one might put it, if stretching a point, he was intending to cheat.

Actually his method of swindling was the same one that he had used in each of his previously victorious years.

On the other hand — perhaps one could legitimately

equivocate the case?

Anyway, the long and short of Lothar's secret was the small bore of his trouser leg. His pants were a mere fourteen inches in circumference at the foot-hole. Once the ferrets were introduced into the unwholesome aperture of his jeans' ankle-hole Lothar would freeze, squeezing and dilating his steely-tough muscles and trapping the beasts at the calf of the leg. He knew that gradually the determined rodents, rendered terrifically bad-tempered and vicious by the compression, would push past his straining ligatures and would attempt to make a bee-line for the most painful biting area, the delicate soft enclaves of his crotch, but to way-lay them Lothar carried in his thigh pocket a rock. It was just a rhodochrosite of about three inches in diameter, but by tensing his thigh and rectal musculature he could impede the ferrets' progress for as much as fifteen seconds by means of this rock. One year he had done this so successfully that the ferrets had bitten through his jean-leg and escaped into the open air. Since the animals do not wish to return once they have escaped he had lain back on that occasion, with no more to worry about and nothing to do except to listen to the agonized cries of those of his opponents who were still trying to win.

'Ready! Ready! Ready! Open yer legs, open yer legs, open yer legs . . . '

The ferret-handlers crouched in their positions with their snapping wrigglers at the ready.

'Ooohh no, no. We mustn't!'

'Open yer legs, open yer legs, open yer legs . . . '

'Ooohh no, no. We mustn't!'

'Open yer legs, open yer legs, open yer legs . . . '

'Noooooo . . . '

It was the twins Panting, Cadr and Idris, who were holding up the festivities. In fits of pure funk that had loosened Cadr's bowels and caused Idris to swoon, weeping and blubbering they wanted to be exempted from their rash decision to volunteer for the ordeal.

There was a pause of a few minutes in order that the Pantings could be cleaned up and stretcher-borne away respectively.

Doris took out her knitting and began to munch on a bean sandwich which was passed up to her from the crowd by the thoughtful Horace.

With six needles and a mess of wools, whose colour-scheme

rivalled a psychodelic nightmare, Doris was knitting a long, striped sock for Horace to wear for the soccer game later that afternoon.

'Open yer legs, open yer legs, open yer legs . . . '

Once again the contestants, now only eight of them, and the officials were ready to start.

'Get ready, get ready, get ready. Go! Go! Go!'

Two ferrets to a leg, quick as a flash they were inserted and the twines wrapped in place. The giant stop-clock was ticking inexorably above the stage.

Lothar Spume flexed his leg, straight as a ram-rod, tight as a you-know-what. He could feel the indignant reaction of Lord Fitzmount Brazenby Lampshutte IV. He squeezed more tightly.

Doris Ontal, knitting complacently all the while, was squeezing also. The ferrets were racing up the baggy leg of her drawers.

'There, there, dearies,' Doris patted the squirming lumps affectionately. 'Ooo'll be all right, duckie!'

Her animals were racing up her leg, not pausing even to take a nibble. But soon they would . . .

Doris leant over onto one haunch and heaved. Brrrrrrrrrrrrrrrrppppppp — brrrrruummmmpppp.
And again she heaved. Brrrrrrrrrrrrrrrrppppppp — brrrrruummmmpppp.

The speedy squirming within her jogging knickers lessened to a feeble fidgeting. Brrrrrrrrrrrrrrrrppppppp — brrrrruummmmpppp.

The movement ceased completely. Unperturbedly Doris continued to knit.

To her left a large, middle-aged lumber-jack and a bank-manager were crying out to the handlers to release them. The clock showed seven seconds of elapsed time and on the other side Doris could hear the strains of Alouette, Gentil Alouette coming from the Royal Canadian Mounted Policeman, who was showing a fool-hardy amount of guts by going close to the ten-second mark while wearing his wide-bore riding breeches (and, of course, the inevitable scarlet jacket and Boy-Scout tit-fer-tat).

At twelve seconds the Mounty, screaming like a nun at a picnic, had to be rescued by the undignified procedure of slitting his ceremonial breeks and up-ending him to turf out the little varmints, which by now had a firm and voracious hold upon his nethers.

With gritted teeth and a look of green determination Lothar held on.

It was fifteen seconds now and Doris was still knitting happily.

A doctor was called for and the familiar freckled face of the tousled buculo-inseminology celebrity and in-bucula-gynaecologist was helped onto the stage. He put some blue-bags on the Mounty's bites and offered the latter a pull from his whisky bottle, which was unfortunately empty.

Twenty seconds.

By now there remained only Doris and Lothar. Doris had almost finished the sock and was foraging in her pocket for a needle in order to finish off the ends.

Lothar was beginning to sweat.

Twenty-five seconds — utter silence from the crowd — otherwise no change.

Only Lothar Spume and Lord Fitzmount knew precisely what was happening. Lothar could feel the movements about the rhodochrosite. Perhaps his Lordship would bite his way to freedom?

Twenty-eight seconds.

Behind the crowd the book-makers were making book. The betting was raging hotly with the odds narrowing on thirty seconds with grievous bodily harm.

Thirty!

Lothar was biting his lip but he had not made a noise.

Thirty-one!

Pandemonium was breaking out with the punters — cursing and swearing from the thousand of losers and cautious, but vociferous jubilation from the bookies.

Thirty-two!

Click, click as Doris snips off the last loose end and looks over to Lothar with a broad smile. And just for safety sake — brrrrrrppppp — brrrrrrpppppp!

Thirty-three!

'Aagh, chrissake git me out,' screamed the capitulating Lothar Spume.

Instantly the handlers were by his side, slitting open his jeans.

He gaped down at the damage and vomited. 'Oh, ma testes! Oh ma testes!'

The cheerful, tousled medic appeared at his side almost at

once. 'I'm here. I'm here. Not Omar, but Dwayne!'

Testes deftly swabbed the victim with calamine, blue-bags and deftly manipulated splints and tourniquets.

'Don't worry, old fellow, it's far better than pulmonary odoema. With a bit of luck the little devils will get tetanus.'

At that moment Lothar Spume passed out and simultaneously Dwayne Testes pulled out the rhodochrosite from Spume's pocket.

'What's this?'

It did not take the judges long to determine the rhodochrosite strategy, to pronounce it unfair and to heap calumny and disqualification upon the head of the legendary local ferret-fighting hero-figure with the result that Doris's victory was greeted with even greater cheering and congratulations when finally she indicated to the handlers that she was done, having passed the Drewcastrian record with a staggering total of forty-five seconds.

The twine was cut and Doris shook out from her pant-leg two very groggy, somnolent ferrets.

As a result of the disqualification a bar tender came in second and behind him the Mounty scraped into third place, as is meet, right and proper.

Norman the Mormon and Roddin Corpse jumped onto the stage and lifted the triumphal matriarch, with her knitted sock in one hand and another bean sandwich in the other, high above their shoulders. They turned her around so that every one could see the stretched slogan — Join The Trinomial Plan.

The crowd roared.

Doris replied with a smile. Brrrrrppppppppppppppppppppppp!

The foot shoot followed. This was habitually the afternoon's most popular event and over fifty people, coming from near and far, marched over to the swift stream at the edge of the sports field to try their hand, or rather their feet, at this one.

Each entrant was required to supply himself with a pistol or hand-gun which was loaded with blanks. A stout pair of boots were advisable, although some wise-guys preferred to take their chances in canvas-topped boating sneakers.

The object of this combat was to remain upon a slowly rotating log, which traversed the stream, until all the others had fallen off or had been pushed off or had been induced to jump off by means of shots fired at their feet. The shots were, of course, intended only to be blanks. However, even a blank cartridge, when detonated behind the unsuspecting, otherwise occupied concentrating log-roller can have the effect of startling him (or her) into an unpremeditated leap for the water.

The competition was a pale imitation of the original struggles in which Ontario lumberjacks amused themselves by doing the same thing, but with fully loaded six-shooters and a belly-full of rye whisky. In those authentic and more straightened circumstances many a lumberjack was known to shoot himself in the foot in an excess of gun-slinging zeal.

In this event the favourite of many seasons of successes was Cantor Spume, the third and youngest of the Spume brothers. Cantor was determined to uphold the honour of the Spumes, which had taken such a dusting in the previous games.

Cantor wore high boots with metal cramp-ons at the toes and a small heel and with these he was adept at spinning the log, at stopping it and reversing the direction and at varying the speed. In addition, he had already put in a lengthy practice on the log that very morning, around dawn. He carried a snub-nosed, twelve-shot Mauser in a holster by his right arm-pit.

Representing the visitors in this event was none other than Norman the Mormon. He wore thick-soled black shoes with steel toe-caps to dispel the effects of toe-stomping and, unlike the others who were dressed as lightly as possible, Norman had on a very large, black overcoat. Within each of the two deep inside pockets of the unbuttoned coat he sported a low-calibre sub-machine gun. He reasoned that the ballast would come in handy, and that he would not have any need of the gun until near the end of the test, if he lasted that long!

The log was held still by the judges and the contestants were helped to file out onto the log. While they were still under starter's orders a rope was lowered to just above their head height to which they could cling in order to maintain their balance.

The book-makers were giving three-to-one Cantor Spume and ten-to-one the field otherwise.

Norman paused at the end of the log before mounting. He beckoned Jaime Laudenklier to his side and pressed into the latter's hand a bunch of bills, briefly whispering some instructions to him and giving him a push in the direction of the betting stands. Taking a notch in at his belt and giving the coat one last shrug to ensure that it was floating freely on his shoulders Norman stepped onto the log and strode out into the middle. By the time that the rest of the contestants had followed him space was very cramped on that log.

Cantor took a grip on the log with his cramp-ons, adopting a stance whereby he was facing along the axis of the log. He eased the Mauser loose in its holster.

The crowds were jostling for a place from which to get a good view. The starting pistol was raised high in the air.

'Ready, ready, ready. Steady, steady, steady. Go, go, go!'

Bang! The balance-rope was jerked away out of the reach of those on the log.

They were off, a few of them literally so!

The log slowly began to turn, stiffly at first since there were two schools of thought concerning the direction of revolution.

While his neighbours and the less tactically-minded were trying to get the log on the move Norman, maintaining his balance with ease, set about making some room for himself by propelling his immediate neighbours into the water. He pushed two teenagers off with a sweep of his arm — they were still chatting to each other about pop music and did not have time to notice that the game was underway before they landed in the stream. Next Norman turned, smiling, to face an old farmer and his wife.

'Hi, how do?'

As the old gentleman raised his hat Norman bent forward, butting the man in the face with the top of his head while reaching through between the farmer's thighs to grab the old girl's dress. As the dizzy, agonized agriculturalist wobbled Norman tipped him and his goodwife into the drink with a final heave on the old lady's dress.

The neighbouring log-lovers, seeing this manoeuvre, paused in their concentration and before they had awakened to what was happening Norman pushed the first one against the rest and sent four people flying from the log.

Shots were beginning to ring out all around him, but Norman was not to be disturbed by noise. He dismissed a large negro by giving the latter an intimate squeeze and began to speed after a good-looking young girl, who voluntarily dived into the water when sue saw the approaching gleam in his eye.

There remained only three people on the log.

By now the log was rotating quite fast and it was in the control of Cantor Spume, who had the position farthest from the judges. Norman was nearest to the home bank and in the luckless middle position was another Royal Canadian Mounted Policeman, a short, broad, young fellow, probably of Lowland stock. He was facing Cantor Spume and dancing furiously up and down on the timber in an attempt to synchronize his movements with Spume's.

Norman strode towards the Mounty, who was humming, in French, the customary tune and did not hear the footsteps behind him. Drawing a small, pineapple-shaped object from the pocket of his long coat Norman pressed the gadget into the policeman's right hand.

It was a computer-programmed hand grenade of local manufacture, which Norman had picked up en route at the plant which formerly had been cow sheds.

Norman whispered in the man's ear a message which Elsquaird had composed for the purpose.

'It's programmed to go off in one minute, unless you can break the code! It's a simple trap-door code that requires only that you factorize the number ninety-eight thousand, five hundred and eighty-seven into its two constituent primes. The only other key variable that you need to know is that today's magic number is three! By the way, it takes more than a lifetime to crack it without a computer!'

The cop paused in his stride, his thumb going into the corner of his mouth and his eyes closing momentarily.

''Bye, sucker,' laughed Norman with a grin and a push. 'I forgot to say that it's not switched on!'

Those were the last words that the Mounty heard prior to his landing in the water.

Norman drew his left-hand gun and shrugged off his coat, negligently letting it fall into the torrent below. He cautiously watched Cantor Spume, who was edging nearer, firing blanks like a madman in order to distract Norman's vigilance from his activities with the log.

Norman flipped the safety-catch off and fired a round into the wood at Spume's feet.

As the splinters flew Spume's face registered a moment of surprise. Chrissake, real bullets!

Spume span the log faster and began to edge away.

Norman was after him, shooting as he went. The gun had

several hundred rounds in it and Norman was letting fly all around Cantor's head with as many of them as he could squeeze off.

Spume's hat was clipped off and sent spinning into the river.

When the terrified Spume momentarily slackened the pace of the log Norman ran at his adversary, cannoning into him and sending them both sprawling. As he fell, he dropped the machine-gun and grabbed at the log, embracing it with all his might.

Norman held on, underneath the log, like a tenacious limpet. Spume was not so fortunate. He missed his footing as the big Mormon crashed into him and tipped over backwards into the water, surfacing with a yell.

'Real shells. He had real shells!'

Well, of course, the judges looked into the allegations but the log was so chewed up by the feet of the frenzied contestants that no-one could say for certain that any of the splintering was due to gunfire.

Roddin Corpse kindly retrieved the coat with the machine gun still in its pocket — there was no mention of two weapons and, in fact, Jaime and Stanley had retrieved and secreted the loaded one even before the judges realized what they were trying to corroborate. The gun in the coat was mostly spent but the few shells that remained in it were blanks, as per regulations.

All this time Norman was grimly hanging on tightly to the log by his arms and legs, calmly waiting for the moment to come when he would be pronounced the foot-shoot champion.

Finally — to cheers from most of the crowd — the judges came to their verdict and recognized his victory.

Doris cheered. Brrrrrppppppppp, brrrrummmmppp!

For Preston Pans, however, the soccer challenge, in which the Mayoral entourage had routed the Drewchester Fireballs by a score of one hundred and seventeen to nil, had been his personal triumph.

The Gang of Eleven, each clad in heavy work boots and a long black overcoat, except for Doris who was to play goalie wearing her pink jogging suit, had assembled first upon the pitch. Their faces were set and serious as they watched the opposition run out on to the field.

It was a good soccer field by the standards of Southern Ontario. The climate made for the inevitably thin turf but the potholes, although deep and numerous, were not in the important areas of the pitch.

Elsquaird's coat was literally two feet too long for him, despite the fact that it was a child's raglan that Doris had picked up at a Goodwill Sale at the Fergus synagogue. In its pockets he carried an assortment of his favourite species of programmed grenades. He had flares, smoke bombs, tear-gas and strong-odour hand-grenades which were all detonated by setting off the encoded programme and could only be stopped by punching in the deciphering of the coded programme which was visible on a minute display monitor. The deciphered message contained the instructions for entering in the antidote command. The professor had designed this procedure himself and, with its combination of a trap-door code and digital displays, it tickled his fancy considerably.

In practice, even using a mainframe supercomputer and the most modern graphical techniques that he could devise or had read about, Elsquaird had never, try as he might, managed to crack the antidote message in a sufficiently short time to stop the detonation of a hypothetical grenade, which was a particularly satisfying state of affairs resulting in considerable boosting of sales of the grenades, which were, of course, a product of the Gasville consortium of the Gang of Eleven.

The others, in their long coats, concealed various accessories of a similar nature.

Sid Ra'in had the sights for a middle-range, large-bore bazooka, which resembled a sort of latter-day arquebus, for which Zhilin and Penz concealed the rest in two pieces. Jaime and Horace, who were to be defenders, carried short lengths of chain while Eli and Stanley O'Vayshun concealed spare footballs. Stanley had, in addition, a raw-hide bull-whip wrapped around his waist.

Norman the Mormon, who was the Captain for the Gang of Eleven, and Pans and Roddin Corpse were to be the forward line. They carried no weaponry and wore regular football attire beneath their coats in readiness for a quick strip when and if the need should arise.

The referee, an impartial outsider from Elginturd and a former celebrated centre-forward for Orianensburgville Third Team, called the two captains together. He placed the ball on the centre spot. Norman recognized the opposing captain as the gentleman whom he had expulsed earlier from the foot-shoot log, in the company of his elderly wife. Around his right eye the old gentleman had a very wide-spread, black-and-blue contusion with a hint of yellow about it. Behind the opposing captain were ranged his forward-line and foremost among these, clearly anxious to begin, were the three Spumes — James, Lothar and Cantor. They glowered ominously first at Norman and then at the ball.

That was probably the last really good look that the Spume boys got at the ball. The old gentleman, whose right eye was essentially closed, was not going to see much of it again either!

The referee took out a silver dollar and tossed it up high into the air. 'Heads,' called Norman as he and the other captain watched the graceful orbit of the shining coin. Up, up, up it went and then began to drop back. The coin passed between the expectant faces of the two captains, who had edged closer to see the outcome.

Bang! Norman's head, quick as lightning, had inadvertently butted the old gentleman in the left eye. 'Oooh, my God.' The old man clutched at his face.

'Sorry! Does it hurt?'

Norman, even as he spoke, followed the coin to the ground, covering it with a hand as he dropped on to all fours over the dollar coin. As his left hand covered the original coin his right revealed a second silver dollar.

'Heads it is!' cried Norman jubilantly, jumping to his feet and turning to examine the buttee. 'Oh, that's looks nasty. Have we got a doctor? I'm surely damn sorry, eh?'

The old fellow muttered something which was hardly audible and permitted himself to be led away to the trainer's bench.

Thus it was that Drewchester began the game with only ten men, since substitution was not a part of the local tradition.

Elsquaird, because of his diminutive stature, did not participate in the rough-and-tumble of the game but rather loitered on the Drewcastrian goal-line. By dint of remaining stationary when the ball came near he avoided being caught offside. Indeed, the professor's strategy was to engage the goalkeeper in pleasant conversation during slack moments and to distract his attention at crucial ones by drawing the latter's attention to such objects d'art as activated chlorine grenades in the goal-month.

A blow-by-blow account of this titanic struggle is out of the question. Suffice it to say that each of the Gang of Eleven had a strategy or two which they used with telling effect. For example, Stanley proved himself to be an excellent whip handler and bazooka aimer. The bazooka was used to propel the substitute balls which Eli and Stanley carried during the course of the caber caper, a stratagem of Preston Pans' origination. The ball would pass to Pans in mid-field and at once the scrum, consisting of Stanley, Zhilin, Penz, Eli and Sid would form ahead of him, between him and the opposing defenders. In the scrum the long coats would conceal the rapid assembly and loading with a football of the bazooka. Pans would toe the ball gently into the scrum once inside which it would be pocketed by Eli. Pans, turning, would receive the racing form of Roddin Corpse by cupping his hands to support Corpse's foot and then, launching him in a backward caber-toss, Preston Pans would project his sturdy colleague up and over the line formed by the scrum.

Simultaneously, as Roddin appeared over the top of the scrum with a blood-curdling cry of 'Aaaaaaaaggghhhhhhhsheeeeeeeet!' the bazooka-borne ball would be fired, through a gap in the gaggle of overcoats, at the Drewchester goal.

The aim of the gun-crew was first-class at the start of the game, by dint of considerable practice, and it improved to near-infallibility by the end of it.

As the ball arced its inexorable path towards the opponents' goal-line the scrum dismantled the bazooka and dissolved itself as speedily as it had formed. On most occasions the ball soared high and dropped into the net, which was momentarily left unattended by the goalie whom Elsquaird had distracted.

One hundred and seventeen to nil! That is enough said, except perhaps to remark that Doris had virtually no defending to do since few of the Drewchester forwards managed to find a successful retort to the referee-blind-side chain and iron knuckles technique of Horace and Jaime.

Once in a while things had required Pans' helping hand in defence.

The recollection of those sweet moments caused Preston Pans to smile as he sucked his sore knuckles and soaped them in an attempt to remove the congealed blood.

Finally Pans turned off the shower and stepped lightly out

onto his towel mat. As he dried himself off in a self-satisfied, leisurely manner he became aware that two pairs of eyes were focussed upon him. Frankly he returned the gaze of two grey-haired old ladies, who seemed to have no compunction about invading the men's shower-room and merely watched him calmly.

Neither side spoke, so Pans continued to massage himself as if nothing untoward was happening.

The two old ladies approached nearer. One of them spoke. 'Esss-cuse-moi, 'ooo ees dee way-ee to zee sexy terapeeeste'

'Sex terapeeeste!' corrected the other old lady.

The foremost one was holding in her hand what appeared to be a phrase-book or dictionary, because from time to time she would emit an English word with a strong Quebecoise accent.

'Str-awng. Bu-doh-flahee. Stray-ee-p.'

'Pas stray-ee-p, mais strock, stupide!' corrected the second lady.

The second speaker was a trim figure, a little bent in her stance perhaps, but nonetheless quite tall — about a hundred and ninety millimetres, as Pans noted with surprise.

Her companion was much more erect, which made it evident that she was at least two metres. Two very tall old ladies! The taller one was carrying a long brown-paper parcel, which looked as if it might contain fishing rods. She turned on her companion, wagging her finger coyly.

'Méchante! Méchante, Augustine-Phillipette! Aucune que tu veux, ma chérie, mais pas stupide!' She gave Augustine-Phillipette a rather powerful nudge in the left breast with the end of the fishing rods.

'D'accord, chérie,' muttered Augustine-Phillipette, nursing her bruised chest. 'D'accord, Josephine-Christabelle.'

'Bien!'

Augustine smiled at her companion and lighted two Gauloise, giving one to Josephine and taking the second for herself.

'Air yae t'th' fishen, lassies?' Pans enquired aimiably, nodding at the parcel.

The old ladies smiled at him in a kindly manner but did not deign to reply to his question. Josephine-Christabelle was consulting the phrase-book once more. As she concentrated on the book she lit two more cigarettes, passing the second one to Augustine-Phillipette. Across her tee-shirt Josephine-Christabelle bore, in fading calligraphy, which she had probably done herself, the words, Vive Québec Libre. She dragged heavily on her Gauloise and then threw it down, crushing it vigorously beneath her running-shoe. Augustine-Phillipette handed her friend a further cigarette, which she had lit in readiness.

Pans watched patiently while Josephine-Christabelle got her phrases ready. Augustine had moved away to the side and had taken a seat upon the bench which ran the length of the wall.

Josephine coughed and spat. Augustine-Phillipette got painfully to her feet and brought over yet another cigarette, lighting another for herself as she went slowly back to her seat.

Josephine-Christabelle cleared her throat and began to speak in English. She spoke straight at the naked Preston Pans, who was waiting calmly clad only in a towel. ''Ow 'bouta goo tam, chérie? You a goerrrr, swiddy pah? You a goerrrr zenn?'

'Onla' a kirk gooerrr, lassie,' replied Pans, laughing loudly in her face.

Augustine-Phillipette, ignored by the other two, was opening the parcel of fishing tackle.

'Not zo zaucee, lill man,' retorted Josephine-Christabelle, evidently a little bit rattled. She straightened up, looking down upon Pans from a surprising two metres ten! Again she consulted her phrasebook. 'Ouerrr zee fuck is zee restaurant?' she read. 'Ou-y is you so ugly, sheet-fez? Can ah strock yo' size? Eh, goo'tam, Sharlie, eh?'

'Eh, lay off, lassie, D'y' ken yure tue auld tae b' duin' tha' sort o' thung tae me!'

Pans slapped Josephine's hand which was reaching for his thigh.

'Aaagghh, all rat!'

Pans turned to see that Augustine-Phillipette had risen from her seat. In fact, in the brief glimpse that Pans got of her, he noticed that she had changed considerably. Gone was the old lady-like appearance. Actually, gone was the old lady. Her hairpiece lay on the floor along with her dress and the brown paper which had wrapped the fishing tackle. In her place was standing a very tall negro upon whose torso Pans caught sight of the words: GEORGIA TECH, before the lights went out, to the command, which was issued in a deep masculine basso-profundo.

'Hit dem larts, Josephine.'

A second negro voice laughed out of the darkness. 'Rart oh, man!'

The last intelligence that Preston Pans gathered before the room became almost totally dark was that the 'fishing equipment' consisted of two large spears — two-metre assegais. As the lights went out Augustine-Phillipette tossed one of the assegais to her/his pal, who caught it deftly as he flicked the light-switch.

The only light in the shower-room was coming in through the door leading to the changing rooms and the shiatsu massage-parlour. Usually there was someone in there having a massage, since the noble art of 'finger (shi) — pressure (atsu)' was the latest nine-day wonder with the rich, city-working commuters of Drewchester, who swore by shiatsu as a cure for their fatigue, tension, ennui and period-pains.

'He-elp. He-elp!' Pans shouted, vainly hoping that someone was in the massage parlour to help him. In point of fact the cry was scarcely very realistic in view of the effeminate nature of the individual whom Drewcastrians had chosen to shiatsu them.

At any rate, before Pans could call a second time the door slammed shut, kicked closed by an extremely agile negroid person whom Pans had once understood to be Josephine-Christabelle.

There was no further opportunity for meditative reflection because the point of an assegai passed very close to his body at that instant, ripping the towel away from him and narrowly missing him. This left no margin for doubt about the intentions of these two swarthy beanpoles.

Dropping the towel, twisting rapidly to one side and out beneath the spear Pans gripped its shaft and used it to propel its owner painfully against the far wall.

'Ugh, shee-ite man!' came a curse from the darkness in that direction.

Not waiting for the other negro to try to turn him into a kebab Preston Pans ran, ducking low, towards the door of the john. Fortunately he found the door rather than the wall and slid silently across the floor, beneath the partitions and fetched up, panting hard but trying not to make a noise, in cubicle number three!

5

RESCUE

Norman the Mormon and Roddin, still clad in their drab, black coats which they had worn for the soccer game, rounded the corner of the corridor leading to the shiatsu parlour in the Drewchester arena. Confronting them was a large group of strangers, who were milling around outside the entrance to the office of the shiatsu masseur. Roddin pushed his way through the crowd in order to read the notice which was pinned to the parlour door. Written in a scrawling and uneducated hand, on expensive notepaper which bore the letter head and escutcheon of the Department of Physical Education and Mental Health, Georgia Tech, he encountered the following message: OUT TO LUNCH, MAN, JUST MANIPULATE YOSELF TIL AH GIT BACK.

''Is at to lurnch, mon ami,' Roddin called to Norman the Mormon over the din of the strangers, who were singing.

The strangers were rather tall negroes, apart from which they might have been mistaken for Scotsmen, since each one was wearing a kilt, a sporran, a tam-o'-shanter, gillies and was sporting a neat tartan waistcoat and a tee-shirt carrying the words, Georgia Tech, across his chest in large red lettering. Bulges in the strangers' socks evidenced the presence of a dirk down each black leg. In deep and melodious voices they were rendering a version of the well-known Scottish drinking song — John Barleycorn.

> There was once a ponce
> Who drank a sconce
> Of delicious nut-brown ale.

162

Hey, John Barleycorn,
Ho, John Barleycorn,
Old and young thy praise have sung
John Ba-ar-el-eycorn!

At the end of their number the strangers collapsed into mirthful jollity all round.

'Hey, man. Number one, man!'

'Damn fine song, man.'

'Need-oh, need-oh, man!'

Then one of the throng noticed Roddin in their midst. 'Hey, fellah, wot's yo name, man? Yo fro' rahn hee?'

'Sho thing, don yo 'member dat guy fro' dat limey foo'ball game?'

Roddin turned and confronted his inquisitor squarely. 'Roddin Corrr eez ma nem. When will zis op-pen, do you sink?'

'Roddin,' the man seemed to disregard his question, being far more preoccupied with the name. 'Roddin? Roddin, eh? Wassortov name's dat, man? Hear dat, fellahs — dis dude done colt Roddin!'

'Ahh.'

There were nods all round and murmurs behind stealthy hands. 'Is there something goddam funny?' Norman the Mormon asked as he roughly elbowed his way to the side of his companion.

'Somethin' funny, for chrissake, all of a sudden, eh? Chocolate, eh?' he stared up defiantly into the surrounding strangers' wide, round-eyed gazes.

Evidently the newcomers sensed that here was a righteous christian soul who was better not messed about, for there was an almost universal outburst of shrugs and grunts from the kilted ones.

'No way, man!' smiled down the negro. 'It's just that yo name remarnds me of the tale of Oggin the Nog.'

'Aye, thae heeland teeel o' Oggin the Nog.'

'Och, a' rumm-emember weeel th' teeel of wee Oggin the Nog.'

All around the negroes had suddenly become very Scottish, shaking their heads sagely at the recollection of the legend, sucking their lips back against their teeth with loud slurping noises.

Unanimity!

'Wort a larrrd, Oggin the Nog!'

'A' ken him weeel, Oggin the Nog!'

'Sich a fine braw laddie, Oggin the Nog!'

'His maether's ainly son, Oggin the Nog!'

'His faether's praede — Oggin the Nog!'

'Wa' he no dark o' th' heeer? Young Oggin the Nog?'

'Nae, he wa' feeer o' th' heeer — yo coonass — he wa' feeer o' th' heeer wa' Oggin the Nog!'

'Aye, an' taw wi' it. Mickle taw wa' Oggin the Nog!'

'Nay, he wa' verra wee — dinna y' bide him weeel — an' don' yo go colin' no bo' dumb coonass. Ah don' thing yo all know no Oggin from no Noggin. Yo lettin' this wart guy sure as hell make some fool art o' yo!'

'Yeh, man. Wot the hell yo all mean, a-comin' in he' wid all dis goddam crap 'bout Oggin dis and goddam Roddin dat?'

'Yeh, wot yo mean, man?'

By now the bilingual banter was heating up all around Roddin and Norman. Voices were mingling angry Georgian invective with the chanted attributes of Oggin the Nog.

The overall effect was one of bedlam.

It was surprising, therefore, that over all the din Norman heard a noise. It seemed to come from the massage parlour.

Norman shouted at the top of his voice. 'Roddin, did yer hear that? It was Preston — in there. He shouted help — I swear he did! D'yer hear it, eh?'

Instantly the shouting of the afroid Scotsmen ceased. There was total silence.

Norman, his senses attuned to danger, did not need to look around at the strangers' faces in order to realize instantly what was in those curly-haired, woolly tam-o'-shantered heads.

Roddin may not have had the experience of his friend and may thereby not have had such a highly-developed sense of survival, but he could read plainly enough the determined and slightly elated expression that was spreading over Norman's face. He looked round at the 'Scotsmen', who were watching them.

From the press two kilted heavies detached themselves. They were each carrying, one in each hand, a pair of sections of railway track to which handles had been attached, giving each the appearance of a briefcase. The sections of track must have weighed about two hundred pounds each. The carriers were grimacing and sweating with the strain as they advanced upon Norman the Mormon and Roddin Corpse. The weights were similar to the kind to be found regularly in weight-lifting competitions of the highland games which abound in south-western Ontario.

For one brief moment the Gasville duo looked at each other, nodded, glanced around and then simultaneously hurled themselves, shoulder first, at the door of the shiatsu parlour.

With a splintering and a loud crack the door flew open and the two leapt through, slamming the door to again in the faces of the pack of their pseudo-Caledonian pursuers, all but two of whom were hammering on the door against which the pair were pushing with all their might. The two who were otherwise engaged were the weight-lifters, who had each put down their pieces of track rather carelessly and precipitously with the intention of hounding after Norman and Roddin but with the unintentional effect of stopping their carriers in their stride — pinioned by four hundred pounds of steel on the hems of their kilts!

Norman, while keeping all of his weight desperately against the door, was the first to disengage his submachine-gun from the inside pocket of his coat. Disengaging the safety-catch he jumped clear of the door, turning as he moved.

'Down, Roddin.'

Roddin dived headlong for the floor, slithering away from the light as their pursuers burst open the frail door and burst into the darkened room. Norman let fly with a round of shots that sent the incomers into a disarray of scrambling outgoers.

By now Roddin was armed also. He sprayed several rounds of bullets through the open door.

'Don' you day-re commmme in 'ere, or you get wafforrr!'

Feet could be heard running briskly away down the corridor.

'Aaagghh!'

'That was Pans, eh? Quick — this way!'

At the double they raced for the entrance to the shower-room; Norman instinctively flicked on the light as he ran into the room. The sudden light caught Augustine-Phillipette and Josephine-Christabelle unprepared, blinding them momentarily. They were poised before the cubicle which contained Pans, one either side. The wooden partitions of the cubicle were splintered and gaping from the assegai-stabs. Josephine-Christabelle had pushed an assegai through the wall of the john and was probing for Pans with it. Augustine-Phillipette, who was between spearings, turned at once and launched a well-aimed and deadly projectile, which caught Norman through his flowing coat and pinned him to the wall. The machine-gun was wrenched from his hand and went skidding across the floor towards Josephine who was on the point of levelling it at Pans' pals when Roddin got off the final few rounds of the conflict.

The two erstwhile old ladies slid ungracefully to the floor, where they adopted sitting positions with their backs against the cubicle partition which they had so thoroughly mutilated. Josephine keeled over at once while Augustine just sat there with a glassy-eyed expression on his/her face, looking down at his/her hands, held at stomach-level and bearing the weight of steaming viscera.

Augustine whimpered, making a sound rather like that of a new-born puppy.

'You all right, eh? Pans?'

A head appeared, grinning, over the top of the cubicle wall. 'Och, mon, 'M fine. A' ah hard to du war tae lift masel' high up 'n let them wee sassenachs stab arooond wi' th' wee stick thangs as mickle as th' liked!'

Pans was laughing uproariously as he dropped to the ground. 'Ach, th've made it unco messy hereaboots, d'ye ken?'

Norman was kneeling beside the two slain, would-be assassins, looking at their blood-stained tee-shirts which still displayed, GEORGIA TECH, just like those worn by the strangers which they had recently encountered in the hallway!

'Umm, Georgia Tech,' was all that Norman would vouchsafe for the time being.

6

INSOMNIA

It was a steamingly hot night and Eli Baktrian, Mayor of Gasville and its surrounding adoptions and enclosures, subdivisions and recent acquisitions, leader of the Gang of Eleven, co-conceiver of the Trinomial Plan and public general factotum, was lying, wide awake, in bed. He was sweating profusely and about his head, which rested uneasily on his pillow, the material was soaked with his perspiration.

Beside him he could hear the slow, regular and heavy breathing of Sarah. He had started from his dream in a panic, his sleeping mind screaming, 'Where is Charles Watson Chrissake? Where's Susan Ashcroft?'

What of these figments of his past? Did they marry? Were they still in the country? Perhaps they had gone off somewhere else in the Commonwealth? How could he get them back? Just a minute was all that he wanted. A mere instant that would give him a morsel of control over the flux of time. If they were in the USA perhaps he could find them with an advert?

Charles had been a skinny little runt when he was only eleven, but by the time they were both eighteen he had become two centimetres taller than Eli.

Sarah was getting used to these outbursts to the extent that she no longer woke up to participate. She no longer pressed cool cloths to his brow or murmured reassurances in his ear.

Tonight the weather was so bloody humid!

Eli's sensitive nose told him that sex was out of the question — it also told him that one of the boys in the next room was awfully shitty, but he chose to disregard the latter intelligence. Maliciously he looked over at his wife. Sexually, he reflected, she had dried up on him pretty damn soon after they were married. She had been a hotter prospect when Paddy Delaney had still been alive. Now her love was like old parchment — one of those many changes which were besetting him and over which he had no control.

Eli climbed out of bed and went over to the linen cupboard, opened the door and pulled out a fresh sheet. They were sleeping without covers. Walking back to the bed he gently hauled Sarah up and moved her, still eighty per cent asleep, or so it seemed, to a sitting position on the bedside chair.

Moving slowly and deliberately he proceeded to change the sweat-stained sheet for a fresh one. He was halfway done when he noticed that Sarah was awake and helping him to tuck in the hems of the bedclothes. 'Thanks,' he grunted, tumbling irritably back onto the bed. The cool, clean sheet was a small consolation. Already Sarah was back in the bed and fast asleep!

It has been said that there is an hour for love and an hour for hate, Eli reminded himself. That seemed like fifty-eight minutes too much for the first and light years too little for the second.

For example, there was the little matter with Mandola Magabutne. The Georgia Tech fiasco, which had occupied the Gang of Eleven in a debate lasting all the afternoon, was clearly the work of Magabutne. The whole thing smelt of a double-cross. So far they had only manufactured weapons for him; they had not handed over to him any of the blue-prints of production which they were obliged by the contract eventually to return to the black villain.

Well, he damn well was not going to get those blue-prints back now.

It was always very difficult to understand those negroes — it was not even clear to Eli whether it was just Pans who was the object of Magabutne's hatred or whether it was all of them.

Here was another change which was attempting to get out of control. However, out of control or not, it seemed better to say nothing at the moment providing that that was consistent with holding on to the blue-prints.

Starting with that night's shift Eli had doubled the guards at the munitions plant.

Suppress, oppress, bribe and capitalize upon the decentralization of the provincial governing processes — those must be his slogans. Kiss and kick, sing and suppress, buy and bribe; Eli had found himself repeating this litany virtually every day recently. However, he was determined that the build-up of the Trinomial Plan and all its developing side-lines, such as the armaments production, was not going to become one of those things that were going to change against his volition. It was his will that had brought developments this far and that self-same will was going to keep the Gasville show on the road. Sure, he needed Elsquaird's brains — and those of Penz and Zhilin, too. Sure, he needed Preston Pans, Stanley, Sid Ra'in, Jaime, Roddin, Norman the Mormon and the Ontals. He needed them in the manner that one needs tools, but if the worst came to the worst and Mandola got some of them, even under his very nose — perhaps even demanding some of them, right out in the open with a gross, tooth-gleaming smile — they could be discarded. The only thing that was essential in the final analysis, the ultimate adhesive in the whole fabric of his machinations, was his will. If it were possible to disembody his will, possible to put it into someone else, then the plan would be able to develop under the protection and surveillance of that transubstantiated will.

And he was not about to bend that will!

Things were going too well. The response against the city-slicking ownership of the Ontario farmlands had exceeded all expectations. There had been none of the anticipated resistance or objections from the police authorities or from the Gasville councillors. A few bribes had been passed around, but mostly they were under control because they owned farms, too. And if they did not then the Trinomial Plan organizers were in a position to help them get one.

Once or twice Norman, Roddin and Pans had had to resort to practising the orthodoxy of the protection rackets. But even that had not been too serious — for example, those who were being 'protected' by Pans and the boys showed no signs of resentment or recrimination and appeared to be thoroughly resigned to their lot. If they were disaffected they did not seem to be able to find a hot-bed of dissident opinion in common with theirs with which to fire up any trouble.

The plan was not going to end up gutted like some yearling stirk on the abattoir floor, its cortex blown out by the percussion of the humane-killer. It was not going to be trivial to keep their current momentum, but he could withstand a few murmurings against him, he could retaliate against outbursts of obloquy. He had a strong arm.

Ontario was young and beautiful. Ontarians, like their land, had youth and beauty — and dumb-ass minds — superb bodies that were only good for being screwed. And, left to their own devices, the Yanks would see to that! So, rather than the Yanks, why not the Gang of Eleven? The beneficent screw! From the Trinomial Plan, in the long run, would come development and prosperity. Already, after only months of munitions production, Gasville was showing a balance of payments that was sufficient for them to annex the whole county.

Sarah passed wind in her sleep, causing Eli to turn over to face in the other direction, towards the wall.

Baktrian closed his eyes, squeezing them tightly shut and then opening them wide, as if he was trying to focus on something. He continued to rehearse his accustomed litany of success, the backbone of his will.

Continually reviewing the situation kept him tense, kept him alert, maintained his sensitivity, strengthened his resolve. It enabled him to look upon the possibility of resistance with a nonchalance which virtually approached good humour.

Who was going to unsettle him? What alien intrusion? The invasion of the killer tomatoes? Let them stay put in the salad-bar, preying on those boondocks fatsoes who frequent the steak houses — may the fleas of a thousand camels infest their armpits! Or vice versa!

Eli turned onto his back, pillowing his head on his arms and gazing at the ceiling in the darkness. He smiled to himself, maybe the invasion of the killer tornadoes?

He must fasten upon the pressure-points of the communal consciousness, gripping so tightly as to daze and glaze its perception. Public relations, advertising promotions and fund-raising social events were the appropriate 'pressure-points' and well they knew how to manipulate them — suppress, oppress, bribe and capitalize, kiss and kick, sing and suppress, buy and bribe.

The bed was warm and, despite the heat and humidity, the proximate warmth of Sarah's large and affable body was very soporific.

Eli's eyes were closing, finally succumbing to the inexorable urge to sleep . . .

The crookback hight Baktrian, Lord of the Cinque Rocks, Factotus generabilis mundi, 'Bassador of the Mighty and Amicus Populi was seated, advanced away from the working throng, borne upon the shoulders of an immense host of tiny toilers. Around him in plenty careered a pandemonious multitude of jugglers, mountebanks, lascars, sword-swallowers, cut-purses, vendors and trades-people, each crying his wares and challenging all comers to step up and sample.

Baktrian was pursued, close at hand, by his retinue of the eleven — Elcius the Midget, Zhilincus, Pansard the Giant and Penzard the Wise, Stanius Ovox, Horatio Ontalox and his vapid, stinking shrew of a goodwife, Doratia, Laudacus the Sycophant, Mormon de Norman, Rodius Corporis and Hassidicus Ra'in.

Elcius, perched upon the giant's shoulder, bore at his wrist the master's peregrine, Night, and his vigilant kestrel, Day. The midget lurched as the restive peregrine essayed urgently to launch itself against the will of its master.

The procession made its way within the house, the jostling crowd pressing with difficulty through the postern gate.

The raucous crew disappeared within, its din dimmed until finally there remained no evidence of the merry-makers and the bright, dawn morning was abandoned to the punctuating grunts of the labouring night-watch, which was coming to the end of its travail.

The dawn was waking into a plaintive, slate-grey sky and above the bent forms of the labourers, oblivious of them and quite without self-consciousness, the cow-birds, crows and cardinalis malinoctis were giving full-throat to their strangled day-break chorus.

Over the centuries of the Knight Baktrian's rule of the place, from time immemorial as it now seemed, the village of Gascoine and its surroundings and environment had followed the same relentless regime of industry. The village was divided wholesale into three ridings and to each was ordained a duty or watch of eight hours of the clock during the span of which these self-same ridings, being each one equal third of all men, women and children advanced above the age of nourishment at the breast, having their habitation within the village walls, must labour at the Rock.

None save the knight himself, and perchance his reeve, David, could any longer call to mind the precise beginnings of the labouring. But the need for it was clear as water-crystal to every freeman in the fiefdom. For in the beginning, when the first elders had settled the village and the first Knight of the Cinque Rocks had held court in the mansion, the Rock, which perched massively upon the hillside above the cottages, had presented an obstacle. For this mighty stone, which on this particular day merged into a tranquil firmament of a hue much similar to its own, barred and blocked a potential cart-track which the elders had wisely sought to swathe through the woodlands, over the hilltop and down into the next valley. The alternative route, which was the one by which they had found the settlement originally, was narrow and difficult, having to circumvent the marshy verges of the lake which filled widespread the valley downstream from Gascoine. Accordingly the elders had sought to clear the Rock from its position in a manner sufficient at least for the swathing of a broad track over the hill-brow.

With this project in mind harnesses had been crafted of all sizes and of the finest hides, also a fine ram had been sculpted, in similitude to the battering rams of the ancient tribes of the region. The ram was wrought in the firmest oak and decorated with the many signs which augured prosperity and plentitude and success. The priests had blessed the ram. A full moon of incantations and inhalations of hallucinatory potions had been invested upon the enterprise to ensure its well-being. Finally, at least so it was reported, twelve virgins of impeccable purity and beauty — seven maidens and five youths, as was the tradition, had been lain side by side along its awful length and summarily sacrificed, each one stabbed but once with a single, swift blow of the ballocks dagger, whose smooth, triangular blade of swift steel pierced leaving a neatsome wound and from about whose boxwood handles the Elder's hand never slipped. Bowls of their blood, still steaming and dark as the juice of pomegranates, was massaged into the surface of the ram until it gleamed with a sinister flush which glowed around each of its weals, axe-welts and knot-holes.

The harnesses were painstakingly fastened to yokes positioned along the length of the ram, two by two down each flank of the ram whose dimensions were such that in this manner full two hundred haulers might so harnessed strive at the labour of propelling the ram.

The head of the ram was brought into contact with the front surface of the immense rock and shored up upon lesser rocks lest its purchase might slip while the people pushed it forward. By this means it was originally thought to move aside the offending obstruction — so goes the history of the beginning of the toil, according to the tellers of tales.

Whether this tale be falsehood or veritude makes little difference now to the serfs of Knight Baktrian, for the truth of the matter, which is as plain to see in the pale light of this current dawn as it had been at each dawn down through the centuries of struggle, is that the Rock did neither move nor yield one mite in its position.

Undeterred they had striven. Night and day members of successive watches had manned the pushing of the ram. When the watches were changed the procedure was performed smoothly to a slow, relentless beat upon a goatskin-covered tambourine. At each stroke one pair of serfs interchanged their places. After two hundred beats by the drummer the watches would be completely changed, so smoothly and with so little interruption that the Rock never so much as moved!

Meticulous were the villagers in their attendance and only one reason was countenanced by which a person might be absent from his post when the time came for his watch.

And that was the reason which eventually excuses us all.

Through aeons of tenacity the Gascoinois did not falter nor pause in their labours. Indeed, as time passed and they saw no movement of the Rock, the elders, advised by Knight Baktrian — then a young man, broad and straight and in his prime — realized that to rest, diminish or cease their travail could only result in the Rock beginning to roll towards the village. Such an eventuality would plainly demolish Gascoine, its mansion and all who dwelt therein.

Once realized, the imminence of the rolling of the Rock spurred the inhabitants of Gascoine to further and more severe diligence. For now, as Baktrian the crookback explained to them, they were toiling for their very survival!

Slackness and doltishness in regard of these matters were not permitted by their Lord and he, Baktrian, would oft be seen personally to flog or maim any idler who was brought before his manorial court on such a charge. For the crime of oversleeping he had castrated Johannes Sturman, for falsely excusing himself by reason of the ague he had taken the thumb from Thomas Brewer and over Mistress Sawston, who had mendaciously claimed that her menstrual time was upon her, he had exercised his Lordly rights, thereby begetting a bastard. A small and bent brat this offspring was, twisted to the left like a false stem of yew which is of no good for bow-making.

Such was the Lord's scrupulousness in this regard that few folk dared risk malingering in their duties at the Rock.

Should a serf hope to pass unnoticed in some misdemeanour at the work-place his chances of escaping detection were slim indeed, for at all times the labourers harnessed to the ram were observed with close scrutiny by one or both of David, the reeve, or his bum-bailiff.

And there was neither a gamin nor a loafer within Gascoine that would dare defy their gaze!

7

CHESS

Within the Great Hall the Knight Baktrian was shouting at the top of his voice, reclining on his dais the while.

'Stupid oafs, get those birds down! Odds bodkins, what in the name of damnation did you loose them in here for?'

Everyone was calling simultaneously.

'Night!'

'Day!'

'Nighty, night!'

'Down hither, shite hawks!'

And so on.

The result was cacophonous and pandemonious bedlam, down upon which the two peregrines gazed with a mighty disdain.

'Send the bearers up there,' bellowed the Knight at David, his reeve, who was gazing with puzzled wonderment up at the two birds. The like of this had never befallen him before.

'Let them mount, one upon another, until they can reach the beam, David.'

'But sire, the bearers have carried you throughout all this long night and the better part of yesterday. They are extremely buggered, my liege.'

'By whom? 'Twas not I!'

'Exhausted, my Lord. They are full tired and could not methinks, encompass such a task.'

'What then, dolt-brain, is to be done?' The Knight glared at his reeve challengingly.

Elcius stepped forward. 'Master?'

'What is't, tiny? All this was your doing, midget!'

'Might I have the lures, m'lord? I can resolve this matter in a trice, if thou wilt permit it?'

'Damnation 'pon you! Do it then, and in a trice or faster.'

'My gratitude to you, sire,' murmured Elcius, taking the two lures and attaching to each firmly the corpse of a mouse. The gnomelike man carefully fastened each animal by a reef in its tail, tying the black mouse to the lure of the peregrine, Night, and the white mouse to that of the falcon, Day.

Having checked the lures one further time the dwarf stepped out into the centre of the hall and began to swing the lures slowly about his head. He turned as he paid out the thongs, gradually increasing the speed of his spinning and simultaneously calling out in a high-pitched whistle which was close kin to that of a boatswain's pipe.

The hawks watched. The miniature man span. The mice skimmed the marbled floor of the hall while the crowded retinue held its breath and waited.

As the birds attended more closely Elcius shortened each thong, wrapping it over his wrist as he whirled. Eight feet, seven feet, six feet was the length of the lures when, simultaneously and without a sound, the hunters left their perches and set upon the mice. Night took the black and Day took the white, moving so swiftly that they had the animals in their beaks before anyone could so much as cry out, much less move.

No-one, that is, except the midget, Elcius, for at the moment that the birds dived, as if he were able to sense the instincts of their very souls, he pulled hard at the thongs, causing their revolution to stop and pulling in the mice-laden lures towards his body. As the hawks swerved to compensate for the change in direction of their prey they each must needs pass within an arm's length of the midget, for one split second. That was sufficient. Though the peregrines sped like lightning past his head, each travelling in a different direction, Elcius' disproportionately massive hands moved as surely as if he were picking medlars from the tree.

Snap! Snap!

Elcius turned towards his master, his face wearing a look of grim satisfaction, seasoned with a smile, and in each gauntleted hand he held out a hawk.

'Sire, your falcons I return!'

The Knight beckoned to the handlers to come and hood the birds. He grunted his admiration.

The crowd was less equivocal about its feeling and a cheering burst out on all sides.

'Well caught, Elcius,' called David, laying a congratulatory hand upon the other's shoulder.

'Well done!'

'Bravo, Elcius!'

'Blue blood!'

'Good, good, good, good,' barked the Knight irritably. 'That is noise enough. Now, midget, let us finish that game of 'checs of which you have made promise so oft.'

'Certainly, sire,' replied the gentle-mannered Elcius.

'Clear the floor, save those who are the pieces.'

The multitude pressed back against the walls, thereby leaving a clear space in the centre of the floor. Upon this space the floor had been carefully and exquisitely wrought in the likeness of a board as is commonly used in the playing of echecs and draughts. Each square, being alternately of sea-green or of wax-grey marble, was of a size to be occupied by an human being of adult stature.

'Let the playing pieces come forth as I call,' shouted Elcius above the clamorous murmurings of the crowd.

'Art all ready?'

Elcius began then to call forth the people who were to represent the pieces upon the board, signalling each one to his place.

'White queen — Doratia Ontalox to C one!'

Ontalox smiled proudly as his goodwife strode firmly and determinedly to her position.

'White king — Horatio Ontalox to G one.'

Smiling all around, Horatio paced firmly over to his square.

The rest followed, one by one at the appropriate summons.

'White pawn — Laudacus to A two.'

'White pawn — Hassidicus to F two.'

'White pawn — Ovox to B three.'

'White rook — Zhilincus to C three.'

'White rook — Mormon de Norman to E three.'

'White pawn — Penzard to F three.'

'Black queen — Susan Ashcroft to H three.'

'White knight — Pansard to C five.'

'White pawn — Rodius to D five.'

'Black pawn — Barbara Brown to E five.'

'Black pawn — Sherloch Humes to F five.'

'Black bishop — his Reverence, Michael Chreist, to D six.'
'Black pawn — Raymond Bennett to G six.'
'Black pawn — Mandola Magabutne to H six.'
'Black rooks — Ms O Kanada to E seven and Paddy Delaney to D eight. Black king — Charles Watson to G eight.'

'And I need two more black pawns. Hey you, yes you — the little girl with the horns. Get onto A seven. And you, boy, the bent one -no, not you, the one beside you, go to B seven.'

Hand in hand two children, dirty as coins, edged forward. The boy was slightly crookbacked, being wan of complexion and hesitant of manner. The girl was very small, blonde about the head, with rosy cheeks, and at her temples were two patches of darker skin, smudges of rougher texture than the rest and looking remarkably like a pair of incipient horns.

'There you have it, sire. Is this the position as you remember it? If it meets with your satisfaction then we are at the twenty-sixth move and it is my turn, m'lord.'

'Thank you, Elcius. This position seems meet and right. Where are my advisers?'

Two servants stepped forward, took hold of the immense chair in which the Knight was seated and bore it down to the fringe of the board, setting it down with extreme care so as not to disturb their master's concentration. Once the seat was in its place five advisers came forward from the throng and arrayed themselves around the Knight, leaning over to hold a whispered consultation concerning the progress of the game.

'Where is Antonius?'

'Antonius, sire?'

'No, dolt! Antonius Neale, he was to have advised my play in this frolic with the 'checs versus Elcius.'

'I fear that your Lordship must play without Antonius, for he is not anywhere apparent at this moment in time, sire.'

Baktrian wagged his head in clumsy imitation of his reeve. 'He is not here, sire,' mimicked the Knight. 'He is nowhere to be found, sire, at this moment in time sire! Knowest thou not how to say NOW, fool! At this moment in time!'

David, the reeve, gazed placidly back into the face of his master, knowing only too well when to bide his peace.

'Ah, well. I suppose that I can manage well enough with these five.' Baktrian grumbled, waving a hand contemptuously to indicate his hovering helper-harpies.

'Let the contest resume!'

From the end of the Great Hall the musicians sounded a mighty alarum. Elcius assumed a standing position upon his chair, in order better to survey the board.

'White to move!'

'Move twenty-six!'

'Make thy move, Elcius the midget,' bellowed the reeve, David, who strode purposely from the board as soon as he had completed the ceremonies.

Elcius, his eyes narrowing down to the merest motes of blackness in his large and pallid face, stroked his chin and gazed thoughtfully down upon the players.

'And beware lest thou take all day!' bellowed his opponent.

Elcius did not reply. It was neither from lack of respect nor insolence, but was engendered by the slow perception by the midget of a merry move to play against his master!

The midget scrutinized the Knight. What species of testiness was he in today? Had he not journeyed a full twenty-four hours, all that time going without sleep? Elcius well knew the risk that he was hazarding should he play the combination which he had just conceived.

His attention was distracted by a commotion. The bent boy, who was slightly crooked and twisted to the right, had slipped to the floor, thereby ruining the position.

'Smite that child!'

'But, sire,' protested David, 'perchance he is tired, as are we all.'

'Dost want that I should smite thee, David?' menaced the Knight Baktrian.

Whack! Whack!

'That is better, David. And you, boy, remain standing henceforth.'

'Yes, sire.'

'Do not answer back, you twisted little pig. And stop fiddling with your fid. Put it away! If there is one thing that I abhor above all things in this putrid firmament it is fid-fiddlers!'

The boy nodded ashamedly and slid the fid, a small wooden, pointed gadget in the shape of a church spire, back into its scabbard.

Elcius clenched his teeth and through them spake. 'Pansard — go thence from C five, thither to E six!'

The giant strode slowly to the square of his commission. The move was made!

There was a complete void of soundlessness hanging in the air, heavy as a cloak, as the crowd awaited the reply from their master.

Eli, the Knight, did not hesitate for more than a second. Resentfully he spat out: 'Paddy, thou must needs shift. Get thee hence from D eight to D seven.'

Instantly, smiling as he balanced atop the chair, Elcius made reply. 'Penzard the Wise, from F three get thee to F four.'

The Knight paused for a second to survey the move, then he shrugged and pointed to the comely maiden at H three, the Black Queen, whose rightful appellation was Susan Ashcroft.

'There you are, Susan, my dear. I will be looking for you e'relong. Wouldst thou, prithee, move to G four and give check to that midget?'

The young lady, attired in a fine long dress of velvet and muslin, tripped genteely to the appointed place.

'Here, sire?'

'Precisely there, my sweeting!

'Check!'

'Ha!' retorted Elcius, immediately calling out to Mormon de Norman. 'Monsieur, take thyself from E three to G three, d'accord?'

'Pox on't,' cursed the Knight, beginning to anticipate what was in store for him. Reluctantly he growled out his response. 'Susan, m'dear, I must needs get thee from G four. Go to H five, lass.'

'Press on, monsieur. From G three go to H three.'

There was a groan from the Knight and his retinue alike.

'Susan, canst move once more for me? Get thee from H five to E two.'

The maid smiled and demurely did as she was bidden.

'Monsieur,' Elcius was enjoying himself without reservation by now, jumping up and down upon his chair and pointing vigorously at the negro, Mandola Magabutne.

'Monsieur Mormon de Norman, get thither from H three and smite down that Black upon H six.'

Mormon de Norman did just as he was instructed, felling the black pawn with a cuff with the back of his fist.

'And throw that pawn in the moat,' the Knight shouted in

disgust, for he was considerably disenchanted with his prospects by this juncture.

Desperately the Knight tried to escape the midget's trap. 'Charles! Charles Watson! Move the black king from G eight to F seven, at the double!'

'Zhilincus, get thee from C three to G three,' barked Elcius, going in for the kill with evident relish.

'Chreist!'

'Sire, I am wont to be called Your Holiness.'

'To me, son, you're just plain Chreist, so get thyself from D six, out of the goddamn way, to B eight!'

The cleric shambled away to the square at B eight, muttering into his cassock, in high dudgeon, concerning the rights of clergy and the many respects in which society was becoming very decadent. In particular, what about the morals of the young? What about the lusts of the flesh? . . .

'Silence, your Reverence,' David advised firmly, from the position, which he had occupied, at the corner of the board.

'Zhilincus at G three,' commanded the midget. 'Take thou the pawn, Ray Bennett is the one, which standeth at G six.'

'Paddy Delaney, from D seven takest thou the pawn, Rodius, at D five, And, by the 'bye, cast Ray Bennett, the other black pawn, into the moat also!'

'In that case, Master,' called out Elcius. 'I announce checkmate within three moves!' The midget flung his cap into the air and jumped down from his chair, catching the falling hat, by its large feather, in his teeth and performing a no-handed somersault at once thereafter.

'Master, I would fain give thee check! Zhilincus! Thence from G six to give our master check on F six.'

'Righto! Oy-yoy!' giggled Zhilincus, sliding sidewards from one marble square to the next, like a young child enjoying itself on the winter ice.

'Charlie,' Baktrian sighed wearily, 'Move thyself from F seven to E eight.'

'Mistress Ontalox! Come thee forward from C one, wherein thou hast done little for some while! Get thee, prithee, to C eight and give check to our Liege Lord!'

'May the fee simple take thee, midget,' cursed the Knight.

'Paddy, there is nought for it. Get thee from D five to D eight.'

'And finally, Mistress Doratia, turn the final screw upon our

Knight, Amicus Populi and Keeper of the Cinque Rocks. With due respect, my liege, Mistress Ontalox will move from C eight, to take thy rook, Freeman Delaney, at D eight. Thereby is the checkmate given!'

Elcius raised his hat in the air as a signal of victory and David lifted the small man onto his shoulders, rotating slowly so that the crowd might clearly see the spectacle of the victor and his concluded game.

The Knight Baktrian was not nearly so enchanted with the prospect. He stalked slowly along the front of the crowd, resembling Saint Longinus — tall, strong, twisted, in sandals and still wearing his breastplate — rendering to those from whom he suspected a smile a mighty blow across the shoulders or a knee-punch to the codpiece. Momentarily he paused before a smiling, fresh-complexioned young farmer's wife, thoughtfully tracing the embroidery of her bodice and gazing distractedly upon her rural bumpkin's cleavage.

As if his attention had been cut through with a sword, the Knight spun round and fixed his gaze once more upon the chess game. None of the pieces had dared to move although each and every one of them would rather that they had been anywhere else but right there, right now!

'Where was Antonius Neale? With him I could have won!'

David, the diplomat, agreed at once and vehemently.

Elcius stepped forward and although he was wearing from ear to ear the broad grin of a pleasant victory he added: 'Next time, sire, I divine that you will have your revenge. Henceforth I must be on my guard!'

That would be very wise, shiteloins, agreed the Knight, to himself. A little man has only a limited amount of usefulness in him.

'David.'

'Sire?'

'We have travelled all night,' yawned the Knight, 'and I am tired and needful of some relaxation. Get me a big woman, a giantess and black as Hades.'

'Yes, sire.'

'And David.'

'Sire?'

'Get me an infusion of ginseng.'

'I fear, my Lord, that we have no ginseng within the Manor,

at this moment in time.' David took a cautious step away from his master. 'I, er, mean, we have none now, sire. Perhaps, you would like some Solomon's Seal? I am told that my concoction of that meets with universal favour.'

'Do not tax my patience, David. Art thou a dolt-brain? I want an aphrodisiac, not contraceptive tea! Why is there no ginseng?'

'My lord, I believe Elcius used the last sack of the weed on our recent travels.'

'Elcius!'

'Sire?'

'Thou art running the very risk, small man. Whence went all the ginseng, scurvy-balls?'

'It was used by the men, sire.'

'Really?'

'Yes, sire. I am mindful that I myself used less than a third of the sack.'

'A third, odds sodkins! Put this midget upon a diet of Solomon's Seal! And while engaged thereon let him be given lactuca virusa, the wild lettuce, till he drippeth with women's milk! Give him also a hogshead of snakeroot, a sialalogue which will make his saliva drip until he drooleth like a dotard. Pour into him sudorifics and diaphoretics until he sweats like a cow in labour, drown him with draughts of febrifugious mixtures of herbs — antiscorbutics and macerating infusions until his brow puckers like an old prune, until he cannot hold the sphincter of his bowels and, most importantly, until this fool regrets full dreadfully that he has used up all my ginseng!

'And now, David, get me that maiden. And David!'

'Sire?'

'With tits of steel.'

David did not get time to make reply concerning the prognosis for metallurgical superstructures for into the hall burst a breathless servant — the bumbailiff who was supposedly on duty at the Rock. The man slithered to a halt, prostrate at the feet of the Knight, scattering the 'checs pieces in all directions.

Vlov One-Leg was bumbailiff extraordinary to his lordship, Knight Baktrian, Lord of the Cinque Rocks and so forth. Vlov was the most wonderful opportunity that the lip-serving exercises in humanitarianism ever presented full merrily to a liege-lord — be he ever so over-bearing, hideously barbarous and endowed with the cruellest of cruel tendencies, egad! For any person or persons, be they tyrant or martyr, be they lion or mouse, be they courageous or faint-hearted who would engage into service this Vlov could, without fear of reproach, claim to be centuries ahead of his time in regard to the employment of the underprivileged and down-trodden minority. Such a liege-lord, had he known how so to do, upon taking into his retinue this Vlov, could lay claim to being history's first equal opportunity employer!

For Vlov had many setbacks and disadvantages which made him far from an ideal servant.

As his name suggests, Vlov was missing several things of which the first, and most obvious, was his right leg. Vlov travelled with surprising rapidity by means of a pair of rough crutches, which he had picked up from the corpse of a legless beggar on the banks of Paris's Seine. The beggar, to tell the truth, was floating face down some twenty feet below Vlov when he took the crutches; the beggar having made some disparaging remark about Vlov when the latter had refused to share his meagre crust and having been tipped into France's finest swirling effluent for his roguery.

Vlov was wild-eyed in visage, his hair was grey-white and wispy, being only a fringe about the cranial rim, which stuck out in matted and untidy sheaves of shagginess from the edge of the enormous sock which constantly resided upon his skull in place of a hat. In fact Vlov wore upon his foot several similar socks of the roughest and most pungent unwashed wool, for it was the custom of the Gascoine goodwives to be perpetually busy about the business of knitting socks. Socks were necessary, even ideal, for wearing by the workers at the Rock for they afforded great purchase for the pressing, pushing feet of the straining labourers who strove constantly to budge the ram. Socks were also warm and practical for the hands, for scarves and finally for the headgear of the lower classes.

Truly, such was the rate of sock production that every man, woman, bairn and domestic animal within the confines of Gascoine had a complete set of socks for feet, hands, neck, head and appropriate private parts, in addition to a clean set for Sundays and High Mass days. Furthermore there was a steadily growing surplus of this woolly commodity, since sheep were obliging and plentiful and labour was ever willing. Unfortunately the population had not increased one jot over the centuries of

Knight Baktrian's rule because he was so strict and righteous that whenever a babe was born in Gascoine a man left town.

Nevertheless, although socks were superabundant to the point of crisis Vlov could not be accused of failing in his duties in that regard. At the moment of his entry into the Great Hall, as he careered across the slippery floor, with vestiges of the recent snowfall on his neck and narrow shoulders, Vlov was wearing a total of fifteen woollen socks of varying colours.

He turned his ugly face upward to gaze into the stern countenance of his lord.

Vlov was an extremely ugly Mishite of Latvian extraction. His face was irregular and his right eye wandered aimlessly about in a manner that irritated the Knight, for he could never be sure in which direction this malodorous manservant was looking. On Vlov's right hand only two fingers remained, the others having been lost in an abortive attempt at highway robbery when he was a young man. The missing fingers, trapped in the door, had departed in the escaping coach. The driver had shrewdly taken the measure of the young foot-pad and judged him to be an inexperienced novice, kicked Vlov in the chest, leapt onto the box and lashed the team of horses into a gallop for safely. Vlov had stupidly attempted to board the coach as it raced away; had he not done so he would probably still have had all his fingers.

In addition to his other drawbacks as a servant, there is to be added the fact that Vlov could not speak a word of the King's fair tongue. In order to conduct his duties successfully Vlov had to be accompanied on all occasions by an interpreter, a slow-witted and lazy youth whose only talent seemed to be a miraculous ability to understand the muttering of Vlov, even when the latter was drunk or excited.

Lars was the name of the interpreter, Lars Minitt, and this tardy treasure-house of turgidity trundled into the Great Hall, panting and perspiring, despite being covered generously with snowflakes, in search of his master, the bumbailiff.

If the Knight found Vlov to be distasteful he found the corpulent, effeminate, dirty and disobedient Lars to be beyond the pale, the utmost of Lazars.

'God's filth,' spat out the Lord, sneering down his nose at the two servants, 'what hast thou here?'

Baktrian gazed heavenward in despair, as if looking for an

explanation for these detestable intruders. 'Why art thou not bummin' and bailiffin', Vlov? Do not answer that one. I need not to know. The squire who would keep a steed must be willing to suffer steed-shite! And he who has steed-shite must put up with steed-flies! Just tell me simply why thou art here.'

'Tell, er, him, er, sim-err-ply why thou'rt here,' Lars Minitt slowly translated for Vlov.

The differences between the lingua regis, which was favoured and used to the exclusion of all other tongues and dialects by the Knight and his household, and the language of this ugly Mishite of Latvian extrusion, was a very subtle one. Perhaps this was the reason for Lars being the slowest interpreter in the realm. However, Baktrian had no choice save to employ the man, for what is a bumbailiff when one cannot understand him?

The differences 'twixt the two tongues lay solely within the pronunciation, a distinction that was at that time to be found nowhere else between two such distant types of speech. Consequently it was the very similarity of the vocabularies — almost to the point of precise congruence — combined with fiendish and outlandish switches of the phonetics which made the interpreter's task so formidable.

This, at least, was the manner in which Vlov and his obese interpreter had presented the problem to the Knight at the time of their supplication. When the wary Knight had seemed inclined to dismiss their case as too complicated to be worthy of consideration, and when the Lord had seemed about to disregard Vlov's credentials as a seasoned bumbailiff, the duo had added that a further difficulty lay in the fact that when a word meant one thing in Mishite-Latvian it was apt to mean the opposite in the lingua regis.

The manner in which the pair had made this last plea for the special consideration of their odd philological plight was what had finally captured the Knight's attention and obtained for them their posts. For, while the simple Lars was intent upon explaining to the Knight the antithetical, paradoxical relationship between the two languages, Vlov had been trying, by means of gestures and physical intimidation, to silence his partner, whose babblings he deemed only to be making worse their chances of gaining a station within the retinue of the Knight Baktrian.

As it had turned out, the capering couple had caused the

Knight to burst into uproarious guffawing as a result of which he had decided to engage them on the spot.

'Sire,' continued Vlov, shaking the snow from his sock . . .

'Er, sire,' responded the interpreter.

Gradually the tale was begun, Vlov speaking and Lars struggling painfully through a translation, proceeding so slowly that the latter lost ground with each sentence.

'Some wonderful things will take time at the Pebble, sire,' Vlov explained.

'A calamity, er, has taken place,' Lars interpreted.

'Some rain was rising sporadically then and some conditioners will be soft and warm.'

' . . . at the, er, Rock, sire. The snow is, er, falling steadily now and . . . '

'Some mangle-up of time when none of the idlers will be in some best spirits, you are ignorant, my Liege?'

' . . . the conditions are hard and, er, cold. The sort of weather when all, er, the workers . . . '

'Over somesuch impossibilities some person will go to hesitate, which was scarcely familiar from my ignorance.'

' . . . are in their worst, er, mood, you understand, my Liege? Under these circumstances, er, a thing has come to pass . . . '

'Outside lies they will always hear nothing dissimilar to that afterwards.'

' . . . which is entirely, er, foreign to my, er, knowledge. In fact . . . '

'Some old fatso, sire, absolutely insufficiently young not to be idling outside some loose garment, far from some tickling ewe, flew into their flapping toga except for joining some circle.'

' . . . I have never seen, er, anything like it before. A young, er, stripling, sire . . . '

'They demonstrated without us vapidly, and unlike the very wimps, and with mighty effect, my Lord. That enormous adulterer, some large and muscular giant, straight of spine, fragrant of foot but splay-kneed, left their arrival from some tickling ewe but ran towards, appearing in front at some Pebble, whence everyone who was crazy goes all the time, and has never wished to, for several seconds.'

Vlov paused, looking round at Lars, who was perspiring copiously, holding his head to assist in his memorization. Lars began, speedily for him, to intone the next passage in an attempt to catch up with the narrative.

' . . . hardly old enough to be working in a harness at the ram, slipped from his harness and left the line. I remonstrated with him in forceful manner, but without avail, my Lord. This tiny child, a small and weedy mite with a crookbent back, athletes' feet and pigeon-toes, took his leave of the ram and walked away, disappearing behind the Rock, where no-one in his right mind has gone, or even wanted to go, for centuries, sire.'

'My God,' exclaimed the Knight, not pausing to remark that Lars was improving with practice. 'David, quickly, summon the guard. And get my weapon — no, 'pon reflection of the second kind, give me that fid, boy.'

The Knight stepped across the board and wrenched the pointed object from the grasp of the bent boy. Vlov was gesticulating wildly at his master.

'What dost thou want, now?'

'Not to sing him less, sire.'

'To tell, er, you more, sire.'

'I do not need to hear further. Come, David, we will arm further as we go thither. As for you, Vlov, tell the hindermost part of your tale to Elcius, who will not be coming with us, and to any of the others who may wish to remain for its telling. Come!'

With that the Knight Baktrian exited with great haste, followed by the entirety of his household, saving Elcius the Midget and the servant, clad from head to foot in a multitude of socks, who was ordained to guard the wrongdoer. Thus it was that this quartet — guard, midget, Mishite and interpreter — remained within the Great Hall for some substantial period during which the duo concluded their tale. After ramblings and red herrings, to the snoring of the disinterested guard, Lars limped to the end of the saga.

'Well, I noted his departure in my log-book, although scratching with a quill is almightily difficult with the snow falling so heavily. After that I thought, Good riddance to bad rubbish, and left it at that. Unfortunately the urchin returned shortly and came back to the line, where he stopped and stared at the workers. He just stared at them in a very eery way. I can tell you that I likest it not at all. Then, God have mercy 'pon us all, he began to speak, and he did so, not in the tiny voice of a shrunken little snippet with a back that twists to the left like a bent twig, but in the mighty roar of a great authority, who is angered exceedingly! Well, Lord, I do not mind admitting that I was scared. There was this infant shouting furiously at us as if he was our master, beggin' your pardon, Lord, or something, and behind me the workers were in no mood for listening to some child ventriloquist telling them off about their work. The kid said that they should all stop work. He said that they were stupid to go on pushing a shitty piece of Rock that was so damn big that nobody could move it — unless they were to use dynamite, which was dangerous and would have killed many a fool Irishman from the village 'ere this except for the fact that it had not been invented yet. His manner of speech was so amazing, Lord, that it made my poor old head spin. He said that they should all stop and just take a look behind the Rock to see what he meant. He said that they would find more, and even bigger, rocks back there in such multitudes that no army, be it as large as all of mankind, could hope to move it even the tiniest distance. Well, I can tell you that the workers were mightily irritated by this manner of talking and they began to dispute hotly between themselves, remaining the while in their harness at the ram. I, we, Lars and me, tried to calm them down. Finally it began to look as if there was nothing that we could do. A group of black Scotsmen were intent upon beating this child black, blue and witless — (this Vlov rendered, 'white, green and intelligent') — right then and there, even if they had to risk punishment for leaving the ram in order to do it!'

Elcius applauded heartily, clapping with his widespread palms when Lars had finished.

'Well done, Lars! Well done, Vlov! A capital tale! And waggishly recounted!'

The midget glanced over to the reclining, somnolent heap which had been commanded to guard him.

'And since it seems that I am no longer fettered, let us go and see this miracle which has come to pass. Let us take by the ear this miscreant who has committed the unforgiveable. Having twisted off his lobes let us then forgive him! Hurrah!'

Jumping to his feet the midget raced out of the room, with the one-legged Vlov, and the ungainly mountain of wobbling fat that was Lars, in hot pursuit.

8

CHILD

The snow was falling very heavily by the time Knight Baktrian led his group of followers from the Manor, across the drawbridge and started down the track which spanned the intervening mile down to the Gascoine village work-place at the Rock. He strode at a great pace, widening the gap between himself and his followers, despite the uncertain, slippery conditions of the courseway beneath the snow. He fell to his knees several times, rising at once each time, but only with a great effort, as the sleepless night of travel was beginning to take its toll of his strength.

Behind him the Knight could hear the curses of those who fell and the jeers of those who helped them to their feet. Although he was incensed with anger at what was happening at the Rock, still he made no sound. His lips were bitten tightly closed, the flesh white with the strain. He refused to lose control.

The falling flakes had caused the bright morning sky to darken again, almost to the point of night-time. Instinctively Baktrian looked up, as if expecting to see the appearance of stars in the heavens.

Would that not be a wondrous portent? He remembered as a child being told of a day upon which his grandsire had seen a reddened, full moon at the hour of noon. That same afternoon all the cattle in Gascoine had died, choking upon their own cud!

There were no stars this morning.

His attention snapped back from its brief recreation to the problem in hand. Surely, he thought, he could control a stripling, a mere lad?

Damn these farmers! They had no discipline! They had to

be taught! Kiss and kick, sing and suppress, buy and bribe — he would woo them with a tale!

He would catch this queer fish, which had dared to leave the work-line, with rhetoric. He would bait the line with a red herring. There would be no trouble — and, within the time which a candle takes to gutter, he would have them back, peaceably, to work. These were harmless, gentle people and it would take more than a boy to frighten or inflame them.

Suddenly, because of the falling snow, almost unexpectedly for both parties, Baktrian was upon the assembled workers at the Rock. They were silent. A group of black Scotsmen had left their places at the pushing-ram! They were standing about twenty feet away from their empty harnesses! The vestments of these strange barbarians from the north were tight lineaments, having neither sleeves nor any sort of ruff at the neck, which stretched over their muscular torsoes and bore the legend, GEORGIA TECH.

The Knight had come upon the workers unnoticed. Where was the twisted waif of whom Vlov had spoken?

The crowd of heads now turned towards him, crystallizing from snowy blurs into smudges of faces with white pinpoints of wide-eyes as his eyes became more familiar with the poor light.

'Is this not a full merry morn?' Baktrian bellowed cheerfully, giving the impression for all the world of a genial squire out for his early constitutional. He did not appear to have remarked the fact that the work was at a standstill and that the labourers were away from their posts.

''T minds me well of the volunteer incorporative militia battalion of the Glengarry infantry fencibles to see such a score of kilts out in this darkness,' he continued.

''T minds me of the dark night when I went with those very soldiers to see the salmon speared. For, being proud Scots, they were fine salmon ticklers every one. Large torches of white birch bark were being carried in the boat.'

At this point the Knight waved his hand in the direction of his torch-bearers, who had just caught up with him. 'The blaze of light attracted the fish. And the Glengarry men were wondrous dextrous in spearing.' The Knight paused. When he resumed his voice had risen and he was shouting, his face twitching uncontrollably. 'Now it is your fish-like attention that is attracted by the torches! And what have you been about? Let me see!'

The circle of gathered figures opened to reveal the prostrate and motionless figure of a slim youth, lying in a pool of blood between the congregated feet of the crowd. The Knight took a step closer; he did not need to examine the figure more to know its destiny. 'Those who fight against our sons, our daughters, our sisters and our mothers strike their filthy blows against our Father the King!' he cried.

'And they who are to blame are double-dyed damnable, for they are those who came to us hungry and they cut off the hands of our brothers, yet we gave them corn! We gave them rivers full merry with fish and in return they poisoned our fountains! We gave them the mountains and the valleys, the jugged hare and the scrag-ends of game at our table and received back, to our little warrior, perchance strong drink, perchance trinkets, and without dubiety a grave! The shades of our slaughtered ones can find no rest, their closed eyes see no herds in the hills of light, neither do they see flocks of plentitude in the pastures and the hunting grounds of the dead! Until such enemies are no more we must be as one under that mightiest arbiter whose name is Death!'

The crowd gave ground as the Knight stepped closer to them. He pointed at them menacingly with the fid. 'Mandola! Magabutne! Get these your men hence from here and flay them, in the deepest dungeon. Dost thou hear me, thou black pawn?'

'Yessuh!'

'Go to, then. And, as for the rest of you,' he paused and glanced slowly about him. 'Get back into the harnesses before the Rock starts to roll!'

There was a flurry of movement as Mandola Magabutne led away the assassins of the boy, whose body lay untouched as the rest of the throng scrambled about to fill all the spaces at the ram. The vacant places of the Scotsmen were unobtrusively filled by uncomplaining members of the following which had come down from the Great Hall with the Knight Baktrian.

As Eli, the Knight, turned back to look upon the slain youth he saw that a shadowy figure was bending over the lad's collapsed form. The Knight called out, half recognizing the person. 'Antonius? Antonius? Is that you?'

The figure straightened and stared directly at him, making no sound in return. The Knight looked wildly all about him for the Black King and cried out in a loud voice. 'Charlie, do you see him? Is that Tony?'

Smack! A falcon flew straight into the Lord's face, momentarily blinding him. When he could see again Eli gradually realized that Sarah's arm had fallen across his face.

'Are you still screeching for the missing hordes from your schooldays?' she grunted, opening one eye to look at her husband. 'Who was it this time? Not Tony Neale again?'

Eli did not reply.

9

DEATH

On the afternoon of his undignified demise Dean Smoothe was entertaining three of his colleagues at a discreet and tasteful medical barbecue.

The list of guests consisted of his friend and companion, Dwayne Testes, of Buculo Inseminology, together with his new wife, Anthrax, a bouncy, middle-aged blonde from Biloxi and two interns, each with his sister, girlfriend, wife or mother — Smoothe had no idea which, except that the pregnant one was probably not a sister. The interns had surnames which Dean had forgotten and specialities, which he could remember with ease. The first was a tall, bearded young man by the name of Fidelio, whose subject was infra-radiography and the second man had all the markings of a New York banker — elegant, well-mannered to the point of becoming patronizing, fragrant and slightly portly. The latter was called Eustace and his field, which was at that time quite revolutionarily novel, was masculo-gynaecology, which centres around the treatment of the gestating male.

Smoothe was blissfully content with his current preoccupation, which consisted of cooking eight extremely large slices of steak with the aid of his newest acquisition, which was a barbecue that operated on the same principal as a flame-thrower and was, in fact, one of those peace-time benefits to come out of the assiduous development of napalm during the Cambodian war. Standing eight feet from the suspended pieces of raw meat, Smoothe was directing broad, licking tongues of flame back and forth across them.

It was a wonderful afternoon. The heavens were heavenly

194

and everything in the garden was roses. The ladies were far away at the end of the garden, inspecting the roses. At least, Thelma Smoothe had taken the other three ladies down there to admire her display of hybrids, but Fidelio's pal, the pregnant one, had soon found that the heat was too exhausting for her and she had accordingly retired to a flotation device in the centre of the Smoothes' olympic-size pool.

Inexplicably Smoothe had never been so cheerful. Perhaps, he mused, it might be connected with his imminent fiftieth birthday although that surprised him considerably since he had experienced only misery ten years before at the occasion of his fortieth anniversary. It could hardly be the alcohol, since he was quite used to that.

He could hear the girlish, high-pitched giggles of Thelma and Anthrax. He turned his head, meantime keeping a steady flame on the meat, and gazed lazily over the immaculate greensward. Beyond the pool he could see the babysitter entertaining Bucolia, who was eating the grass at the edge of the hydrangea beds. The little girl looked quite charming in her freshly laundered dress with a golden bow tied around her temples and knotted behind the ears. Bucolia had taken quite a fancy to chewing the lush grass of the lawn, which the gardener allowed to grow to eight inches during the hotter summer months.

'Shall I make us four more whiskies?' called Dwayne, his voice trailing out onto the patio from within the lounge where the cocktail bar resided. Testes had already begun to mix the shots, measuring them carefully and pouring the Glenlivet until the tumblers were full to the brim. Pensively he marvelled at their golden, convex meniscuses.

'Great menisci, these whiskies have,' he chortled.

'I see,' replied Smoothe, having to shout to make himself heard above the roar of the flame-thrower. 'So you've filled them to the brim again, have you?'

'Sure,' grinned Testes, emerging onto the patio with the immaculate round of alcohol.

'Here y'are, Eustace, me boy — that'll put something on your chest and it might even be hair!'

From the house was heard the sound of a toilet flushing. Fidelio's heavy footsteps could easily be made out as he stumbled up from the basement apartment. He paused at the bookshelves in the bar. 'What are those li'l oriental guys, eh? The carvings, you know? They some sort of Chinese stuff, eh?'

'Damn right, Fidelio,' laughed Testes, raising his glass in a mock toast. 'Here's to Dean's Chinese stuff, eh! And here's to the sweet little pile of plunder that each of those tiny stocking stuffers will fetch.'

'I'm not selling,' replied Smoothe smugly.

'Ah, but you just wait until we've stretched you out in the old box and winched your oh-so-weighty remains up on the old catafalque. Then, after we've set that flame-thrower to the blue touch-paper, we'll be off toute de suite to the nearest auction rooms. We'll sell the lot!'

'It's a good job that I know when you're joking, Dwayne,' responded Smoothe, just a trifle testily.

'I'm always joking ol' feller, isn't that what they say 'bout me all over the Institute?'

Whoosh! Smoothe loosed a particularly large sheet of flame, whose loud expiration drowned his reply.

'Are they really very valuable?' asked Eustace wonderingly, turning over in his palm the small carving which he had fetched from the bar while the others were talking.

'Certainly, that one's worth about three grand,' answered Smoothe.

'All in all,' he continued proudly, 'I've collected about one hundred and fifty during the past ten years.'

'Yeah,' interrupted Dwayne, 'you young guys will have to start it sometime. We all do — collecting I mean. Any medical guy worth his salt — and, by God, aren't we all? — has to start collectin' some expensive and appreciatin' stuff before too long. It's the only way to keep the ol' I.R. off your back and to keep the pile that you've earned by the sweat of your brow and your armpits! And it has to be somethin' pricy 'cause yer gonna have a lot to save. Dean has netsukes, like the li'l guy in yer ape-like mitt — be careful now. I've got houses and horses. I've known guys who saved porcelain, paintings and purses, Louis Quatorze of course. The only thing you mustn't collect too many of is women — wives are the devil when it comes to taking away your wad.'

Testes paused to scratch himself intimately. He screwed up his brow, trying in vain to recall something.

'Say Dean, thinkin' of them netsukey doo-dads reminds me of that Jap surgeon you had visiting the Institute. Wassisname?'

'Who?'

'Ya know, that li'l hunchback guy?'

'Oh, Yamaha Zung?'

'Yeah, thassim! Yamaha Dung.'

'Spelt Dung, pronounced Zung,' Smoothe corrected. 'And he was Vietnamese, not Japanese.'

'Yeah, sure,' chortled Testes, singing softly to himself, wearing a wide grin.

'Ding, dong merrily on high, Zing, zong merrily the sky.'

'Hodannah in excelsis,' added Eustace, with a self-satisfied laugh.

'Tell these young fellers about the operation.'

Smoothe slowly shook his head, smiling ruefully to himself at the recollection.

'Aw, go on. You tell it damn fine! An' if you don't then I will. You don't want to hear it botched up d'you?'

Smoothe cleared his throat. Eustace and Fidelio gazed fixedly at him.

'We-e-ell,' Smoothe drawled, starting very slowly, 'you can imagine this small, dignified but, sad to say, extremely wall-eyed oriental gentleman in the operating theatre. Strong hands — efficient — polite — his winning smile turning the dissecting room into a seminary of frivolity, a jostling bran-tub of adulating young votaries of levity gathered about the distinguished, diminutive surgeon. The order of the day is amputation.

'Concentrating on the prosthesis of the procreative organ, Yamaha Zung and his colleagues lean forward over the operating table in a conspiratorial, praeterorgasmic repugnance of uterine brotherhood. Every whispered opinion is weighed, every sanctified phrase is successfully eviscerated. Questions are asked — answers given. Can a prosthetic beget Siamese twins? A topic for a paper there, Yamaha pronounces, but what of the question of primogeniture, foetus in foetu? What of Caesareans, risk of blemishes, harelip and breastmole? A barrage of insolent questions are volleyed at him from every corner. Zung takes a firm hold of the organ. What of the incidence of supernumerary digits? What of Minotaur's ankle, asymmetry of the testes, of Menelaus' kneecap? What about crossed-eyes?'

Smoothe paused and smiled at his rapt audience.

' "Who said that?" snaps Zung, whipping round to locate the evil-speaker. "Yakimoto, shit!" he screams out — glancing down at the objet detaché, which is still in his hand. He looks around the watching interns and says, cool as you please, ''Now, look what you have made me do!'' '

'No kiddin'?' asked Fidelio suspiciously, looking alternately at each of the two older men, who maintained their straight-faced composure for several seconds before disintegrating into a series of choking guffaws, as they both invariably did at the credulous reception of this anecdote.

As abruptly as he had begun, Testes stopped laughing and gazed thoughtfully down into his glass, which was nearly empty.

'I'd bedder gedda fill-up,' Testes grunted, rising to his feet and pausing for a moment to gain equilibrium.

'Doctor Testes doesn't seem too happy on the subject of the fair sex,' remarked Eustace, watching the elder man pass tentatively through the open screen door and disappear again into the bar.

'He's had his knocks,' Smoothe explained. 'You know how it is.'

'Sure,' Fidelio put in. 'It's the same with all them woman novelists, you know, eh? They just gotta take it out on the poor guy ev'ry time. It's like they only god one fuggin' tale, you know?'

'You mean the angst of the treacherous, double-dealing male, who puffs and grunts his way through an infinity of sex acts, always missionary position, which his intellectually superior wife, from her inferior vantage point, finds dreadfully tedious?' asked Smoothe, lowering the flames for a moment in order to turn towards his guests without scorching them.

'That's it all right,' agreed Eustace. 'Tedious interruptus!'

'Well, it sure makes movies,' urged Fidelio.

'Yes, the Canadian School of Shuddering — that pillar of the cinematographic and repertory professions — swears by it,' replied Eustace.

Smoothe changed the subject adroitly. 'The netsuke,' he indicated the tiny statue in the other's hand, 'is a fascinating art-form. You wouldn't be able to guess just how much time it took me before I could find anything as suitable as that to collect. I tried musical instruments, particularly the violin and violoncello, but they were just too bulky. And they collected dust, as well as being too expensive to insure!

'They are Japanese miniature ivories. Most of those which

I possess date from the last century. It is quite a delight in itself merely to track them down. For example, I knew about the existence of that one, from catalogues and antiquarian books, for almost three years before I could get to see it face to face. The Japanese used to wear them fastened to the end of their sashes or belts. The lacquer is called urushiol. Sometimes as many as thirty coats have been applied. It is the sap from the urushi tree — in fact, it's C fourteen H eighteen O two, if you really want to know.'

By now the two young men were beginning to wonder whether they really did want to know. They exchanged an expressive glance.

'The lacquer is mixed with oil and dries very slowly by oxidation. The finished product is polished endlessly with magnolia ash or powdered hartshorn.'

'It sounds like a very time-consuming labour,' Eustace put in, obligingly.

'Nice lawn,' Testes half-shouted as he emerged with another full tray of full drinks, which he carried as confidently and steadily as a churchwarden with an offertory plate.

'I always say — ''Don't seed it, sod it!'' '

Laughing gaily at his own wit Dwayne proposed a fresh toast and then drank to it, wobbling somewhat before sitting heavily down again beside Fidelio. He put his warm hand on the young man's knee and breathed malodourously in the latter's face.

'Them things weren't hacked out by no flint hatchets, matey! In fact, there's more to makin' them things than to brain surgery, and I should know, 'cause I messed up at both!'

He guffawed so hard that he almost fell sideways from the patio bench.

'Them's finely chiselled out, man. They're not bludgemmed — pardon me, blud-geoned out with a quartzite mallet or Onondago chert. No sirree! No cherts for them guys, not Saugeen, nor Selkirk or Vanport. Well, 't stands to reason, don't it? We wouldn't do a trepanning with a hammer made of greywacke!'

'Nor any other paraphernalia from the flint knapper's toolkit,' added Smoothe.

'That reminds me,' Dean Smoothe continued, 'of Sophonisba, the lady of Grecian times who hammered a nail into her hubby's skull. She must have been the first brain surgeon.'

'Bedder lug nex' time,' commented Dwayne, 'maybe nex'
time she'll screw him to death!'

Eustace and Fidelio laughed raucously and appreciatively at
that one. After all there is a sense of relief, of being put at ease,
which comes with beholding one's superior behaving like a drunk
with a risqué line in scurrilous humour.

'You know,' added Eustace, 'here we have anecdotes in the
making. When the hospital holds your joint fiftieth birthday
celebration conference next year I will be able to deliver the
encomium for you both. In it I will be able to recount this
afternoon, with it's witticisms, and I'll say that it just shows
how quick Doctor Testes was, retaining all his faculties well into
his thirtieth year, and all that sort of thing. Yes, I'll say,' he
sighed and exhaled forcefully, 'Testes was quick, always ready
with the lightning riposte, but Smoothe? When Smoothe asked
a question it was *the* question, yes indeed, Smoothe was deep!'

'Perhaps we should exchange a few more epigrammatical
gems, Dwayne. What do you think? Just for the record, since
we know that we're "on stage", so to speak!'

'Yeah, less show 'em tha' we cansssti' put up a good stack
o' sail.'

'After all, you wouldn't want that conference to flop for want
of ammunition.'

'Usually, with those after-dinner speeches you have to keep
watch for the dagger in the back. Perhaps we should resurrect
the Elizabethan tradition, that when a man rises from the table
to drink a toast his neighbours rise with him, weapons at the
ready, to safeguard his flanks.'

'Quite right, Eustace,' agreed Smoothe. 'For that reason, no
toasts at the conference banquet. Just make it a quick and zesty
speech and then wheel out the boar's head, like Judith with the
head of Holofernes on a silver platter with the you-know-what
in its you-know-where.'

'An' Herpes, the winged messenger, god of liars, eh, can bring
on the topless girlies, eh?'

'Hermes, Fidelio,' laughed Smoothe, giving the steaks a blast
from the other side, 'Hermes, you fool! The god of science and
bastard of Zeus, and, in many ways, the Olympian who best
represents our scholarly profession.'

'Ah, so,' agreed Eustace, in a mock-oriental impersonation,

setting down the netsuke, with which he had been fiddling all the while, upon the table.

'Ah, so,' responded Dwayne, rising unsteadily to his feet once more, intending to replenish their whiskies. 'There yer've god the only two words that mean the same damn thing in English and Japanese! Ah, so — here ah go!'

'Can yer gemme an apple, like, you know, from the bowl in the bar, eh?'

Testes rounded on Fidelio, who had spoken, with surprising rapidity, responding in a loud, almost bellowing baritone.

'Boy, I'm just a brain with sexual organs attached. I don't pick fruit!'

'There, now you know,' put in Eustace, who was not usually so free with his well-built contemporary. 'That's it in a nutshell. It's the way of all floss, as the dentist said to the hooker when she tried to get her teeth into his ... '

Drrrinnggg! The telephone from the bar put an untimely end to Eustace's story. Dwayne answered the call, being nearest to the phone by virtue of his glass-filling commission at the bar, on which sat the telephone, disguised as an orange model of a World War II Junker.

Testes addressed the pilot's cockpit. 'Yeah? No, this is Testes. Eustace who? Oh, him! Sure, he's here. Ya wannim? Whaffor? Hey, Eust, the hospital's on the line. C'm'ere, feller.'

Dwayne Testes continued to take the call which was intended for Eustace. It turned out that the kidney ward was hunting for someone to do the day's schedule of ten operations, which had been overlooked by the programme director, who had been in a hurry to leave for Acapulco for the day.

Testes called Fidelio into the bar as well, holding on to the telephone all the time, preventing with an outstretched arm all Eustace's attempts to wrench the Junker from the hands of the inebriated senior physician.

'OK. Hang on, an' I'll ask.' Testes turned to Fidelio and Eustace, covering the cockpit with his palm. 'They want ten ops doin' right away. Kidneys. Dead easy.'

'Give me that phone. They called looking for me, not for you.'

'Wrong, buddy. They were lookin' for you 'cause they couldn't get a hold of Smoothe or me at the Institute. Anyway, I don't wanna work my ass off when I could be eatin' a nice steak, an' drinkin' an' havin' a fun time!'

'Wodda they payin'?' asked Fidelio. Testes spoke down the receiver. 'What's the rate. Whadyasay? Jeeze, I can'd hear. Fellers, shut that damn door a minute. Thad goddamn flame-thrower's drivin' me nuts!'

Fidelio hastily slammed shut the screen door which led onto the patio and then, since the roar of the flaming barbecue was still too loud, with an expression of considerable irritation on his face, crashed shut the glass door.

'Now, wodda they payin'?' he reiterated.

'C'mon,' Testes addressed the person at the other end of the line, 'you can do bedder than that. Three hundred? Each? Ged lost, wadthehell doya thin' we are? Make it five — four seventy-five, an' thad's as low as we damn well go. Don't kid me. Stuff the dick yerself! Ya know damn well there's no-one else around at this time of day. OK. So we's agreed, just a sec, let me ask the guys. No, I don' wanna do it — at that price? You kiddin'? Hang on.'

Testes turned to the young men, who by this time had gathered closely around him at the phone. Neither Eustace nor Fidelio saw, behind them, Dean Smoothe tugging strenuously at the patio door, which had locked itself automatically when Fidelio had closed it.

Taking no notice of the man outside, Testes continued his negotiations.

'OK. I got you four seventy-five per op. Now which of you two tyros is goin'a do 'em?'

'Waddisit?' asked Fidelio.

'You heard,' put in Eustace, 'kidneys.'

'Why don'ya do five each. OK? Thad'll be ... er ... '

'Near twenny-five hun'red,' Fidelio helped him out. 'Don' ya wanna few yerself?'

'Shit, nod at thad price!'

'Right!' said Eustace. 'Get the car. We will take five each and, with luck, we'll be back in time for dessert.'

Eustace strode to the door and turned expectantly back towards Fidelio, as if surprised at the other's dilatoriness.

'What's the matter?'

'I never done kidneys, eh? Do ya, you know, do a fron'al incision?'

Testes pushed the reluctant man in the direction of the door.

'It doesn't madder. Just cut in to 'em somewhere an' see

where ya got to when you're inside 'em, see? Waddya thin' I do all the time?'

'Just a moment,' Eustace had stopped in the doorway, his overcoat half on, and was gazing pensively at Smoothe, who was on his knees, beating against the fly-screen with his fists. Tears were rolling down his face, which was extremely red. Sweat was streaming down his face, filling his eyes and mingling with his tears.

'What on earth is Smoothe doing?'

The answer was, plainly and simply, that Smoothe was choking to death.

All alone, despite being surrounded by guests and indirectly because of the flame-thrower barbecuer in his hand, he was choking out his last few tortured breaths.

For, since the steaks were cooking nicely and nearing completion, Dean Smoothe had taken a large Argentinian steel hatchet and sliced off two small pieces of meat. The smaller piece he had tossed to Bucolia, who had crawled closer, having tired of eating the grass, to watch her guardian at work.

The larger piece of steak he had tried for himself.

Such is the tenuous grasp that mere mortals have upon the spirit of life that it can, at times, take no more than a slight hiccough to loosen their grip irrevocably. While blowing his nose on a tissue and simultaneously throwing a few final flames at the meat, Dean Smoothe had just one such hiccough. The result was instantly to lodge the sample piece of gastronomic delight firmly down his windpipe.

Dean knew the score. He had seen the video several times and had even lectured to medical frosh on just such an eventuality. His colleagues would know the drill, too. So it was with comparative calm that Smoothe briskly crossed the patio, still spitting flame and thereby wilting several innocent rose bushes en route, and tried the handle of the door.

It was stuck!

Smoothe could see the men inside the house, but he could not make them hear. Now he was beginning to panic. How long had he got? What did the video say? Why didn't those three shit-heads see that he was asking them to open the door?

Bang! Bang! His fingers were bleeding and the sweat, hot as acid, was pouring into his eye-sockets. He was becoming dizzy.

Ah, at last! They had seen him. Three faces looked down at him, painfully kneeling before them on the rough patio.

'The door's locked,' shouted Testes. 'Where'd'ya keep the goddamn key?'

Dean Smoothe could not speak because a providential hiccough had rammed a piece of char-burned Canadian-number-one steak down his refined throat.

Instead of replying Smoothe, very dizzy by now, staggered against the wall, turned through one hundred and eighty degrees and collapsed in a heap.

Behind him his frenzied friend and collaborator, Dwayne Testes, was shrieking, 'Quick, for Chrissake! Le's ged round the side of the house.'

However, although he sprinted like an athlete out of the door and around by the side of the house, Doctor Testes arrived too late to do more for his mate than to close the lids of his bulging eyes.

Meanwhile, as Testes panted round the side, Smoothe, leaning against the house, could see the ladies at the foot of the garden. Thelma turned her head in his direction. Her lips moved, speaking to him, and as they spoke they detached into a meteor shower of lip-particles that sped towards him, a kaleidoscopic sprinkle of points of every-coloured light. Her eyes, large, warm, solicitous and etched with mascara, looked softly in his direction. As they looked they grew. And grew. And grew.

What was she saying?

Smoothe tipped forward onto his face. Thelma, turning to Anthrax and the pregnant lady, pointed to the patio. 'I think that Dean has just fallen down.'

10

SMOOTHE EXIT

With the passing of Dean Smoothe the village of Gasville experienced, sightlessly and unwittingly, the turning of the second, and perhaps the most formative, page of the Yukiad.

At the time this change was not apparent, in much the same manner as a boxer cannot determine the moment at which he becomes a southpaw or an embryonic composer cannot tell when he starts to become a genius.

If one were to attempt to pinpoint the moment of change, which one would do as reluctantly as one would if one were asked to specify when a cloud-burst began to rain, then one would perhaps choose to select the meeting of the trustees of the Sorores Mundi Calamity Fund, which took place scarcely two weeks after the demise of Gasville's much-mourned, celebrated, buculo-inseminologist. For when the trustees' meeting fell due it became apparent that its three members each had to offer his apologies for absence.

The trustees of the Calamity Fund had been originally ordained to be Dean Smoothe together with Yukio Kanada and O'Toole Delaney. The last two were unable to attend because it was their feeding time and Smoothe, quite reasonably, could not attend posthumously.

In fact the meeting took place on schedule with Eli Baktrian deputizing, as he customarily did, for the baby boys and with Thelma Smoothe standing in for her late husband.

Smoothe had been in the habit of convening the meetings of the trustee committee, of which he was the only member in attendance, thereat murmuring to himself the arithmetic which described the current state of the now quite colossal fund for

205

the support of the down-trodden, the deprived, the demoralized and the destitute survivors of explosions in Southwestern Ontario, pouring himself three whiskies, signing the minutes and calling his broker to place the latest windfalls that had been collected, house-to-house and condominium-to-condominium, by the Fund's volunteer representatives.

However, on the occasion of this, the last regular and official meeting of the trustees of the Fund, the venue was not the usual Institute of Buculo-Inseminology at nine-one-one Bucolox Drive at WHU; instead it took place in the inner sanctum of the Mayor's chambers.

Thelma Smoothe arrived punctually at nine pm in the new black Porsche sports convertible of which she had that very afternoon taken delivery, right after affixing her signature to the final document which pertained to the sale of the Smoothe residence, the Smoothe yacht, the Smoothe cottage on Lake Winnebago at Port Standard's Happy Holiday Acres and the Smoothe helicopter, which was kept at the WHU Medical Faculty Airstrip.

The sleek black automobile, its trunk replete with the sale's proceeds, in cash, in matching black portmanteaux together with an over-night bag and thirty-four changes of clothes, harmonized tastefully with Thelma's widow's weeds. The weeds in question consisted of a black silk suit of jogging pants and blouse, a black panama hat together with veil and black velvet gloves. Beneath the panama bounced her tumultuous, newly-bobbed hair-do and from head to blackly manicured toe she had lavished a newly imported, expensive perfume entitled Descent.

As she swept into the Mayoral office Thelma smelt, looked and felt, for the first time in years, like a Real Woman.

She would have given the impression of a Real Woman, if there had been anyone present upon her arrival whom she could have impressed. However Eli Baktrian arrived carelessly five minutes later to find Thelma already comfortably established in his padded, patent leather, black reclining-rocking-swivelling chair, smoking a Black Sobranie and reading his blacklist.

Having spent the afternoon at the opening of Gasville's new Armadillo Safari Park, Eli was sporting his agricultural bib-fronts and was carrying five bottles of champagne and thirty-two kilos of oysters — Thelma's favourite food (she had renounced steak after The Unhappy Event).

Eli grinned evilly at the sight of his chic caller. 'Glad yer could come. I thoughd yer'd missed m'call. Here, have an oysder.'

Eli took three oysters from the first bucket and set the other containers down on the desk, dangling the three above Thelma's bright-white, orthodontically perfected choppers.

In his tumescently tight trousers, which were redolent of armadillo excrement, the Mayor smelt like a Real Man.

The committee meeting was adjourned the following morning at approximately three am. No minutes were taken. All that is known of the meeting is that after its conclusion Thelma left for foreign parts — presumed to be Montréal — never to return, and Bucolia Smoothe became a ward of the court, which is to say that, since Eli had by now appointed himself to the Gasville Local Court for Anomolous Events Not Covered By The Farmers' Almanac Nor By 'World Sports News', she went to live in the Baktrian household.

And no questions were asked. Or answered, for that matter.

* * *

Thus it came about that Bucolia Smoothe, upon Dean Smoothe's death the third infantile trustee of the Sorores Mundi Calamity Fund and contumelious fruit of the conjugation of Dean Smoothe's and the posthumously tortured loins of Felicite Sox, came under the guardianship of Eli Baktrian and his strangely begotten wife, Sarah (formerly Delaney, that was).

Although she had not been consulted about the matter, the warm-hearted Sarah was delighted to have her complement of tiny charges increased from two to three.

'Oi'm thinkin', it will be a dandy thing for them boyos to have a sister, don't ya know?' she told Eli, when he brought the baby home for the first time.

'Yep,' agreed the Mayor.

Historians of the Yukiad, while invariably recording the pertinacious prophecies of Grandma Martin, universally show no mention of apprehension on the Mayor's part, concerning the weird trio of which he was, in several senses, in loco parentis.

Perhaps the Mayor was too engrossed with the praxis of his expansionist policies for the town and its armaments industry.

This point of view is upheld by the evidence of several large capital transfers, made by Eli on behalf of Yukio Kanada, O'Toole Delaney and Bucolia Smoothe, from the Calamity Fund to the weaponry manufacturing business, which was discretely enlarged, at this period, to occupy new buildings which were speedily erected in the parking lot adjacent to the seminal cowsheds which Eli had originally appropriated.

At about this time, too, it was noticed that the oracular Grandma was no longer resident in the basement of Martin's Byre and gave every appearance, by giving no appearance at all, of having gone for good. With the old girl gone, she was soon 'out of sight, out of mind' for the Mayor, who never again gave thought to those quaint, horn-resembling shadows upon Bucolia's forehead — although they became more and more pronounced as she grew, but were dismissed as symptoms of some undiagnoseable allergy by the family physician — nor to Grandma M's warning about the winsome, awesome, tiresome threesome.

11

LAKESHORE

What will these children do when I die?

It is foolish to continue calling them children. One is a beautiful, serene and saintly young lady, whose loveliness chills my blood and the other is a handsome and helpless young man. Why do they trust me, allow me to take control of their lives as if I were a doting parent? After all we started on opposite sides. None of the Gang's other survivors so much as gave a thought for the effects. What did I expect? Some of them were simply animals — Pans, Norman, Roddin and the rest of those killers. The murderousness of the Scot and the mercenary were somehow expectable and therefore acceptable, but I have to admit that I disliked the Quebecois from the moment I set eyes on him. There was more to those emigres. There was a hint of culture and sophistication about that duo. In other circumstances they might have evolved into very fine scientists. Instead they, and I, all wasted our time with politics and the panoply of power.

It is pleasant and tranquil by the lake this afternoon. The reading antenna on Yukio's helmet is moving quickly over the page as he reads while I push his wheelchair. He is still engrossed in the lives of Robespierre and his colleagues. This is the largest and most difficult volume that has taken his fancy since he became a vegetable. As we walk Yukio is squirming in his seat with discomfort. This is the recurrent effect of the shrapnel, which was never completely removed. I imagine that the surgeons did their best under the circumstances, but there were such a lot of repairs needed at once. The specialist told Bucolia later that an older man would not have lived. I am sceptical of such intuitive tommy-rot but there is nothing to be gained by asking these fellows to prove their claims — scientific certainty is just not that important. Although for myself I find its presence a great comfort and when it is missing I lose sleep.

As usual, I am holding Bucolia's hand as we three make our perambulatory tour of the lake. I have brought them here to the cottage to escape the summertime bustle of the town. Through our contact I imagine that I can feel the devotion that engenders their trust. I fondly like to think, conversely, that she can perceive my feelings through my touch on that cool, smooth faultless flesh.

Bucolia seems to be in high spirits today. As we strolled she chattered on about her childhood. Often she has been coy with me about the matter of telepathy. She is shrewd enough to surmise that that would fascinate me and today, for the first time, she gave me some actual details.

I have been mulling over possible explanations for the disappearance of this skill. Certainly it is something which Yukio, who was apparently the best of the trio, could benefit from now. I do not understand it. Mundane skills, such as that of being able to ride a bicycle, survive the most calamitous accidents. Telepathy must be different — more like a loan than a gift.

Yesterday Wolf came for a fleeting visit. He does not often see them these days. I suppose that their state depresses him. Nevertheless, he is the only one to show concern.

I wonder whether Wolf will take care of them when I die?

1

CHILDHOOD

From the Baktrian household's earliest exposure to the three babies it was obvious that their presence was causing changes to it in lots of respects.

To begin with, Sarah was so overjoyed to have become a mother-of-three that she fairly blossomed. Delighted with her new meaning to life, after so many years of wishing for babies with Paddy Delaney, she bloomed. She actually changed physically. Even Eli, who was sexually relegated to being a thing of the past most of the time, noticed that her figure, still ample, seemed to become trim and attractive, taking on the smooth curves of a young mother. Her face, it seemed, had something of that radiance and glossy-haired beauty which Eli had only noticed before in pregnant women.

Sarah's new appearance commanded respect with a serene dignity which even the hunchback Mayor felt obliged to respect. She was as tranquil as trees. Even when the nursery was bursting with din, damage and disaster all about her one would have thought, gazing at her calm expression, that all was as quiet as a Bank Holiday Weekend at Port Standard.

It is a mother, evidently, and only a mother, who is privileged to watch the passage of time and to see the minutiae of its effects upon her young. The Mayor was often out on some official errand or other. Therefore it was Sarah, not Eli, who was able to spend hour after summer hour entertaining the trio. She would delight them with the mindless spinnings of an old whimmey-diddle, a rudely carved propellor on a slim shaft, which Eli's great grandfather had originally whittled out of a piece of sumac. It was Sarah who got to while away autumnal evenings, the yellow-red light of the changing woods speckling across her musical score, by playing tunes to the children upon the old harmonium that stood in the entrance hall. She piled them all on her ample lap and let them pull and push the stops while she pedalled. How they giggled to hear the resulting groans and belches that issued from the wheezy old contraption as they wrenched out the Forte or the Diapason, squelched in the Vox Humana or yanked simultaneously on the Viola, the Flute and the Melodia stops. It was amazing to Sarah to witness the harmony that prevailed between the three and the sympathetic manner with which they learned. For example, it was clear from the earliest moments of Bucolia's exposure to the instrument that hers was an affinity for music which was quite out of the ordinary. The little girl was able, before she could even manage to walk, to imitate small passages of music, which Sarah would play for her. Bucolia was especially fascinated with the hymn Amazing Grace and was the master (or mistress) of it — including a rudimentary left hand — before she was two years old.

The liaison between the children was exhibited by the manner in which they absorbed what their mother had to tell or to show them. It was not so much a question of each child being extremely capable at learning swiftly but, and it had precisely the same effect, it seemed as if whatever interested any one of the babies was at once comprehended by the other two, as soon as the first one had got it. Amazing Grace is a very good example of this, for it was hardly a week after Bucolia had become able to play this two-handed ditty that Sarah found all three of the babies — at this time they were scarcely two years old — perched in line along the piano stool in front of the harmonium, O'Toole taking care of the pedals, Yukio the left hand and Bucolia the right. In addition, all three had somehow miraculously picked up the words!

The same thing happened again, about a year later. One rainy afternoon in November, the other two being exhausted and fast asleep, Sarah had chanced to show Yukio a photograph of El Greco's Laocoon. The lad had appeared quite absorbed by its grim lines, being found later on several occasions that day with the book out upon the floor and opened at the El Greco section. Partially hidden behind a door Sarah had gazed at the child. Such was his absorption that she need not have taken the precaution of concealment. She wondered how it was that this ancient master, once an agonisingly sad . victim of rough treatment by life and by the Inquisition, could still be holding rapt the attention of such a baby, such a novice — an innocent, who could not possibly have been sensing the massive cathedral of pain which the pictures embodied. However, Sarah had scarcely shrugged off her strange impressions when she came across the children, just three days later, together in the playroom, working away jointly with brushes and pencils at an enormous sheet of paper on which they had enscribed a series of hideous heads, each quite reminiscent of the Greek genius. The faces were twisted, agonized like those of the lunatics which attracted El Greco so much.

'What are yowse all drawin' there?' asked Sarah.

'Mad men,' giggled Bucolia, who was the best talker of the three.

'Yeff, mammen,' echoed O'Toole. His brother vehemently nodded in agreement.

With rapt attention Sarah had seated herself down silently to watch the sketching children for the rest of that afternoon. They persisted without relent until dinner, which was late because she had been unable to leave the spectacle of the diminutive trio of artists. Later that evening, the children being all asleep, Sarah had brought out the sketches for Eli to see. He squinted at each one slowly, wearing a rather cross expression, which was really the product of inadequate eyesight and of concentration. When he got to the last one Eli looked up at her with a wide grin on his face. Sarah half-expected some dirty joke or at least some dismissive stupidity from her man. The Mayor was not noted for his interest in either babies or the arts.

'Shide, Sarah! So them kids done all this? Well, jeeze, sure beads me where they godden them brains, but hod shid, they did!'

Sarah gave him a breast-smothering, spontaneous embrace, relieved that he was as enthusiastic as she was.

'So them tiny dudes bin copyin' El Gree-eco himsel'! Well, I'll tell yer, Sarah, maybe they takes after granpa', he was kind'v ardisdic. He useda tell me, when I wuzz a kid, thad music an' ard are th' thoroughfare of mankind. Sonny — he allus called me thad — Sonny, he useda say, if yer only can draw, pain'

or play some goddam instrumen' when yer growed up, then
yer'll meed all sords o' folks. An' Sonny, yer'll nod be meedin'
'em in th' streed with yer ard 'n music, yer'll be meedin' 'em
in here — an' he useda poin' t' his ol' heart'n' give me a grin.'

Eli sighed, shook his head and turned away from the drawings
to turn on the radio. The couple gazed silently at each other
and Eli added, 'Too bad I didn' take th' ol' guy's advice.'

Between them, unheeded as each watched the other, a phone-
in dialogue from Radio GAS960 continued. ' . . . I wanna ask
you the inevidable quession. Whad aboud my future relations
and my prospecds in business?'

'I'm glad you asked that question, Peter. So, I see you as
a business man. Am I right?'

'No, 'M'in farming.'

'Yes, that's what I see. And you're doing (spoken tentatively)
quite well?'

'Well, 'm nod workin' righd now.'

'Ah, but I see lots of work coming to you in the near future.
Yes, I think I see you on a farm. Yes, it's a farm. I can see
you running through the fields of wheat.'

'Corn!'

'Ah, maybe you're right, corn — yes, I see you running . . . '

''Ve only god one goddamn leg! God th'other caughd in th'
bailer, thas why I losd th' farm! I don' thing yer damn
predictions are no damn good. Farms, pah! I losd m' goddamn
place to thad sdinkin' Trinomial shid, an' if yer ask me yer jus'
a f . . . '

Eli switched off, scowling and quickly stomped out of the room
to the phone in the front hall.

Sarah knew what Eli was doing and to whom he was phoning
without having to eavesdrop to find out. He would be calling
Preston Pans, or if not him then Penz or Zhilin or Norman or
one of the thugs. Through the open door she caught the phrase,
'Yep, ged his address. Sure. They'll have id ad th' goddamn
station. Bud ged id! Beads me how they led thad crap oud over
th' air, haven' you warned them enough? Well, do id again!'
And with that remark Baktrian had slammed the phone down.

These irate phone calls to the rest of the Eleven, late at night,
at weekends or otherwise in the middle of the family's rightful
time for Eli's attention were becoming more and more frequent.

This was a further change that was taking place within the

Baktrian house. For Sarah could sense the latent violence behind the calls.

She could detect in her man's tense attitude the aggression which he was spending upon the rest of the world. At home he plainly tried his best to leave the rigours of government behind and to become the conscientious, cheerful and careful father. She did not pry into the activities of the Gang of Eleven but it would have been impossible to ignore the presence of such tell-tale signs as gasoline cans, grenades, automatic weapons and crow-bars, all of which she had seen, at one time or another, incongruously stacked within the trunk of the Mayoral limousine.

At the early signs of the violent undercurrents associated with the Trinomial Plan Sarah had tried to divert her attention. In an attempt to avert the incipient alienation which she was beginning to feel towards Eli she had thrown herself into such projects as the decoration of the old, small bedroom at the back of the house.

Sarah decided that this room would be ideal for Bucolia, who could not share with her brothers forever.

'To be sure, she may be but a mite today, but Oi've a mind that she'll not be staying that way forever.'

As a result one day she brought home several patterns of pink wallpaper to show to Bucolia, who was supposed to choose her favourite for her new bedroom. Not a one to do things by halves, Sarah had fifteen rolls of pinks to select from and a similar number of blue rolls for the boys, who could not be expected to stand by while their sister's room was given a new décor without having their room, which the trio had formerly occupied, receive the identical treatment.

'A lick o' th' paint, and a smidgeon o' th' love don't cost a pund. But they's th' way to th' heart of me babies,' she confided one day to the deserted house, which had no intelligent reply to make.

When Sarah showed the choice of wallpaper patterns to the two boys they began by entertaining themselves unrolling the paper and laying the strips out on the floor like a carpet. Yukio lay down on one roll, whose pattern consisted of large, blue maple leaves and giggled while O'Toole rolled up the paper with Yukio inside the roll.

'Lessave thissone, maw!' they chanted in unison.

'Thissone, thissone, thissone!'

'Ah, now, look at the mess youse made for me, an' me havin' to take back to the store them rolls Oi don't use, to be sure.'

However, her mild reprimand was, as always, accompanied by the broadest of understanding smiles.

Sarah did not trouble to show the boys' choice or, in fact, any of the blue rolls when she set about helping Bucolia select her choice of wallpaper. Much to her surprise, however, Bucolia displayed no interest and did not even attempt to look at the treasures which her mother brought into her room. The little girl just gazed out of the window, behind the back of Sarah, who was holding the choices of pink patterns, one by one, up against the wall to estimate their effect.

'Don't this one look so beauteous, bedad, 'twill make a saint weep.' No reply from Bucolia. 'An' what about them darling little divils? Don't yer think them's the prettiest flowers?'

No reply from Bucolia.

Eventually Sarah realized that her audience was inattentive. She was rather disappointed with her little daughter, who was usually such a good friend.

'Hey, you little miss! Come on now an' pay attention. Why am Oi supposed to think that raisin' youse is such a joy. Oi'd like to know. Such a privilege, such a miracle, Oi'm thinkin'! If yer don't think that havin' me for yer mother is worth a fig — well, maybe Oi'm thinkin' the same way about yerself!'

To Sarah's amazement Bucolia looked calmly up at her and replied with a smile. 'Mom, I want the blue maple leaves, too, please.'

'Well, stap me jiggers! Why did yer not say so? An' me thinkin' that yer didn't like them colours.'

So that was the manner in which the decorating turned out.

Apparently Sarah did not notice that her daughter had chosen a pattern which she had never been shown. This inexplicable tale may be apocryphal, of course, but it is quite well authenticated in the sense that even today visitors to Baktrian House can still find the two blue-decorated bedrooms in their original maple-leaf-forever glory. Just inside the room which once belonged to Bucolia hangs a plaque which relates this tale of the telepathic children's choice.

A similar occurrence happened in the spring, about eighteen months later. By this time the Mayor's 'eccentricities' were developing to the point of noticeability, of which more shortly, and Sarah was alarmed and desperate to the stage at which she was considering separate beds and perhaps even separate existences. The upshot of the widening rift with Eli was to draw her closer to the children, who made better and better companions as they grew. As yet they were still not attending school. In fact, Sarah found that she needed their presence like a drug, like an addiction, so that when Eli, who was trying as best he could to maintain his responsibilities and to be a good father, despite an ever more demanding schedule of official or corporate duties, found enough time to take the kids swimming at Port Standard or fishing at a provincial park Sarah found herself resenting her temporary deprivation. Later she was to come to resent these trips further when, as they got older, Eli would take the trio hunting, sometimes using goshawks and peregrines or black eagles or, worse still, sometimes using small arms, gas-shell launchers and grenades, whose origins she could not guess, although she suspected Zhilin and his unshaven friend, Penz.

The incident took place when Sarah decided that it was time to give her children each a garden of their own. By now they were no longer toddlers but, rather, small people. Who knows when that happens exactly? Anyway, articulate young humans was what they were, which will serve as a rough estimate of their age. It is true that at this stage O'Toole was a leading contender for membership, and even official office, in the A.A.A.A. (the All-American Autists' Association, that is). Nevertheless, even O'Toole could make himself well enough understood and the other two were as fluent as Sarah herself and, in addition, they could do one thing to which she could never bring herself. They could curse like Eli.

Sarah had picked out three small plots right beside the south-facing wall of the barn. This was a place sheltered from the wind and rain, while catching the sun, and the soil was very nourishing for plants just there, because of the ample manuring which it had received, intentionally as well as inadvertently, over the seasons. She cleared the ground and turned over the top-soil several times, revealing fine black earth replete with worms, and then called the children, who were climbing in the nearby orchard, to come over to her for a surprise.

'Oi think its well nigh the time for youse to be growin'

somethin'. To be sure, if yer niver grows nottin' then yer niver knows nottin', as yer man used to say. So Oi've marked out for youse the daintiest little gardens right here, d'yer see?'

Sarah indicated where she had affixed signs bearing their names to the wall of the barn over their respective plots.

'Tis the flowers with which youse goin' t' start, don't yer think that's a dandy ideee?'

'Aw, mom, I'd sure like some flowers of my own,' Yukio replied enthusiastically.

'Me, too!'

'Me, me too!' echoed O'Toole.

'Well, look yer in my palm here,' continued Sarah, 'Do you know what these little divils are?'

The children crowded round but, of course, they had never seen seeds before and had no notion of what they were. They shook their heads.

'These is seeds, to be sure. These ones is flower-seeds. But in this world there's every kind of seeds — why, there's cow-seeds, there's cabbage seeds, there's tomato seeds and there's even man-seeds.' She looked round at her audience and gave them a sly wink.

'What do they do?' Bucolia asked.

'Flowers grow from these seeds,' responded Sarah. 'All we have to do is to put them in the ground and water them and soon they'll produce the nicest flowers.'

'If you put man-seeds in the ground will they grow into men?' asked Yukio.

Sarah laughed, and blushed. 'Now let's get to the workin',' she replied, without addressing his perspicacious question.

'Oi've the little darlings of some seeds right here in me apron pocket,' she began to extract the first of a series of small packets, laying them out in a line on the ground. 'These little divils is every one an annual ... '

'What's an annual?' O'Toole butted in.

'They're the poor wee chappies that can't last it through a Canadian winter — so they die off and have to be replaced next year. But they make the best show, just look at them pictures, d'you see. And best of all, next year youse can all try some other types of flowers in yer garden. So, now, what's it goin' to be? Just look at them pictures now an' tell me which yer fancy. Oi've got the petunias, zinnias, candytufts — an' a fine display they'll make to be sure — pansies — them's bright-eyed little beggars, eh? Oi've got nasturtiums, calendula an' antirrhinums ... '

'Yeah, yeah, the snap-dragons! Oh, please, snap-dragons,' the children chorused simultaneously, jumping about and clapping their hands.

'The snap-dragons. Wha ... ? Oh, yer meaning the antirrhinums, is it? Why youse crafty waggers had me goin' for a moment there, I dare say. Snap-dragons is it?'

Sarah picked up the packet of seeds from the front of which stared out an assortment of ferocious flowers with their mouths opened snappishly and their stamens stamenning with dignity, their pistils perky and their sepals separated. But nowhere on the packet did it say that 'snap-dragon' was an occasional epithet for an antirrhinum. No, no, Sarah was wrong, here it was in small print on the backside of the packet. Therefore Sarah shrugged, a trifle puzzled perhaps, and handed out the trowels with which the children were to plant their chosen seeds.

Strange to say, however, that there is no suggestion in any version of the Yukiad that the kids had the slightest inkling of how to read. But let us not make a mystery where none ought rightfully to exist, although the incident is a further illustration of the harmonious, virtually telepathic, union within the relationship which the Baktrian children enjoyed from an early age.

One last example of this unanimity is afforded by their first exposure to the far away animal kingdoms. This took the form of exploring glossy, coffee-table picture books containing photographs of many of the wild species of Africa. For example, they would sit together on a white-outed, blizzardly day, when school was closed, and they would look at and discuss the relative merits, the characters and characteristics of the animals of the Serengeti, the creatures which live in the kopjes — the austere, flaking granite rocks of that region. When Bucolia discovered that the minute guinea-pig-like hyrax was the constant prey of the Serengeti eagles she burst into floods of tears, and all three sat there bawling mightily and cursing the black eagle vociferously. On the other hand, when O'Toole cast his vote for the bird-slaughtering, pointy-eared caracal — a gymnastic cat, which plays havoc by leaping six feet into the air and sending some poor bird, which he has been stalking, to oblivion with a blow of his claw-filled paw — the other two. without a moment's pause agreed with him. What a lovely, sweet pussy! Similarly their collective unity threw up several more unanimous animal opinions: the harrier hawk was such a nerd, despite his double-jointed legs, because hawks were meant to be princes of the air, not ground-grovellers; they preferred the cliff-springer to the pancake-tortoise, because the former stood out proudly on the hill-side in their picture-book, while the latter could scarcely be seen as it cringed in a cowardly fashion in a crevice, the meat in a rock sandwich; they favoured the gecko over its predator, the tiger-snake for, although the latter was prettier, none of them could bring themselves to like snakes very much and finally they dismissed the puzzle of whether or not they liked the wrinkle-lipped bat after straining their eyes, with the aid of a magnifying glass, to detect the wrinkles upon a specimen which was photographed in very dark shade, hanging from one of the candelabras of a large succulent called a euphorbia.

At the end of the book was an impressive picture of two noble, gleaming, proud — and completely naked — Masai, a man and a woman, both very tall and dignified. At this photograph they gazed in silence. It was replete with things which they had never seen or suspected to exist before. It was not necessary for them to put their thoughts into words; as usual they were thinking the same thing.

Notwithstanding Sarah's steadily increasing, all-consuming preoccupation with the children and their growing curiosity concerning Masai genitalia, an inquisitiveness which led the children at an early age into the scientific, mutual organ investigation during the course of which the three agreed fervently that the female body was much more interesting, and far less hideous, than the male, there was not one of the family who failed to notice the encroachment of Eli's 'eccentricity'.

In the beginning it manifested itself in little more than the occasional day-dream. The children saw no more than this, except that perhaps, had they been older, they might have noticed the intrusion of several archaic exclamatory turns of phrase such as 'Pox on't!' and 'Avaunt!' which increasingly crept into the Mayor's everyday speech. Sarah noticed more of this because it showed itself during his ramblings, which were a frequent concomitant of nightmares. These were the familiar nightmares in which Eli cried out, enquiring the whereabouts of some long-lost school-friend or relative. Sweating copiously he would rise up in his sleep, not actually sleep-walking, but rather raising himself on one elbow and staring sightlessly straight at his wife.

'Where is Sylvia?' Eli demanded belligerently on one such occasion.

'Who is she?' murmured the somnolent Sarah.

'Every swain admires her,' confided the Mayor, sinking back onto the bed, pulling the corner of the sheet up to his mouth and nagging at a corner of it with his teeth.

'I sure don' know where t' find them Mennonide chicken flippers,' he added, immediately collapsing into a fitful sleep, leaving Sarah to muse over his remark. Later, simply by asking him over breakfast, she was told that in the nearby Mennonite villages, when Eli was a boy, the outstanding event of the year was a grand sale and alfresco chicken-bake. Everyone came from miles around to buy pastries, handicrafts, tools and animals from the Mennonite community. The main street would be cleared and down the centre a couple of dozen metal barbecue pits would be set up over which the chickens would slowly bake, each one held between two wire-mesh plates which had two handles at the corners and were laid over the flames. Every ten minutes two men would run down the length of the row of chickens and deftly, one by one at great speed and with superb dexterity, they would flip over the chickens in order to prevent the meat from becoming charred and burnt.

Sarah nodded with comprehension as he recounted the spectacle of the sprinting chicken-flippers, amazed that what could seem so eerie in the middle of the night could be reduced to such a commonplace event by the light of day.

'Ah, surely we'll take the kiddies to see them flippers one of these foine days, bedad.'

On another occasion Sarah awakened to hear Eli murmuring a tale to himself, speaking at times in the first person and at other times as narrator or as the object of his search.

' ... Th' limousine redurned, bringing th' kids home,' Eli said very quietly, almost a whisper, spoken as from the depths of the deepest sleep. 'Methought it would be Stanius Ovox at the wheel. I went forward thither to meet them. "Get thee down, my good children and embrace thy father" I commanded unto them, and down they dutifully alighted, even as they were bidden. Embracing them in turn I happed to look upward, glancing a glance at the ostler at the wheel. Behold, it was none other than Antonius Neale, whom I have sought far and wide this ten months. "Antonius, Antonius Neale, old friend" I gave him gladsome greeting. Sending home the young ones I climbed up on the box beside my old friend and bade him tell me whither had he disappeared this long time. He sat there only — slouchy, grouchy-quiet — with his stringed instrument beside him, which minded me well of the many times when we had whiled away an evening with the playing of the sackbutte, the cymbals and the viol-de-gamboyes. "Wilt thou play?" I enquired of him, but he answered only with a listless "No". I was much disappointed, I can tell thee, but I didst not let it show, starting instead the engine and offering to deliver him safely to his home again. "Dost live in the town of Gascoine?" I asked of him as we journeyed thither. He made no reply that I couldst hear. "Art thou married to a goodwife?" I persisted. There was a long silence and then, drawing out the longest, saddest sigh, he indicated to me that I should stop. As he stepped down he looked long at me and made reply "I do not know!" then, turning, walked away. I have not seen him since, 'though I sought him at the 'checs match.'

This last remark surprised Sarah, who could vaguely remember Eli recounting to her a vivid chess-game nightmare, but that had been some years before. Overwork, she thought to herself, too much overwork; it was confusing his mind, apparently. She was not surprised, although a small cloud of incipient sadness hovered over her warm heart at the thought, for how could a decent man engage in all this incomprehensible Trinomial business without it damaging him? She had resentfully watched her man harden and sometimes, when she did not despair of him altogether and abandon him to his lot, Sarah thought that if only she could somehow get Eli free from that evil little mathematical dwarf, that wretched Elsquaird, that she might yet rescue him from the soul-hardening, spiritual plaque with which the machinations of that wicked midget were embalming the Mayor. He had gone into politics to help people, she reflected, and now he was hurting them. Even torturing them, she suspected.

2

LUST

The children aged steadily, as they will inexorably do, and were ten years old when Sarah found out about the Mayor's ultimate mediaeval mannerism. She caught on to the secret from a chance remark of Doris Ontal.

Doris had inadvertently let slip the fact that she was finding it increasingly difficult to find secretarial, single girls for work at the Gasville Town Hall, who would submit themselves to the F.A.D.S. test. The test was serious business, despite its sounding like a fashion quiz. It was a medical screening test designed to detect the presence of Fractal Armature Disease Syndrome, a fatal disease which had been discovered about a decade earlier. It had originated in Honolulu and was a viral strain which was transmitted by such intimacies as coital coupling. Such was the voracity of this epidemic disease, which had spread first into California and then travelled east like wildfire, that it was not uncommon for employees of attractive young ladies to ask that they should take the test as a pre-condition of employment. Indeed, such practice had become virtually mandatory in the show business profession, the fashion world and in the high-level executive environs.

Therefore Doris's remark was hardly unusual and might have been taken to demonstrate simply that F.A.D.S. had encroached slightly further down the social ladder. Nevertheless, for some intuitive reason Sarah had pressed the other woman mercilessly to find out more. The scene had ended with Doris in tears (fortunately Horace Ontal was not there for had he been he would have been enraged to see his goodwife so abused) confessing the whole story.

225

This tale directly concerned the Mayor, Doris had said, 'Such a great man, but a bull with the girls.'

As Doris explained the facts Sarah clarified and brought up to date her own conception of her man and his 'eccentricity'.

During their married years Eli had been resorting increasingly to the verbiage of a strip-farming, feudal landlord cum Squire of the Manor. Possibly this was the influence of the Trinomial Plan, which did indeed base its agricultural operations upon the European strip-farm-cycle method of the Middle Ages. However, there was nothing old fashioned about its profit margin or its rate of expansion. Nonetheless, Eli had apparently taken to stalking the corridors of the newly-enlarged Gasville Rural County Town Hall, cornering isolated young secretaries and falling upon them to have his seigneurial, Squirely Will.

As usual, it was Elsquaird who had put two and two together. He had observed the Mayor, a gaunt stalker wearing a Napoleonic shako on his head and carrying a lance-like object, which turned out to be an Indian atlatl, a device formerly used for launching thrown projectiles such as hunting spears, regularly set off at coffee-break time to walk the halls. Confronted with any young piece of femininity the aging Mayor would playfully lift their skirts with his atlatl and make some jocose remark.

Possibly the Mayor had struck lucky in his first few essays of lordly lust, but soon word came back to Elsquaird and the other executives of the Gang of Eleven — Pans, Zhilin and Penz — and the word was 'complaints'. Girls had to be bought off. Other, more compliant ones, had to be found and their whereabouts at coffee-break times carefully organized and monitored on a large map of the building, which Elsquaird supervised, covered in significant coloured flags which indicated the location and cooperativeness of each nubile maiden in the municipal employ. Soon Elsquaird realized the danger to the Mayor from F.A.D.S. at which point he instituted the testing and added the outcome of the test to the information carried by each coloured flag. Girls who were F.A.D.S. carriers were dismissed at once, with a disability compensation and the demand, reinforced by threats, for absolute secrecy. Every flag indicated clearly whether the girl's test had been conclusive or not. The test was reckoned by the medical profession to be eighty per cent reliable but, based upon calculations made using the statistics which appeared in the *Lancet* and other professional

journals, Elsquaird concluded that the reliability could not
exceed thirteen per cent. However, what else could he do? The
Mayor must be protected at all costs since he was the personality
whom the people respected. Eli Baktrian was a much loved man,
in several senses, and was indisputably the only figure-head who
could successfully represent the Trinomial Plan to the populace.

Elsquaird, while confident that his intellect made him essential
to the Gasville project, harboured no delusions concerning just
how long the set-up would last if the boss was a midget!

Therefore, whatever the level of reliability, the F.A.D.S. test
had to be administered conscientiously and discreetly. The
details were taken care of by Dwayne Testes, who could be
depended upon, for a price. A high price, in fact.

There were also the fruits, of course. The fruits of these
corridoristic conjugations of corny concupiscence, the mediaeval
metaphor of Mayoral lust. In other words there were bastards
— lots of little bastards — who had to be taken into care. Their
semi-reluctant mothers certainly did not want them, for one can
buy only so much cooperation and Elsquaird did not want the
victimized young women to spill the beans. It was arranged that
the horde of bastards would be put into the custody of the Sorores
Mundi Calamity Fund for the downtrodden, the deprived, the
demoralized and the destitute survivors of explosions in
Southwestern Ontario. To accomplish this Penz, Jaime
Laudenklier and Stanley O'Vayshun had to fabricate a series
of loud, but harmless, explosions — one for each new bastard.

Meanwhile the Mayor, oblivious of the major operation which
was woven about his web of copulatory caprices, continued to
have his way, every day, in deserted corners of the Town Hall,
in which he would chance upon likely lasses as he shuffled along,
sometimes hauling with him the metal-detector, which he had
picked up at the liquidation sale of a Trinomial farm. Sweeping
slowly from side to side, Eli would inch his way along the
carpeted floors, picking up dimes and pennies which had been
distributed with meticulous care by Norman the Mormon,
Horace Ontal, Sid Ra'in and Roddin. Just the top of his head
would be visible to the sacrificial maiden, who would be watching
the Mayor's approach as she waited her turn, according to
Elsquaird's instructions. The girl would study the nearing shako,
as it nodded from side to side.

Elsquaird was supremely satisfied with the manner in which

he had careened the hull of his leaky craft, tarring up every gap from which a whisper of scandal might escape. Inconspicuous gifts from the Trinomial Plan to the Calamity Fund saw to it that the dozens of issuing bastards did not cause trouble.

However, being a man unaccustomed to the making of mistakes, Elsquaird did not notice one, not even a sizable one, when he made it. He did not question a second time the advisability of collecting under one communal roof all the off-spring of his Mayor's dalliance. Without thought, Elsquaird ordered an extension to the Sorores Mundi Calamity Home and as a result an entire new and spacious wing had been built (this was seven years before Sarah had learnt the truth from Doris, and at the time she had given it no thought whatsoever) and into it these special individuals had, one by one, been placed for safe-keeping.

The solution effected, the Gang of Eleven executive breathed a sigh of relief. Now, so they thought, they could relax.

3

TELEPATHY

Teenage is the best of ages and it is the worst of ages. It brings with it more stirrings, startings and changes than the mere outcrop of pus-crested, pimply facial suppurations. It brings more than suggestions of stubbly chins, foul breath and sweaty corporeal curvatures. It heralds in the urges for which the means are still denied.

In the case of the Baktrian children this did not mean sex!

In fact they progressed into the senior year of their high school careers, which were exemplary and identical, all three, without the slightest taint of physical urges. That is not to say that they did not have the normal, acute awareness of the bodily changes, needs and suggestions. It is probable that the cohesion of their unusual trio immured them against the intrusions of their contemporaries for much longer than is customary for a Gasville teeny-beany.

Of course, with the development of their faculties had come responsibilities. In fact, predominant among these were their positions, which they assumed with Eli Baktrian to advise them, as the members of the Board of Trustees of the Sorores Mundi Calamity Fund for the downtrodden, the deprived, the demoralized, and the destitute victims of explosions in South-Western Ontario. As members of this board they had encountered a steady, small but significant stream of unfortunate cases over which they had to arbitrate. Particularly touching, for example, they found the cases of babies, apparently abandoned as the result of some devilish detonation. Such cases happened regularly every few weeks.

Perhaps it was this, their role as benefactors, that caused the

229

early maturity in Yukio and his two siblings. This is not to say that they developed into morose, overbearing, tense little calculus nerds, for example. In fact, during the lessons on mathematics, science and natural philosophy, which Professor Elsquaird had kindly volunteered to give to the trio, an intellectual regime which had begun when they were five and had continued — clandestine from the viewpoint of (and therefore kept secret from) the Board of Education — to the great benefit and delight of both teacher and pupils, he had deliberately encouraged his young charges away from nerdiness.

'Before we start with our equations today, kids,' Elsquaird would commence, 'let us conjugate that very important verb — "To be a calculus nerd". Here we go, all together, no slackers!'

And they would all chant.

'I am a calculus nerd,
You are a calculus nerd.
He, she or it is a calculus nerd.
We are calculus nerds,
You lot are calculus nerds,
They are all calculus nerds.

I'm not a calculus nerd,
You may be a calculus nerd,
Person, person, person may be a calculus nerd,
But we are not calculus nerds,
You're all calculus nerds,
And they are certainly calculus nerds.

But I will never be a calculus nerd,
You can't help being a calculus nerd,
He, she or it will always be a calculus nerd-person,
We will never succumb to the nerdiness calculorum,
You lot will never escape from the calculus nerds,
But neither will they fail to be ensnared by the
calculus nerds.'

And so on. For ten minutes at the start of each lesson they would purge any recalcitrant proclivities which might encourage, foster or otherwise nurture nerdiness.

As a result they were all normal and clean as a whistle, free from psychoses or complexes about their past or their future. These three became thus very close approximations to the proverbial blank slates upon which Life is attending in the wings to scribe its Holy Writ.

Returning, chauffeured by the Mayor, from a Sorores Mundi Board meeting they would often resort to cheerful singing, which testified to the mature and light-hearted, in an adult some would say 'laid back', approach which the children took to their challenging responsibility.

> 'Sorores Mundi Calamity Fundi,
> Fish on Friday,
> Church on Sunday.'

They were not entirely spiritual to the extent of completely disregarding their bodies and the alterations therein and thereon. In fact Bucolia, and her brothers, were particularly proud of her already-large and still-developing breasts. On lazy summer weekend afternoons the trio would repair to the hay loft and there they would recline together, Bucolia chewing some blades of grass while Yukio and O'Toole suckled a breast apiece. Occasionally they would help each other masturbate, more out of scientific curiosity than from desire.

Even as Bucolia was becoming womanly, so the boys were growing. Yukio, quite unusually for one with his semi-oriental features, had grown to be about a head taller than the stocky, broad-shouldered, barrel-chested O'Toole. Yukio was even a shade taller than Eli who, being a hunchback, was gradually curling like a leaf with old age and was therefore shorter than he had been in his youth. Both the boys had twisted backs, although not as much as their father, and it would not have occurred to anyone to call the boys hunchbacked but they might realistically have been termed 'twist-backs' for Yukio's spine was twisted so as to turn his shoulders fractionally to the left in relation to his thorax. Similarly O'Toole's abdomen was wrung a little round to the right.

Neither boy took his infirmity to heart.

As Bucolia developed, her face had become serene and maternal. Her skin was olive, seeming almost radiant and positively captivating to those unused to seeing this Byzantine type of beauty. Her brow was still adorned with the two shadows at the temples, which now gave her appearance an aspect of further mystery and allure but which, when she was a small child, had reminded the casual observer of a pair of incipient horns.

On those torrid afternoons they would lie in the hay, moving as little as possible while indulging in a variety of guessing games. Their favourite was simply to guess the number which was in the head of one of the others. To an outsider there would have seemed to be very little point in this exercise; indeed, they were almost perfect at it.

'One.'

'Yes.'

'Two.'

'Quite right.'

'Seventeen.'

'Yep.'

'Fifty-nine.'

'Damn, you cheated!'

'No way!'

'One hundred and twenty-three.'

'Yes.'

'Bucolia always picks primes.'

'Three to the power sixteen.'

'Neat, eh?'

'Who'd ever think of exponents?'

'The natural log of the inverse hyperbolic cosine of point six six recurring!'

'Hot stuff, man, that's the best you've ever guessed. I think we're improving.'

The identities of the individual speakers are unknown and quite irrelevant, because when it came to this game — or, indeed, to any intellectual skill — Bucolia, O'Toole and Yukio shared the same prowess. As with their tastes in décor or of plants for their gardens when they were small children the threesome continued to share all that they learnt, at the instant of learning or so soon thereafter as to render the time-lag to be undetectable.

The apparently idle game of guesswork was a case in point. To the inattentive observer, for example to any of the Gang of Eleven making his or her occasional visit to the farm, this was kid's stuff — like playing 'I spy' on long car trips — but to the trio it was even more mundane. To the Baktrian brood it was simply training. When they had finished with numbers they would begin to guess other things. They were flawless on the guessing of chemical formulae of which one of the others was thinking or of quotations, not to mention movie stars and newspaper headlines.

'Giant waves down ship's funnel.'

'Brilliant.'

'Woman gives birth to herself.'

'Well done.'

'Droughts doubts routs sprouts.'

'Superb!'

'Where d'you find all that crap?'

'Hell, I didn't get that one.'

'No, no. That wasn't meant to be a puzzle. It was a comment.'

They were just as good at the divination of music phrases and at jokes, which tended to ruin the impact of the latter.

'Why are all orthodontists called ... '

'Dennis!'

Yukio, who was more than slightly sensitive about the clarity of his diction, did not like that one very much.

Yukio's obsession with good diction had germinated in a most innocuous manner. It had occurred during the High School Debating Society's annual public speaking competition, in which he found himself defending the indefensible — namely, the advocability of the pursuit of the 'Political Life'. Yukio had contended that a politico, an orator first and foremost, must have articulate diction. It was, he had assured the assembled multitude, for the 'Men in the Public Eye' a sine qua non, a tool of the trade.

'They're all tools in that trade,' had echoed from the middle of the crowded audience. A titter ran through the throng.

Catching O'Toole's eye, as the latter nodded in the direction of the row behind him, Yukio had, from his brother's telepathic prompt, retorted instantly:

'Pipe down Lukar! Better to serve God than Mammon — filthy Lukar!'

'Ugh?' queried the puzzled Lukar, an anthropoid from the football team, who would not normally have been at anything so demanding as a debate, much less a political debate, had it not been for the fact that his sexual strategy regarding the skinny, grey-complexioned, presently-breastless girl beside him required that he submit to all her intellectual interests. Lukar was vaguely aware, from the speaker's expression, that Yukio was only too ready to torch him with his tongue, so Lukar wisely lapsed into silence, gazing at the ceiling as if his very existence depended on it.

Yukio waxed so fervent during the course of that encomium for parliamentary democracy that he had entirely convinced himself by the end of it. And thus, by the trio's penchant for mutual assimilation, he had also convinced Bucolia and O'Toole as well, thereby imparting to the group its political bent and its humanitarian conscience.

Just as the smallest suggestion of water in the desert — the shortest spring shower in the Northern Sahara or a freak electrical storm in the Kalihari — brings forth vegetative life, so political awareness came to Yukio. For, generally speaking, Gasville was apolitical, an electoral backwater, a watershed of parliamentary apathy where an opposition member pounding the hustings could kiss babies until Armageddon and still have no hope of persuading so much as one vote to switch parties. It was a community of vehement democratic abstainers. A town of honest people who honestly did not give a damn!

What put political pepper into Yukio will never be discovered now. Perhaps it was some tale of his step-grandfather in Eire?

As the youth's speech ran on his ardour was lubricated, liberated and out came his heartfelt pleas, departing from the lines which he had prepared. Out came the words, in the demanding diction which he was recommending, crisp and clipped, clickety-ticketing off the end of his ticker-tape tongue.

' . . . you cannot abrogate your responsibilities forever! Get the bit between your teeth, in fact, get out and get the lot between your teeth, eh? You can study biomathematics as a regime to improve your mind. A spell at a university will train your body (at this point he paused with the aplomb of a professional to permit the audience a small, disciplined laugh) but politics is for training the soul! I do not mean that we all must needs become fanatical Eastern mullahs, or join some paramilitary Black Squad of political assassins. But we cannot expect the world to continue to function without our taking part in it. And if you have an interest in something, in the uninteresting sense, then you had damn well better take an interest in it, in the interesting sense.

'I am told that religion and politics are different spheres of life. But I would say without a moment's hesitation, and yet with all modesty and without fear of contradiction, that those who claim this do not know what religion is. Nor do they know what politics is! For it *is* a religion, for religion is a question of belief and so is politics. Without political belief we are free to be blown whichever way the strong and the determined will dictate, be they good or evil. Without a political faith we are an inviting prey to mobocracy and the unbridled passions of the powerful people, the people whose identity we cannot and will not know until it is too late. Hope is the sheet-anchor of every man; when hope is destroyed great grief follows, almost equal to death. I think that hope is bigger than a mountain and all its trees, rocks and promontories.

'When our political labours are over and the task that has been appointed to us, the task of forming our environment responsibly, when that project to which we are called to put our hand to is accomplished then it will all melt away again and no one will care to know what it was that we did or how it all came into being. But we will know! We will understand what we have accomplished in the widening search for democratic system and symbol. For the sake of our children and for that of our children's children we will have acted. Acted politically and not in vain. The choice is yours! Do you vote today or do you quietly go on chewing your groundnuts?'

When Yukio had finished his speech he had slumped to his seat, exhausted by his ingenious outpouring. The audience responded with a hearty round of applause, which was led by O'Toole.

Nonetheless the debating prize had gone to the captain of the girls' physical education team, a well-endowed platinum blonde by the name of Liselotte Kleinwunder, for a speech entitled My Dog.

Afterwards Bucolia and O'Toole had greeted Yukio as he descended wearily from the school stage.

'Yer done good, man.'

'Well done,' seconded Bucolia with a broad smile. 'You know what I think?'

'Of course I do,' smirked her brother.

4

WALKING WOLF

'Yer talkin', boy, sure geds righd on m' dids. Id's like having some goddamn, chicken-shide Englishman in th' back of th' car. And Chrrrrr-isd, ain' I up t' here with them guys this week. They done me good, I can tell yer!'

Yukio thought to himself that he did not need his father's coarse invective. He was on the point of telling the old man that having him in the Mayoral limousine with them was like picking up a hitch-hiking bum when he felt Bucolia's gentle, cautionary touch on his sleeve. Do not say it, she looked at him with a frown.

'Okay,' Yukio sighed aloud with weary resignation.

'Wassadd?' Eli rounded on him irritably. 'Wadya say? Yer being smardass or somethin'?'

'Well, I was only expressing my political opinion,' Yukio continued defensively.

'Ad thy age, yer shouldn' have polidical opinions. In facd, I doubd thad yer should opine ad all, dill yer's full-growed. An' even then id's wiser t' buddon yer lip.'

'Oh, come on, father! You may play the simple farmer, but you have views. You are a politician; you are the Mayor.'

'Oh, father, father,' Eli imitated sarcastically. 'Whad's wrong with "pa", like everybody else?'

The wrangle, which was an unpleasant, hostile augury of what the rest of the family outing to Port Standard might become, was fortunately curtailed by their arrival at the Gasville cemetery, at which they were to stop in order to let Sarah spend some time at the headstone which was all that marked the prior existence of the late Paddy Delaney.

O'Toole leant forward and tapped Stanley O'Vayshun on the

shoulder. 'This is the place, Stan. Turn in here and stop by the gates. It's a pleasant day, we can walk from there.'

Stan turned the smooth, noiseless, black ghost of a car in through the gates of the Gasville Acres of Peace and drew up at the kerbside. Behind him, Eli's four-wheel drive truck and the Ontal family motorbikes followed suit. The Ontal's offspring Boris, Norris and Maurice helped their father, Horace, to manhandle the machines off the road and to park them discreetly among the tombstones.

A turn through the tombs is guaranteed to calm any family squabble. For one thing the sobriety of the surroundings has an initial effect of reducing everyone to a contemplative silence. The group was quite large, consisting of the entire Gang of Eleven and both the Baktrian and Ontal families. The plan was to venture to Port Standard for an afternoon of recreation and relaxation, despatching a few matters of Trinomial government en route and pausing briefly at the Acres of Peace.

Sarah had brought flowers, complete with a flower vase and a container of water, as she had continued to do each week of each summer since the Great Gasville explosion at Sorores Mundi, which had claimed her Paddy for the Other Side. Eli, Bucolia, Yukio and O'Toole formed a semi-circle about the headstone while Sarah worked. Their attention wandered over the surrounding graves. There were many Martins: Moses Martin, Maria Martin, Martin Martin, Pincas Martin, Radok Martin, Mildred Martin, Mordred Martin, Maximillian Martin, Murdoch Martin and many more Martins.

'There seem to be more dead male Martins than female,' Yukio remarked casually.

'Well, them Martins are a forgetful bunch,' suggested O'Toole.' I bet yer that their menfolk die first and when the women go, old crones by that time mostly, they have forgotten which one was which guy's wife. Since they can't git the right tombstone to put the name on they just leave it.'

'Sometimes them old gels just slide away, unbeknowns' like.' Eli added. 'Sometimes they don' die ad all, nod reg'lar like. I've a mind of ol' gran'ma Martin, her thad lived in th' basemen' of th' Old Byre, thad useda be th' Down Hall. Nobody knows nothin' aboud where she disappeared t'. I remember thad 'twere she done tol' me all aboud how t' gid up an' go become th' Mayor. T'were her thad perrrdicted thad I'd bead oud ol'

Dom Snuze, th' ol' dude whose lyin' over thar'.'

Eli pointed at an overgrown grave which was barely visible, about twenty yards away. Yukio strolled away in that direction.

Tomas Mordecai Schnauser was the name upon the gravestone which went on to describe this man, better known as Tom Snuze, formerly of AusfarhtHimmelberg Pa., who had worked hard and long for his fellow man, both as a warm-hearted neighbour and as a local Gasville Town Councillor. Yukio remembered a little of Snuze from fragments of conversation which he had overheard between his parents. Snuze had been a prominent figure in local politics, although he was quite the antithesis of Yukio's own idea of a politician, having as he did the dreadful diction which is the inevitable result of the phonetic confusion which obtains in an Eastern European household transplanted to Pennsylvania. However, Snuze had fallen from power when Eli had annulled the town council. He had taken the blow rather badly. Eli had uncharitably remarked at the time, over the obituary, that Snuze must have belched himself into an early grave.

Yukio lit a cigarette. Leaning against the legend of Tom Snuze he gazed about at the other epitaphs. The names which he picked out were often familiar — Dean Twain Smoothe, he had been Bucolia's father. Felicite Sox, he remembered her name from the files of the Sorores Mundi Calamity Fund because it occurred in the description of the explosion in a narrative whose flowing and colourful prose occupied pride of place on the first page of the Charter of the Calamity Fund. Beyond Ms Sox, Yukio could see the life-size effigy of a cow. It was Grace the Childbearer, the locally celebrated cornerstone of paediatric medical history who had been Bucolia's natural mother. Yukio inhaled deeply on the cigarette and let his mind stray back and forth over the prospect that his aunt had been a cow, Amazing Grace. Beside the monument to the redoubtable Grace was a statue of Stan Steel. To Mister Steel's posthumous left Yukio could make out the lines:

> Euphoranastasia Anthrax,
> Gone to rest with Grace,
> The culprit was a careless
> cranial catheter.
> (O.H.I.P. 20076732)

Out of sight on the other side of Euphoranastasia Anthrax he knew that there lay the remains of his mother, Ms O Kanada. The grave was placed in the leaf-fluttering, cool shade of a large maple tree. Should he walk over and look at it? Yukio did not often visit the burial place of his mother. He felt no urgency to do so and on the rare occasions when he had been there with all the proper paraphernalia of mourning he had only come away depressed and enervated. Besides, he told himself, there was hardly time for that sort of thing on this afternoon; in any minute the Mayoral caravan would be getting under way again. On the other hand he did feel a certain enormous perambulatory vigour, of the sort that a politician needed on walkabouts in his constituency.

Yukio changed his mind. He would walk over to see his mother.

Picking his way through the weeds he began to intone a mock speech, feeling as he did so that he was being watched. He looked around but could see no one.

'What should we dare?' Yukio put to himself, rhetorically.

'And do so that there would be nothing before us except a choice of victory or death? The Gasville farmers are an unsophisticated and credulous bunch. Brave they are, as a matter of course they are fearless as lions. To kill and to get killed is an ordinary thing in their eyes. And if they are angry with someone, why — they will thrash him. And there's an end to it. But consider instead the dark and brooding menace; is he not much more to be feared?' Yukio paused and smiled to himself, imagining applause and cheering from the assembled members of the Party.

'That type may be here within our midst — and he is not to be trusted! For who can be wise, amazed, temperate and furious . . . '

'Loyal and neutral in a moment.'

A voice behind Yukio joined him to finish off the sentence. He whirled round to confront a tall, swarthy individual who was standing not a yard away from him and who had apparently materialized there without making a sound. The stranger wore moccasins on his feet and had, Yukio felt, an obsolete air about him.

'That was Shakespeare, eh? I don't often encounter quotations from the Bard of Avon in this cemetery! You're Yukio, aren't you?'

'How did you know?'

'I come here a lot and I've seen you before, at the Kanada grave. So I knew who you were, even if I hadn't seen you with all that mob,' the Indian stabbed a disdainful thumb over his shoulder in the direction of the parked Mayoral limousine. 'And in any case, I bin brought up at the Sorores Mundi Fund Home, an' all the kids there know you by sight and by name. We all know yer sister and brother, too. Are they around here someplace? I saw them all arrive.'

'Bucolia will have gone to see her dad's grave and to have a look at Grace, the cow. O'Toole's still with mother.'

'Why were you quotin' Shakespeare?'

'Oh, I just practise from time to time, you know?'

'Sort of political speechin', eh?'

Yukio nodded, reddening a little as he did so.

'Yer don't need to be shy about it,' the Indian reassured him. 'I knew what you was doin' when I snuck up on yer.'

'What is your name?'

'Oh, I thought yer'd remember me from Sorores Mundi. Ya know the rhyme?

> Sorores mundi,
> Calamity fundi,
> Fish on Friday,
> Church on Sunday.

Anyway, I'm called Walkin' Wolf.'

'Oh, now I remember your name. You live at the Sorores Mundi Home.'

'Used to. Now I've got a job, see, as projectionist at the Alhambra.'

'I did not think that anyone else knew that verse.'

'About Sorores? Yeah, all the kids in the Home know that one. I dunno where we picked it up. It just came into our heads one day and there it was. Suddenly we all knew it. Seeing you somehow brought it back into my head.'

'Do you keep in touch with the Sisters of the Home?'

'Not much. I don't say that they weren't nice ol' ladies, but I don't go back there much. On the other hand I see all the braves and squaws what were in there with me. They always

know where I am, and they often come and find me, whether
I want them to or not. It's like we were all brothers and sisters,
know what I mean, eh?'

'Yes, it is like that with Bucolia, O'Toole and me. Whatever
one does, the other two know at once.'

'I thought so. Yer see, it was just like that at the Home. Which
was a real pain if yer wanted to go off and quietly pull yer
puddin' in the showers.'

'You are an Indian, I think?'

'Half-breed, they never found m'paw. I'm just an
anachronism, eh? What could be more so than a "breed" who's
bilingual? Sometimes it used to make me wanna laugh right
back in the white faces of them saintly Sisters. They'd say —
"C'mon, yer gotta practise yer French to get on in the world".
Well, I'm helluva fluent, as a result — for an Injun, that is —
but all it's gotten me is a projectionist's job in a flea-pit movie
theatre that should've been condemned and shut down years
ago!'

At that moment, without warning three men leapt from
behind a nearby mausoleum and set upon the Indian, knocking
him to the ground.

'Zat iss himp.'

'Ja, holt him gut. Ziss iss der von, himmel, see hiss face vot
I told you off!'

Penz and Zhilin were the first two of the assassins to reach
Walking Wolf. Jumping on him they sat on his back, pressing
his face into the long grass.

'Ho'd the wee beggar doon, will ye. A'l gae throo his trews
wi' m' hands. Wha' th' he-ell ha' y' got here, laddie?' asked
Preston Pans as he pulled out on to the ground the contents
of the youth's jacket pocket.

'Hey, gedoff yer fuggers. Chrrr-ist tha's my money. Give id
bag.' It was very difficult for the Canadian Indian to make a
very convincing and cogent argument from his prone position.
By way of a hint in etiquette, Pans kicked him in the ribs.

Tossing away the cigarette stub Yukio jumped upon Pans
broad back. The latter responded with an sharp elbow-jab into
Yukio's right ear, which loosened his grip sufficiently for Pans
to turn and get a clear view of his assailant.

'Och, lay off, laddie. This is no business o' your'n.'

By now the others had arrived on the scene, their running,

arriving feet causing the blades of grass to sing out as if under the blade of the scythe.

'Let him go, you brute.'

'Piss off, Yukio,' grunted Norman the Mormon, pinning the boy's flailing arms against his sides.

Jaime Laudenklier, Stanley, Roddin Corpse and Sid Ra'in had the Indian's coat off by now and were ransacking the garment. Sid ripped open the lining with his knife and felt inside.

'Shit-head, ged out. Coats don't grow on trees, buddy, yer finker!'

Pans grabbed the Indian by the forelock, forcing his head back as far as it would go.

'Och, pea-brain, d'ye want me tae scalp ye, lad? If no' then chew yerrr tongue, ye swarthy sassenach.'

Yukio opened his mouth only to find Norman's large hand come over it, stifling his words. Out of the corner of his head, without quite being able to see them, Yukio felt the presence of Bucolia and O'Toole. He heard his brother quietly, but firmly, say, 'Led him go, Norman. Or else.'

Norman looked over his shoulder at O'Toole and seemed about to retort with some spirited invective when he met the latter's blazing gaze. At that point Norman seemed to think better of it.

'Just tell yer brother to keep quiet,' Norman replied, relaxing his grip.' It's none of your business.'

Yukio massaged his arm, which had gone quite numb under the bully's strong grip.

Horace Ontal pushed to the front of the circle of witnesses, followed by Eli Baktrian and Elsquaird, who carried a peregrine falcon upon his wrist.

'Boy,' Eli bellowed, looking down at Walking Wolf, who was allowed enough freedom so that he could sit up. 'Hast Mandola Magabutne sent thee, varlet?'

'Whathehellyermean?' exclaimed the frightened and angry victim, looking around from face to face among the group as if to estimate from which direction the most danger was going to come. His gaze settled upon Yukio.

'Shit, man! Whad are them ass-holes tryin' t' do t' me? Is this some police sdade, or whad, eh?'

'I will not beseech thee thrice, eagle-shite! Didst Mandola send thee?'

'Mandola shpandola, wassall this crap? Mandola my arse!'

'Leave him alone,' cried Bucolia, glancing at Yukio as she spoke, 'he clearly has no idea what you're talking about.'

'They all say that, Bucolia, my dear,' explained Professor Elsquaird. 'You see, we've had to deal with these spies before. Regrettably, we have no choice.'

'What didst that blackamore asketh thee to report upon, yer scurvy turd. Sent he thee in search of the plans?'

'Plans? Get lost, dad. Wassall this plan-crap?'

'Blueprints, you buffoon. Is that what he wanted?' Elsquaird continued. 'You know, of course, that it will be useless for you to insist upon your innocence. We know all about you. This time you are not wearing the Georgia Tech tee-shirt, but that doesn't fool me. Do you think I am so simple as not to expect a change of tactics?'

'Verily, 'tis the time of thrice telling knave,' said the Mayor, frowning as he addressed the prostrate Indian youth. He nodded to Elsquaird and added ominously, 'Unhood the bird!'

'What are all you people doing?' protested Yukio, in a loud voice. 'Is this some sort of demented generational complex, driving you, who are all old enough to know better, out to beat up young kids? You are supposed to be our good example. What is this lunacy?'

'Silence, my son.'

'Silence nothing! If he were a spy, do you really think that he would be this inept — as conspicuous and foolish as a penitent who hits himself on the head in public, just to make a noise?'

'Quiet thy insolent, intellectual tongue, son.'

'No, father!'

Eli scowled at Yukio, who pressed on. 'You are all making idiots of yourselves. What is this stupid game? It is as pointless as fools cursing, swearing and F-wording one another outside a movie theatre — practising in readiness for a film that is rated ''obscene lingo''. What are you clowns doing? This is not real, man!'

Very slowly Eli turned and reached out for the gauntlet on Elsquaird's hand. With one swift movement the Mayor pulled the glove free. He stepped over to his son, his movements light and almost dancer-like.

Before anyone could move the older man struck his son along the side of the head with the studded gauntlet.

'Oh!' Bucolia shrieked, as if she had been hit. O'Toole steadied her, putting his arm about her shoulders.

The group was silent, each one looking at the confrontation — a conflagration of hatred and contempt — between father and son.

'There's nothin' I do thad's okay, anymore, in yer smard-ass eyes, kid. So don' ged so goddam uppidy. You're mighdy fearless, boy — on paper!'

Yukio opened his mouth to reply but a move from O'Toole stopped him.

From the back of the group Sarah spoke up. 'Come now, boyo. Will yer trate yer old man daycent, Yukio, now?'

5

CONFLICT

Yukio was sprawled out on the couch in the living-room of the Baktrian farm-house, picking his teeth after dinner. Out of the corner of his eye he was watching his parents. Eli was sitting at the table, making marks on a prototypical legal document with the aid of an extremely short pencil stub with which he stabbed here and there at the page in a short-tempered, irritable manner.

> 'Hormones, rich-mones,
> Beggar-mones,
> Thief.'

'Whath'fuck's thad supposed t' mean, smard ass?' Eli snapped at his son, who made no reply, save to repeat the phrase under his breath, exploding into audibility only on the last syllable.

'Aw, shide,' shouted Eli, picking up his scattered pages and stomping out of the room, slamming the door.

Since the incident at the Acres of Peace father and son, or more accurately father and children, because Bucolia and O'Toole shared their brother's sentiments, had confronted one another as little as possible, and then only in silent resentment on the part of Yukio and in disturbing detonations of distemper on the part of the Mayor.

Sarah watched all this argumentation with the quiet and pondering wisdom of a woman who did not know what to do about it. She was certain that whatever it was, and however it was, between her man and her children the omens were not

246

propitious for the peaceful reconciliation which she wanted so badly to see. It had been so much simpler when the kids were small, for then when Eli had started to become bad-tempered with a child or vice versa she had always been able to distract the child with some new sight or sound — a flower, the spectacle of an animal in a nearby field, an envelope bearing a dazzling foreign stamp or a snatch of a song or a hymn. But nowadays she no longer knew what to do to keep her brood from flying at each other's throats. She knew that the imminent election — the first that Eli had permitted since his accession to power and a concession which had been forced upon the unwilling Mayor by the steadily growing resistance to the Trinomial Plan — was weighing heavily upon her husband, making him irascible and unreliable with everyone, not just Yukio, but even the closest of his associates in the cabalistic Gang of Eleven. Desperately she wished to mould him back into the potentially good man, who had serviced her lawnmower when Paddy was away and whom she had recognized and taken to back in the council chamber of Martin's Byre. To stand by and submit mutely to this internecine warfare between father and children was fast bringing her to that sacred moment when her faith in Eli, atrophied almost to nothing by the alienation wrought by year after year of his violent methods of government, would be placed upon the anvil.

She had never spoken of her feelings to her children, for it was not her style to cry on the shoulders of others, and no-one among her acquaintances ever voiced the slightest reservations about the Mayor and his methods, but she knew, deep within herself, just what was right and what was wrong.

And Sarah knew, for her father had told her this many times as he had sat by the fireside, gazing into the flames in the hearth and plotting his revenge upon the guards from the Ulster camp that had crippled him, that even if you are a minority of one the truth is still the truth.

Sarah did not look up from her absorption in her intuitions, which persisted in her mind like an ether while her deft fingers were occupied with her knitting. Had she glanced up she would have met the steady, observant gaze of her son fixed upon her face.

Sarah was not old, Yukio reflected. But her face was beginning to age. Thin ridges of skin had formed, crossing below the eye-sockets and visible when Sarah took off the spectacles which she had recently been obliged to wear. A tiredness had crept into the grey gaze of her eyes. Her once cherubic, rounded head had become thinner. Pouches of subcutaneous fat had allowed themselves to form beneath the facial skin in the places where its elasticity had vanished. Crowsfeet haunted the corners of her mouth and eyes. The mouth had narrowed, the lips shrinking from rouge-red abundance to a thin line which showed none of its lip-stick anymore, since her lips were clamped determinedly, tightly together. All in all, that once vital source of love and good-naturedness, which had been his mother, had lost its glowing immanence.

When Yukio looked at the gentle lady who had turned into his step-mother he could see all too clearly that bony skull which lay behind her features. Finally the young man spoke. 'Did you hear him? What the hell am I supposed to say to a man like that?'

'To be sure yer man's yer fayther, an' 'tis an end to't all,' Sarah replied quietly, without either looking up or relenting in the headlong pace of her clicking needles.

'But mother, surely you know what that bugger is doing out there? Are you blind to what he and his cronies are getting up to?'

'Boyo, methinks yerself's bin gossiping with that idjit Injun again?'

'There is nothing wrong with Walking Wolf, although the way that Eli has treated him would make one imagine that he was some sort of guerilla insurgent, hell-bent on the downfall of the Baktrian regime.'

'Yer fayther's basically a good'n, and daycent too. He's just got hisself in too deep, diddling wi' th' politics, yer know? An' himself has done that foolish thing fer the foinest motives, don't yer know?'

Yukio snorted, turning away and walking to the door.

'Generations to come, son, will think more kindly on yer Da. They'll find it impossible to believe, Oi'm thinkin', that one such as himself ivver walked upon the Earth.'

'My arse!' exclaimed Yukio, slamming his way out of the house.

Sarah paused to brush from her cheek the solitary tear which rolled slowly down it and then she took up her needles once more.

6

GANG HOME

The Strategic Reconnaissance Room in the basement of the Gasville Town Hall was very crowded. This room, whose walls were covered by maps which in turn were covered in coloured flags and modelling pins, was usually used only by Professor Elsquaird and his immediate Chiefs of Staff to keep a monitorial eye on the Mayor during his daily seigneurial peregrinations in search of the planted, pert pretties which the Professor arranged for him to encounter en route.

The Mayor had never been into this room, which was labelled Extremely Smelly Garbage and Worse on the door in order to reduce the chances of his straying into the place by mistake when hounding up and down with his metal-detector, which was rarely far from his reach these days.

'What lieth in yonder sanctum, Elcius?' the Mayor had enquired one day of Elsquaird, who cringed beneath his boss's use of the eerie epithet, about whose origins he had no clue.

When, in the early days of this mediaeval eccentricity the Professor had protested: 'What is this ''Elcius'', Eli?'

The reply had been. 'In sooth, though we have been close, Elcius, I would fain have the appellation ''Sire'' 'pon thy lips.'

'Yes, sire!'

Thereafter the professor kept a close rein upon his opinions concerning the state of the mental health of his employer. He maintained a strict vigil, searching daily in the countenance and behaviour of his leader, expecting imminently that change to lunatic variability and dangerous, violent caprice which so often attends incipient madness in history's great figures of destiny. However, these daily inspections had thus far not revealed any traits which were too alarming, in the Master.

At this moment Eli was, of course, not there, being held at bay by the ominous legend on the door, and the rest of the Gang of Eleven were listening attentively to Elsquaird.

The little man was standing upon his accustomed packing-case and at his feet lay his four-legged friend, Roland. Roland was a bull-mastiff, which was slightly taller than its master, upon whom it doted as if he were a delicate little child — to be protected and cherished — and to whom it was devoted.

In his left hand the midget dramatically held up a piece of crumpled paper. It was a letter, which had been expertly pitched through the window of the Mayoral limousine, landing on his lap scarcely an hour earlier. Upon reading the ungrammatical, scrawled and partly illegible contents of the note Elsquaird had hurriedly conferred with Eli and arrived upon a course of action, a precursor to which was the present paramilitary briefing.

'So how you know zees ees nod an hox?' asked Roddin.

'Hocks? What the devil are you blithering about, Corpse?'

'Merde! Corrrr, en Québec we say "Corrr". Zat's so, hox — eet rams weed jocks, zem funny sings, d'accords?'

'Himp minz H-O-A-X,' Zhilin interrupted.

'Of course he does,' snapped the professor. 'Do you think I didn't understand? It is certainly no hox — er, hoax — I know, because we have been receiving several of these notes lately and the police have informed me that they have invariably proved to be reliable.

'The po-lis?' grinned Preston Pans, who was reclining on the right-hand-most three chairs on the front row.

'The notes! Now stop fooling about!'

The group did not appear to be fooling about. In fact they did not appear to be in particularly high spirits at all; rather the opposite. The chairs were arranged in a semi-circle about the speaker's packing-case podium and the members of the Gang sat on these chairs, which were of the uncomfortable, plasticated, rudimentary kind which seem to be intentionally designed to keep inattentive audiences awake, by a combination of discomfort and intermittent sliding off the seat, through boring lectures in draughty lecture halls — How we re-designed our house, Five ways to plan a holiday in Chad, The history of AusfarhtHimmelberg in slides.

'I assume that this note originates with Magabutne and his

boys. As you may remember, we have come to a deadlock in the re-negotiation of the arms contract with that old black fraud. I have been trying to apply some pressure by cultivating other possible Third World parties. This, I imagine, is part of his manner of response. Although I cannot think, from past experience — the attack on Preston, for example — that he is going to stop at vulgar notes.'

Elsquaird waved the paper in the air.

'Vat's it zay,' growled Sid Ra'in, who was sitting beside Pans, leaning forward so that his sidelocks hung pendulously about his face as he stared at the floor. Carelessly, as he spoke, Sid sliced a magazine into strips with a large, sharp hunting knife.

'I was coming to that, but firstly it is important to be clear about the authorship and the motives behind this missive. It seems to me, and you can judge for yourselves in a moment, that all these notes are designed to demoralize us. They always bring intelligence of some farm or farmer for which the Trinomial scheme has gone wrong. Anyway, here is what it says — I have taken the liberty of rendering my own translation, the original is written as if by a child, and a very illiterate one at that! It is addressed to "Hey, you white trash" and roughly it says "What are you lumps of white worse-than-turds going to do about the squatters in the abandoned farm on Blair-doon Road?" Actually, this is the second note which I have received. I had a previous message, in much the same literary style, concerning this Blair-doon farm. It is one of the numerous cases of desertion by the tenant. There are so many of them that we have not managed yet to get replacements in all the cases. I have had the O.P.P. keep an eye on these places, but sometimes one slips their notice.'

Horace and Doris Ontal, who were sitting at the back, holding hands and quietly paying attention, disengaged themselves. Horace stood up.

'Can I see that note?'

Elsquaird passed the paper into the audience to Jaime Laudenklier, who glanced at it, shrugged and then handed it over to the Ontals.

'Und vot you zink vee am goink to do?' asked Penz and Zhilin simultaneously.

'Cut zem bastazz,' suggested Jaime vehemently.

'Oy, yoy, sure vee cut zem. Iff vee ketch zem! How are vee

ketching zem going to, already?'

'Yer man, Penz, has a point,' agreed Stanley O'Vayshun, snatching the note from Horace Ontal's hand.

'Bejaibers, man, have yer seen how many toimes that nigger calls us trash, bedad!'

'Deplorable, isn't it?' Elsquaird agreed.

'Th' dee'll come when a'th'wee golliwoggie-fellers are rate weer a'can belt th' boogars. An'then am goin't'mordrrrre tha' Mandola and a'his pansy-chappies, tu-uue.'

There was a general murmur of approval for Pans' sentiments.

Elsquaird clapped his hands and announced:

'Right, then let's go. We have to meet Eli and the police. It is important to move fast. I would not put it past that double-dealing Mandola Magabutne to forewarn the squatters. He is certainly no friend of ours. He only wants us to feel that he is bringing chaos to the Trinomial Corporation. Which he will never do! Come on, let's go. In the words of Shelley, it is time to:

> Rise like lions after slumber,
> In unvanquishable number -
> Shake your chains to earth, like dew,
> Which in sleep has fallen on you -
> Ye are many, they are few.

Come on, quickly now. Up, Roland.'

With that the professor climbed onto the back of the obliging bull-mastiff, which had risen and stationed itself by the packing-case perch of its master. With a smart kick of his heels the midget set Roland in motion and, riding at the head of the group, set off to rendezvous with the Mayor.

7

FARM

Since the spectacle in the cemetery Yukio had begun regularly to meet with Walking Wolf and the two had become quite good friends. They shared a sense of incompleteness and inconsistency about their lives, which was tinged with that oh-so-common feeling that political action was somehow the solution to the problem of rationalizing their plight.

As a result of this kinship, and being unable to find his brother and sister, who apparently had gone off somewhere together, Yukio headed in the direction of Walking Wolf's place, feeling inexplicably disgusted with himself and in need of company. Wolf lived in a commune comprised of a group of friends who had been his companions during the days when they had all been inmates of the Sorores Mundi Calamity Home. The commune occupied — in the capacity of squatters — a farm which lay about ten kilometres outside Gasville, along a little travelled road on which Yukio had to wait for fifty minutes before he succeeded in hitching a ride.

It was dark by the time that Yukio reached the farm and he stumbled and cursed as he walked down the pothole-ridden, muddy, un-metalled road which led from the main highway down to the gates of the farm.

The place looked stark and deserted, although a second glance around the spot revealed the presence of many trucks and rusting old jalopies parked here and there, with no obvious system, all over the front lawn and throughout the farmyard at the side of the house. The building itself looked to be in complete darkness, but this was to be expected since the members of the commune tried very conscientiously not to attract attention. This was the third such abandoned farm in which they had taken up residence and, from bitter experience with the Ontario Provincial Police, they knew what to expect should they be caught. In fact, the vigilance of the O.P.P. was increasing all the time because the number of farmers who abandoned their homes, and the Trinomial Plan by which they held their lease, was growing alarmingly. This was one of the factors which were forcing the Mayor into holding an election.

As Yukio walked up the gravel drive he found himself imagining the familiar, smoke-filled and heady, incense-laden atmosphere of the large living room around which, in the dense-dark penumbra of greasy light from a shaded forty watt bulb, thirty or more shadowy shapes would be sitting on the floor, leaning back against each other or the walls, discussing, embracing, fondling or exchanging back-massages and foot-rubs.

He paused outside the screen-door. The inner door was open and he could catch indistinctly the conversation of those within. He stopped to listen.

' . . . shit, man, don'yer criticize me till yer've walked a moon in m'moccasins, loafed a league in m'loafers and broken bread in m'brogues!'

Several voices broke into laughter. Yukio recognized the voice as that of Walking Wolf, evidently keeping the peace by preventing the debate from getting too heavy.

'Aff-der all, how yer gonna punish these guys anyway. D'yer thin' they should be condomned to death?!' More laughter.

A muffled voice said something which sounded like: 'Time to insult the trottoir.'

Yukio frowned. He could not tolerate the muddy speed-mumble of the regional dialect shared by the county's inhabitants. It was no wonder that they had taken a perfectly good Indian word for village — kanata — and turned it into the nation's name. They did that sort of thing all the time, turning T's into that abject apology for a consonant, the D.

'It is my firm belief that in the er, er . . . ' Yukio recognized this voice, despite its nervous tremor, whose familiar cadence accompanied by pronunciation which was as clear as a cow-bell belonged to his sister, Bucolia. By now he had also sensed the presence of O'Toole in the room with her and the others (how had he missed their car out in the yard?)

Bucolia was groping for her words, unaccustomed as she was

to speak out in the face of such a large audience. Yukio concentrated, in order to help her out. O'Toole, he reflected, could have helped out just as well but probably did not trust his vocabulary. Yukio knew precisely what she was trying to say.

'Er . . . complex constitution under which we are living in this county, the only safe and responsible course of action for an honourable person is to submit without protest to the penalty of disobedience.'

Bucolia's words drew some grumbles from the grey grousers.
'Pacifist crap.'

'We don' need thad sen'imen'al slop.'

Disregarding these malcontents Bucolia looked up, her face wearing a broad, beaming smile of welcome for the brother whose arrival she had by now intuited.

Yukio halted in the doorway and looked slowly around the room, which was precisely as he had imagined it — envisioning it, as he now realized, through the senses of Bucolia and O'Toole — while en route. Stepping carefully over the prostrate forms he made his way to his sister's side and sat down.

'How did you know about this place?' he whispered. 'You have never been here before.'

'But O'Toole and I always know where you go,' Bucolia smiled into his puzzled face, passing her hand over his shoulder in a light brushing movement, as if in reassurance.

Walking Wolf came to Bucolia's defence.

'Yer won' find me no pacifism-pusher, man, eh? Nor'd yer be if yer was an inden-churred Injun, see? Bud I don' agree thad yer should drive outa thief by just any ol' means. No, sirree! If 't's m' paw as comes t'steal I'd be so damn glad t'find oud who he wuzz thad I'd use one means. If 't's an acquaintance comin' t'steal I'd use another means. If 't's a whide man, some paleface shit as comes-a-stealin', yer'd 've me use some goddam differen' means 'n if 't were an Inuit. If 't were a weaklin' then I'd beat him shitless, but nodso if 't were a guy whad's stron'er'n me. An' if the guy's armed to the teeth then I'll stay quiet. Git me?'

Yukio's gaze came to rest upon the open, smiling face of his sister.

Sometimes he simply could not bear to look at her face. The expression he met there was often like that of a meek cow and gave him the feeling, as a cow occasionally does, that in her own speechless, dumb manner she was saying something. He saw, too, that there was a selfishness in that suffering expression of hers, a selfishness which wanted him for her own — protectively, perhaps, but passionately, silently in a manner which was different from that of his mother or O'Toole. Even so, her gentleness overpowered him, just as her music, played for him at home when they were alone in the farmhouse, melted away his frozen resolve.

What would he do without Bucolia?

Yukio shrugged the recurrent question aside and addressed his Indian friend.

'That's just pseudo-speciation, Wolf,' Yukio began. 'You do not need to be intimidated by it. The term just denotes the fact that, like your metaphorical villain, mankind comes in many different kinds and has to be treated as such. Man, while he is obviously one species, continues to appear on the scene split up into groups of one sort or another. Tribes, castes, clans, families, religions, ideologies — you name it! These groups provide their members with a firm sense of distinct and superior identity — of immortality, if you like. This demands, however, that each species invent for itself a moment when it is the centre of history!'

Everyone had paused to listen and the last sentence was quietly uttered to a collective that was literally holding its breath.

'And this group?' asked O'Toole, sensing what his brother was thinking.

'Whad's our momen' in the cen're of hisdory, man?'

'I'll tell yer that,' volunteered a tall, slightly bent, slim young man with thin, untidy, long ginger hair.

'Yeah,' added a second voice, 'yer tell'em, eh?'

'We're gonna screw them Trinomial friggers!'

'Oh, yeah? An' how yer gonna do thad?'

Voices volunteered opinions and solutions from all sides.

The sandy-haired individual shouted over the hubbub caused by the rest of the crowd. ''S'easy, man, we just blow up their munitions dump, you know whad I mean?'

'What munitions?' asked O'Toole. 'I don't know what yer mean.'

'Tell him, Jack,' laughed another man, rising to his feet. He, too, was tall, slim and slightly twisted about the torso.

'Yeah, tell him, Jack. He doesn't know whad yer mean. Yer

know whad I mean?'

'You didn't know about the munitions factory?' asked the incredulous Jack. 'Chrrrist, guys, d'yer hear this dumb bastard? Where yer bin, feller? You know whad I mean?'

'What does he mean?' simultaneously responded Bucolia and Yukio. 'What factory?'

'In the disused cowsheds at WHU, man!'

'What?'

'Where?'

'Whose factory?'

Bucolia and her brothers gazed at one another in wonderment and surprise.

Walking Wolf and Jack were looking at the trio with a silent, stern concentration and simultaneously within their collective three-fold consciousness formed the words ELI BAKTRIAN.

'Not pa?' ventured O'Toole at last, glancing helplessly at Yukio and Bucolia.

'Didn't yer know?' Walking Wolf asked Yukio.

'No. I never thought . . . I suppose it is obvious . . . now that I think about it.'

'It explains the secrecy,' added Bucolia.

'It explains why he's never let us go there with him,' agreed O'Toole.

'I do not think that we can bomb our own father's factory. Can we?' asked Bucolia, non-plussed.

'A reformer cannot seek to have close intimacy with him whom he seeks to reform.'

Yukio turned to look for a long moment, which was full of intelligence, at this last speaker, who was a stocky young woman, with the friendly rotundity of a milk-maid and the slightly twisted abdomen which she shared with most of the others in the room.

'But yer can't 'xpect us to bomb our own goddam pa.'

'They do,' Yukio answered quietly, with a sigh, to his brother. 'That is just what they do do.'

'Yukio,' Walking Wolf took his friend by the wrist. 'I know what yer thinkin'. And I know that yer know that I know, yer know what I mean, eh? Yer pa is nod a good man, man!'

'Even the devil can quote Marx for his purposes,' Yukio replied testily, pulling his hand free.

'Man, you know whad is wrong and whad is righd. So don'give me that balls! Yer godda train yer body to be as tough as steel, if yer gonna fighd them forces of decaden' capidalism. An' yer mind's godda be as supple as a blade of grass, eh? If yer gonna live wi' principles then yer godda give ungrudgingly yer unequivocal suppord, man.'

'The labour unions will be behind us, see?'

'Sure thin''

'But' Yukio protested half-heartedly, 'The violent approach is impossible. It is unachieveable, visionary and Utopian.'

'Crap, man.'

'Stuff thad stuff, eh?'

'Thad's just whad the proletariat collective has always done, man! Violent action in the cause of social justice. An' we're gonna do it again, just yer wade and see.'

'You cannot just corrupt Communist ideals to the populist viewpoint,' Yukio continued. He looked desperately around the room for assistance. In each gaze which he encountered it was clear that the group had formed its communal opinion and strategy before ever it met up with Bucolia, O'Toole or him.

'Pipe down yer bourgeois intellectual!'

'We are *not* that,' snapped Bucolia, 'Whatever else we may be. And it is not just because it is our father, who is involved, either. The fact is that violence is bad news for all.'

'Who said anything about violence?' countered the man named Jack. 'We can knock out that factory without a single person being harmed. After all, hisdory works dialectically, man, it advances through the clash of opposing forces. Thesis, antithesis and synthesis, eh? Yer don't get one shit's worth of progress ouda being pragmatic, conciliatory or shilly-shallying.'

'We got the dynamite right here, man.'

Someone, with a flourish, fetched the dust-cover from a crate that was resting on the floor in the corner and slid it out into the centre of the room.

'Chrrrrist, easy man. Yer don'wanna blow us t'bits.'

'Aw, c'mon feller! Who's s'posed to mess with this stuff if id ain't the ex-kids of the Calamity Homes fer th' big bang brigade? An' thad's us, sweedie!'

Yukio, Bucolia and O'Toole involuntarily recoiled from the proximity of the explosives. Sweat was breaking out on the brows of the two youths at the recollection of the explosive circumstances that had ushered them into the world.

'Fuck!' O'Toole spat on the floor.

'Don'yer worry, man. Id'll be safer'n houses. If we scout them sheds good before we start then there ain't gonna be no slip-ups.'

'No scouting,' barked Walking Wolf.

'Shit, why not?'

'Yer don'wanna tip them guards off, do yer, stupid?'

'Yeah, wise up, man. Them guys god fire-arms. Yer wanna ged shod?'

'Since when don'we know howda use firearms, then, eh?'

'Sure we do, but we are gonna do this without any violence, yer mutt.'

'Who the shit you calling a mutt?'

'You!'

'Hey there, no makin' the fist, OK? It just strains the group. You know our rules, guys. No couplin' off, no fighdin', no covetin' some other dude's woman, an'all thad. See? Don'go breakin' up the group, man. We've god enough hassle wi'the pigs, man.'

'Yeah, the Movement first, d'yer hear?'

'Well, don'bug me. OK?'

'OK.'

'An' they can stuff them rodden weapons. It don't madder how they guard that damn place. We'll ged id, see?'

'OK. OK. So led's ged down to the details,' Walking Wolf insisted loudly.

The group collectively shook itself, pricked up its ears and inched closer into the middle in order not to miss a word.

Yukio, Bucolia and O'Toole were each close to tears as the crowd squeezed in around them, enfolding them into its inimical council of war.

8

RAID

By the time that the Mayoral convoy reached Blair-Doonought farm the night had grown very dark. This feature, they felt, would facilitate the raid. It would give the raiders the element of surprise.

Stanley, whose limousine was leading the string of vehicles, flashed his lights twice, which was the prearranged signal to the drivers of the following six police cars to douse their lights. He switched off his own headlights and pulled to a halt, swinging the car across the lane as he did so. Behind him each of the police cars followed suit. Up ahead, past the gate into the farmyard, another group of cars, which had come in from the opposite direction, were doing the same in order to prevent escapees leaving by that route.

The crescent moon, which had not given much light in any case, seemed to have vanished for good behind thick banks of rolling rain-clouds.

Speedily dark shapes jumped out from the vehicles and ran up to delve into the trunk of the limousine, whose catch Stanley had released. The trunk contained the weapons — cudgels, riot shields and batons, helmets, small arms and heavy rubberized torches. Each policeman took two items and a fibre-glass shield. Norman, Roddin, Zhilin, Penz and Pans were already armed with tear-gas capsules and short-barrelled bazookas, which fired heavy calibre rubber bullets. Sid Ra'in and Jaime both had knives, Eli and Horace each tested his cat-of-nine-tails, which was made of thick hemp rope, by smashing it against the ground.

Elsquaird, with Roland at his side and two falcons on his wrist, was to follow in the wake of the initial charge in the company of Doris. Their task was to detain anyone who evaded the first onslaught.

The Mayor addressed the group in a whisper; standing beside him was a police sergeant with a two-way radio, into which he was hissing instructions to the detachment which was approaching from the other direction.

'Prithee, take heed and gird thy valour about thy loins. In this endeavour th' Almighdy is on our side, for we are th' righdeous ones. Armed with might, we shall overcome the heathens! Christ comes today!'

'Quotidianus Christi adventus,' Elsquaird seconded.

'These cut-purses and footpads thinketh that they can vaunt their sinfulness in our face — that they can cock-the-snook at us, thad they can spew on our running shoes — taking what is not their fiefdom when id is neglected by the omission of some bum bum-bailiff. Just because yer nod reevin' all th' time don' mean thad any ol' jackass shidhead can come in an' sdard takin' farms! OK? So avaunt, my loyal yeomen. Once more into the fray, dear serfs, and let us show these m-fucking vassals who's the boss! T'is the hour for government by the landowners for the landowners! Now t'work!'

With these words the group dispersed, melting rapidly and efficiently into the darkness, according to their plan.

Fortunately for the unsuspecting squatters inside the farmhouse, who were still deeply engrossed in their debate concerning the means whereby to sabotage the munitions factory and whether the ends justified those means, the violent turn of conversation against the Mayor had proved distasteful to some of their crowd. As a result, Bucolia, Yukio and O'Toole were sitting dejectedly on the side porch of the house. Yukio was quietly smoking a cigarette. They were seated on the porch-swing, which was installed far back on the porch and therefore was in virtually opaque blackness. They had been joined by a young man called Simon Dortees, a hunchback who had arrived very late to the meeting, having been working the late shift at the Gasville sewage farm. He was standing at the porch-rail, airing himself off before going inside.

'I'm sorry that I smell so bad,' Dortees was accustomed to say to those whom he met. 'It may smell like shit to you but it's bread and butter to me.'

Yukio found the hunchback very likeable, not nearly the same sort of extremist that he had just encountered in the house. He offered the young man a cigarette.

'Shhh, what was that?' Bucolia held up her hand, as if for silence. Of course no-one could see the gesture.

'What?'

'I thought I heard a car door slam.'

'Yes, you're right,' agreed Simon. 'There goes another. Just a moment, there's someone out there.' He slipped away into the darkness with Yukio at his heels.

'We will wait here,' said Bucolia to O'Toole, responding to Yukio's unspoken command.

The two stood side by side on the porch in the black-out for what seemed like a very long time, straining to catch the noises from the gateway. It was clear by now that there were people out there — far too many people to be merely Simon and Yukio. There was a cough, the clatter of metal dropped on the gravel and twice someone farted.

'What ought we to do?' Bucolia was thinking, debating whether she should tell the others in the house. She was just about to do so when Yukio and Dortees returned. They were running fast.

'Go! Run! It's the cops!' screamed Dortees, smashing in the window of the dining room with his forearm and shouting the words through the shattered pane at the top of his voice.

'This way, quickly,' Yukio pulled his sister away, breaking into a run in the direction of the open fields at the side of the house. 'Keep your head down and run like hell!'

Vaulting the porch-rail, O'Toole followed as fast as he could, taking his direction from the sound of his brother's urgent whisper. Now feet were sounding on the gravel and shapes were racing towards the house, heedless of cover and camouflage. The shapes could be discerned vaguely by the scant light of the slim moon which emerged at that moment from behind the clouds. A boy with a bull-mastiff barred O'Toole's path, carrying two large birds. Evidently the other two, running ahead of him, had avoided the boy.

'Stop.'

'Outa the way, kid.'

O'Toole smashed his fist into the boy's eye, knocking him to the ground. Instantly he felt the sharp pain caused by the dog's teeth sinking into his ankle. The birds were flapping angrily about his head and shoulders. He beat at them with his hands. Desperately he kicked out, loosening the animal's grip. He kicked again, blindly and panic-stricken, and found that he had scrambled free of the mastiff, leaving part of his jeans in its jaws. O'Toole turned tail and fled as fast as he could go. The dog barked and raced a few more paces with him, but fortunately turned back to tend to its fallen master. The falcons had disappeared into the night.

O'Toole ran on recklessly and sightlessly across the barren field. 'Oh, God,' he thought, realizing what he had done, 'I've just smashed Elsquaird! Oh, Christ! Oh, shit!'

Back at the farmhouse the rest of the young people were not as lucky as Yukio, Bucolia and O'Toole, who got away into the fields before the cordon could completely enclose the place. Simon Dortees, also, managed to get clear because he had not been inside either. For the rest of the group, coming as the warning did like a subconscious dream-message in the middle of the self-less and earnest haggling of the debate, the command to flee was not immediately effective. Dortees' cry hung over the squatting squatters like a harmless echo. Even though they were in theory always prepared for raids by the authorities this one did not seem real at first. The group got to its feet in a lazy sort of manner, initially milling around in the room as if they were at a party. No-one spoke. Someone blew out the candles and someone else stifled the light.

'The cops! The cops for Chrissake!'

With that the throng began to move. It started to heave and push in different directions, first towards the back door and then towards the basement stairs, moving like waves breaking upon a beach and then falling back. Everyone was shouting, and the voices of police could be heard bellowing through loud-hailers outside in the darkness. Some dived out of the back door, only to be met head-on by a charge of policemen. The squatters turned back, some running down into the basement with the intention of escaping through one of its narrow windows; others made for the second storey, hoping to get out onto the roof of the porch. Dogs were barking from all directions.

Walking Wolf led the charge out of the kitchen door, right into the arms of Preston Pans, who broke the youth's nose with a swingeing, two-handed blow from the barrel of his riot-bazooka.

'Yer bastard!' cried the man behind Walking Wolf, aiming an ineffectual blow at the more experienced Pans, who dodged to one side and smote his attacker over the head with his fist.

'Silence, laddie, when y' speak tae me.'

There was the sound of shots. A girl's voice screamed. More shots. Shouting, screaming, crying. The sirens blared out from the top of three police cars which came speeding round to the front of the house, their lights full on and directed towards the farmhouse. A voice addressed the scrambling hubbub.

'You kids are illegal squatters. Give yourselves up and come on quietly. If you resist there's gonna be trouble.'

The melée began to ease up as the police and the Gang of Eleven started to get their prisoners under control. Many of the kids had been pushed, shoved and kicked from the house over to the police cars, where they were ordered to place their hands on the roof of the car and to lean, face down with legs spread. Zhilin and Penz dragged a wriggling, abusive man over to the maple in front of the house. Slamming the fellow's head back against the trunk of the tree, Penz hissed:

'Von moof an' I'm gonna cut you mit ziss,' he held his strop-razor close beside the man's ear. 'Iss zat vot you vont? Ja?'

Doris was helping the crumpled Elsquaird, who was holding his hand to his eye and wincing from the effect of O'Toole's blow. Doris led the midget to a four-wheel drive that was parked in the drive, picked him up and placed him atop the hood.

'You'll soon be feeling better, Professor,' she said in a comforting, motherly manner as she examined his face under the light of her torch. 'You'll soon be all right.'

Roland brushed around and around her legs, licking them and jumping up against the vehicle on which his master was seated.

'I recognize this,' the professor said slowly. 'Give me that torch. Why, its Eli's wagon, Doris,' he exclaimed.

'Oh, my, whadya make of that, professor?'

Elsquaird did not reply, knowing full well the explanation for the car's presence there. Despite the darkness he had recognized O'Toole. 'Ummm,' he said at last, 'Better not to mention it to Eli, Doris. Not now, anyway. I will tell him later.'

'Aieeeeeee!'

Elsquaird and Doris broke off, glancing in the direction of the scream. They could see nothing. The sound had come from deep within the impenetrable gloom under the trees.

The scream had emanated from a police sergeant, who had been shot on the far side of the house. His assailant was not one of the squatters. As was discovered later, he had been hit and mortally wounded. The sniper had been watching, motionless in an oak tree on that side of the house. Having hit his target the man — a tall, wiry negro — folded his weapon in two, removing the sights and stowing them in the leg-pocket of his jeans, and dropped noiselessly to the ground. Silently he moved away in the direction of the open country. Beneath his black leather jacket he wore a white tee-shirt, which was visible as the front of the jacket parted when he began to run. Across his chest was written the legend, GEORGIA TECH.

9

RALLY

Eli Baktrian, Mayor of Gasville Ontario and munificent benefactor of that city and all its surrounding satellites, appendages and attendant paraphernalia, had determined to hold a summer fair to mark election day. This event was to be held at the Gasville Hockey Arena and Symphonic Auditorium for the Promotion of All Things Pertaining to the Arts and Cultural Rebus of Gasville. This last-named edifice was an enormous hall, which was reserved exclusively for the holding of the basket-ball matches of the Gasville Senior Citizens Club. The place had been constructed at great expense by Mayor Baktrian, using the proceeds from the Trinomial Plan and its munitions side-line.

On this election day the place was crowded; never had so many crammed themselves within its walls since its original barn-raising. Crowds had come from all over the county and even further — from as far afield as Elginturd in some cases — bringing with them their entire families, right down to their household pets and babes in swaddling clothes, to see the lavish event. In one corner of the hall a miniature-gauge train was giving free rides around a dizzy-making, miniature circular track. Kids, cats, dogs, pet pythons and even a pet skunk were piling into the newly lacquered carriages to get their turn on the ride. Truth to tell, when the skunk's turn came every prospective passenger seemed to lose interest in their trip, with the exception of the skunk's mistress, a tiny, bespectacled girl with braces and ginger hair hanging in long greasy bangs.

The ballot boxes had been set up at the far end of the hall, where they would be under the gaze of the dignitaries on the

266

stage. Nearby to the polling booth the bar had been erected and from behind the bar, in a spirit of jovial conviviality, Jaime Laudenklier, Norman the Mormon, Preston Pans, Zhilin and Penz were dispensing free beer to all prospective voters and their kin.

'Och, stape reet oop an' wet th'whistle, lassie. C'mon, lads, t'is a' free,' giggled Pans, holding half a dozen frothing tankards high in the air and waving them about.

On all sides the crowds were laughing and jostling genially, children offering a taste of cotton candy to their grandparents and the grandparents declining demurely, protesting that the sugar would gum up their dentures.

Eli Baktrian and the remainder of the Gang of Eleven — Professor Elsquaird, Sid Ra'in, Roddin Corpse, Stanley O'Vayshun and the Ontals — Horace and Doris — were clambering once more onto the stage for a further bout of official speech-making. Doris was wearing her best seasonal hat, which took the form of a towering straw construction topped with plastic flowers and vegetables. When the hat was brand new the vegetables had been authentic and fresh. The brim of this handsome headgear had supported courgettes, carrots, cauliflowers, soya beans, water-cress, haricots verts, haricots rouges, haricots noirs, haricots bruns, haricots bleus and several species of Jack-by-the-Hedge.

Unfortunately, for this had been in their courting days, Horace Ontal had been irresistibly drawn towards this cornucopia atop his beloved's cranium and, as a result, had eaten it all. In order to ensure that he kept his hands off her head and his mind on the more important business of her body Doris had been obliged to cease replenishing the edible decorations and to replace them by plastic imitations. In the first instance this substitution had proved quite indigestible to Horace, who instinctively persisted in sampling his beloved's produce, carelessly attending to the matter with only half his mind, the rest of it being centred upon his darling Doris.

The folks on all sides cheerfully chuckled with good natured ribaldry, raising their glasses in a toast to the midget professor as Elsquaird came forward to the microphone. For some moments he played around with the thing in vain, tapping it with his knuckle and blowing into it, as well as whispering, 'One, two, three testing', several times without effect. The little man climbed down from his packing-case and went over to the sound engineer who was randomly raising and lowering rheostat switches in a desperate attempt to produce some amplification.

'I dunno whad's up. We sure had sound las'dime, eh?'

'Get on with it!'

'Aw, cool yer arse. Cain't yer see I'm dryin'?'

The midget went back to his place to wait by the microphone. At last the electronics expert got the system going with a vengeance and a terrific, high-pitched whistle was emitted with such volume that the sound drove everyone's hands to cover their ears. After several more minutes of fiddling with knobs and fumbling with electrical cable connections a compromise level of amplification was found and Elsquaird was once again able to stride purposefully to the apron of the stage, climb up onto the packing-case, clear his throat and commence to address the crowd.

'Brothers and sisters in Love,' began the professor.

This incestuous opening caused a little stir from those near enough to hear him.

'In love with service, in love with the community spirit, in love with progress and political and sociological challenge — to you I speak here today. We are gathered here, under this roof and on this hallowed ground, to give expression to our love for all these good things of life. And how are we going to articulate that expression? We are going to say it all with the power of our vote. For today you are called upon to give expression of your support for Mayor Eli Baktrian — (pause for applause, the Mayor stands, modestly and bashfully, he takes his bow and waves at the audience) — who has been serving this community for more than twenty years and in that time has brought to this area industrial prosperity and agricultural stability. It is by means of Mayor Baktrian's masterly Trinomial Plan that we have been able to return the farmlands to their rightful owners, the farmers, to tend and care for in the traditional, ecologically sound, sociologically meaningful, strip-farming manner of their European forefathers.'

Listening to the professor's speech one might have formed the idea that the day's election was to be a hard-fought, democratic example of competitive politics. In fact, no such thing was even remotely true. The only position which was up for election, in this, the town's first election for over twenty years, was that of mayor. However, the post was not being contested by an alternative candidate since all the potential opposition candidates had recently and mysteriously withdrawn from the fight. Therefore this election was an exercise aimed at seeing just how much support the community would give to Eli Baktrian and to spot those who withheld their blessing.

'Once I visited one of these modern, strip-farming ventures,' the professor continued. The professor squared his shoulders and cleared his throat with a short cough. Although he realized fully the disingenuousness and the suspect nature of these, his oratorical crowd-manipulations, he tried not to tell downright falsehoods.

'And I paused in my tour of the small-holding to ask the farmer what the Farmer's Almanac said about the coming season's soil erosion and climate. The man replied in a kind and cooperative manner ''I have only the copy from last year, but it is very good. Stay here and I will get it for you.'' To this I replied ''Is this how you practise? Why, when I resolve to shave I buy myself the latest shaving apparatus!'' And that is what this community must do, good people. We must buy ourselves the latest shaving apparatus OF GOVERNMENT! And by that I mean the Trinomial Plan and all its benefits. And the only way to receive those benefits is to vote for Mayor Baktrian. For only he has the power to run the Plan, and to run it well!'

The professor paused for the cheering, much of which originated from the barmen at the nearby bar.

'Every day we are being weakened,' Elsquaird went on, 'Every day our leaders look more and more like terrified men! They no longer have the guts to attend to our cries for help. They lack the traditional remedies of petition and they no longer represent the people. But that is a false indictment when it is directed at our Mayor. For Eli Baktrian is the one politician for whom it is not true that he has abandoned the people. He *is* the people! It is he who is holding this community together. It is he who is upholding law and order. It is he and he alone who is bringing the prosperity to this area — a prosperity which has allowed us to expand until our county is the biggest in Southwestern Ontario. And all this he has done because he has had the Trinomial Plan. And this has not been an easy task, good people. For I know this well — that if one thousand, if one hundred, if ten men whom I could name, if one honest man

were to withdraw from the Trinomial Plan it would mean the
end of civilization as we know it in this county!'

'I withdrew from the goddam plan,' called out a voice from
the back of the hall. At once there was a scuffling in that vicinity
and someone was ushered out of the hall in the company of two
policemen.

The crowd in the auditorium waited for the long arm of the
law to do its work. Everyone was standing in silence except for
the occasional genial ripple of comment:

'Who is it?'

'It's the R.C.M.P., right?'

'No kiddin'!'

The onlookers were straining on tiptoe to catch a glimpse of
the activity and the speaker on the stage waited patiently for
the restoration of order.

However, order did not restore itself immediately, for at the
moment when the police exited with their charge another group,
about sixty people in all ,entered at the opposite end of the arena.
They were chanting as they advanced.

> 'Hold your tongue,
> Play it dumb,
> Suck your thumb,
> Here we come!
>
> Sorores Mundi
> Calamity fundi,
> Fish on Friday,
> Church on Su-u-unda-a-ay!'

This new group consisted of young men and women, former
inmates of the Sorores Mundi Calamity Home, who entered
the meeting in the wake of a figure who limped along on
crutches. This figure was Walking Wolf, wearing a swathe of
thick bandages about his skull. Immediately behind him followed
a group carrying a banner bearing the legend:

> 'Home-Rule is Self-Rule!
> Self-Rule is Self-Control!'

In the throng behind the banner were Yukio, Bucolia and

O'Toole Baktrian. The members of this new band wore resolute expressions. Besides their leader several others of them still wore the bandages which covered wounds which had resulted from the raid on the Blair-Doonought Farm or from the sentences of imprisonment which had followed.

The holiday-making masses gave ground to let this new entourage enter.

Elsquaird caught sight of Yukio — tall, twisted and gaunt — in the crowd. The professor cast a nervous glance in Eli's direction but the latter did not yet seem to have noticed his son's presence. Hurriedly Elsquaird took the microphone in his hand and stammered into it.

'Now I give you the person for whom you have been waiting, for whom you have been voting. The man who has worked for this town more than anyone else. I give you Eli Baktrian! I give you the Mayor!!'

Pans began to cheer, Zhilin began to clap. The crowd erupted into noisy appreciation. Much of the din came from the frenzied tintinabulation of the crew of youngsters who had entered with Yukio and Walking Wolf, most of whom where a little twisted and hunchbacked in one direction or another. They were blowing whistles and horns. Some had baseball bats with which they beat a staccato tattoo on fibre-glass riot shields.

Eli stepped with slow dignity up to the microphone. Gripping the lectern firmly with both hands he calmly surveyed the expectant throng. The applause died down but not so the crashing and whistling of the newcomers, who doubled their efforts.

The professor was starting to look uncomfortable, glancing uneasily back and forth — now at the Mayor, now at his children.

In contrast, Eli's calm gaze swept over the crowd in a manner of apparent authority but which did not take in the details. To the Mayor this hubbub was just one more political rally. Had he not handled a hundred like it in the past? Had he not quelled the querulous, been offensive with the abusive, been eluctant with the reluctant and seductive with the reductive?

The professor was relieved to see that Eli still did not notice the presence of his children in the crowd. When the bedlam and racket did not subside Eli sought out and found the gaze of Preston Pans; with a decisive nod he prodded the air with his

forefinger, indicating the noisy mob before him. Pans registered
his comprehension and turned at once to those beside him,
hurriedly whispering instructions which sent Zhilin, Penz,
Norman and Jaime hastening through the crowd in the direction
of the disruptive kids. The troop of policemen followed at their
heels, elbowing and shoving their way into the crowd.

'Tell those kids to pipe down.'

'Let the man speak.'

Angry voices called for silence.

Pans and the police arrived to confront Walking Wolf's
followers. Now, for the first time, the gigantic Scot spotted
Yukio, Bucolia and O'Toole. He stopped his squad and both
sides squared for a clash. For one timeless moment Preston Pans
and Yukio glared at one another.

'Soo-oo it's y'sel', laddie.'

Yukio did not reply, instead he raised his hand high above
his head and the din ceased instantly.

'Led the bugger speak,' shouted Walking Wolf. 'Led's hear
what these robbers, these farm-stealers have t'say.'

'Careful, Injun,' snarled Pans, with Norman the Mormon
at his elbow, holding an axe-handle in front of him with a two-
fisted grip.

'Hey, waart man, who's yuh callin' dutty names, man?'

Pans felt a sharp prod between his shoulder blades and turned
to see, immediately behind him, six tall negroes in tartan kilts.

'This tarm, man, yuh don' gonna haard in no shit-haass
latrine, fellah.'

Tall as he himself was, Pans was looking straight at the words,
GEORGIA TECH, displayed six-fold upon the chests of
Mandola Magabutne's men.

Stalemate. Silence. At a nod from Yukio, O'Toole gently
began to lead Bucolia out of the crowd.

Eli Baktrian, nostrils pinched and eyes closed, began to
address the multitude.

'How are yer, brethren? Doing good? How's id feel t' live
in Gasville? Does id make yer — proud? Does id fill yer guts
wi' piss n' vinegar t'know yer've god th' besd goddam li'l cidy
in Canada?'

Roars of applause greeted the Mayor's opening remarks.

'Lis't'me, then, an' lis'n up damn good. Ontario hath too
many men of subsdance, wealth and riches; men who taketh

away but do not give, men who owneth the land and do not husband it, who leave it fallow and turn the serfs away from their hospitality. Manifold such villeins exist, I say to thee, and their time has come! Under the Trinomious Plan it has become their privilege and bounden duty to assume the role of benefactors to those who can make Ontario great! The farmers!!'

The Mayor paused, rocking gently on his heels as if in a Newtonian reaction to the tumultuous applause.

'While I am thy Mayor, while I am thy liege lord and have thy fealty these noisome men will neither prosper nor thrive. To them I will never bend the knee. To them I will never bend the back.'

'Yer back's bent shitless a'ready!'

'Yer evil ones may tordure me, revile me, break my bones, even kill me homicidally. Then yer will have m'dead body, evildoers. But, by the welkin, yer'll nod have my obedience! I will not harm these men, for the Trinomious Plan seeks neither to harbour malefaction nor malediction. For myself I have found that we are all such sinners that we should leave punishment to God. Yeah, will I suffer for you — good swains of Gasville. For real suffering, bravely borne, melts the evillest heart of stone — such is the potency of suffering. By seeking not to punish, but only to correct these iniquitous squires and their Toron'o-brokin' reeves, I do not seek to apportion blame. This, good free-men and goodwives, saves me from attributing motives to my opponents, detractors and critics. Today, as I correct them, as I take from them those farmlands which are not theirs by descent, I can love them because I am gifted with the omniscient eyes to see myself as others see me. And vice versa. If I wish to devote myself to the service of Gasville, I will and I must relinquish the fleshly desires for children, for wealth and for notoriety and I must, and will, live the life of one retired from household cares.'

'He's not goin' to do anymore washin' up!'

A few people laughed but many just frowned at the interrupter.

'It is time for action! It is time to let the ripe fruit fall! Fun and frolic are permissible during one's years of innocence. Once one's eyes are opened one must look Truth full in the face.'

Eli inhaled deeply, spreading his arms wide in a majestic, universal embrace. His eyes were tightly shut, like those of one in a trance.

'I do not labour for Gasville for personal gain. I am willing
to reduce myself to zero, for a politician must put himself last
amongst the people. My conscience is clear. I can now give
myself the certificate that hardly ever does a thoughtless word
escape my lips.

'But I warn you all that everything is not pomegranates and
plaisance. You might not be aware that there is in this county
a body, a very powerful body in its way, a very united body
whose intent is averse to the Plan Trinomious. A body of
resistance, a body of unwillingness, an uncooperative body which
I must cast into the dungeons of oblivion — for the choice is
to set at risk all that we, the community, have worked for for
twenty years. I sense elements of this body here with us today
and to them I must say as was spake of old. If you, I say unto
them, tremble in the law courts of thy liege or are terrified by
hardships in gaol then so be it. I cannot find fault with you.
But what choice do I have but to deal thusly with thee? If I
concede to thee, how couldst I thereafter look the world in the
eye? So beware, sons and daughters of Beelzebub for I have
seen thy face. In our civilization there will naturally be progress,
retrogression, reforms and reactions, but one effort is required.
And that is to drive out oppressors!'

Cheers. Enthusiastic stamping of adulating feet.

'I am a man. Only a man. But I am first and foremost thy
man! I am humble! I am pure! I count myself as worthless —
for you! I love all mankind, except that I hate all men — all
overweening, selfish men — who do not hate themselves.'

As the resultant cheering died away Eli opened his eyes and
stared at his listeners in silence.

Inside Yukio's head two voices were tugging, protesting,
striving to push back the resurgent bubble of an idea.

'Don't say it Yukio,' insisted the voices.

'Bucolia, O'Toole,' thought Yukio, 'Surely you will
understand?'

Yukio opened his mouth and shouted at the top of his voice:
'If you hate all men who do not hate themselves — do you hate
yourself?!?'

Dead silence.

Here and there a sort of whispered, sporadic, syllogistical jig-
saw puzzle began.

'He can't ... '
' ... Hate himself, because ... '
' ... Then he wouldn't ... '
' ... Hate himself!?? ... '
' ... But he ... '
' ... Can't ... '
' ... Not hate himself ... '
' ... For ... '
' ... Then ... '
' ... He'd hate himself ... '

The paradox slowly crystallized in the collective mind with the effect of a sort of intellectual frisson, a tickling of the Gasville intellect.

People began to chuckle, then to snicker, then to laugh out loud. They repeated the argument over to themselves. They laughed more.

It was Elsquaird who was the first to realize what was about to happen, but even as he did so the hall erupted into multitudinous guffawing. Jumping onto the packing-case the midget grabbed the microphone from Eli and, pointing at the young intruders, screamed: 'Get them!'

In a trice blows were falling, feet were kicking, Georgia Tech biceps were bulging and an irrevocable brawl of biting and belting was underway. Waves of violence surged back and forth as the police chased Magabutne's men, who in turn pursued the Gang of Eleven, themselves after the warriors of Walking Wolf. Mothers, screaming, grabbed their babies and ran, while the flailing axe-handles dealt out black eyes and cracked ribs to left and right.

Tall and twisted, seemingly immune in the midst of the fray, Yukio burst into tears.

Watching the sobbing youth, Elsquaird fiercely gnawed his lip in anguish.

10

RETALIATION

It was the hour of midnight on one of those very dark nights on which those who like raiding go raiding, saboteurs go sabotaging while the rest of the populace is sleeping peacefully.

Noiselessly Mandola Magabutne's chauffeur-driven black Mercedes, with its lights extinguished, glided into the parking lot adjacent to the former cow-shed complex of the Institute for Buculo Inseminology. Since the days when cows had been inseminated therein, to Haydn-esque harmonies, the scattering of low buildings had expanded greatly. The original shed in which Grace had begotten Bucolia Smoothe had long since been converted into the central headquarters of Gasville Munitions Incorporated. Now there were twenty buildings, secured behind a tall, electrified perimeter fence. A conning-tower, manned twenty-four hours a day, dominated the munitions precinct from its position on top of the guard-house. Secured on the roof of the tower a rotating search-light projected its inquisitive forefinger into every quarter, scanning the perimeter fence with a frequency of one cycle per minute.

The negro, older now, coughing and wheezing, pressed the button which lowered his window and expectorated hugely out into the cold night air. With his poor health he did not like to be out this late; it was bad for his lungs. However, this evening was special. Magabutne had been waiting to get even for nearly twenty years.

From the bushes at the far end of the parking lot a group of shadows silently and swiftly moved in the direction of Magabutne's car. The leader of the group, crouching low as he ran with cat-like agility, was a black, kilted figure wearing

276

a GEORGIA TECH tee-shirt. He was followed closely by
Walking Wolf, Simon Dortees, Yukio, Bucolia and O'Toole.
This last trio did not crouch as they moved, nor did they run.
Their movements had a desperate air of indecision, almost as
if they did not know why they were there.

'All set, Justine-Christabelle?' barked Mandola, addressing
the other negro by his code-name.

'All set, boss. All dee guys are in dere places, man. You got
dee trolley?'

'In dee trunk, Justine-Christabelle. Get dee ting quick, I
wanna ged dee hell ouda here. Fast!'

Justine-Christabelle motioned to another negro, who had just
run up to the car, and together they moved to the rear of the
Mercedes. From the trunk they lifted a four-wheeled trolley,
a sort of extendible, dexion-type construction which they quickly
set up. Fully extended the gadget resembled a light-weight fork-
lift truck. It possessed a vertical frame on which could move
a spring-loaded platform large enough for a man to stand on.
Dexterously Justine-Christabelle and his companion finished the
contraption's erection, tightening the two quick-release wing-
nuts which rendered it rigid.

'OK, man. Go,' ordered Magabutne, moving to shut the car
window.

'An' dee trucks, boss?'

'Yuh do yo stuff, felluh. Dey'll be here, don' worrah.'

As he finished speaking the electrical window of Mandola's
car clicked to and the car, its lights still extinguished, quietly
moved away.

Walking Wolf produced a two-way radio from his jacket and
spoke into it. 'Yer all ready?'

'Yeah, eh?'

'Ardillery in place?'

'Yeah, man.'

'Jumpers ready?'

'We're here, man.'

'Ready, man.'

'I'll coun' t'ten then we go as soon as the lighd's passed. OK?
Yer know whad I mean?'

'Gotcha, Wolf.'

Walking Wolf looked once around the group beside him. 'Yer
all ready t'run like hell?'

They nodded. He began to count. 'One, two, three ... '

A question-mark still hovered in Yukio's, Bucolia's and O'Toole's collective mind. Reading their reluctance, Walking Wolf scowled at them, unseen but telepathically registered, in the darkness. ' ... eight, nine, ten. Go! Guys, go!'

At that instant the smoothest, most minutely planned paramilitary sortie ever plotted in the peaceful paradise of Gasville, was launched into action. The search-light passed and the negroes began to run. Sprinting like basket-ball heroes they pushed the trolley ahead of them, sending it hurtling across the lot to end up with a crash against the fence. Electric sparks flashed and crackled but rubberized stanchions on the front of the machine protected its handlers from shocks.

As they reached the fence the artillery arrived in the form of two girls and a youth who ran up with a small field-gun on a tripod. The gun was placed on the platform, Dortees jumped on with it and in an instant the platform was spring-ejected to the top of the derrick, enabling the muzzle of the artillery-piece to clear the fence.

'Ready, steady, go!' shouted Dortees. Boom. The gun fired. Crash. The length of chain fired by the gun wrapped around, and took out, one of the legs of the conning-tower, which lurched crazily and toppled with a splintering noise onto the roof of the guard-house.

The reaction from the shot propelled the gun, and Dortees, backwards off the trolley's platform. Dortees fell to the ground, laughing with elation. 'I tol' yer I'd hid id, man!'

With the search-light gone the night was pitch-black. The platform dropped again and the first of ten running figures jumped aboard. The trolley jerked, the spring fired the platform upward and the first man sailed into the air and over the wire, dropping into a crouching position as he made his sure-footed landing.

In ten seconds ten such men were projected into the munitions compound.

'Ged the gates! Here come the trucks! Ged the guard-house!'

Across the parking lot appeared six trucks, hurtling towards the gates, which were released just in time for these juggernauts to smash their way through.

The munitions guards never had a chance. As they emerged sleepily from the guard-house their weapons were confiscated and their keys were taken. Inside, one smart-ass got to the phone, whose wires had been cut. Finding the apparatus dead he gave up and surrendered like the rest of his colleagues. Guarding is just a job, so why get shot?

Within fifteen minutes the six trucks were full of munitions, explosives and the raiders, who put the torch to as many buildings as they could before taking to flight.

The guards had been stripped of their clothes and weapons and chased away into the night.

As the trucks hurtled away down the road the blazing of the huts, exploding like a holiday firework display, lit up the sky. The siren, activated by the smashing of the gates, continued to wail plaintively into the deserted darkness.

In the front seat of the leading truck Yukio gazed stony-faced at the highway ahead. He felt Bucolia's warm hand gently take his own and lift it to her face. In his mind he could hear his sister's soft voice saying: 'Non-violence, non-retaliation, brotherhood, sisterhood — personhood.'

He looked at her and thought: 'For once I do not know what it means.'

11

CIVIL WAR

In the Mayoral suite at the Gasville Town Hall the scene was one of intense activity. Through the window the reddening light of dawn was stealing gradually. The members of the Gang of Eleven, their eyes bloodshot and their faces tired and placid from lack of sleep, were assembling in response to the urgent summons of Eli Baktrian and Elsquaird, both of whom had been there since two o'clock. Eli had been roused from his bed by a panic-stricken call from the guard sergeant of the munitions factory, who had walked into Gasville from the scene of the raid, barefooted and clad only in his underwear, to call his chief with the news of the attack by Walking Wolf and his associates. Eli had jumped from his bed, cursing wrathfully at the world in general and at Sarah, being the only victim to hand, in particular.

'D'yer know whad them kids of yers 've done now? There's been a raid, goddam id. They've been seen raiding *my* facdory. Jeeze, whad in hell they think they're doing? Who'd they think they are — Yukio, O'Toole, even Bucolia — hand in glove with thad damn Injun and thad black bastard, Magabutne.'

Eli dragged on his jeans. 'I'll kill them shidheads when I gid them.'

With that remark he had been gone before Sarah was fully awake, leaving her to make whatever she might of his shouted, incoherent diatribe against her children.

Eli had jumped into the four-wheel drive and raced over to Elsquaird's apartment, virtually dragging the bewildered, sleepy midget from his bed.

'C'mon! C'mon! Gid yer pands on and led's go. Them shids 've

280

sdolen our goddam munitions.'

The pair had driven down to the factory, briefly surveyed the blazing spectacle and then rushed over to the Town Hall to summon the rest.

'Thank God it wasn't all stored there,' Elsquaird muttered to himself as they raced through the deserted streets of the town.

Gradually the Eleven had arrived, straggling in one by one, in the Mayor's office. And now they were all busy. Doris and Horace Ontal had been sent off to Eli's home to get Sarah to make breakfast for the gang and to fetch her and it back with them. Elsquaird, Roddin Corpse and Norman the Mormon were hastily priming the contents of a box of Elsquaird's trapdoor-code programmed hand grenades. Sid Ra'in, Preston Pans and Stanley had been sent to the weapons store in the Town Hall basement and were now arranging the stock, which they had brought up, of machine-guns, bazookas, automatic pistols and boxes of shells and cartridges. Zhilin and Penz were somewhere in the building.

Jaime arrived waving a copy of the first edition of the *Gasville Free Press*. He rushed up to Eli with the paper.

'Have you seen this, boss?' he exclaimed. 'We in the paper already, ja?'

Eli snatched the newspaper and stared at the front page, which bore the headline: GASVILLE CIVIL WAR.

The article went on to describe the raid, detailing many previously closely guarded secrets concerning the munitions factory.

'Damn! Who tol' them all this crap?' snarled the Mayor. 'Them goddam kids musd've goddam tol' th' Press damn quick. Why they doin' this t'me?'

He handed the paper to Elsquaird. 'Whad yer make of id?'

The professor began to read aloud. ' ... a group of determined opponents of the Trinomial Plan of Mayor Eli Baktrian, self-styled autocrat and petty dictator of Gasville, last night attacked and ransacked a secret factory controlled by Baktrian and his thugs ... '

'Shid! An' I thoughd they worshipped me. Chrissake, haven' I paid enough to the goddam rag-bag paper? How can they turn round and say all thad garbage? I bed them kids wrid id! I bedcha they did.'

' ... after the successful raid this band of social vigilantes escaped in the direction of Drewchester ... '

The professor paused. Doris and Horace had returned. They were standing in the doorway, empty-handed.

'Where's breakfast?' Eli screamed. 'Where's Sarah?'

Horace hesitated to reply, glancing round the room at the questioning faces.

'Where's she?'

Still there was no reply. Horace began to blubber like a child.

'Sarah's hanged herself,' Doris answered, her voice choked with emotion at the death of her friend.

Eli smashed his fist on his desk with a loud crash, sending the contents of his desk-tidy flying in all directions. 'Shid on her,' Eli spat out the curse in the manner of one whose tractor has just failed to start. 'An' where's th' bloody food?'

Doris and Horace gaped speechlessly at the Mayor. 'Ged oud an' ged some food. Don' come back till yer find somethin'.' The Ontals turned and fled.

'Where th' hell is Zhilin and Penz?'

'In the ante-room, boss,' Norman replied.

'Ged 'em in here, now.'

Norman slipped out of the door, to return a moment later followed by Zhilin and his crony, Penz, who was carrying their glass perpetual motion machine.

'Zis ist geschtoppen. Ist kaputt!' moaned Zhilin. 'I am not unterschtand vy zis ist nicht gehen jetzt.'

'Sdop pissin' around wi' thad fuckin' thin'.'

In two swift strides Eli had crossed to Penz and wrenched the contraption from the latter's hands. He hurled it against the wall.

Shards flew everywhere as the glass tube imploded, smashing and scattering black, green, blue, red, mauve and white beads in all directions.

Zhilin emitted a gasp and, together with Penz, fell to the floor, scrambling to pick up the precious fallen beads. Eli Baktrian booted the crawling Zhilin violently up the backside, sending him sprawling, face down, amidst the fragments of glass.

'Pox on thy unnatural device!' Eli screamed piercingly, kicking the prone Zhilin again and again.

'Easy does it, Eli,' Elsquaird stepped forward. 'That won't do any good. What we should be doing is deciding what to do. Once they read that article, every malcontent farmer in the county is going to be congregating at Drewchester to help the raiders.'

Eli turned slowly to look at his midget adviser. The Mayor sneered as he looked down at the professor.

'Yer done this t'me, eh? 'Twas yer shiddy advice t' led them kids ouda gaol. An' yer knew aboud my kids, right? Din' yer?'

Elsquaird began to protest about the Baktrian children but the Mayor cut him short. Eli snapped his fingers at Roddin Corpse. 'Sdick this li'l shide in m'dungeon most foul. An' leave him there!'

Roddin Corpse, grinning with delight, caught the professor by the scruff of the neck and hauled him off his feet as if he were a doll. 'Now zen, meester professeur El Queer. 'Ooo ees zee bad guy now, eh?'

Roddin ran from the room with the protesting manikin under his arm. Roland, seeing his master so abused, barked and made to run after them but Roddin slammed the door in the animal's face. The dog, whining, scratched at the door with his forepaws, barking and sniffing the woodwork, as if trying to detect traces of Professor Elsquaird in its austere, polished grain.

'Ged me th' cops,' snapped Eli, 'An' th' troops. I wanna ged all our forces oud there. We're gonna fladden thad drash — th' kids an' th' blacks — we're gonna squash 'em so they'll wish they'd never lived!'

Norman obediently picked up the phone and began to dial.

Roland was flat on his belly by now, whimpering and pushing his muzzle under the door.

'An' shood that goddam crittur!' shouted the hysterical Mayor.

12

BATTLE

It was a damp, dismal, desperate dawn in downtown Gasville. The torrential rain which had been plaguing the combatants for the previous week still refused to abate.

It was the third week of the military engagement which the newspapers persisted in calling, 'THE GASVILLE CIVIL WAR'.

As a result of the publicity the followers of Walking Wolf, Yukio, Bucolia, O'Toole and Mandola Magabutne had been joined by hordes of discontented farmers, who rose unanimously to cast off their yoke and to overthrow the perpetrators of the much-maligned Trinomial Plan, for which no-one any longer had a good word to say. For example, Abdul Akbar Jahman, who was usually a peaceful, patient farmer, now in his late middle-age and pre-eminently respectable, raised a division of farmers from the north. Arming themselves with knives, pitch-forks and fowling pieces the troops of Jahman's division had converged on the contested area, just north of the Drewchester-Gasville road at Eidrood Ridge. Several similar bands had congregated in that region during the course of the three-week long campaign, slipping in under cover of dark, through the woods which Walking Wolf's forces had at their back.

Walking Wolf, whose maternal grandfather, Abraham Limping Wolf, had been an Indian celebrity in Gasville when Eli Baktrian was just a boy, had been christened General Wolf by the *Gasville Free Press*.

'I know this villein, I knew his grandsire, Abraham,' Eli spat out in disgust, when he saw the headlines: General Wolf stands up to Mayor Baktrian.

'Pox on't, dost thou see this? Hight General Wolf, highted of Abraham — ol' Limpin' Wolf — if he fain would contest with me, so be it! I will grind him full mercilessly into small pieces. Then those small pieces I will tear into shreds. Then those shreds I will render unto dust with m'pestle — the powerful pestle *of mightiness*!'

The Press had found nicknames for other segments of the fighting fray. The followers of Walking Wolf, Yukio, Bucolia and O'Toole, being mostly graduates of the Sorores Mundi Calamity Home for victims of explosions, were christened the Calamity Kids. Group photos were taken and displayed in the newspapers, showing a large detachment of young men and women, mostly with some degree of the characteristically twisted torso of their progenitor, whose forces were ranged against them at this moment below Eidrood Ridge.

Since the middle of the night the troops and supporters of Mayor Baktrian had been marching through Gasville's main street, fully armed. Their total number was difficult to estimate, although it was large, for the grim similarity of their facial expressions and their uniforms led one into the illusion that this phalanx of fighters was merely the same band going round a closed circuit again and again, bringing the same faces back over and over to march the length of Gasville's main street.

For days now the fighting had been quiescent, each side dug in well into its defences, and during that period both sides had mustered reinforcements as best they could. By now the Magabutnoi at the Ridge numbered five hundred. In addition to these and the several hundred Calamity Kids there were also many divisions of farmers holding the Eidrood Ridge and the Eidrood Farm which flanked it in a salient at the north-west end of the ridge.

On the other hand the Gang of Eleven, which was now the Gang of Ten because Elsquaird remained imprisoned despite attempts to dissuade the Mayor from this folly, had many divisions of police, troops and militia under its command. There was a large detachment of the Fifth Royal Elginturd Volunteers, usually called the Old Five Hundred, a police troop known as the Old Contemptibles, the Cambridge Constabulary Gymnastics and Bag-pipe Team and an artillery division from the university, the WHU Royal Engineering Reserve.

The Eidrood Ridge was a Place of the Foremost Canadian

Significance. On frequent occasions the two towns of Gasville and Drewchester had jointly hosted the Southwestern Ontario Winter Skiddoo Championships and held them at the spot which was now Walking Wolf's headquarters.

The Eidrood Ridge was visible from the Gasville-Drewchester turnpike. It was a long, low ridge running from northwest to southeast. At the northwestern end lay the Eidrood Farm, abandoned now to General Wolf's men. In this highly fortified farm, lying in a salient of the front system, was Mandola Magabutne's division. The distance from Walking Wolf's line, in a southwesterly direction down the scarp slope of the ridge and across the muddy fields to the front line of Eli Baktrian's forces was about two thousand yards.

The day's campaign allowed Baktrian's troops three hours and twenty minutes to cross this gap and to engage General Wolf's forces. On several days of the campaign the Baktrianites had made this crossing on schedule, at the cost of substantial losses, only to be repulsed and chased back across no-man's land by the end of the day.

Tangles of barbed wire ran hither and thither in no-man's land, trampled into the greedy, clutching, squelching relentless grip of the mud.

Behind Walking Wolf's position, to the northeast, was a dense wood, which covered the gentle slope in that direction. It was through these woods, which were usually a picnic area, that Wolf's reinforcements had infiltrated. This wood curved around to flank the Eidrood Ridge at its southeastern end. Now that all the reinforcements and supplies had passed through the wood the area had been mined and barricades of picnic tables had been erected. Out of sight from Walking Wolf's men the WHU artillery were positioned to the southeast, firing blind over the intervening woods into the trenches of Walking Wolf's troops. More often than not the WHU artillery fire passed right over the Calamity Kids, travelling northwest, and devastated the Old Contemptibles, who were out on the left flank of the Baktrian army, facing the redoubtable Eidrood Farm.

One victim of such a barrage was an old ambulance, fitted with caterpillar tracks and long-range field-radio and radar. This exceptionally large vehicle was entombed, lurching at an eccentric angle, in the ooze in the middle of no-man's land. It bore the legend, TESTES PRIVATE CASUALTY SERVICE, in large, bright red lettering, written backwards in mirror-images along the sides of the van. The ambulance had been one of the first civilian vehicles to join in the battle. Hearing of the civil war, Dwayne Testes had at once risen from his resting place and called around to the second-hand car dealers in the vicinity, until he had located a much-used ambulance — there was no point in using something new and expensive for the task which he had in mind.

Next, Testes had sent out paging calls for a number of impoverished interns and other medical types who were willing to try their hand at anything — including his two subordinates, Eustace and Fidelio, the hapless witnesses of Dean Smoothe's last gasp. Within hours the emergency ambulance service was operational; caterpillar tracks had been fitted which made their outfit the only one capable of cleaning up — financially and surgically — in the neutral quagmire between the troops. All had gone well for a couple of weeks; at each dusk Testes' squad had gone in and brought out as many survivors as they could while the artillery units were pausing for dinner. And so it would have continued, had it not been for the fact that Eli Baktrian had one night convinced himself that he had seen Vlov One Leg, deserting, scurrying about among the corpses in the dusk and ordered an extra round of artillery fire, which had accidentally and predictably scored a direct hit on the ambulance. In the absence of a first-aid team capable of retrieving the first-aid team the bodies of Eustace, Fidelio and Rena Failure had been left inside the crippled ambulance. By now they were beginning to smell.

Each side was dug in well, with Baktrian's men having a labyrinth of trenches and tunnels laid out across the fields to the edge of no-man's land. The unceasing rain was rendering these redoubts increasingly more dangerous and for that reason today was to be the occasion of the Offensively Big Offensive.

Although the Wolf-troops had the higher elevation, even they were beginning to worry about the danger of collapse of their earthworks if the rain did not stop soon.

During the night Pans, Zhilin and Penz had led a little sortie. Taking a small squad selected from the Gymnastics Team they had successfully prepared a large land mine beneath an outpost of the Eidrood Farm. After much controversy it had been agreed to explode the mine at six-fifty am, prior to the start of the offensive proper at seven am. In addition, in order to avoid firing on their own men, the artillery bombardment was to stop at this time. It was hoped that, with the Eidrood Redoubt out of commission and with the main task force of Walking Wolf cowed by the hitherto continual mortar fire, that a strong Old Contemptible push against the farm would break through. Once the farm was breached it was clear to Eli that an offensive along the top of the ridge would quickly push the enemy into the hands of the waiting artillery. To further confuse and inhibit the opposition the rest of the Gymnastic Team and Pipe Band would be spear-heading a direct onslaught by the Old Five Hundred.

Unfortunately, when the mine was detonated the WHU artillery took it as the signal to stop their shelling. Consequently Walking Wolf had a warning that something was coming and ten minutes grace to do something about it.

The first thing that he did was to get Mandola Magabutne on the field-telephone and warn him.

'Jest let th' waart trash come mah way, kid, an' ah'll screw dem, man!'

The second thing that Walking Wolf did was a masterpiece of suicidal, cogent, pseudo-Napoleonic strategy. Leaving the Magabutnoi to defend the flank and Yukio, alone, to monitor the electronically activated mine field to the rear and the right of their position, he took every other man-jack of the Wolf Brigade and struck straight across no-man's land at the enemy's weak spot — the Cambridge Constabulary Gymnastics Team and Pipe Band! The latter, due to some confusion, were still milling around aimlessly, rather than preparing for their attack, tuning their chanters and practising hand-springs on one another's shoulders.

In addition, General Wolf struck just after the Magabutnoi had engaged the Old Contemptibles on his northwestern flank. He attacked at seven oh one am.

Yukio watched his friends from the Sorores Mundi Calamity Home rise from their waterlogged trenches, scrambling, some slipping and falling back with a splash into the knee-deep, scummy, greasy water. Spear-headed by Abdul Jahman's team with Walking Wolf running at its head, the Calamity Kids sploshed and splished their way down the slope towards the enemy.

In the trench containing O'Toole and Bucolia an argument

was raging. Yukio knew this dispute, for the three of them had rehearsed it many times, with Yukio and O'Toole sometimes on one side and sometimes on the other. Not so, however, Bucolia, who maintained with steadfast clarity the same point of view.

'Whatever we think of Father or Trinomiality is irrelevant. All that matters is that violence is evil.'

'Bud id ain't so simple, Sis,' O'Toole was protesting, trying, without hurting her, to tug himself loose from Bucolia's grip.

'Nothing except a battle lost, is half so melancholy as a battle won,' Yukio quoted as he turned away and trudged off in the direction of the southeastern mine-field.

The rain had stopped. Yukio was thankful that he did not have to choose today. His head throbbed with the intensity of his brother's and sister's argument. From behind him there came the sound of rapid-firing small arms, which had ceased momentarily at the instant of attack, almost as if the forces in the field below had to ask absolution before they set to with their devastating work.

Yukio reached the detonation panel and squatted before it, his hands hovering over its red buttons, which could, in an instant, turn the woods and scrubland before him into a jig-saw of screams and sheets of flame. Balancing on his heels Yukio poised himself, his large hands widespread just a few inches over the panel of buttons so that, if a sniper were to get him, he would fall forward and detonate the entire hillside.

His throat ached with that bitter, painful strangulation which accompanies the effort of fighting back tears. Despite his grim resolve a droplet of liquid materialized on his battle-soiled face and began its slow roll down his cheek. Since the rain had stopped this must have been a tear.

Although the noises — the shouts, the shots — were louder now Yukio hardly noticed them. He was vaguely aware that the artillery had started up again and smiled to think that the Calamity Kids were no longer in their entrenched position and that the guns were aimed at an empty redoubt.

Inside his brain, Yukio received the sensation like that of soft grapes being squeezed and of their juicy contents bursting out; the soft, fruit-like falling of his slain Calamity Kid half-brothers and half-sisters.

Let the ripe fruit fall.

Ahead of him hovered a hazy white light — faint and mobile like the legendary min-min lights of the Queensland deserts. Overhead the sky was turning pink, as if someone had released into the sunlight a world of rosy cockatoos — an immense, avalanching flock of galahs.

The shells were whining over his head and smacking into the vacated entrenchment which he had left behind him.

Suddenly there was an exceptionally loud report — a lucky shell had hit the ammunition dump on the top of the ridge. With this same report he registered the fatal squashing of two large pomegranates — too large for squeezed grapes, these — in his head.

Yukio half rose, his eyes staring wide and wild from the sensation. Floods of acidic, burning, scorching tears coursed down his cheeks. Clenching his fists he gave an agonized scream:

'Aa-a-aa-agghh! Oo-oo-oohh!'

* * *

'Ay-yay-yay! Mein Gott! Haff you zeen happening down zer vat iss?' Zhilin lowered his field-glasses and turned, challengingly, towards the others.

'Himmel! Himmel! Himmel!' was Penz' only reply. He was intently training his binoculars on the activity at the crest of the Eidrood Ridge.

'Ziss vould have happennt nie iff vee hat from prison got der Professor.'

'Merde!' retorted Roddin Corpse. 'Ouee can mannish ouizzoud zat mizzhit, El Queer.'

'Och, wull y'a' shut y' faces,' shouted Pans over the squabble.

The group was assembled before the tent which contained Eli Baktrian's field HQ. The flap of the tent was pushed aside angrily and Eli emerged, followed by Norman the Mormon, Stanley, Jaime, Sid Ra'in and Horace.

'Yeah, shud up!' reinforced Norman.

'Yeah, s'no use belly-achin' aboud this cock-up.' interrupted Eli, taking control. 'Yer all know whad's happened, eh? Them chicken-shide gun-guys from th' Universidy have blundered mighdily! If th' sdupid basdards had kep' on shellin', like they was supposed, them kids couldn' even have showed their faces. Now they're sdreamin' down ther' like id's some goddam Sunday picnic. So now we're gonna go an' ged 'em ourselves!'

Horace appeared unconvinced. He was thinking of Doris, abandoned, for safety, in the Gasville Town Hall.

'Do we really have to do it, Eli? Maybe it'll turn out all right?'

Eli ignored the question, attending instead to buckling on his sabre — the family heirloom which had seen service with General Beauregarde — and to adjusting the chain-mail vest which he was wearing beneath his coat. The Mayor picked up his steel helmet — a Great Basnet — and settled it upon his head. The helmet resembled the headgear of a football player, except that the face was guarded by a curved sheet of metal containing multitudes of minute perforations. Unlike a sports helmet, the interlocking panels of metal extended downward to cover the nape of the neck and part of the chest. Finally Eli slung a sub-machine gun over his shoulder. He nodded to Norman.

'Ged yer weapons,' Norman snapped. 'We're gonna go after the leaders. 'Special preference fer thad damn half-breed! But we godda go fast an' we godda go good, eh? So for speed, we gonna move out north and duck in behind the Ol' Contempts — see? Thad'll carry us quick to the foot of the scarp — then we strike south-east into no-man's land and take 'em from the flank or the rear. Ged me? An' just ged me thad Walkin' Wolf. OK?'

Horace seemed about to speak, but Norman silenced him. 'We got no time for questions, Horace. Just be sure thad you — an' Sid, 'cause he's a good sniper, too — take a good audomadic rifle. Lots o' grenades, all of you! Led's go!'

Already Eli Baktrian was on the move.

The others collected their weapons and followed suit. Pans and Norman brought up the rear, wearing grim expressions and holding their automatics trained on the group in a manner calculated to convince even sceptics such as Horace Ontal.

Eli, travelling fast ahead of the group, was no longer paying heed to the conversation. His mind was racing forward into the conflict . . .

Outdistancing his retinue the crookback, Lord Baktrian, cast north-west in pursuit of the vanguard of Contemptibles. Once he paused, brandishing high the fine-chased sword which he had of his father, calling thunderously for speed.

'Faster, rabble! Faster!'

'We are coming, sire, with all speed,' cried Hassidicus in reply. 'T'is a tiresome mire, m'Lord.'

'I know t'is a quagmire,' grumbled the Lord to himself, pressing on towards the ringing sounds of the battle.

Within his own skull, the Knight's voice sounded as fine, young and powerful as ever. Outside, alas, it was but a faint trailing thing, carried rapidly away midst the powerful, forcing gusts of wind. It was the same with his body. Hassidicus was right. The Knight's ageing physique, so powerful in repose, was fast becoming spent in the course of his struggle through the mud. Nevertheless, driven by his will and the desperate nature of the conflict, Baktrian traversed the fields for a distance of some seventy chains in the wake of the Contemptibles. From this point he could catch the reports of the weapons and the cries of his combatants, who were engaging enemy forces besieged within the Eidrood Farm. He could even make out the individual shouts of the yeomen.

Baktrian paused for breath, exhilarated by the sound of the chase above him and the spectacle of the struggle which he could perceive further to his right. There, in no man's land, his Gymnasts and Pipers tenaciously sought to hold the manifold intruders at bay.

Knight Baktrian veered in an easterly direction, intending to engage with the conflict from the rearmost flank of the hostile invaders.

The enemy was not far distant. As he moved forward the Knight was assailed from his right side by an opposing spearman. Simultaneously a blow to his helmet drove the Knight to his knees. It had been caused by a shot that ricocheted away, leaving his brain ringing. Gasping, groping for a weapon, Baktrian strove to regain his stance. He could not see the enemy, who had manoeuvred into his blind spot. Sweat — of fear and of fatigue — was in his eyes as the Knight whirled about, struggling to one knee and firing in a manner almost random. Luckily the shots broke his assailant's spear. The youth advanced on Eli, drawing a butchering knife as he approached. Lunging to his feet, Baktrian faced the boy again, glancing from his mud-smeared face to the haft of the broken pitch-fork which his burst of shots had smashed. The Knight took aim.

Two other enemies materialized at the side of the first.

Eli fired.

The commotion attracted the attention of several more of the invaders, who moved to surround the Knight.

All at once Baktrian was reinforced by the arrival of Pansard, Rodius, Mormon de Norman, Zhilincus, Penzard, Ovox, Hassidicus and Horatio Ontalox.

Jaime had fallen behind; wounded and impaled upon the barbed wire.

The opposing forces were so close that firearms were useless. They set to, viciously, hand-to-hand.

Baktrian smote down two of the aliens who were within reach, dealing them crashing blows with the butt of his sword.

'Burn, crush, flatten, destroy!' cried the Knight, pushing through the conflict with fearsome flailing of his steel-gauntleted fists. He was seeking Walking Wolf.

Behind him, as he hastened onward, his retinue were struggling manfully. Three yeomen smote Horatio to the ground and sought to do him injury. Pansard gat himself atop the trio and kicked out their brains.

The going was almost impassable. Baktrian fell headlong several times into the treacherous, relentless grip of the mire. Scrambling to his feet, he forced himself to press on. His gun was rendered useless by the slime. He cast it away.

Ahead he could discern a lone figure and, sensing the opposing general, he drew two grenades from his belt.

A second figure appeared beside the first, a tall but twisted youth; each one was filth-smeared and as black as a chess-pawn.

* * *

The chance shell that hit the ammunition magazine on the Eidrood Ridge had released a terrific explosion, which spat flame, flying debris and tearing, vicious splinters into the morning air. Dangerous shards went thudding into recently vacated trenches, splashing into ditches half-filled with water, ripping through the rough canvas of tents as if it were nothing but paper.

Fortunately Walking Wolf and the Calamity Kids had moved out minutes before. Only Bucolia and O'Toole had remained at the redoubt, still arguing.

The force of the explosion had caught Bucolia and lifted her clear of the trench, flinging her several yards and dashing her head against the withered stump of a tree. When the blast had hit her, Bucolia had been staring it straight in the face, so to speak, and the last sensation which came to her before she lost consciousness was of a prickling and gritty, unpleasant tickling all over her face. It was almost like the stinging which results from an open-palmed slap in the face.

O'Toole had been killed instantly, slashed through the jugular vein by a flashing jag of glass and smashed on the head by exploding junk.

When Bucolia regained consciousness she groped around for a moment — a painless, tranquil instant of ignorance before her mind clawed its way back to what had happened. With the returning realization of her whereabouts came a chronic, pounding pain in her head and a stinging sensation all over her face. Gingerly she touched the tender skin, shivering at the feel of blood.

Drawing her hand away she looked down at her blood-smeared knuckles. As she gazed at the hand she froze; a shudder of terror engulfed and paralysed her mind — turning every corpuscle within her to ice.

She could not see.

There was no messy palm to inspect, no torn blouse or dress, no bruises. No details.

Bucolia sobbed until she choked, coughed and spluttered and then sobbed some more. O'Toole, the others, everything was put out of her mind, so full of pain at this final fateful trick, which this beastly violence had played upon her.

When her final convulsive sob had been emitted and her misery had no further self-expression remaining, Bucolia climbed slowly, very tentatively and stiffly, to her feet. She began to walk, asking herself, and the morning, the agonized question: 'Yukio Kanada?'

Hither and thither she stumbled, turning her scarred, torn, blood-stained travesty of a face to the new-invisible, brightening sky. She could feel the gusty wind against her forehead, gored now in the manner of the brow of an animal whose horns have been burnt out. She burst into tears once more, her emotions swindled by the juxtaposition of the familiar, delightful sensations conjured by the fresh breezes and the nightmare forebodings summoned by the blindness.

Where was she going? Bucolia stopped — puzzled. She no longer felt that customary sense of presence which directed her to the boys. Were they dead? Suddenly she remembered the forgotten O'Toole and the fact that he had been in the trench with her. Frantically she began to cast about for him, but it was impossible. She had no sense of direction, no idea how far she might be from the dugout which they had both occupied. Above all, gone was the reliable homing signal which had invariably led her to O'Toole and Yukio in the past.

Aimlessly she moved about between the obstacles of warfare, picking her way very slowly down the slope. Often she would fall, or sink into the mud and slide for several feet.

Bucolia had groped her way five hundred yards in the direction of no man's land when Yukio caught sight of her.

Gazing down the hillside he could barely make out her slime-covered form crawling along. Even without being able to see his sister he could sense her cosmological radiance. Faintly he could hear: 'Yukio Kanada? Yukio? O'Toole?'

After detonating the mine-field, Yukio, enraged at the fate of his brother and sister, had turned back along the Eidrood Ridge and hurried off to seek them. Behind him the whole hillside and wood was aflame. The blast had blackened his skin and clothes, leaving him singed and stinking of cordite, but otherwise he was unharmed.

He broke into a run — a shambling, stumbling run — sensing that Bucolia was hurt. Of O'Toole he had no impression.

Spotting her, Yukio paused for a second and then plunged headlong down the hillside towards Bucolia.

'Bucolia! Bucolia!'

Scrambling down to where she was, oblivious of the sound of firing close by, he seized her roughly and embraced the bewildered young woman against his chest.

What would he do without Bucolia?

He surveyed her wounded face, kissing those gashed and blasted, sightless eyes. Her blood and grime mingled with his own. Holding her pallid face between his hands, his own slowly filled with an expression of horror as he realized what had happened.

'Yukio? Is that you?' Aaaaggghhhhhh! A shriek of agony went

off in his brain like a rocket-launcher.

Intent on the spectacle of his gentle, innocent, victimized, overpoweringly adorable girl, Yukio did not hear the approach of Eli Baktrian, until a voice spoke behind him.

'Face me, churl! Art thou this Wolf? Face me and fight, confront me and I will split thee like a twig.'

Yukio spun round, startled by the familiar accents. He realized that he was unarmed, having left his weapons at the mine-field.

'Eli, you shit!' exclaimed Yukio, edging round in a circle, holding Bucolia at his back, in an attempt to keep the Mayor, his quondam father, at a distance. The latter closed in, holding his sword extended before him. Eli did not seem to have recognized his children — perhaps because of their besmirched appearance.

'Wolf, thou coward. Be still, wilt thou? I wouldst fain crush thee like a thistle smote by a morning star.'

The Knight-Mayor smashed the ground with the flat of his sword to give Yukio an impression of that dreadful weapon smacking into the tiny flower.

'It's me, Eli. Yukio. You shit! Look what you've done! Sarah! Bucolia! O'Toole! My God, I'll strangle you with my bare hands.'

The Knight lunged forward. 'Prate not at me, varlet. Is't me, thy Lord, that thou wouldst molest?' Eli laughed eerily from within the basnet. Missing at the first lunge, the Mayor pulled his blade from the mud and the two circled once more.

'Yukio? Yukio?' called Bucolia, whom he had been obliged to abandon momentarily. She pawed the air in search of her brother.

Eli Baktrian lunged again, missing for a second time. However, on this occasion Yukio grabbed at the other's wrist and twisted the gauntlet, causing the sword to drop to the ground. Before Yukio could grasp the weapon, it slid from his outstretched fingers and fell into a water-filled trench at his feet.

'No, no! Yukio! Yukio!' Bucolia screamed again, terrified at the nearby, grunted sounds of combat.

In the moment that Yukio had spared to watch the disappearing blade, the Mayor was on him once more. This time Baktrian struck out with his fists, in each of which he held a grenade. Despite fatigue and age, the Mayor was still the stronger man. Gripped at the wrists by Yukio, Eli forced him to his knees, attempting all the while to deal a blow to the head.

'Wolf, thou monster of creeping insurrection, these jewels in my fists will soon blow we twain to pieces,' hissed Eli, through the visor of his helmet. 'Ah, got thee! I soon will quarter thee, like the knave thou art!'

Eli wrenched his right arm free and raised it high for the final blow.

'Yukio? Where are you? Stop fighting! Stop! Oh, please! Stop it, both of you!'

Bucolia frantically clawed at the air before her in an attempt to find her brother. Stumbling on the slippery hillside, Bucolia lost her footing. Down the slope she rolled, cannoning into the Mayor's legs from behind. Eli was momentarily caught off balance and, as a result of a swift tug by Yukio, he pitched forward into the trench. As the Knight plunged into the water he dropped one of the grenades onto the ground beside Yukio, taking the other into the ditch with him. As the object rolled towards his sister's feet Yukio dived to smother it with his body.

Crump. Crump.

The grenades detonated simultaneously. In the ditch the muddy slime pitched in turmoil about the Knight's body, which disappeared into the deep water, weighed down by its chain-mail and heavy helmet and hampered by the long coat and trailing scabbard.

On the ground, Yukio groaned and whimpered.

Hands outstretched, fingers passing lightly over the ground at her feet, Bucolia edged her way carefully in his direction — groping forward, seeking his body. Finding it, she clutched him to her. She pressed her face into his, rocking him, hoping for him, pouring sightlessly forth that effusion of gentleness that had so often given him the feeling, as a cow occasionally does, that in her own meek, speechless, dumb manner she was saying something.

'Yukio Kanada,' she wailed. 'Yukio Kanada.'

13

TOURISTS

The tour buses had traversed the Drewchester-Gasville road just before dawn. Some bore New York plates, others came from Ohio, Michigan and Massachusetts. They had pulled off the road, driving over the demolished fences bordering the fields below Eidrood Ridge, and there they had parked.

Patiently the passengers had waited for dawn, quietly pouring coffee from their flasks, eating a sandwich breakfast and talking in whispers.

Dawn had come and gone, magnificent and pinky-grey, and many of the tourists had lain back, resting their head on a cardigan or a jacket, and had tried to catch a few winks of sleep before the show.

Shortly before seven am they were roused.

'Hi, holidaymakers. And thank you for choosing O'Halloran's Tours today. My name is Bobby-Joe Blixen and I'm your tour guide for this morning. You're gonna see hisd'ry made right there in front've your very eyes, just like all that ancient old stuff that you learned in college, if you majored in socio-political hisd'ry an' all that. It's gonna be really neat.

'If you look out the right side you'll see Eidrood Ridge an' it's up there that the anti-establishment troops of General Walking Wolf, a full half-breed native person, are defending Democracy as we know it, from the terrors of Imperialism. Both sides have a great dee-fence. D'you see the other team, straight ahead in the field down there? See, just behind that darlin' li'l ambulance with all the neat antennae and stuff — and the caderpillar twacky-things, you know what I mean?

'Those of you who were awake will maybe have heard that

298

big bang just now? That was a mine going off on the ridge and
if y'take oud your binoculars from the compartment under your
seat, which can also be used as a flotation device, you'll see how
the farmhouse is blazin'. That's the start of a day's attack on
them black guys in the farm, who're led by Mandola
Magabutne, a full-blooded negro and a former tee-shirt
manufacturer. Mandola's reported to have said: ''Better death
than dishonour''.

'Hey now, folks, here's some'ing in'eresting. See them kids
running down the hill? Why! This is a real attack, ladies and
gen'lemen! Oh, my! Gee, look at those cute li'l policemen
running up to the farm, way over there!'

The tourists clapped their hands in child-like delight. 'See
how slippery it is oud there — 'cos of all the rain. Aw, too bad,
poor li'l feller, tch, tch.

'If you turn your glasses to the right you'll see the universidy
artillery division.'

'What?'

'Where?'

'Over there, see? They're fighting for the stadus quo and are
supporting Mayor Eli Baktrian, of Gasville, an' his military
Junta. Right now his right-hand man, Professor Elsquaird, a
fully-grown midget mathematician is rumoured to be under
arrest and . . . my God! Can you folks see the woods over there?
Just in fron' of the artillery? Have you ever seen such an
explosion? It must've been every mine in that sweed li'l ol' wood.
My God, have y'ever seen such a blaze?'

Everyone sat in silence for some time, transfixed by the
spectacular conflagration. Finally Bobby-Joe affably broke the
spell.

'Gee! See that guy in the tin hat? He's godda sword, see?
Yeah, over there — where I'm pointing. He looks like one of
them middle-aged guys — ya know? A knight or a squire or
something?'

The tourists watched as Eli Baktrian grappled his way through
the fray and struggled up the slope towards Bucolia and Yukio.

'Hey! See that, folks? The knight's wrestling with the tall guy,'
Bobby-Joe giggled. 'Whose gonna wi . . . - oh, there he goes,
she god him! Yeah! Yeah!'

Bobby-Joe wound down the window and pushed her head
out, laughing effervescently and shaking her short, blonde curls

with delight in the damp morning air.

There came a pause in the racket of the battle and over the moist air she caught the pure, crooning voice of Bucolia's sorrowful wail. 'Yukio Kanada! Yukio Kanada!'

Bobby-Joe pulled her head inside the coach once more and addressed the day-trippers.

'Can you hear thad singing woman? I think thad's the national anthem, ya know whad I mean? I don't think I've ever heard it before. Have you guys?'

The passengers nearest to Miss Blixen agreed that they sure never had.